ARAÑA

NIGHT OF THE HUNTER

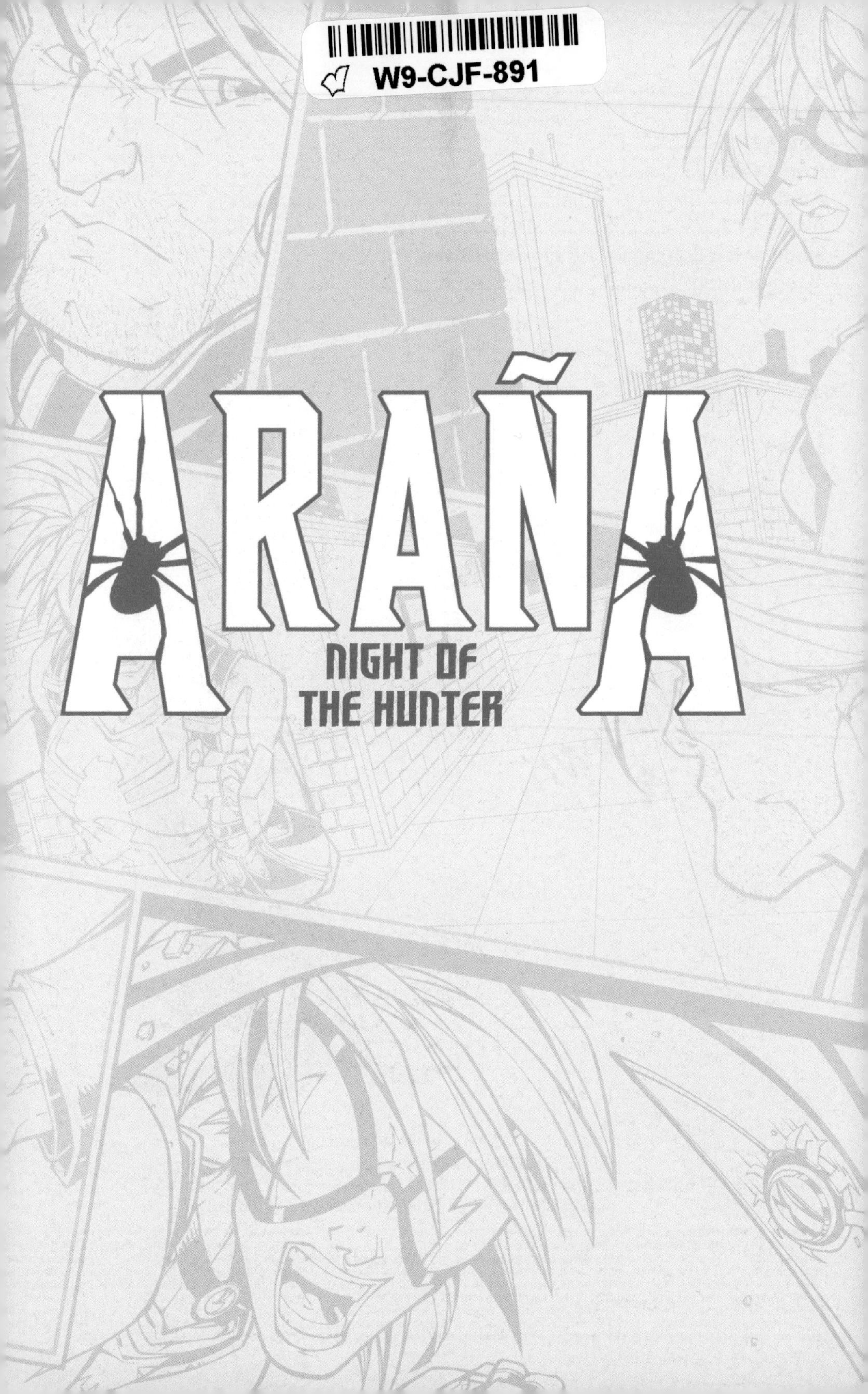

CONTENTS

collection editor JENNIFER GRÜNWALD
assistant editor DANIEL KIRCHHOFFER • assistant managing editor MAIA LOY
associate manager, talent relations LISA MONTALBANO • vp production & special projects JEFF YOUNGQUIST
svp print, sales & marketing DAVID GABRIEL • editor in chief C.B. CEBULSKI

ARAÑA: **NIGHT OF THE HUNTER.** Contains material originally published in magazine form as ARAÑA (2005) #7-12, SPIDER-MAN & ARAÑA: THE HUNTER REVEALED (2006) #1 and CAPTAIN AMER (2004) #602-605. First printing 2022. ISBN 978-1-302-94789-7. Published by MARVEL WORLDWIDE, INC., a subsidiary of MARVEL ENTERTAINMENT, LLC. OFFICE OF PUBLICATION: 1290 Avenue the Americas, New York, NY 10104. © 2022 MARVEL No similarity between any of the names, characters, persons, and/or institutions in this book with those of any living or dead person or institut is intended, and any such similarity which may exist is purely coincidental. **Printed in Canada.** KEVIN FEIGE, Chief Creative Officer; DAN BUCKLEY, President, Marvel Entertainment; DAVID BOGA Associate Publisher & SVP of Talent Affairs; TOM BREVOORT, VP, Executive Editor; NICK LOWE, Executive Editor, VP of Content, Digital Publishing; DAVID GABRIEL, VP of Print & Digital Publishing; S LARSEN, VP of Licensed Publishing; MARK ANNUNZIATO, VP of Planning & Forecasting; JEFF YOUNGQUIST, VP of Production & Special Projects; ALEX MORALES, Director of Publishing Operations; D EDINGTON, Director of Editorial Operations; RICKEY PURDIN, Director of Talent Relations; JENNIFER GRÜNWALD, Director of Production & Special Projects; SUSAN CRESPI, Production Manager; S LEE, Chairman Emeritus. For information regarding advertising in Marvel Comics or on Marvel.com, please contact Vit DeBellis, Custom Solutions & Integrated Advertising Manager, at vdebelli marvel.com. For Marvel subscription inquiries, please call 888-511-5480. **Manufactured between 9/23/2022 and 10/25/2022 by SOLISCO PRINTERS, SCOTT, QC, CANADA.**

10 9 8 7 6 5 4 3 2 1

ARAÑA
NIGHT OF THE HUNTER

ARAÑA #7-12

WRITER
FIONA AVERY

PENCILERS
FRANCIS PORTELA (#7-8, #10), **ROGER CRUZ** (#9)
& JONBOY MEYERS (#11-12)

INKERS
VICTOR OLAZABA (#7-8, #10), **JOHN STANISCI** (#9-10)
& MARK IRWIN (#11-12)

COLORISTS
UDON'S JEANNIE LEE (#7-8),
UDON'S LARRY MOLINAR (#9-10),
JOHN STANISCI (#9) & **SOTOCOLOR** (#11-12)

LETTERERS
VC's RUS WOOTON (#7-11) & **RANDY GENTILE** (#12)

COVER ART
MARK BROOKS, JAIME MENDOZA & DAVE McCAIG (#7, #9),
MARK BROOKS & DAVE McCAIG (#8),
ROGER CRUZ, JIMMY PALMIOTTI & GURU-eFX (#10-11)
AND **TAKESHI MIYAZAWA & CHRISTINA STRAIN** (#12)

ASSISTANT EDITOR
NATHAN COSBY

EDITORS
JENNIFER LEE & MARK PANICCIA

CREATIVE CONSULTANT
J. MICHAEL STRACZYNSKI

SPIDER-MAN & ARAÑA:
THE HUNTER REVEALED

WRITER
TANIA DEL RIO

PENCILERS
ROGER CRUZ
& JONBOY MEYERS

INKERS
JIM ROYAL, MARK IRWIN &
TANIA DEL RIO

COLORISTS
GURU-eFX & IMPACTO STUDIOS'
DEBORA CARITA

TITLE PAGE ARTIST
BYRON PENARANDA

LETTERER
VC's RANDY GENTILE

COVER ART
JONBOY MEYERS & GURU-eFX

ASSISTANT EDITOR
NATHAN COSBY

EDITOR
MARK PANICCIA

"CONJUNCTION"

WRITER
SEAN KELLEY McKEEVER

PENCILER
DAVID BALDEÓN

INKER
SOTOCOLOR'S N. BOWLING

COLORIST
CHRIS SOTOMAYOR

LETTERER
VC's JOE SABINO

ASSOCIATE EDITOR
LAUREN SANKOVITCH

EDITOR
TOM BREVOORT

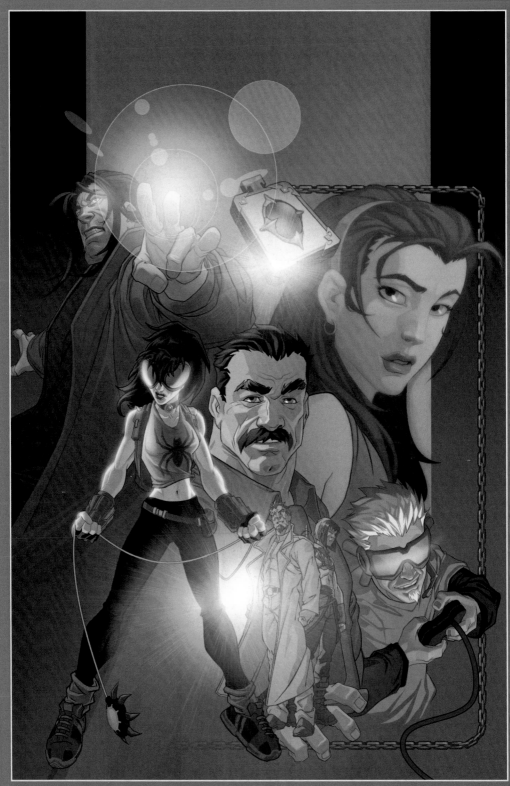

ARAÑA #7

4

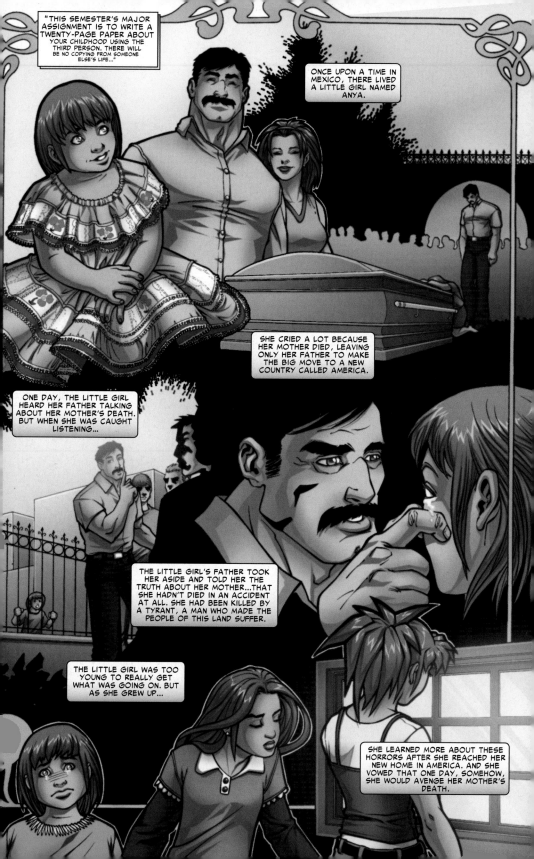

"THIS SEMESTER'S MAJOR ASSIGNMENT IS TO WRITE A TWENTY-PAGE PAPER ABOUT YOUR CHILDHOOD USING THE THIRD PERSON. THERE WILL BE NO COPYING FROM SOMEONE ELSE'S LIFE..."

ONCE UPON A TIME IN MEXICO, THERE LIVED A LITTLE GIRL NAMED ANYA.

SHE CRIED A LOT BECAUSE HER MOTHER DIED, LEAVING ONLY HER FATHER TO MAKE THE BIG MOVE TO A NEW COUNTRY CALLED AMERICA.

ONE DAY, THE LITTLE GIRL HEARD HER FATHER TALKING ABOUT HER MOTHER'S DEATH. BUT WHEN SHE WAS CAUGHT LISTENING...

THE LITTLE GIRL'S FATHER TOOK HER ASIDE AND TOLD HER THE TRUTH ABOUT HER MOTHER...THAT SHE HADN'T DIED IN AN ACCIDENT AT ALL. SHE HAD BEEN KILLED BY A TYRANT, A MAN WHO MADE THE PEOPLE OF THIS LAND SUFFER.

THE LITTLE GIRL WAS TOO YOUNG TO REALLY GET WHAT WAS GOING ON. BUT AS SHE GREW UP...

SHE LEARNED MORE ABOUT THESE HORRORS AFTER SHE REACHED HER NEW HOME IN AMERICA. AND SHE VOWED THAT ONE DAY, SOMEHOW, SHE WOULD AVENGE HER MOTHER'S DEATH.

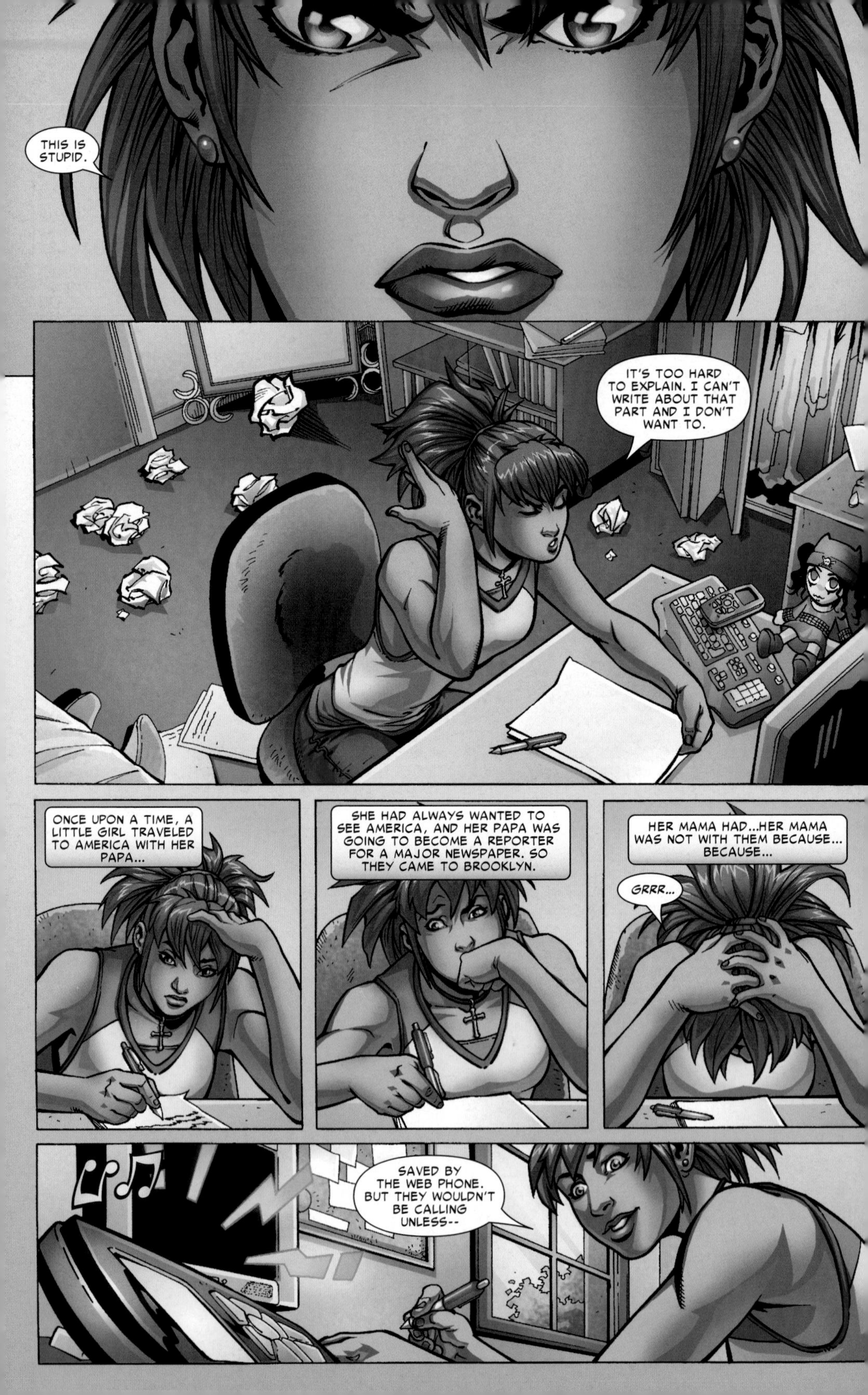
THIS IS STUPID.
IT'S TOO HARD TO EXPLAIN. I CAN'T WRITE ABOUT THAT PART AND I DON'T WANT TO.
ONCE UPON A TIME, A LITTLE GIRL TRAVELED TO AMERICA WITH HER PAPA...
SHE HAD ALWAYS WANTED TO SEE AMERICA, AND HER PAPA WAS GOING TO BECOME A REPORTER FOR A MAJOR NEWSPAPER. SO THEY CAME TO BROOKLYN.
HER MAMA HAD...HER MAMA WAS NOT WITH THEM BECAUSE... BECAUSE...
GRRR...
SAVED BY THE WEB PHONE. BUT THEY WOULDN'T BE CALLING UNLESS--

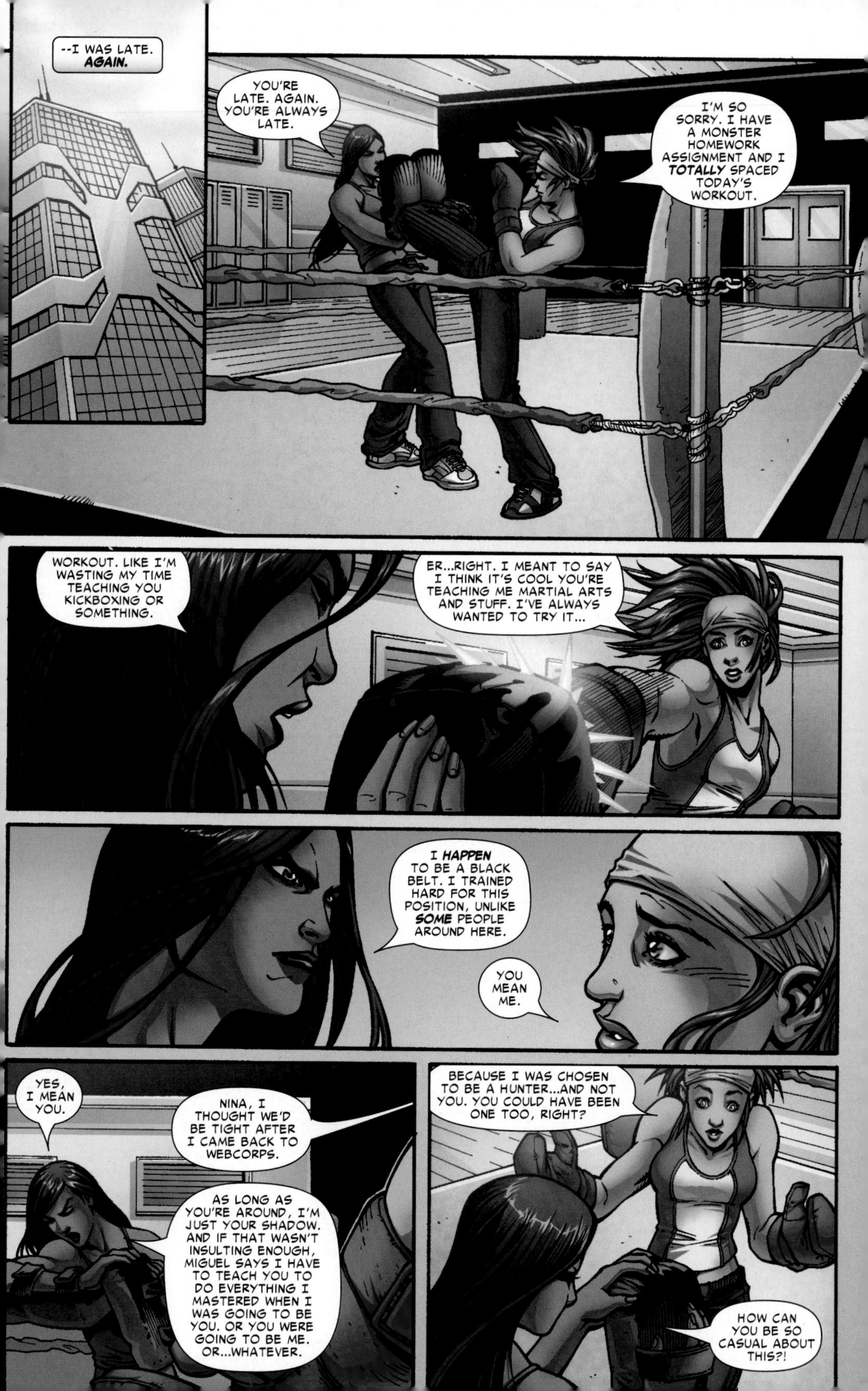
--I WAS LATE. AGAIN.
YOU'RE LATE. AGAIN. YOU'RE ALWAYS LATE.
I'M SO SORRY. I HAVE A MONSTER HOMEWORK ASSIGNMENT AND I TOTALLY SPACED TODAY'S WORKOUT.
WORKOUT. LIKE I'M WASTING MY TIME TEACHING YOU KICKBOXING OR SOMETHING.
ER...RIGHT. I MEANT TO SAY I THINK IT'S COOL YOU'RE TEACHING ME MARTIAL ARTS AND STUFF. I'VE ALWAYS WANTED TO TRY IT...
I HAPPEN TO BE A BLACK BELT. I TRAINED HARD FOR THIS POSITION, UNLIKE SOME PEOPLE AROUND HERE.
YOU MEAN ME.
YES, I MEAN YOU.
NINA, I THOUGHT WE'D BE TIGHT AFTER I CAME BACK TO WEBCORPS.
AS LONG AS YOU'RE AROUND, I'M JUST YOUR SHADOW. AND IF THAT WASN'T INSULTING ENOUGH, MIGUEL SAYS I HAVE TO TEACH YOU TO DO EVERYTHING I MASTERED WHEN I WAS GOING TO BE YOU. OR YOU WERE GOING TO BE ME. OR...WHATEVER.
BECAUSE I WAS CHOSEN TO BE A HUNTER...AND NOT YOU. YOU COULD HAVE BEEN ONE TOO, RIGHT?
HOW CAN YOU BE SO CASUAL ABOUT THIS?!

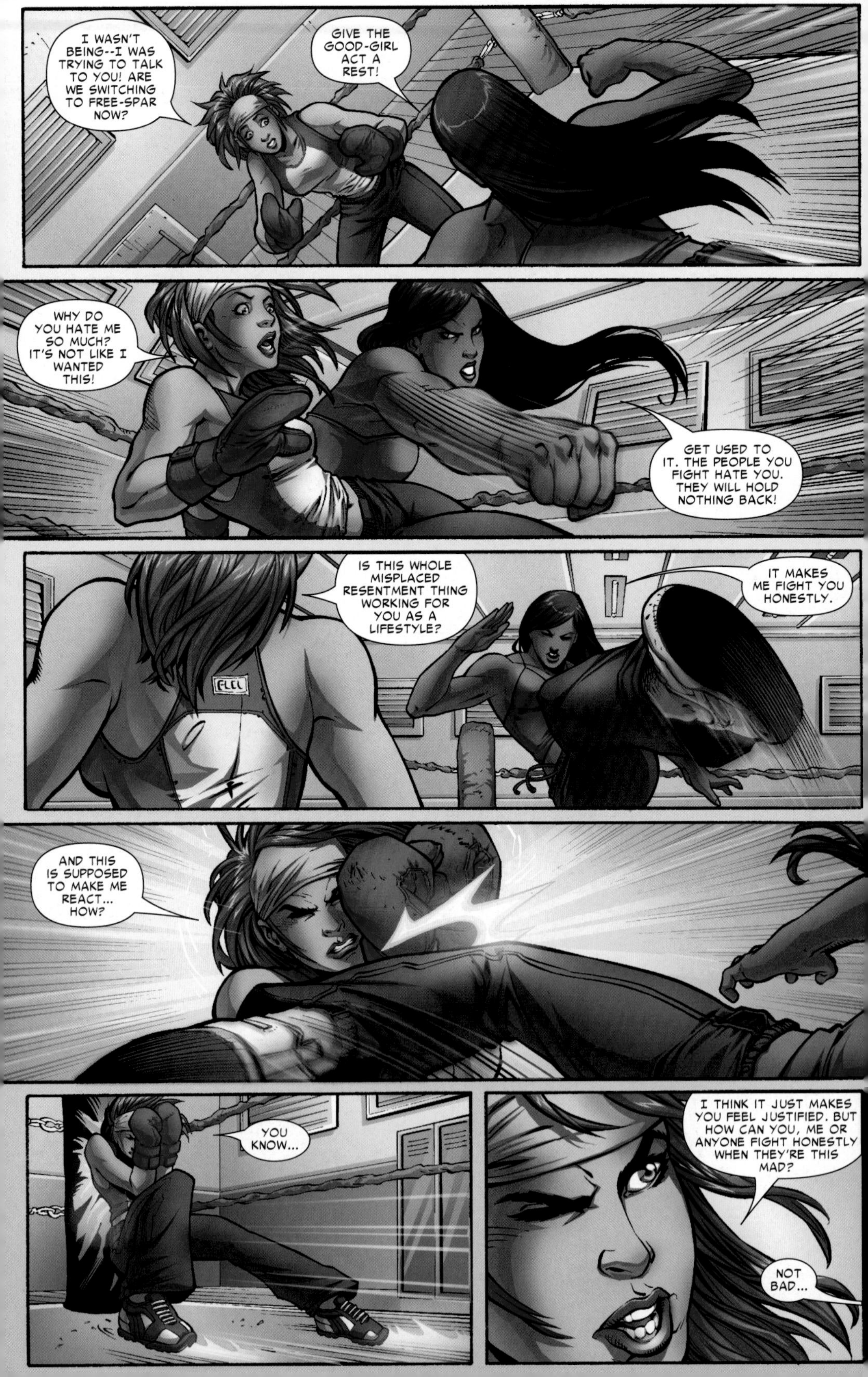
I WASN'T BEING--I WAS TRYING TO TALK TO YOU! ARE WE SWITCHING TO FREE-SPAR NOW?
GIVE THE GOOD-GIRL ACT A REST!
WHY DO YOU HATE ME SO MUCH? IT'S NOT LIKE I WANTED THIS!
GET USED TO IT. THE PEOPLE YOU FIGHT HATE YOU. THEY WILL HOLD NOTHING BACK!
IS THIS WHOLE MISPLACED RESENTMENT THING WORKING FOR YOU AS A LIFESTYLE?
IT MAKES ME FIGHT YOU HONESTLY.
AND THIS IS SUPPOSED TO MAKE ME REACT... HOW?
YOU KNOW...
I THINK IT JUST MAKES YOU FEEL JUSTIFIED. BUT HOW CAN YOU, ME OR ANYONE FIGHT HONESTLY WHEN THEY'RE THIS MAD?
NOT BAD...

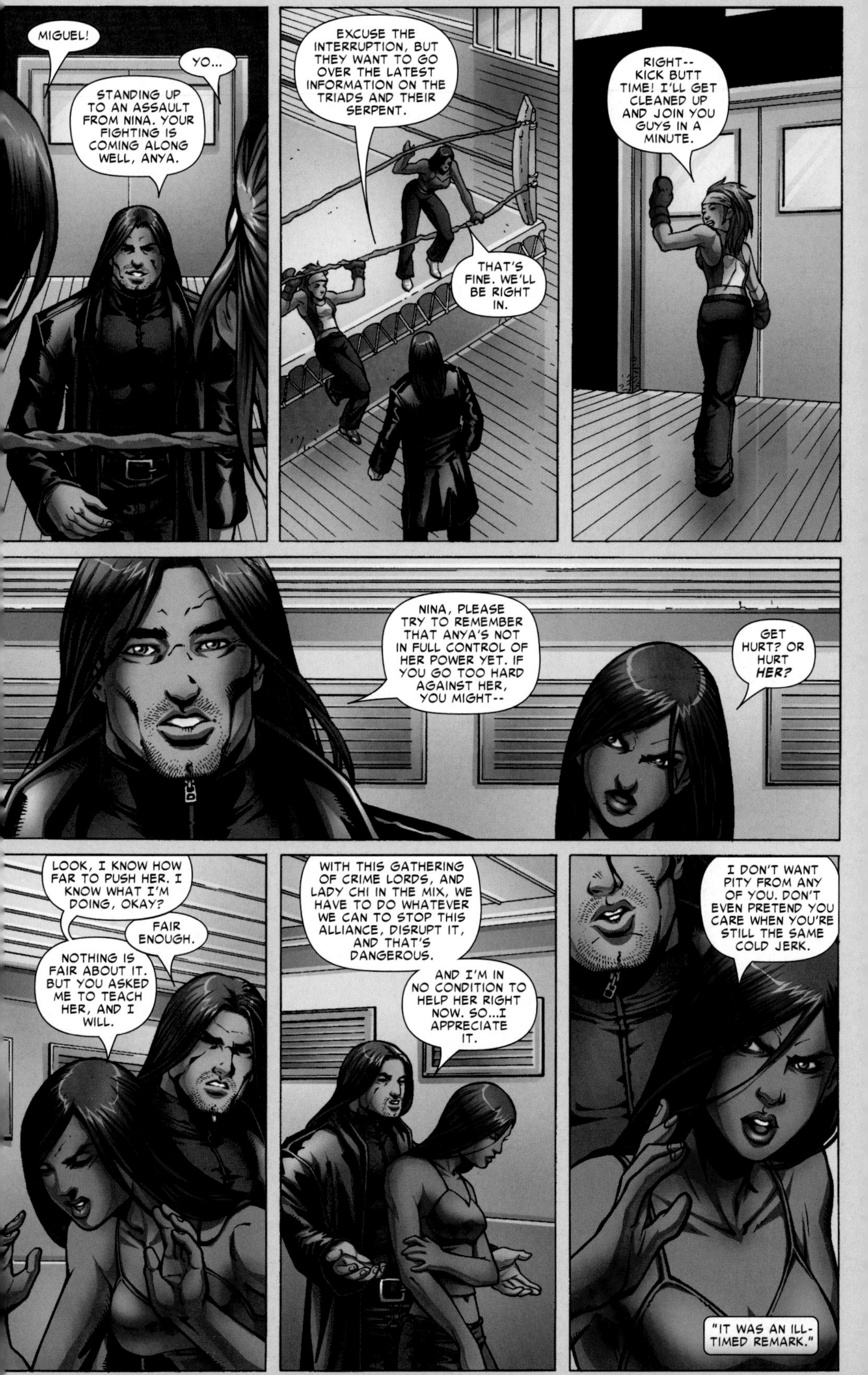
MIGUEL!
YO...
STANDING UP TO AN ASSAULT FROM NINA. YOUR FIGHTING IS COMING ALONG WELL, ANYA.
EXCUSE THE INTERRUPTION, BUT THEY WANT TO GO OVER THE LATEST INFORMATION ON THE TRIADS AND THEIR SERPENT.
THAT'S FINE. WE'LL BE RIGHT IN.
RIGHT-- KICK BUTT TIME! I'LL GET CLEANED UP AND JOIN YOU GUYS IN A MINUTE.
NINA, PLEASE TRY TO REMEMBER THAT ANYA'S NOT IN FULL CONTROL OF HER POWER YET. IF YOU GO TOO HARD AGAINST HER, YOU MIGHT--
GET HURT? OR HURT *HER?*
LOOK, I KNOW HOW FAR TO PUSH HER. I KNOW WHAT I'M DOING, OKAY?
FAIR ENOUGH.
NOTHING IS FAIR ABOUT IT. BUT YOU ASKED ME TO TEACH HER, AND I WILL.
WITH THIS GATHERING OF CRIME LORDS, AND LADY CHI IN THE MIX, WE HAVE TO DO WHATEVER WE CAN TO STOP THIS ALLIANCE, DISRUPT IT, AND THAT'S DANGEROUS.
AND I'M IN NO CONDITION TO HELP HER RIGHT NOW. SO...I APPRECIATE IT.
I DON'T WANT PITY FROM ANY OF YOU. DON'T EVEN PRETEND YOU CARE WHEN YOU'RE STILL THE SAME COLD JERK.
"IT WAS AN ILL-TIMED REMARK."

I'M SURE LADY CHI DIDN'T MEAN TO INSULT US WITH HER REPLY TO OUR OFFER TO PROTECT HER ON THE WAY TO THE SUMMIT. ALL THESE CRIME BOSSES IN ONE PLACE...THAT'S QUITE A TARGET, AMUN.

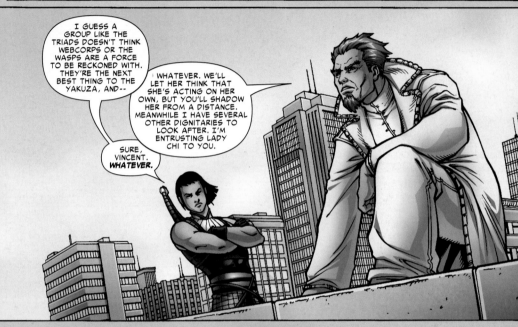

I GUESS A GROUP LIKE THE TRIADS DOESN'T THINK WEBCORPS OR THE WASPS ARE A FORCE TO BE RECKONED WITH. THEY'RE THE NEXT BEST THING TO THE YAKUZA, AND--

WHATEVER. WE'LL LET HER THINK THAT SHE'S ACTING ON HER OWN, BUT YOU'LL SHADOW HER FROM A DISTANCE. MEANWHILE I HAVE SEVERAL OTHER DIGNITARIES TO LOOK AFTER. I'M ENTRUSTING LADY CHI TO YOU.

SURE, VINCENT. *WHATEVER.*

WE ARE READY TO ESCORT YOU, LADY CHI.

TRY NOT TO MAKE A NUISANCE OF YOURSELF.

I'M NOT A LOST PUPPY. I'M PERFECTLY CAPABLE OF PROTECTING US.

BUT, MY LADY. I PROTEST! YOU COULD BE--

I SAID NOT TO CONTRADICT ME.

GOT IT?

AUGH...

I'D LIKE TO SHOP AT BARNEY'S FIRST. THEN TIFFANY'S. PERHAPS ROCKEFELLER CENTER.

AND WE WILL DO JEN AND BARRY'S.

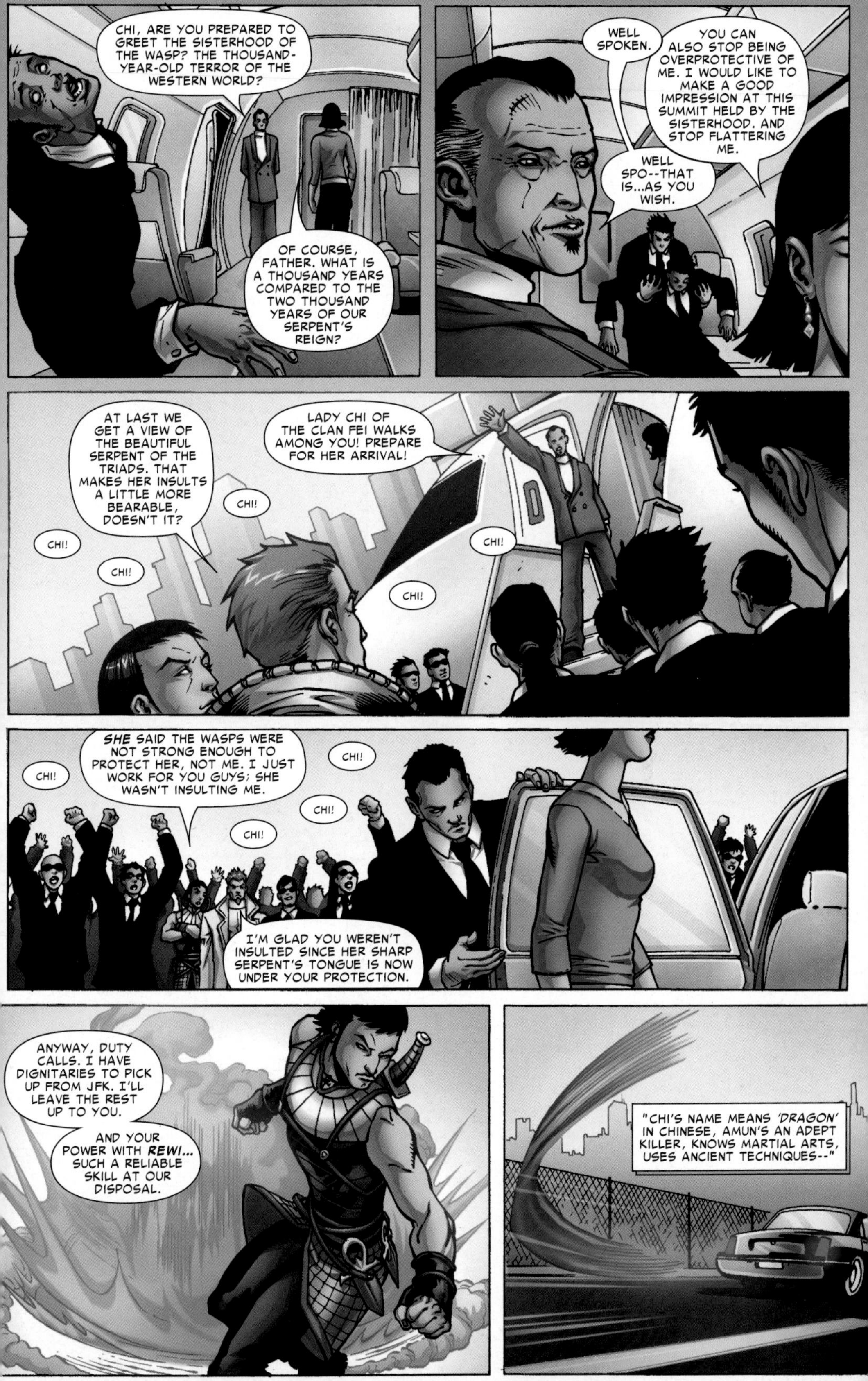
CHI, ARE YOU PREPARED TO GREET THE SISTERHOOD OF THE WASP? THE THOUSAND-YEAR-OLD TERROR OF THE WESTERN WORLD?
OF COURSE, FATHER. WHAT IS A THOUSAND YEARS COMPARED TO THE TWO THOUSAND YEARS OF OUR SERPENT'S REIGN?
WELL SPOKEN.
YOU CAN ALSO STOP BEING OVERPROTECTIVE OF ME. I WOULD LIKE TO MAKE A GOOD IMPRESSION AT THIS SUMMIT HELD BY THE SISTERHOOD. AND STOP FLATTERING ME.
WELL SPO--THAT IS...AS YOU WISH.
AT LAST WE GET A VIEW OF THE BEAUTIFUL SERPENT OF THE TRIADS. THAT MAKES HER INSULTS A LITTLE MORE BEARABLE, DOESN'T IT?
LADY CHI OF THE CLAN FEI WALKS AMONG YOU! PREPARE FOR HER ARRIVAL!
CHI!
CHI!
CHI!
CHI!
CHI!
SHE SAID THE WASPS WERE NOT STRONG ENOUGH TO PROTECT HER, NOT ME. I JUST WORK FOR YOU GUYS; SHE WASN'T INSULTING ME.
CHI!
CHI!
CHI!
CHI!
I'M GLAD YOU WEREN'T INSULTED SINCE HER SHARP SERPENT'S TONGUE IS NOW UNDER YOUR PROTECTION.
ANYWAY, DUTY CALLS. I HAVE DIGNITARIES TO PICK UP FROM JFK. I'LL LEAVE THE REST UP TO YOU.
AND YOUR POWER WITH *REWI*... SUCH A RELIABLE SKILL AT OUR DISPOSAL.
"CHI'S NAME MEANS *'DRAGON'* IN CHINESE, AMUN'S AN ADEPT KILLER, KNOWS MARTIAL ARTS, USES ANCIENT TECHNIQUES--"

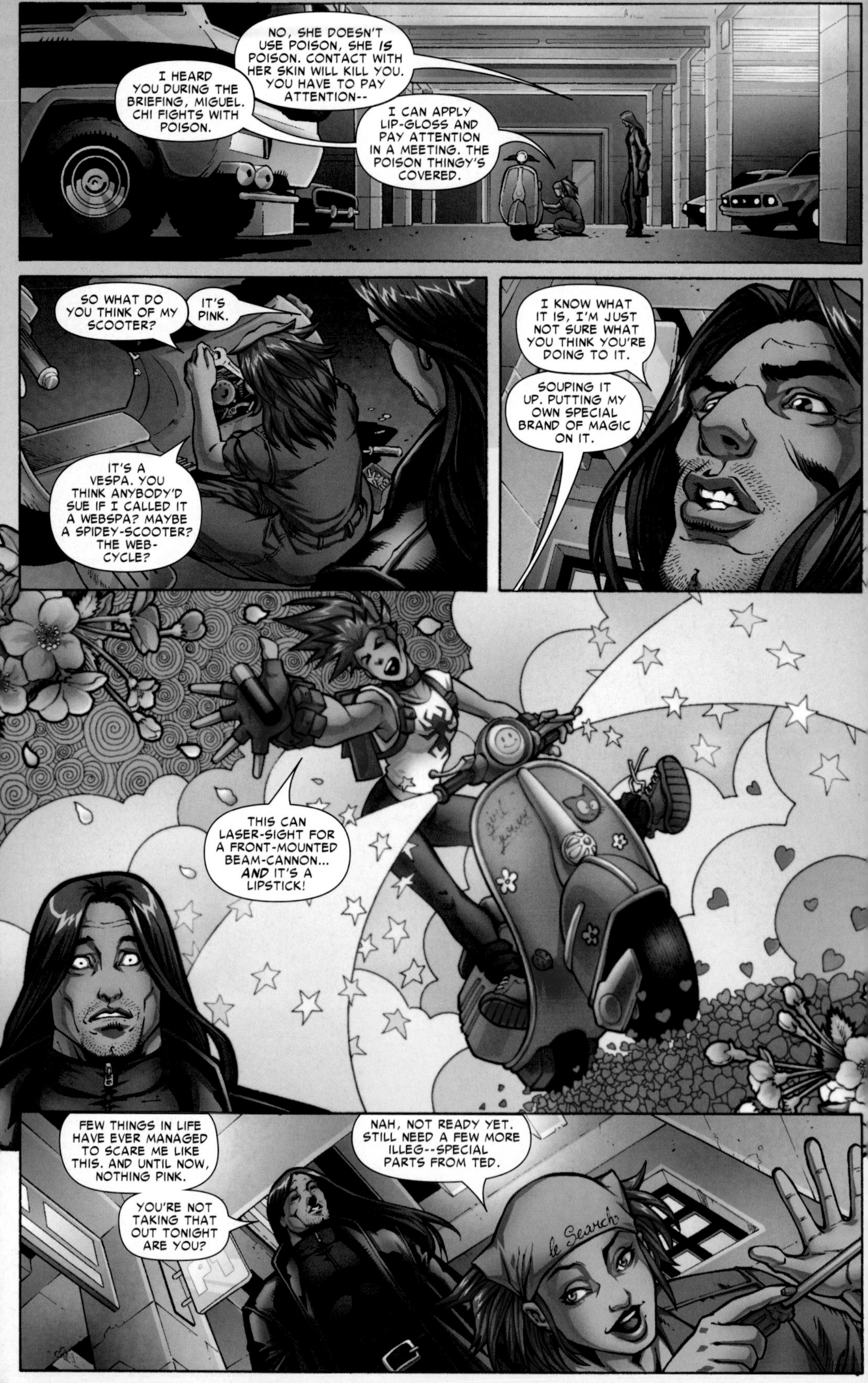
I HEARD YOU DURING THE BRIEFING, MIGUEL. CHI FIGHTS WITH POISON.
NO, SHE DOESN'T USE POISON, SHE *IS* POISON. CONTACT WITH HER SKIN WILL KILL YOU. YOU HAVE TO PAY ATTENTION--
I CAN APPLY LIP-GLOSS AND PAY ATTENTION IN A MEETING. THE POISON THINGY'S COVERED.
SO WHAT DO YOU THINK OF MY SCOOTER?
IT'S PINK.
IT'S A VESPA. YOU THINK ANYBODY'D SUE IF I CALLED IT A WEBSPA? MAYBE A SPIDEY-SCOOTER? THE WEB-CYCLE?
I KNOW WHAT IT IS, I'M JUST NOT SURE WHAT YOU THINK YOU'RE DOING TO IT.
SOUPING IT UP. PUTTING MY OWN SPECIAL BRAND OF MAGIC ON IT.
THIS CAN LASER-SIGHT FOR A FRONT-MOUNTED BEAM-CANNON... *AND* IT'S A LIPSTICK!
FEW THINGS IN LIFE HAVE EVER MANAGED TO SCARE ME LIKE THIS. AND UNTIL NOW, NOTHING PINK.
YOU'RE NOT TAKING THAT OUT TONIGHT ARE YOU?
NAH, NOT READY YET. STILL NEED A FEW MORE ILLEG--SPECIAL PARTS FROM TED.
le Search

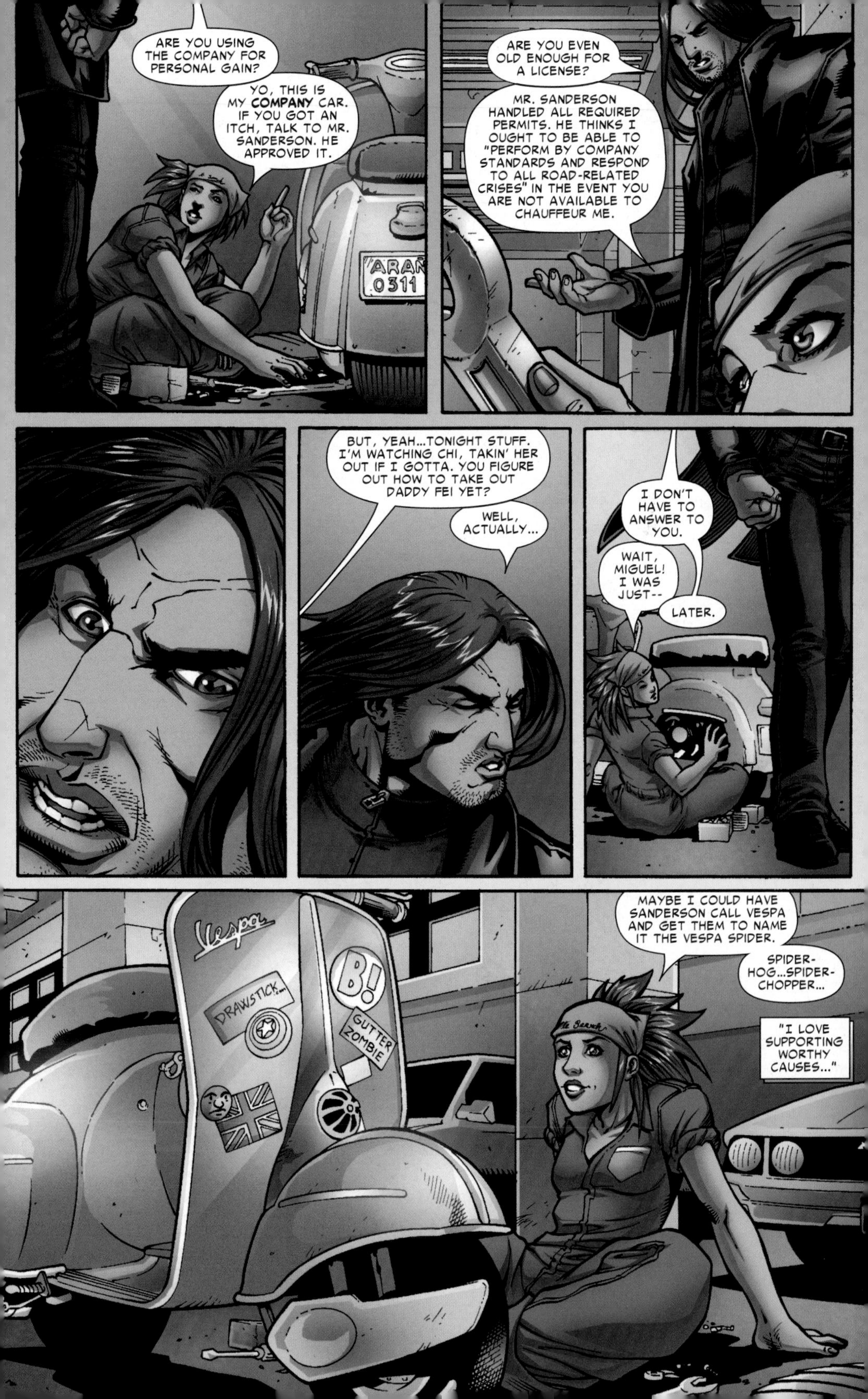
ARE YOU USING THE COMPANY FOR PERSONAL GAIN?
YO, THIS IS MY **COMPANY** CAR. IF YOU GOT AN ITCH, TALK TO MR. SANDERSON. HE APPROVED IT.
ARAÑ 0311
ARE YOU EVEN OLD ENOUGH FOR A LICENSE?
MR. SANDERSON HANDLED ALL REQUIRED PERMITS. HE THINKS I OUGHT TO BE ABLE TO "PERFORM BY COMPANY STANDARDS AND RESPOND TO ALL ROAD-RELATED CRISES" IN THE EVENT YOU ARE NOT AVAILABLE TO CHAUFFEUR ME.
BUT, YEAH...TONIGHT STUFF. I'M WATCHING CHI, TAKIN' HER OUT IF I GOTTA. YOU FIGURE OUT HOW TO TAKE OUT DADDY FEI YET?
WELL, ACTUALLY...
I DON'T HAVE TO ANSWER TO YOU.
WAIT, MIGUEL! I WAS JUST--
LATER.
Vespa
DRAWSTICK.com
B!
GUTTER ZOMBIE
MAYBE I COULD HAVE SANDERSON CALL VESPA AND GET THEM TO NAME IT THE VESPA SPIDER.
SPIDER-HOG...SPIDER-CHOPPER...
"I LOVE SUPPORTING WORTHY CAUSES..."

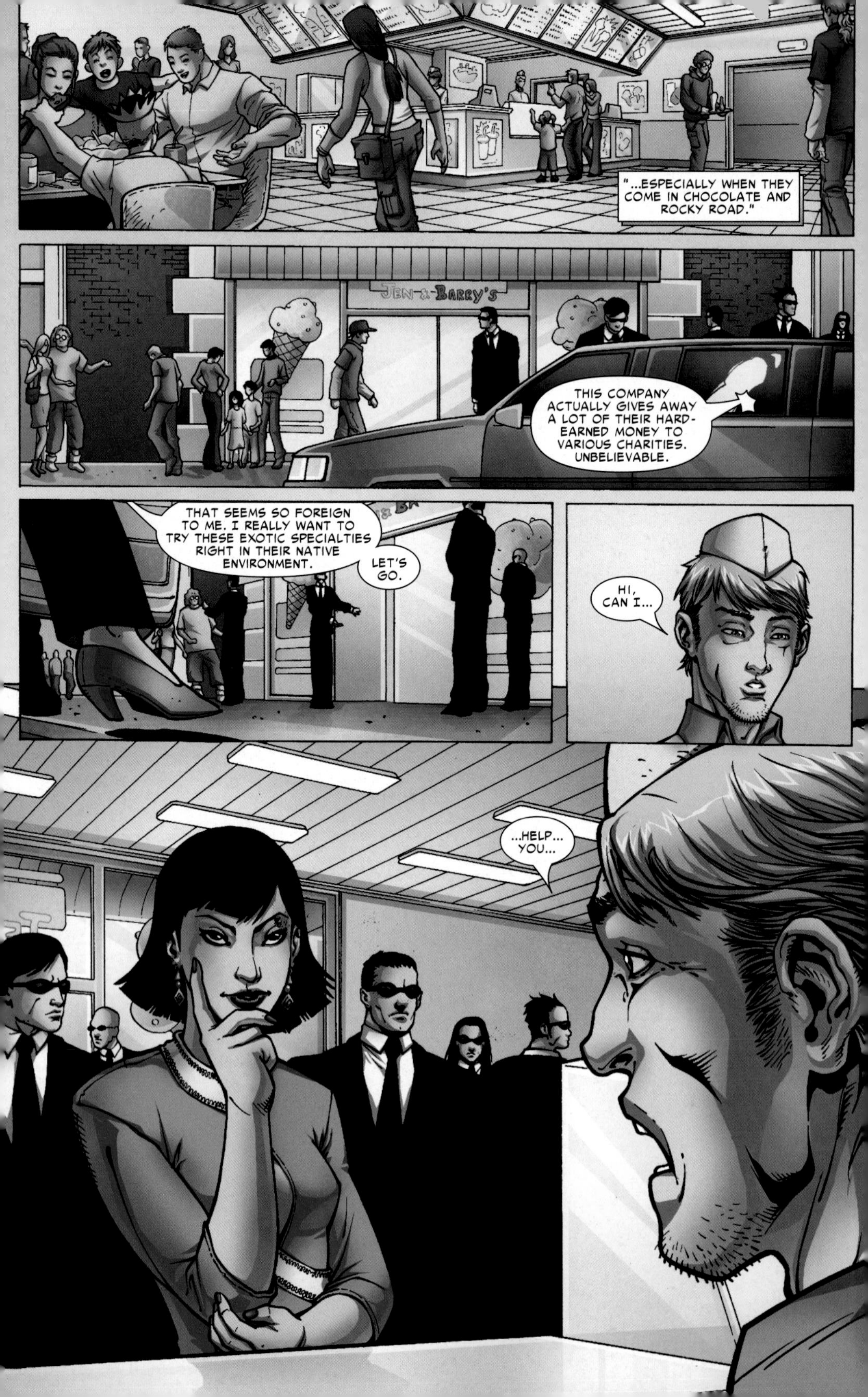
"...ESPECIALLY WHEN THEY COME IN CHOCOLATE AND ROCKY ROAD."
JEN & BARRY'S
THIS COMPANY ACTUALLY GIVES AWAY A LOT OF THEIR HARD-EARNED MONEY TO VARIOUS CHARITIES. UNBELIEVABLE.
THAT SEEMS SO FOREIGN TO ME. I REALLY WANT TO TRY THESE EXOTIC SPECIALTIES RIGHT IN THEIR NATIVE ENVIRONMENT.
LET'S GO.
HI, CAN I...
...HELP... YOU...

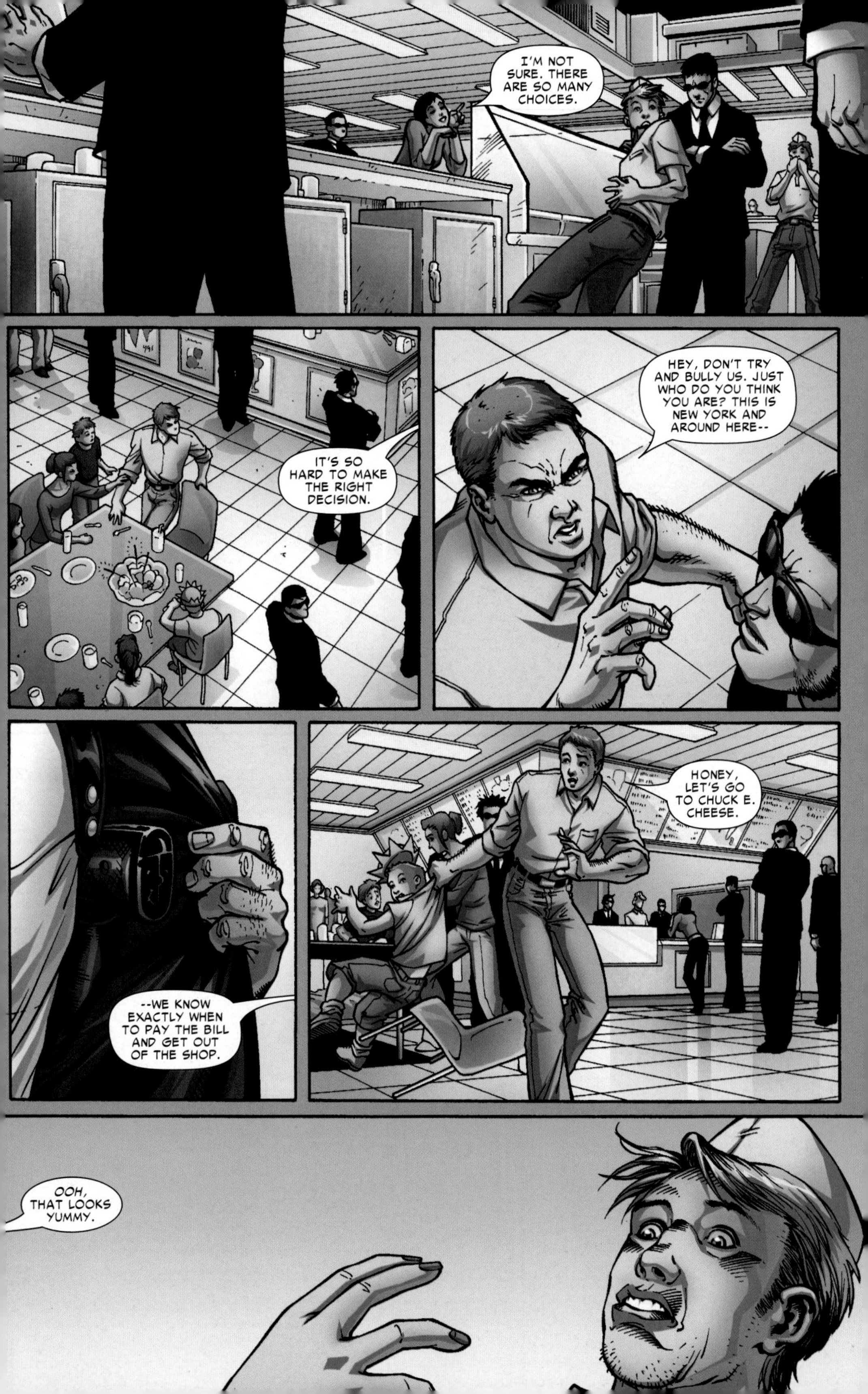
I'M NOT SURE. THERE ARE SO MANY CHOICES.
IT'S SO HARD TO MAKE THE RIGHT DECISION.
HEY, DON'T TRY AND BULLY US. JUST WHO DO YOU THINK YOU ARE? THIS IS NEW YORK AND AROUND HERE--
--WE KNOW EXACTLY WHEN TO PAY THE BILL AND GET OUT OF THE SHOP.
HONEY, LET'S GO TO CHUCK E. CHEESE.
OOH, THAT LOOKS YUMMY.

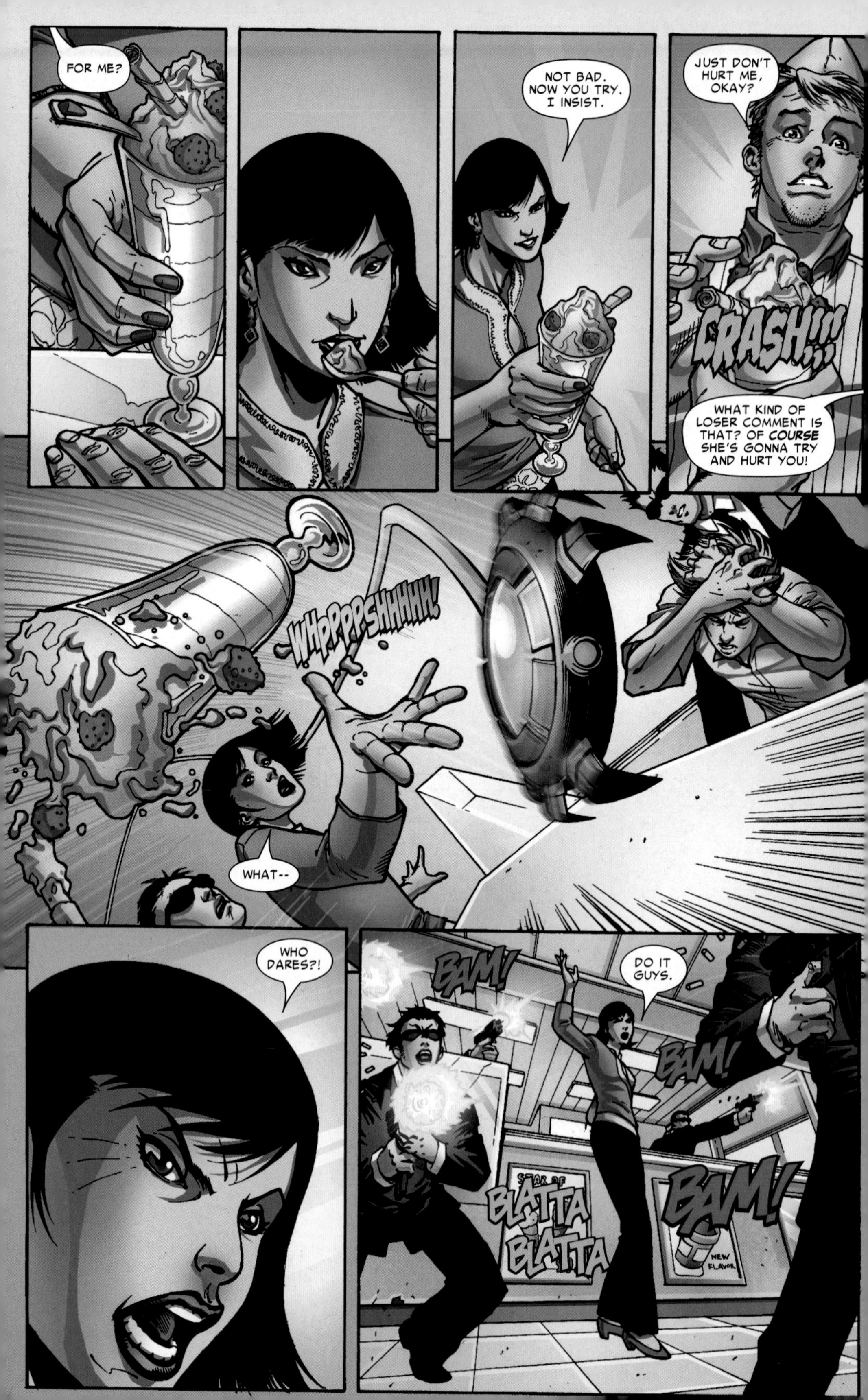
FOR ME?
NOT BAD. NOW YOU TRY. I INSIST.
JUST DON'T HURT ME, OKAY?
CRASH!!!
WHAT KIND OF LOSER COMMENT IS THAT? OF COURSE SHE'S GONNA TRY AND HURT YOU!
WHPPPSHHHH!
WHAT--
WHO DARES?!
BAM!
DO IT GUYS.
BAM!
BLATTA BLATTA
BAM!
NEW FLAVOR

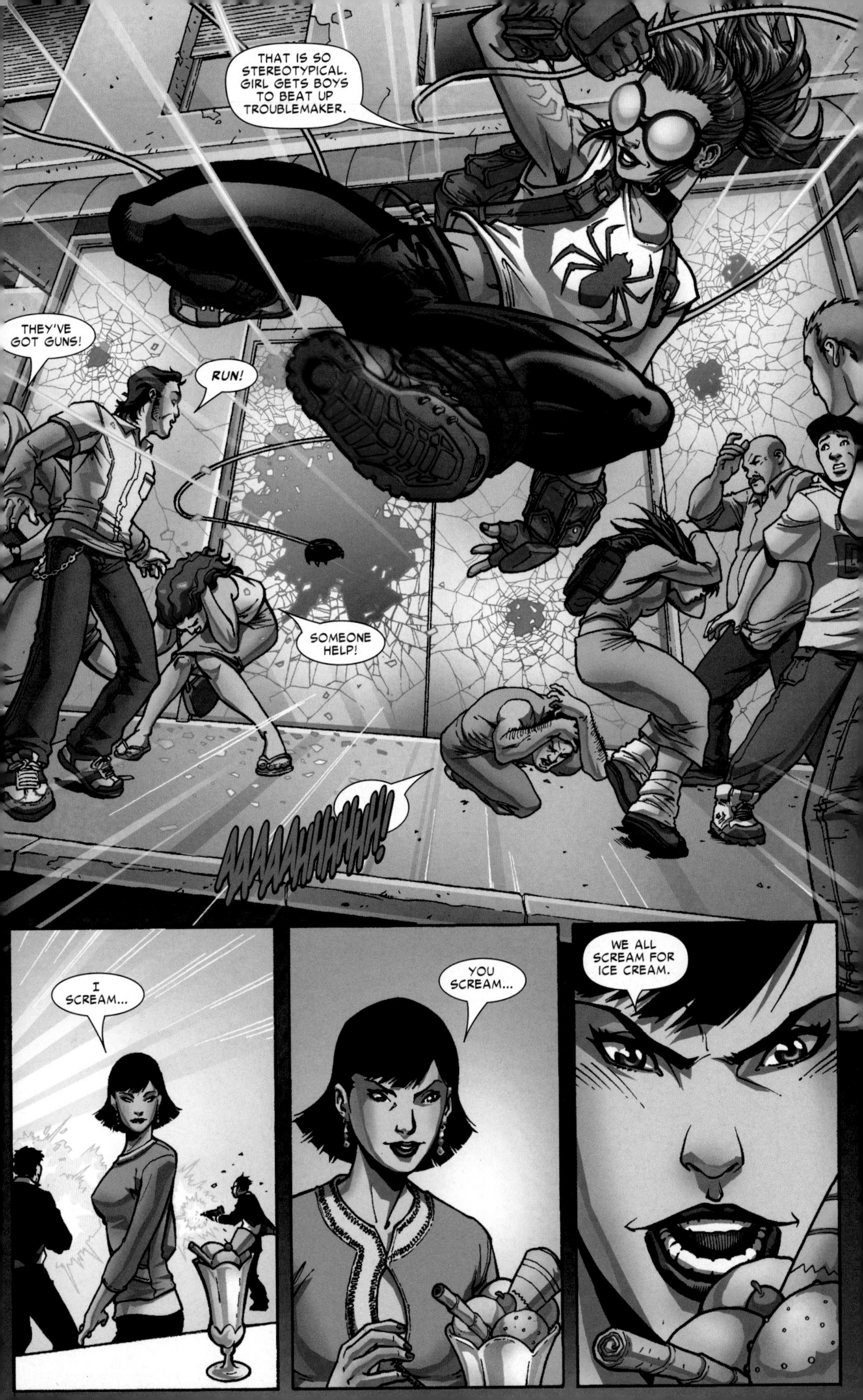

THAT IS SO STEREOTYPICAL. GIRL GETS BOYS TO BEAT UP TROUBLEMAKER.
THEY'VE GOT GUNS!
RUN!
SOMEONE HELP!
AAAAAHHHHH!
I SCREAM...
YOU SCREAM...
WE ALL SCREAM FOR ICE CREAM.

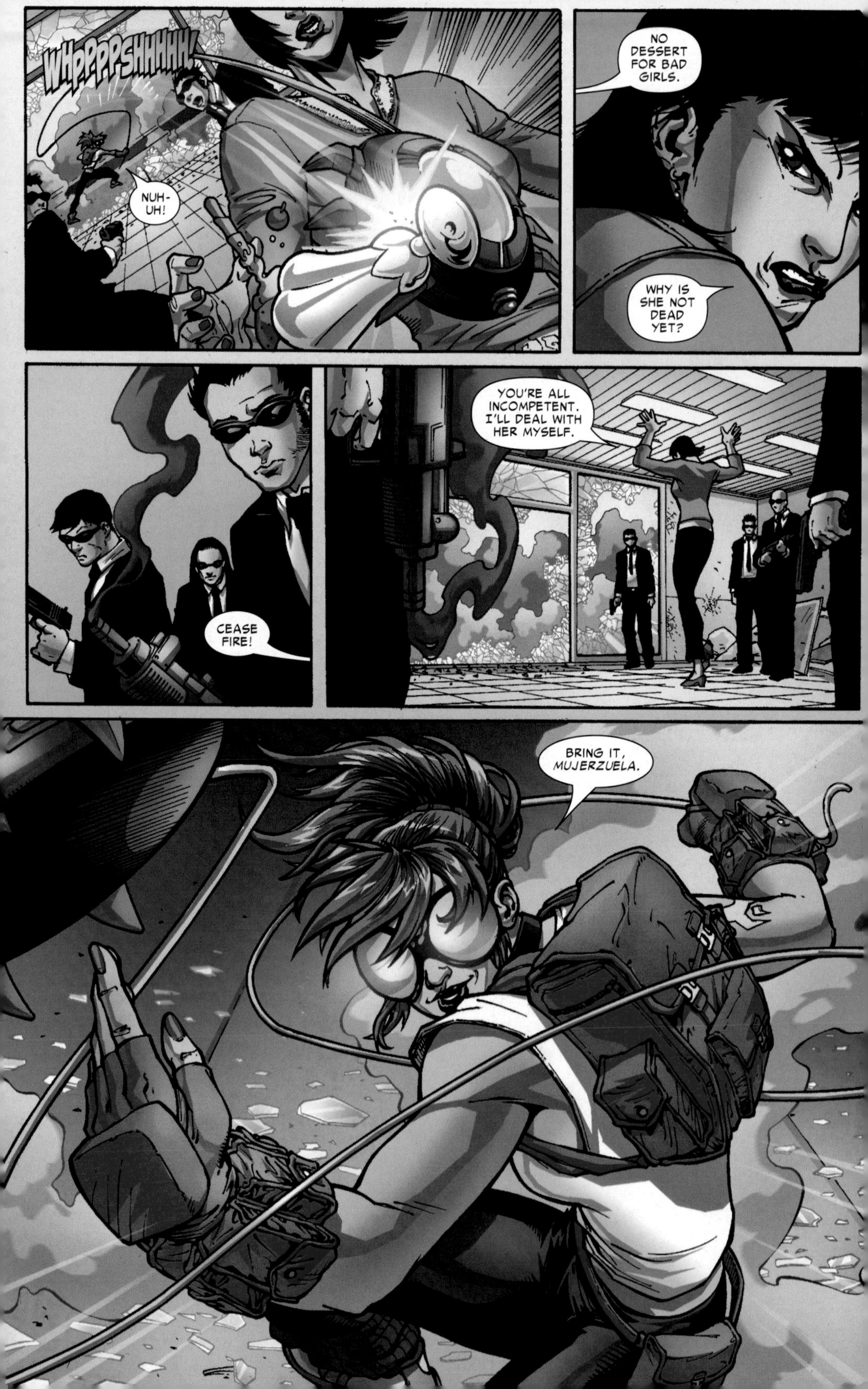
WHPPPPSHHHH!
NUH-UH!
NO DESSERT FOR BAD GIRLS.
WHY IS SHE NOT DEAD YET?
CEASE FIRE!
YOU'RE ALL INCOMPETENT. I'LL DEAL WITH HER MYSELF.
BRING IT, MUJERZUELA.

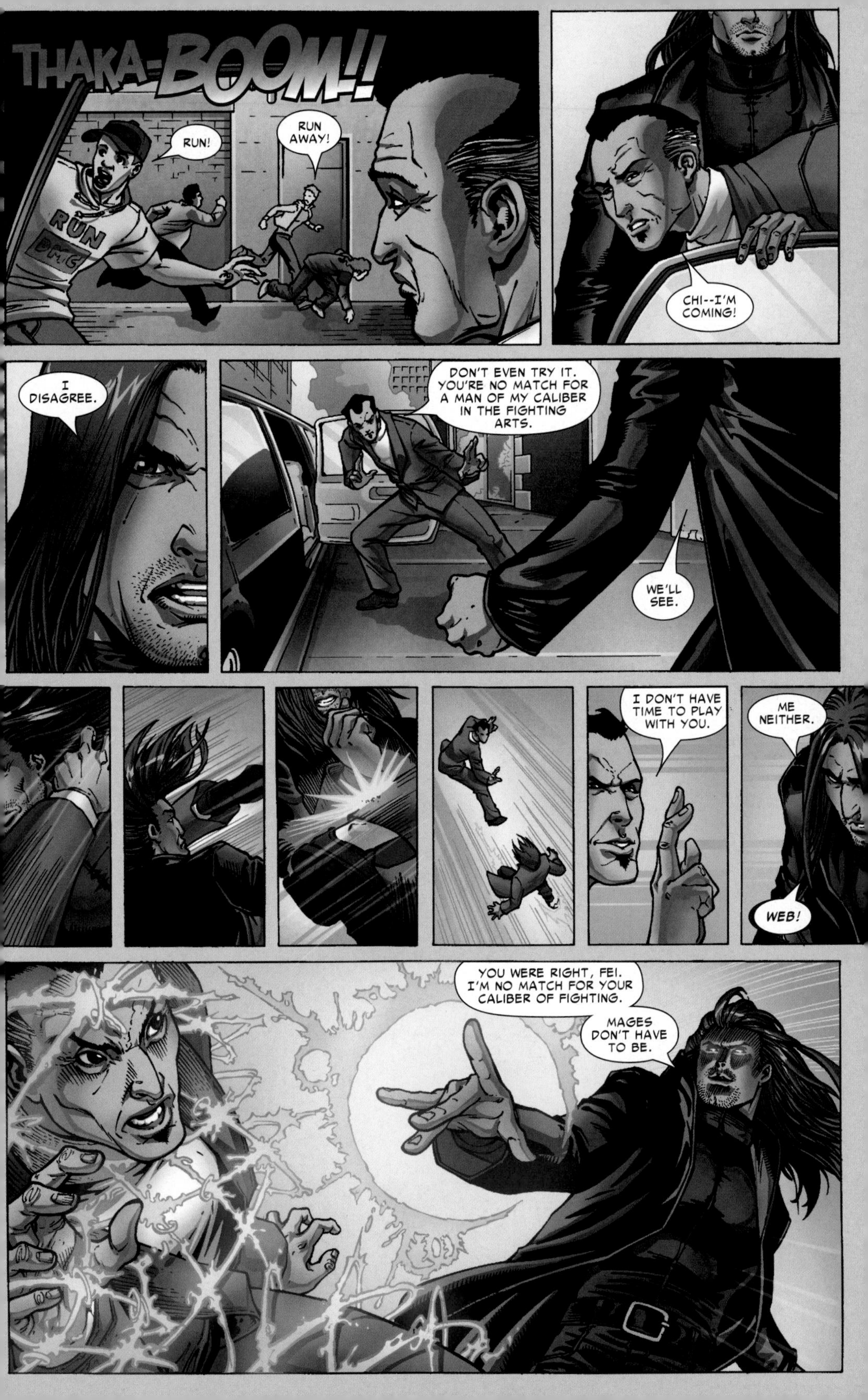
THAKA-BOOM!!
RUN!
RUN AWAY!
CHI--I'M COMING!
I DISAGREE.
DON'T EVEN TRY IT. YOU'RE NO MATCH FOR A MAN OF MY CALIBER IN THE FIGHTING ARTS.
WE'LL SEE.
I DON'T HAVE TIME TO PLAY WITH YOU.
ME NEITHER.
WEB!
YOU WERE RIGHT, FEI. I'M NO MATCH FOR YOUR CALIBER OF FIGHTING.
MAGES DON'T HAVE TO BE.

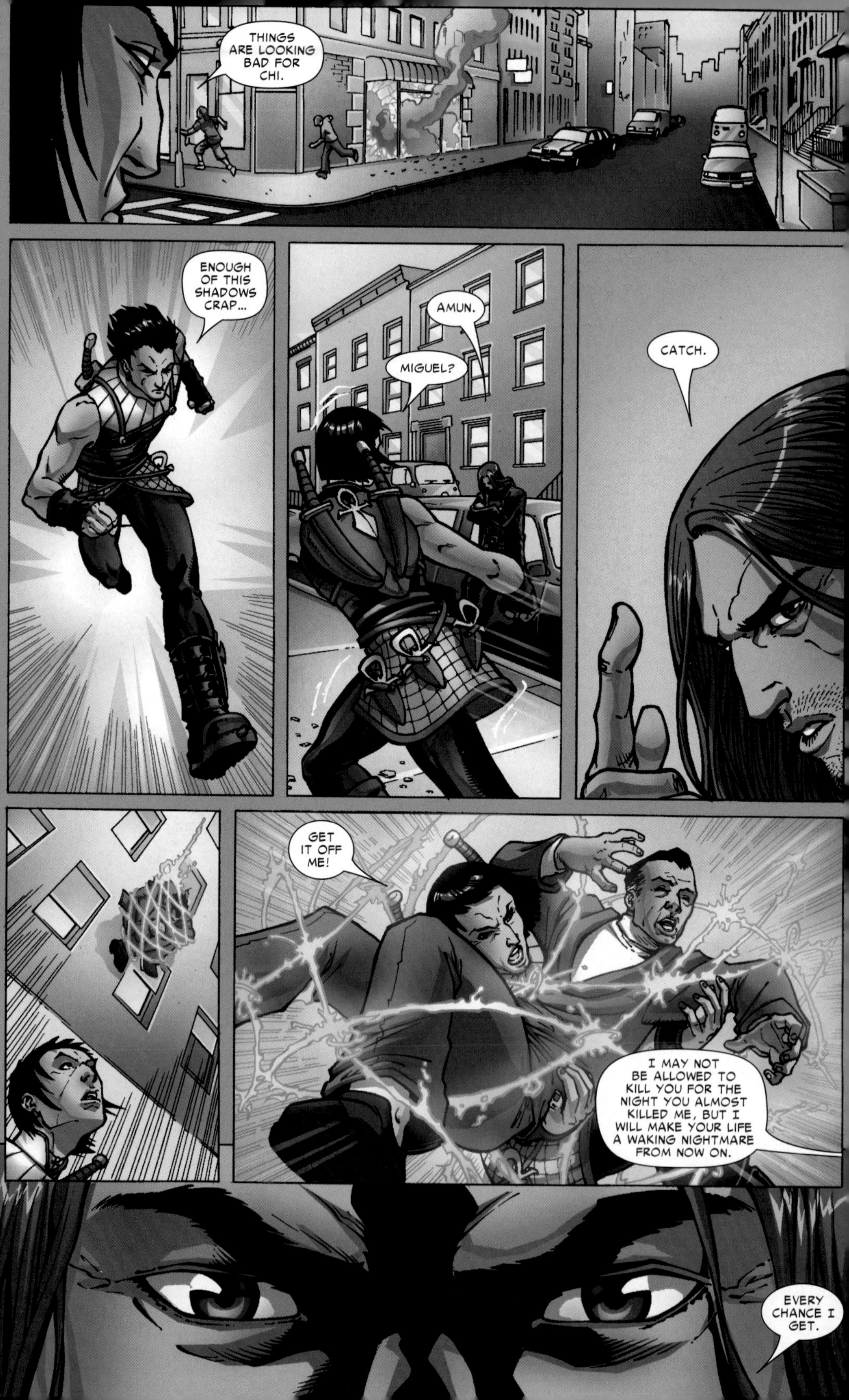
THINGS ARE LOOKING BAD FOR CHI.
ENOUGH OF THIS SHADOWS CRAP...
AMUN.
MIGUEL?
CATCH.
GET IT OFF ME!
I MAY NOT BE ALLOWED TO KILL YOU FOR THE NIGHT YOU ALMOST KILLED ME, BUT I WILL MAKE YOUR LIFE A WAKING NIGHTMARE FROM NOW ON.
EVERY CHANCE I GET.

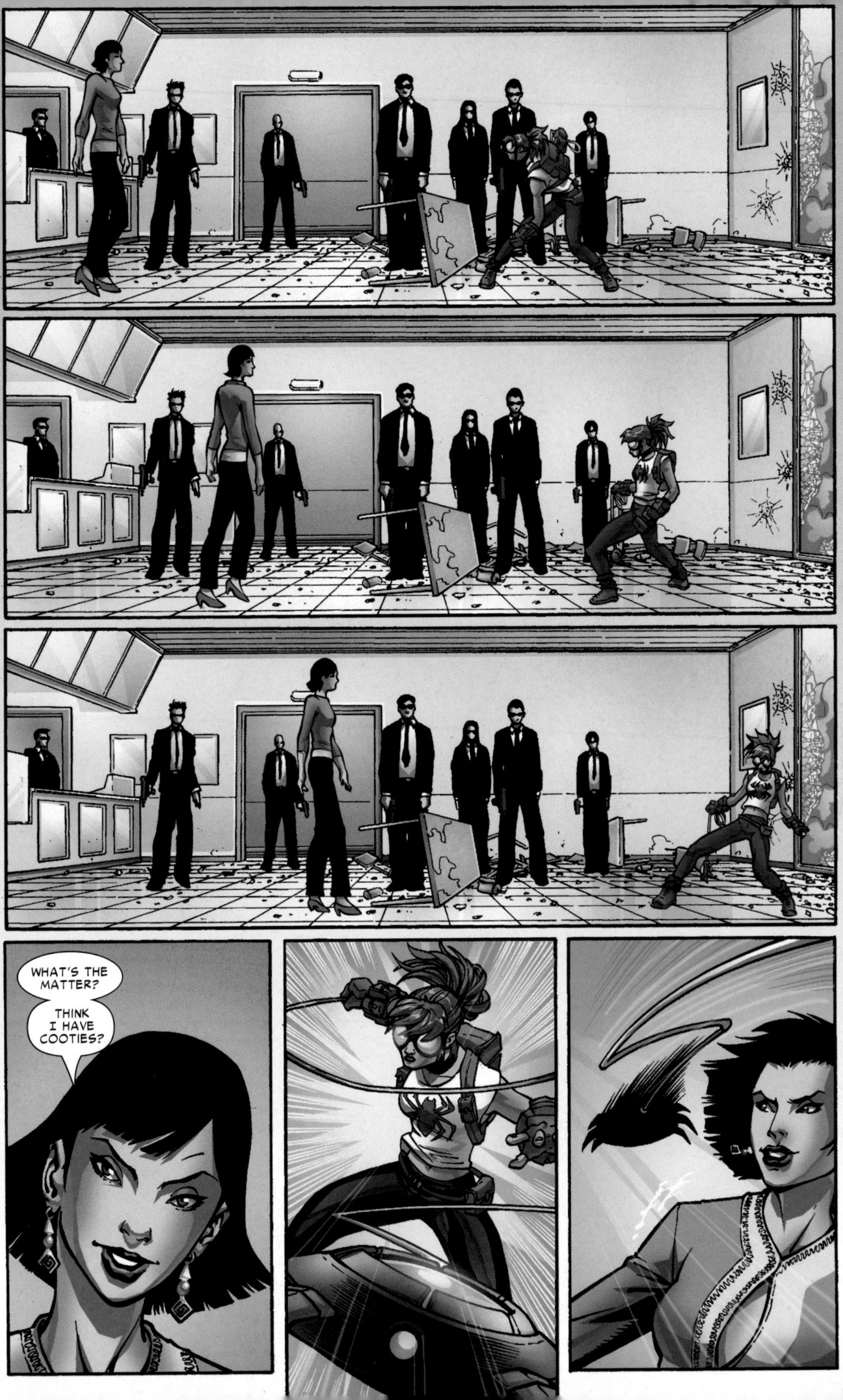
WHAT'S THE MATTER?
THINK I HAVE COOTIES?

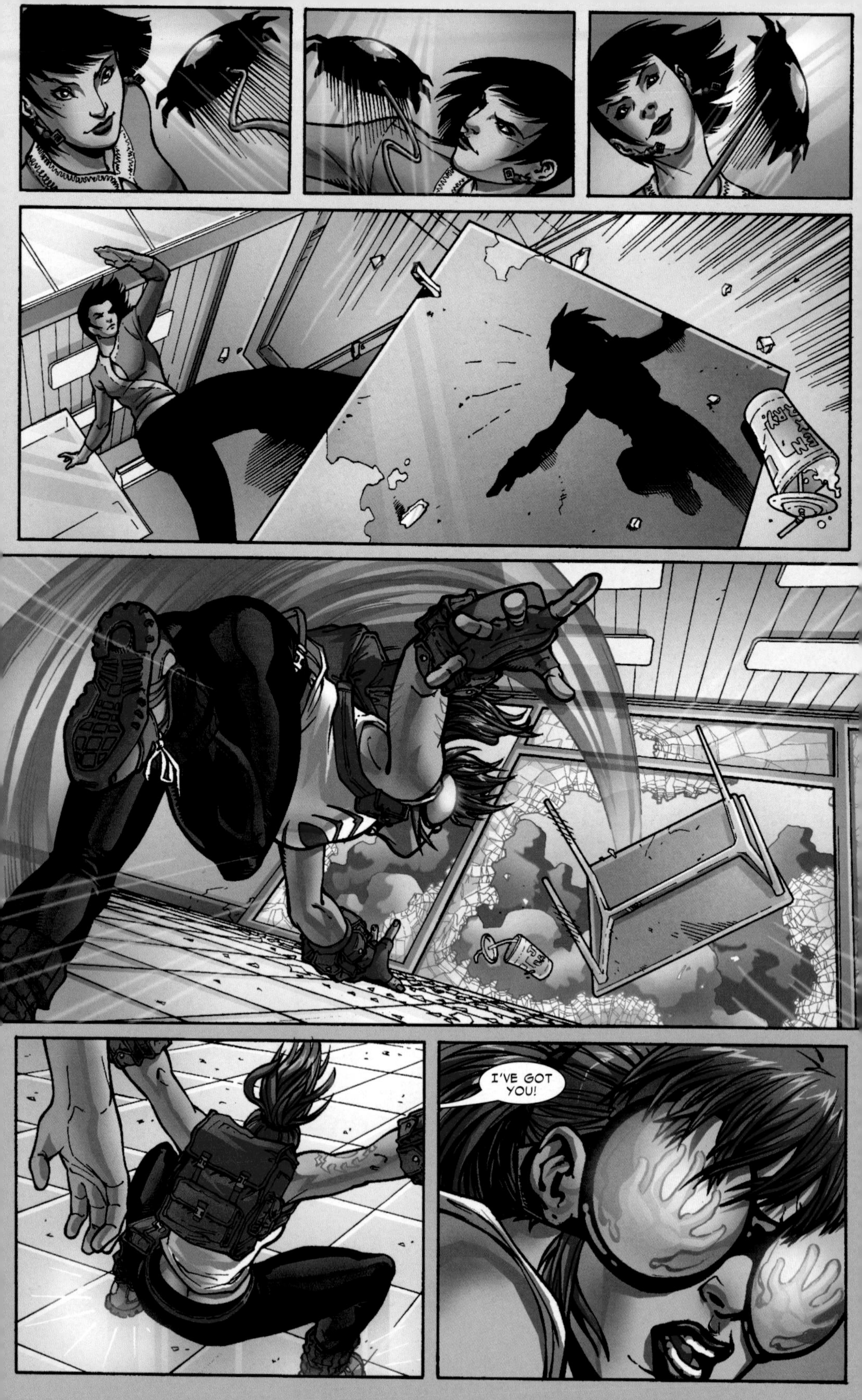
I'VE GOT YOU!

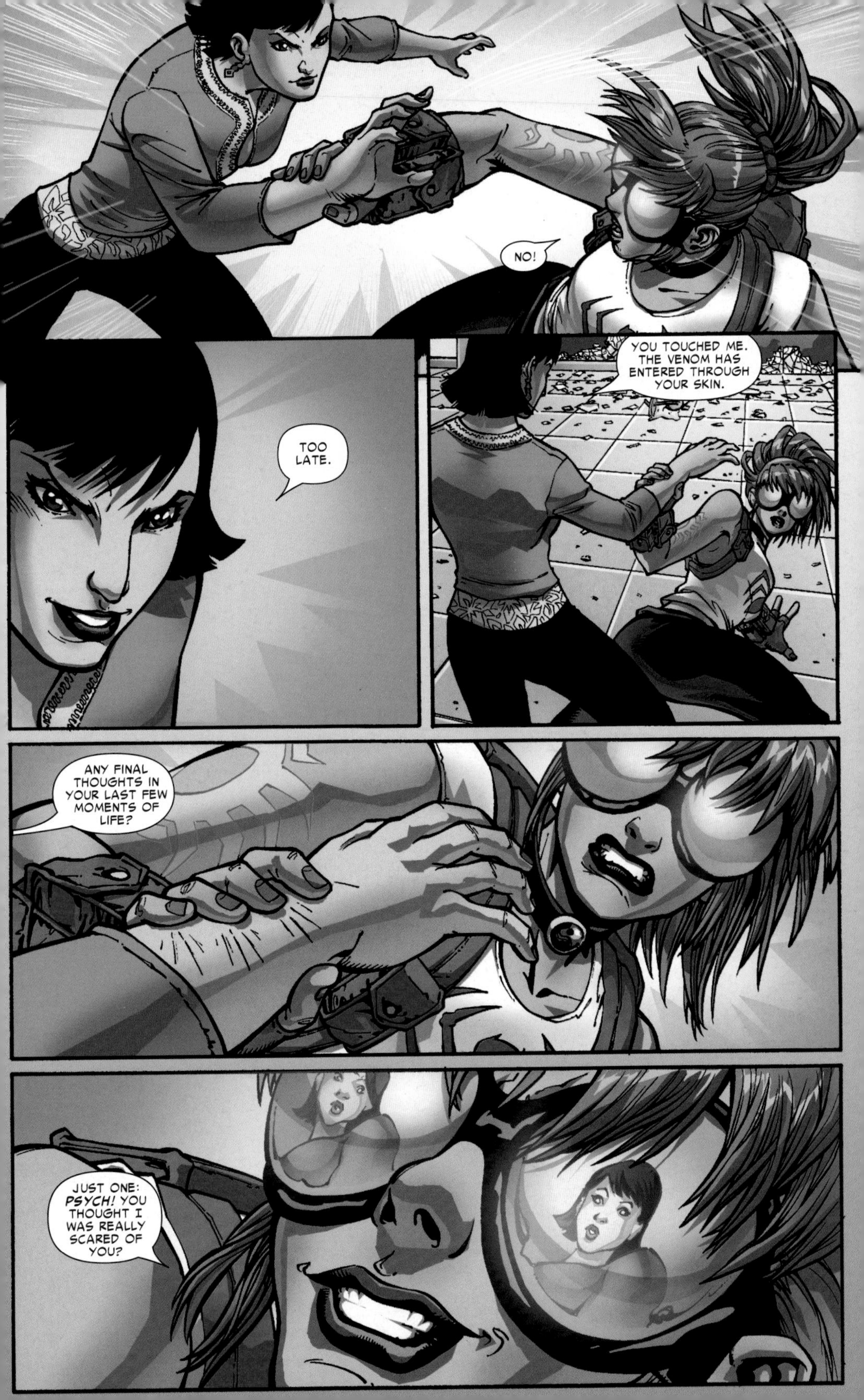
NO!
TOO LATE.
YOU TOUCHED ME. THE VENOM HAS ENTERED THROUGH YOUR SKIN.
ANY FINAL THOUGHTS IN YOUR LAST FEW MOMENTS OF LIFE?
JUST ONE: PSYCH! YOU THOUGHT I WAS REALLY SCARED OF YOU?

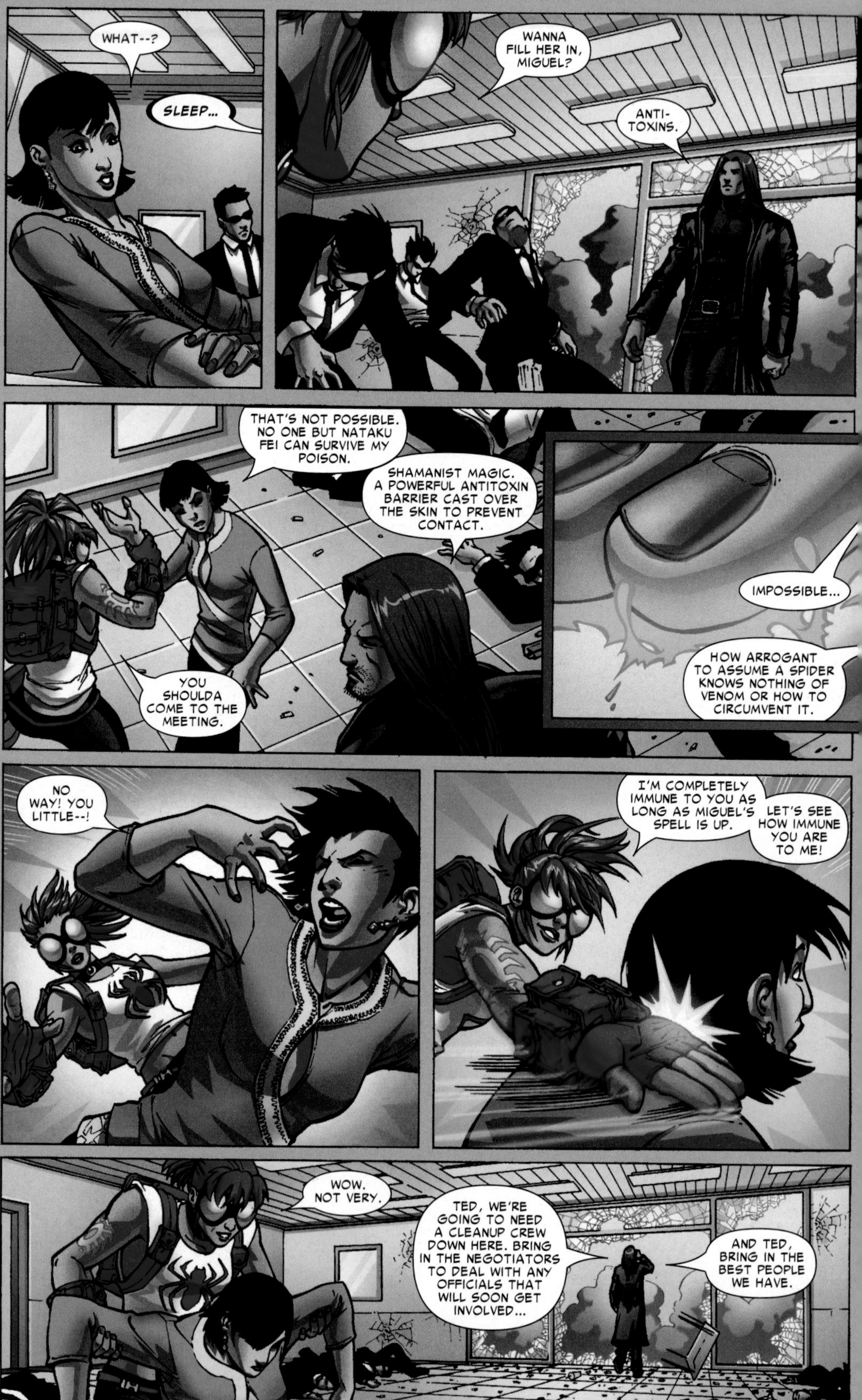
WHAT--?
SLEEP...
WANNA FILL HER IN, MIGUEL?
ANTI-TOXINS.
THAT'S NOT POSSIBLE. NO ONE BUT NATAKU FEI CAN SURVIVE MY POISON.
SHAMANIST MAGIC. A POWERFUL ANTITOXIN BARRIER CAST OVER THE SKIN TO PREVENT CONTACT.
YOU SHOULDA COME TO THE MEETING.
IMPOSSIBLE...
HOW ARROGANT TO ASSUME A SPIDER KNOWS NOTHING OF VENOM OR HOW TO CIRCUMVENT IT.
NO WAY! YOU LITTLE--!
I'M COMPLETELY IMMUNE TO YOU AS LONG AS MIGUEL'S SPELL IS UP.
LET'S SEE HOW IMMUNE YOU ARE TO ME!
WOW. NOT VERY.
TED, WE'RE GOING TO NEED A CLEANUP CREW DOWN HERE. BRING IN THE NEGOTIATORS TO DEAL WITH ANY OFFICIALS THAT WILL SOON GET INVOLVED...
AND TED, BRING IN THE BEST PEOPLE WE HAVE.

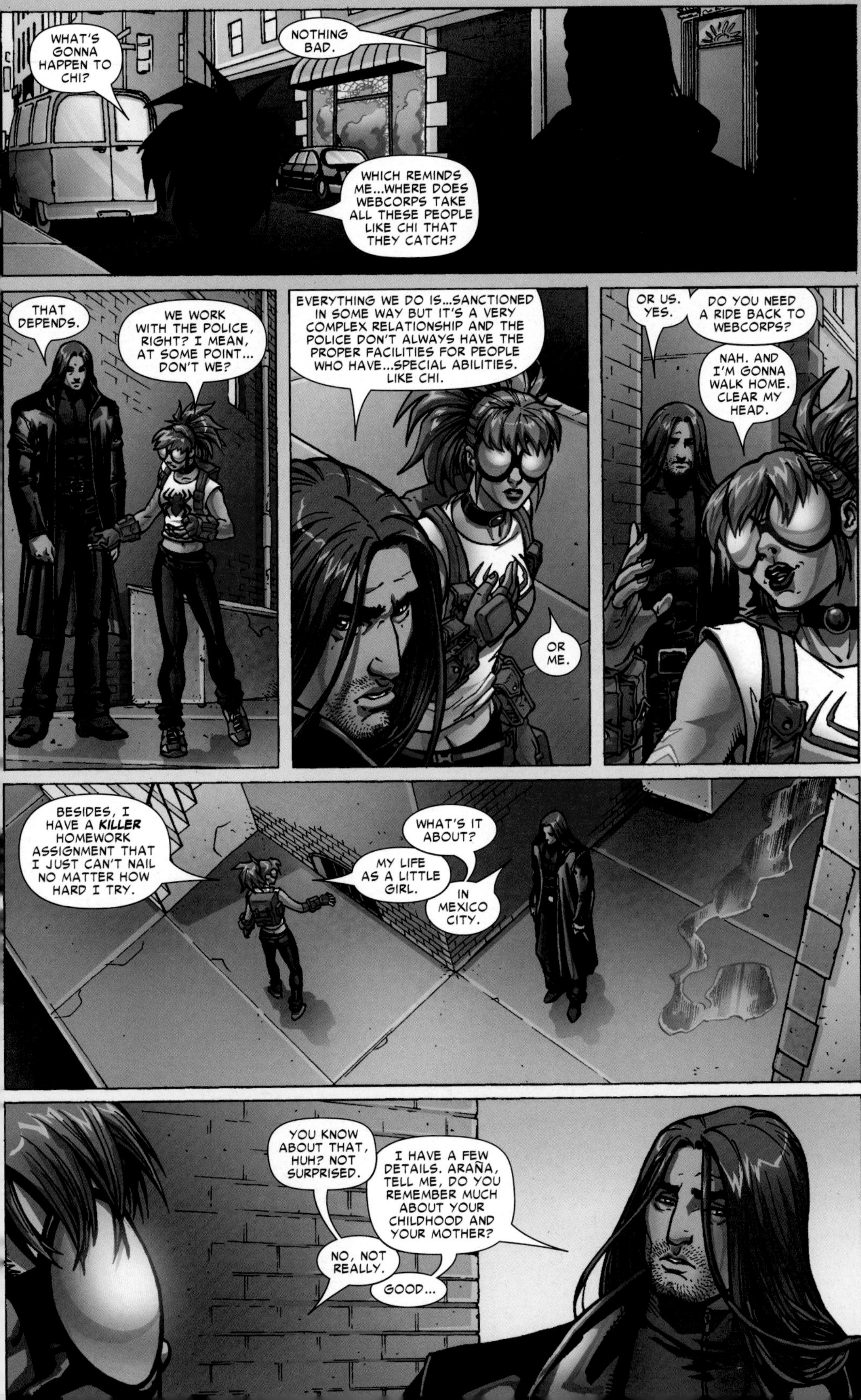
WHAT'S GONNA HAPPEN TO CHI?
NOTHING BAD.
WHICH REMINDS ME...WHERE DOES WEBCORPS TAKE ALL THESE PEOPLE LIKE CHI THAT THEY CATCH?
THAT DEPENDS.
WE WORK WITH THE POLICE, RIGHT? I MEAN, AT SOME POINT... DON'T WE?
EVERYTHING WE DO IS...SANCTIONED IN SOME WAY BUT IT'S A VERY COMPLEX RELATIONSHIP AND THE POLICE DON'T ALWAYS HAVE THE PROPER FACILITIES FOR PEOPLE WHO HAVE...SPECIAL ABILITIES. LIKE CHI.
OR ME.
OR US. YES.
DO YOU NEED A RIDE BACK TO WEBCORPS?
NAH. AND I'M GONNA WALK HOME. CLEAR MY HEAD.
BESIDES, I HAVE A KILLER HOMEWORK ASSIGNMENT THAT I JUST CAN'T NAIL NO MATTER HOW HARD I TRY.
WHAT'S IT ABOUT?
MY LIFE AS A LITTLE GIRL.
IN MEXICO CITY.
YOU KNOW ABOUT THAT, HUH? NOT SURPRISED.
I HAVE A FEW DETAILS. ARAÑA, TELL ME, DO YOU REMEMBER MUCH ABOUT YOUR CHILDHOOD AND YOUR MOTHER?
NO, NOT REALLY.
GOOD...

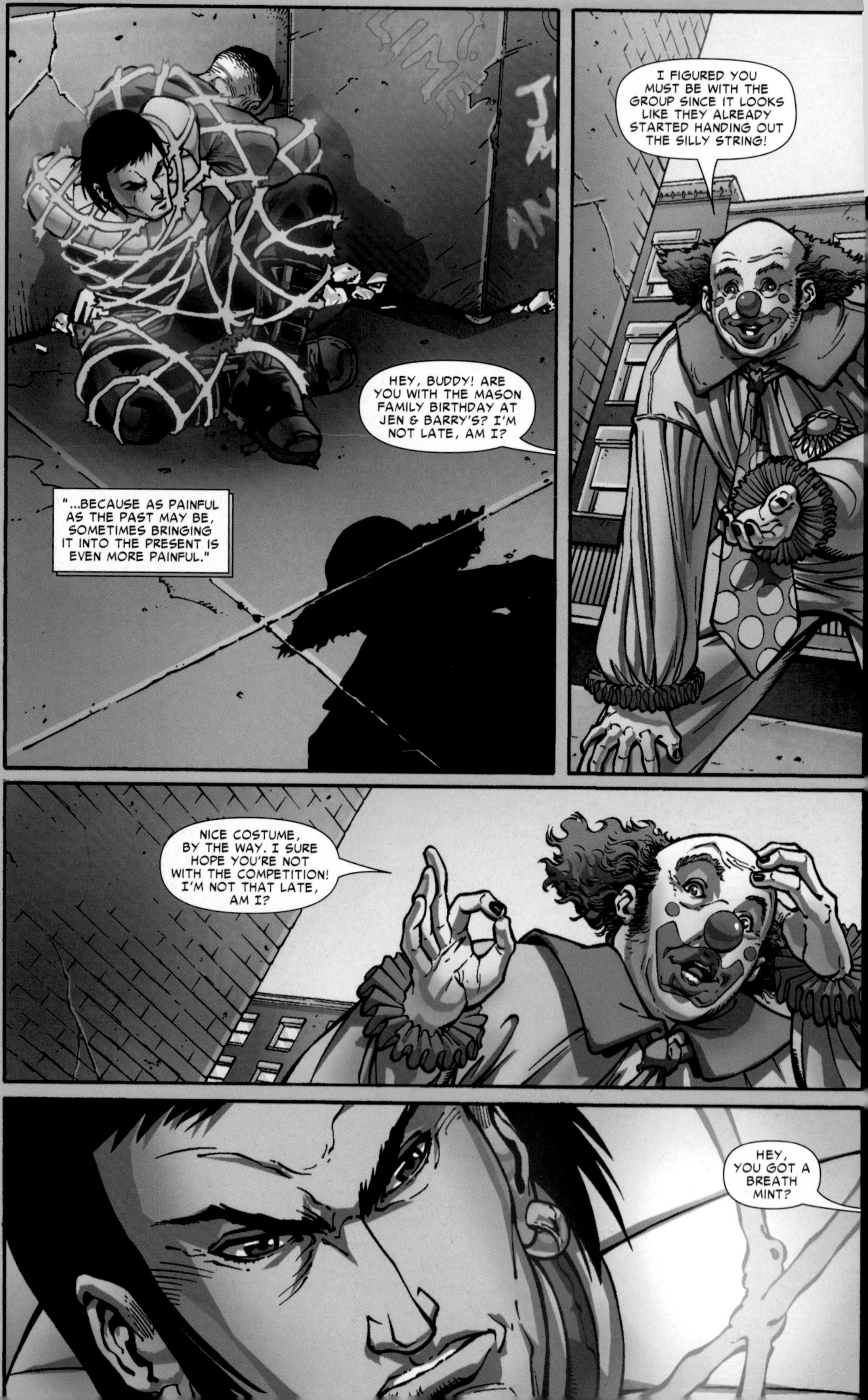
HEY, BUDDY! ARE YOU WITH THE MASON FAMILY BIRTHDAY AT JEN & BARRY'S? I'M NOT LATE, AM I?
"...BECAUSE AS PAINFUL AS THE PAST MAY BE, SOMETIMES BRINGING IT INTO THE PRESENT IS EVEN MORE PAINFUL."
I FIGURED YOU MUST BE WITH THE GROUP SINCE IT LOOKS LIKE THEY ALREADY STARTED HANDING OUT THE SILLY STRING!
NICE COSTUME, BY THE WAY. I SURE HOPE YOU'RE NOT WITH THE COMPETITION! I'M NOT THAT LATE, AM I?
HEY, YOU GOT A BREATH MINT?

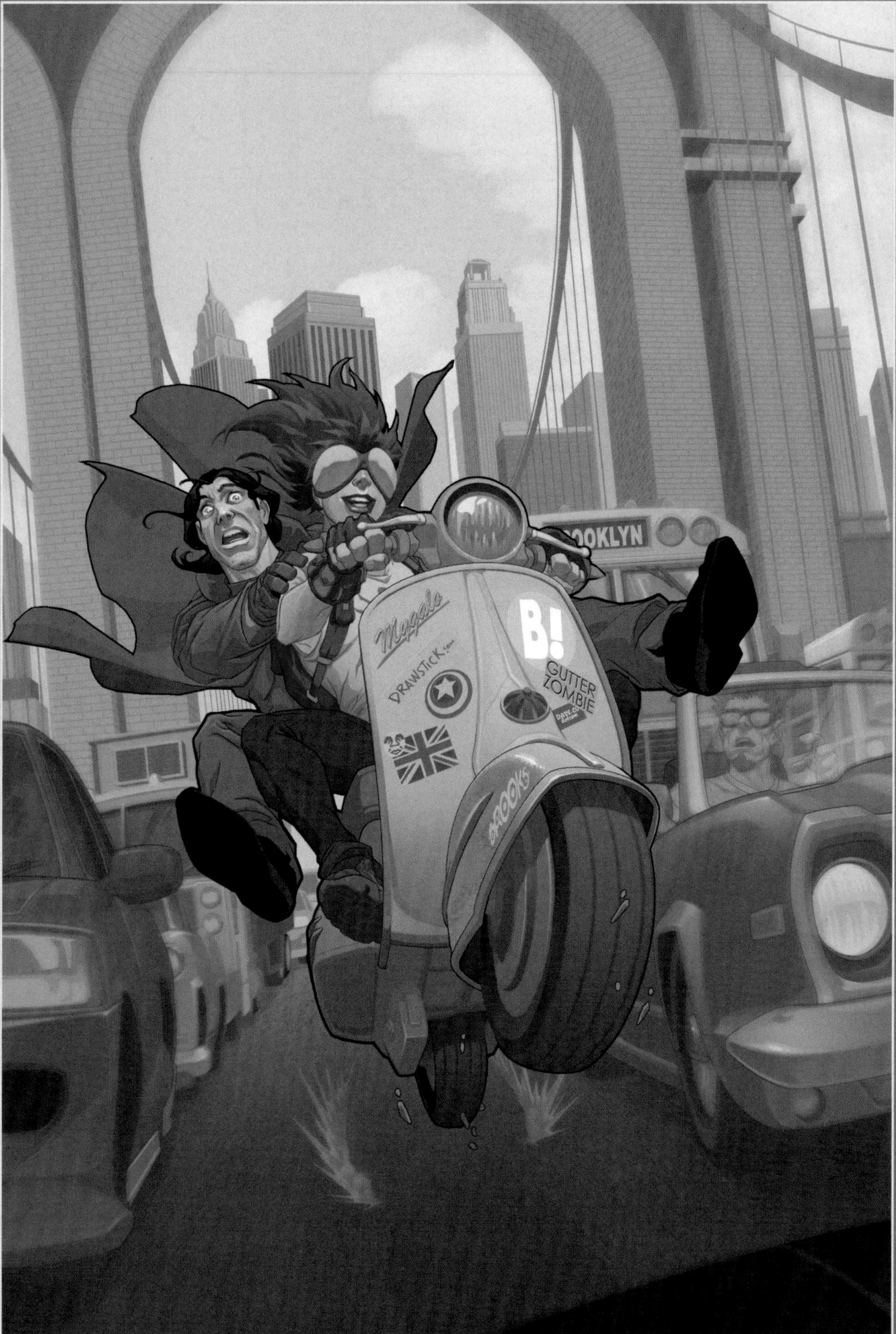

ROOKLYN
Mygalo
DRAWSTICK.com
B!
GUTTER
ZOMBIE
BROOKS

ARAÑA #8

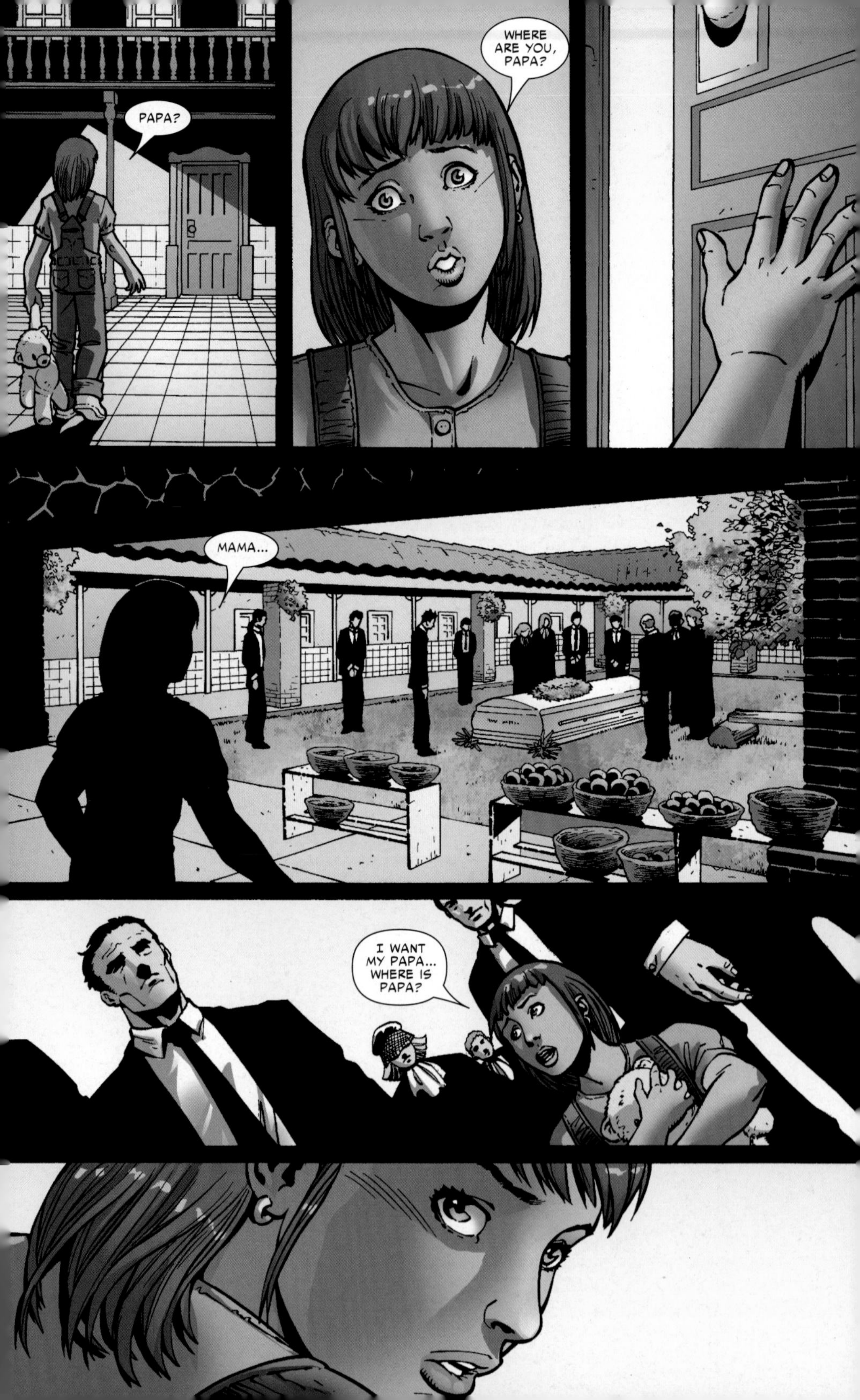
PAPA?
WHERE ARE YOU, PAPA?
MAMA...
I WANT MY PAPA... WHERE IS PAPA?

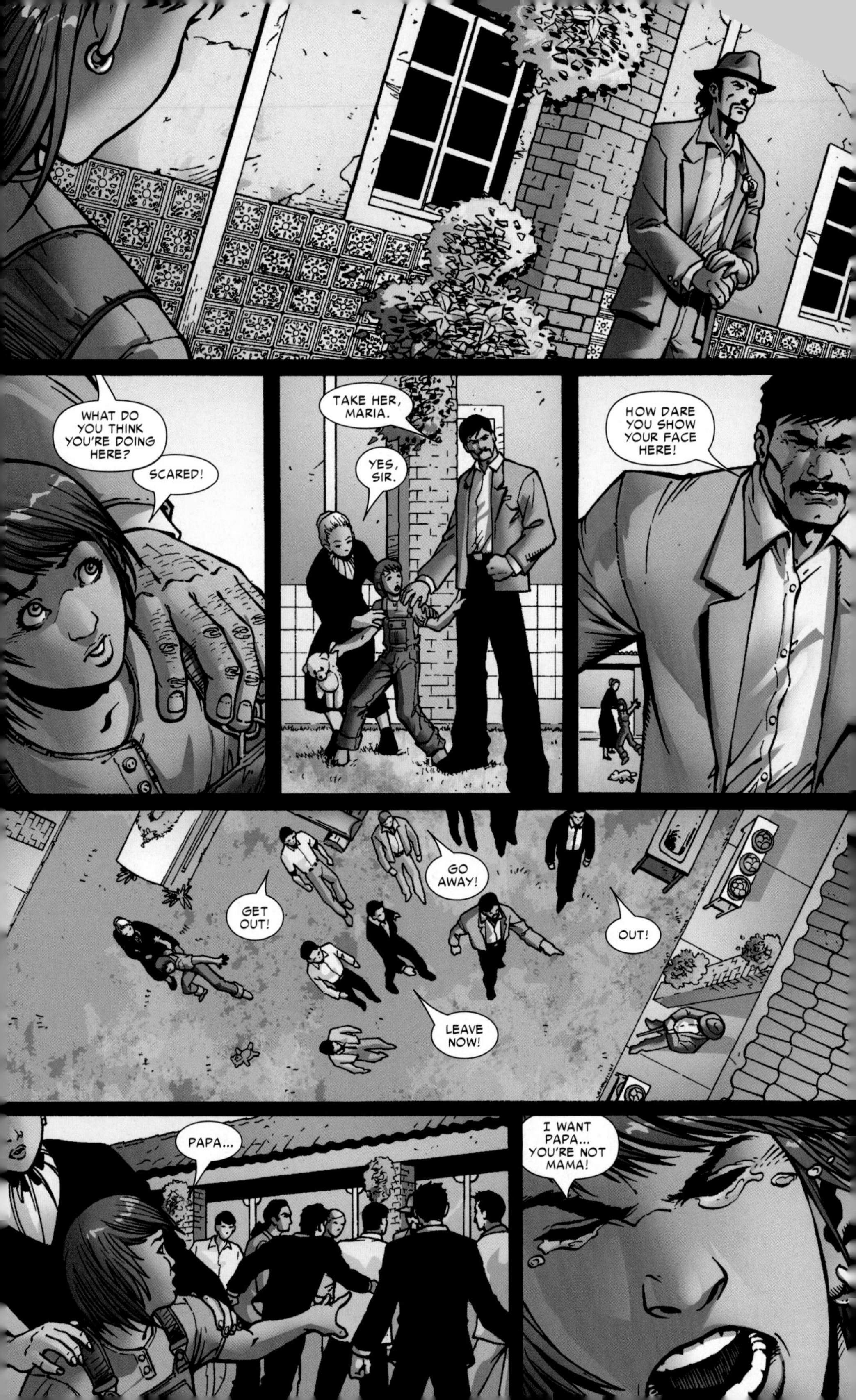
WHAT DO YOU THINK YOU'RE DOING HERE?
SCARED!
TAKE HER, MARIA.
YES, SIR.
HOW DARE YOU SHOW YOUR FACE HERE!
GET OUT!
GO AWAY!
OUT!
LEAVE NOW!
PAPA...
I WANT PAPA... YOU'RE NOT MAMA!

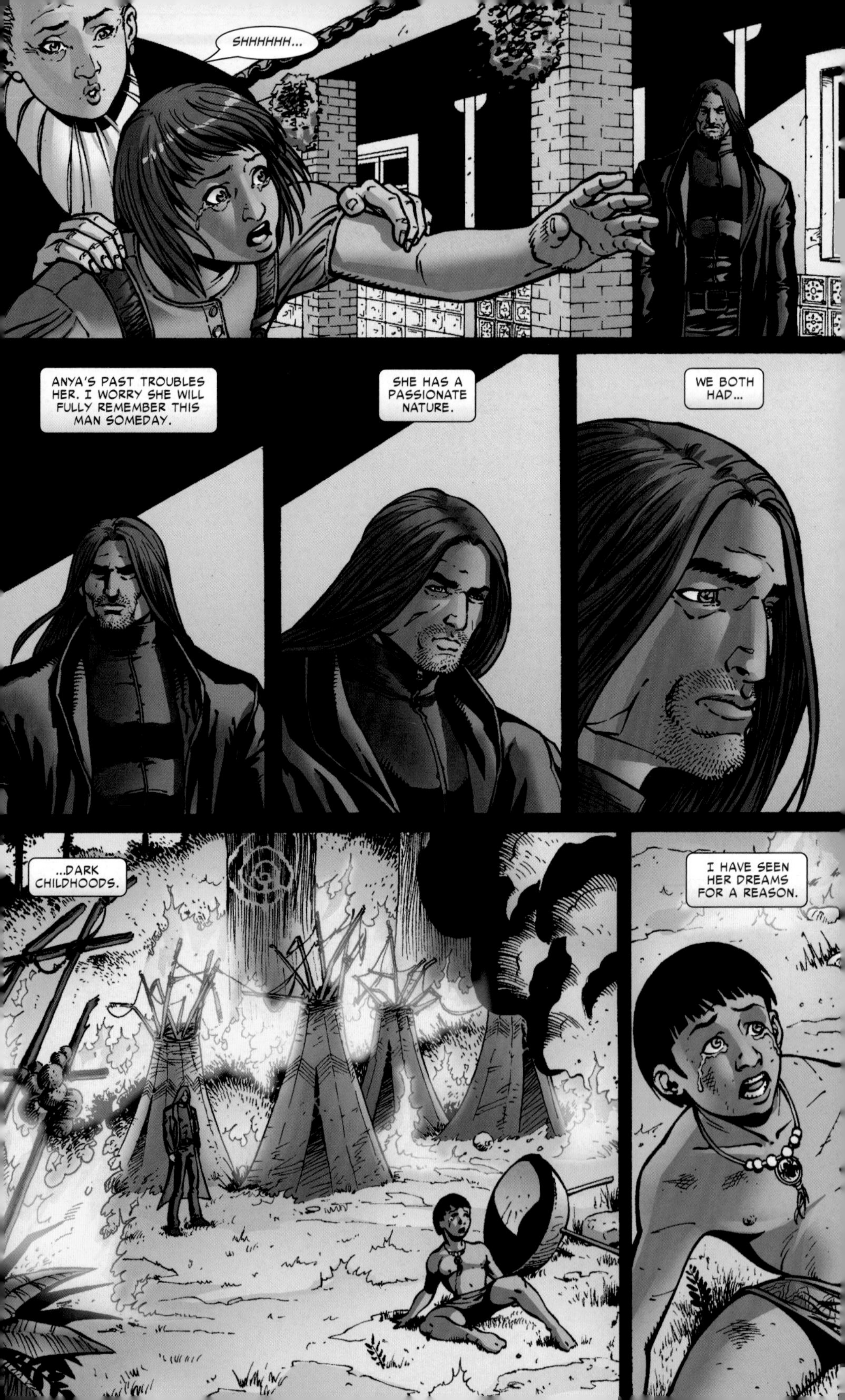
SHHHHHH...
ANYA'S PAST TROUBLES HER. I WORRY SHE WILL FULLY REMEMBER THIS MAN SOMEDAY.
SHE HAS A PASSIONATE NATURE.
WE BOTH HAD...
...DARK CHILDHOODS.
I HAVE SEEN HER DREAMS FOR A REASON.

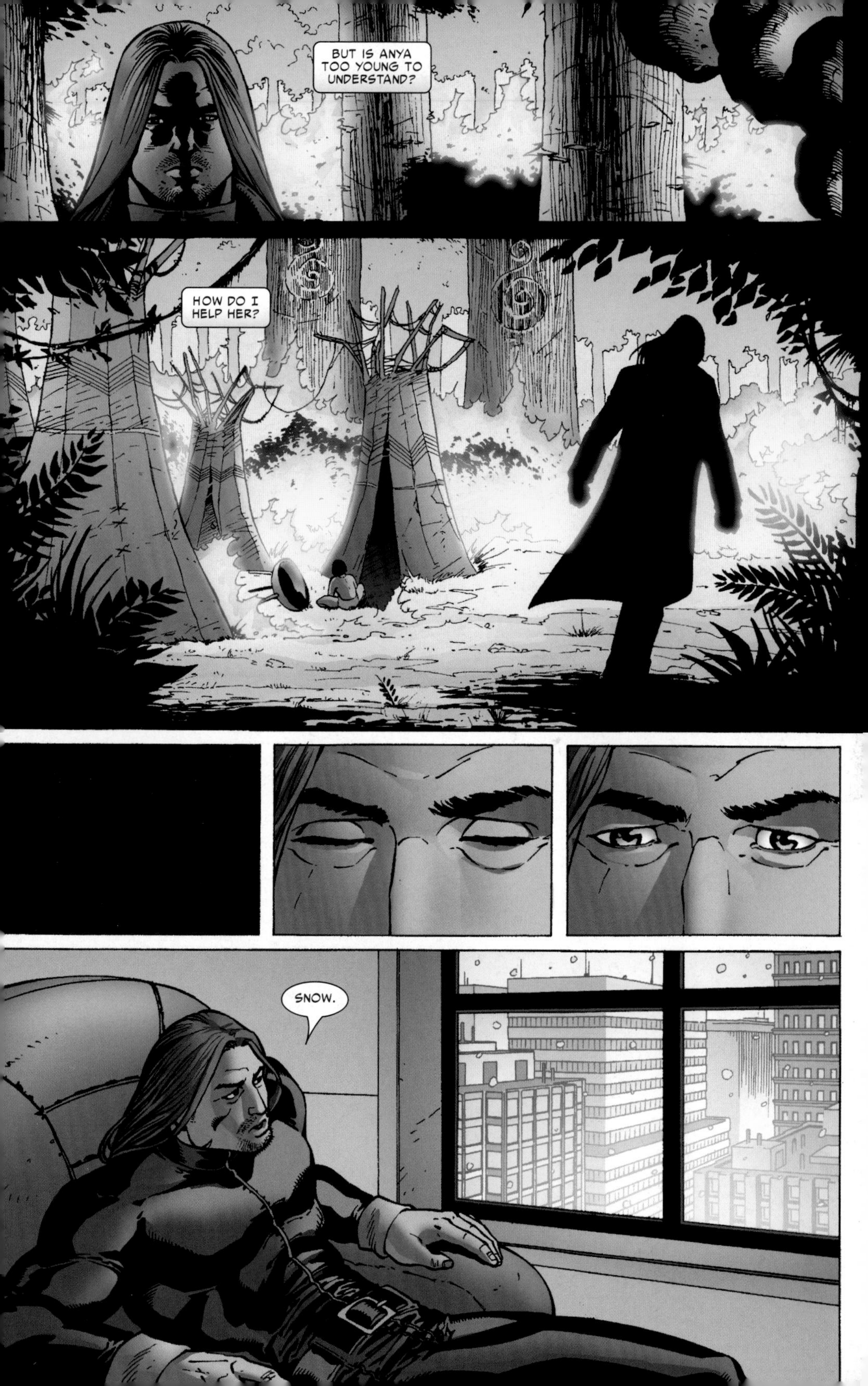
BUT IS ANYA TOO YOUNG TO UNDERSTAND?
HOW DO I HELP HER?
SNOW.

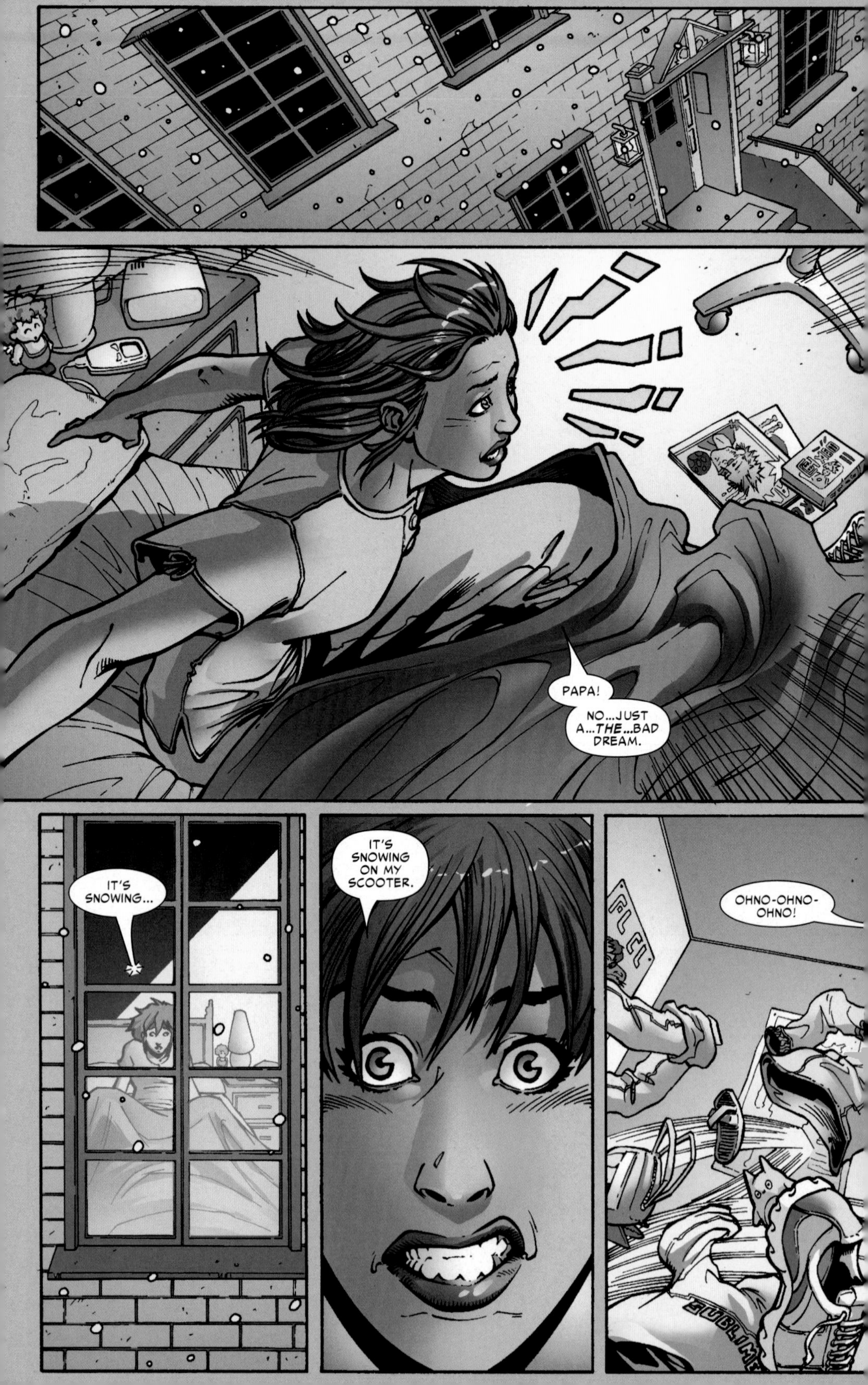
PAPA!
NO...JUST A...THE...BAD DREAM.
IT'S SNOWING...
IT'S SNOWING ON MY SCOOTER.
OHNO-OHNO-OHNO!

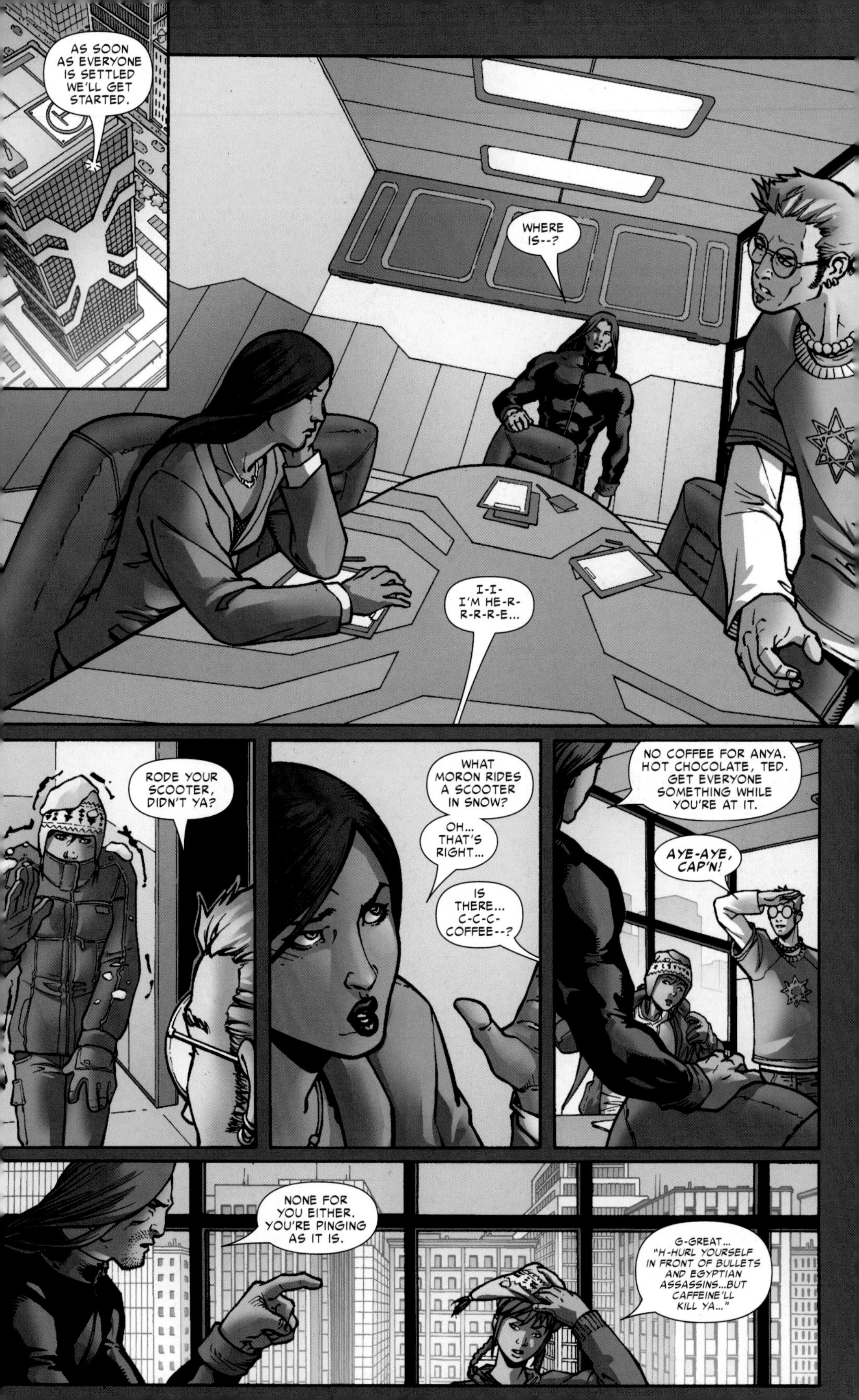
AS SOON AS EVERYONE IS SETTLED WE'LL GET STARTED.
WHERE IS--?
I-I- I'M HE-R-R-R-R-E...
RODE YOUR SCOOTER, DIDN'T YA?
WHAT MORON RIDES A SCOOTER IN SNOW?
OH... THAT'S RIGHT...
IS THERE... C-C-C-COFFEE--?
NO COFFEE FOR ANYA. HOT CHOCOLATE, TED. GET EVERYONE SOMETHING WHILE YOU'RE AT IT.
AYE-AYE, CAP'N!
NONE FOR YOU EITHER. YOU'RE PINGING AS IT IS.
G-GREAT... "H-HURL YOURSELF IN FRONT OF BULLETS AND EGYPTIAN ASSASSINS...BUT CAFFEINE'LL KILL YA..."

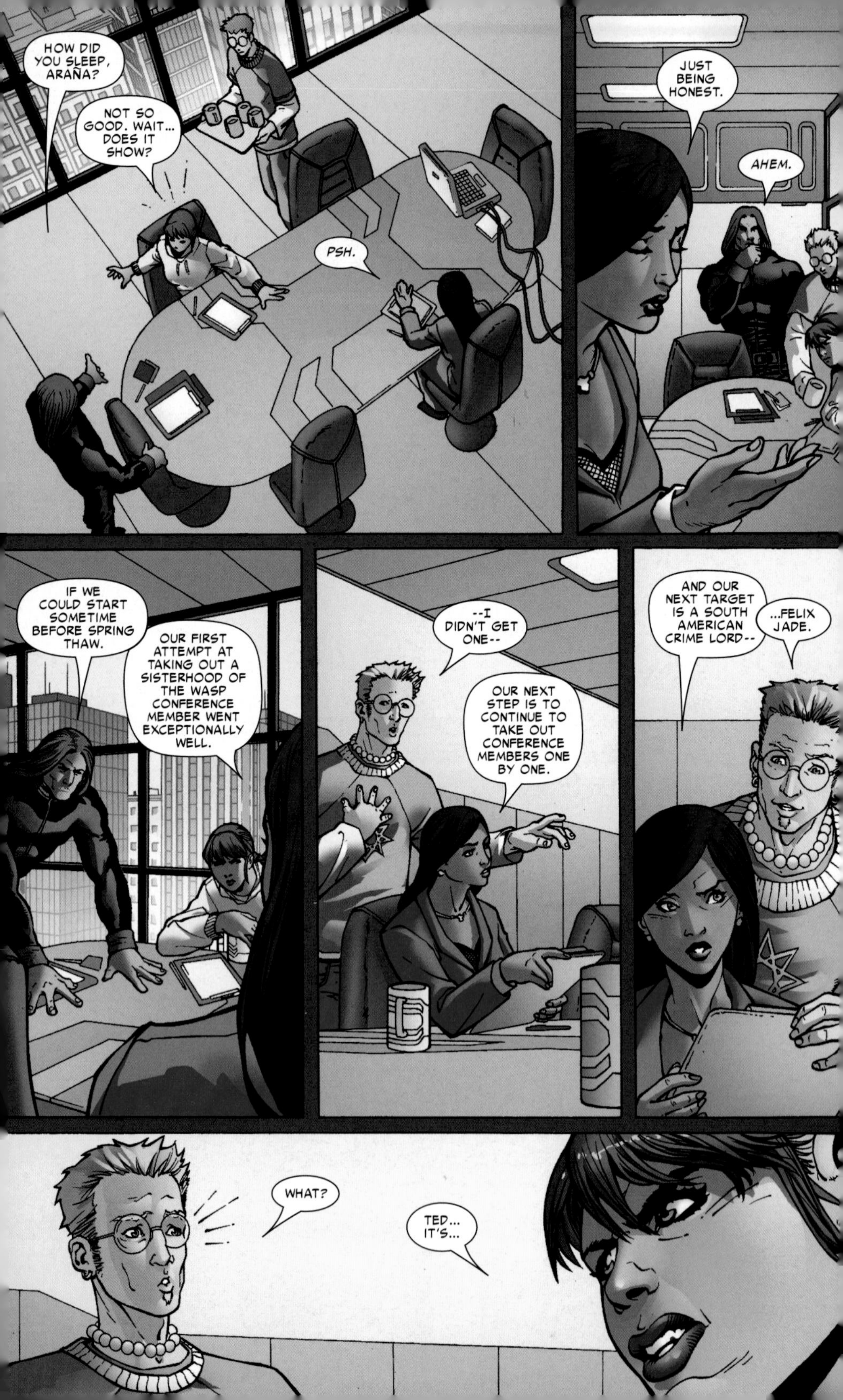
HOW DID YOU SLEEP, ARAÑA?
NOT SO GOOD. WAIT... DOES IT SHOW?
PSH.
JUST BEING HONEST.
AHEM.
IF WE COULD START SOMETIME BEFORE SPRING THAW.
OUR FIRST ATTEMPT AT TAKING OUT A SISTERHOOD OF THE WASP CONFERENCE MEMBER WENT EXCEPTIONALLY WELL.
--I DIDN'T GET ONE--
OUR NEXT STEP IS TO CONTINUE TO TAKE OUT CONFERENCE MEMBERS ONE BY ONE.
AND OUR NEXT TARGET IS A SOUTH AMERICAN CRIME LORD--
...FELIX JADE.
WHAT?
TED... IT'S...

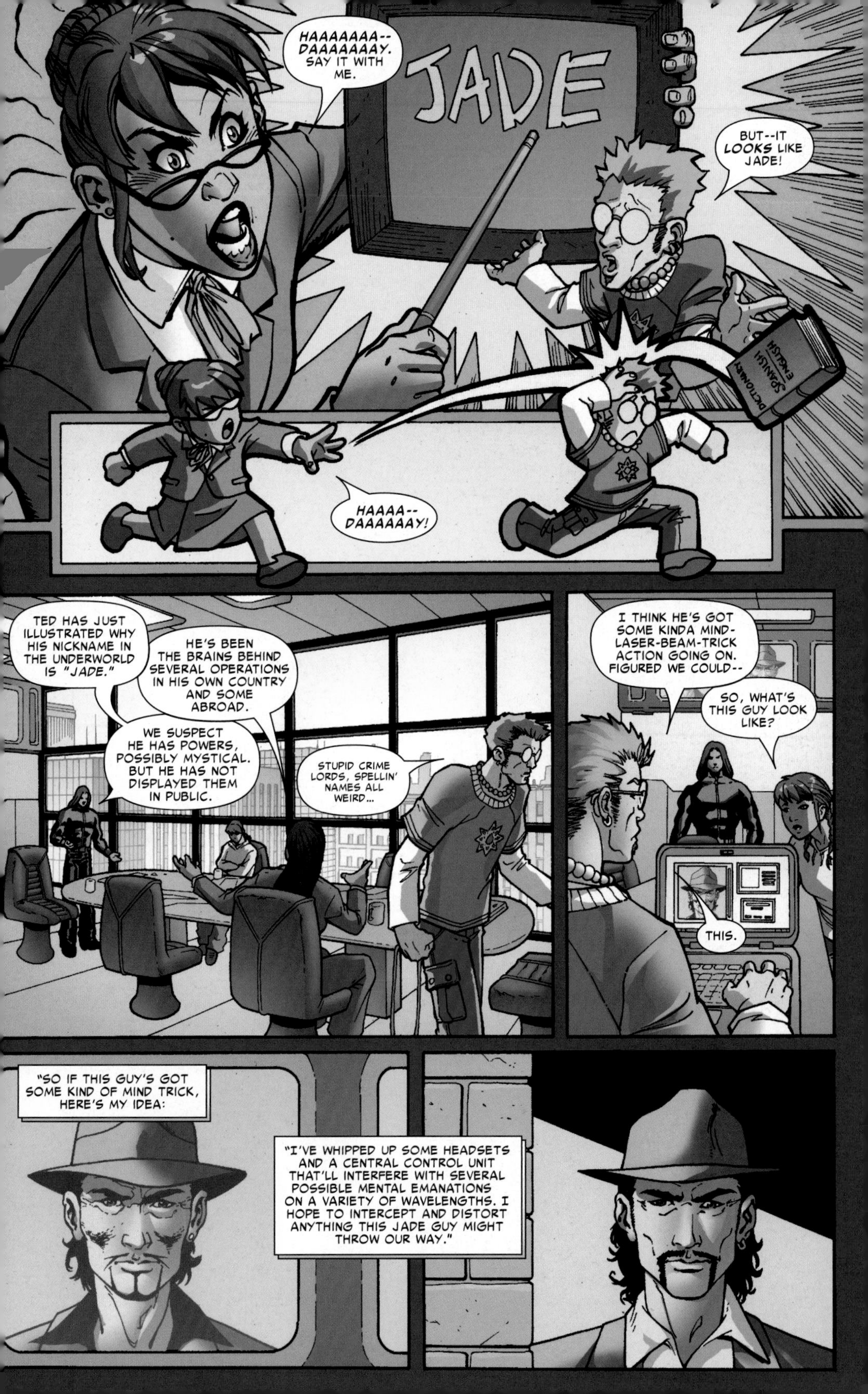
HAAAAAAA--DAAAAAAAY. SAY IT WITH ME.
JADE
BUT--IT LOOKS LIKE JADE!
DICTIONARY SPANISH ENGLISH
HAAAA--DAAAAAAY!
TED HAS JUST ILLUSTRATED WHY HIS NICKNAME IN THE UNDERWORLD IS "JADE."
HE'S BEEN THE BRAINS BEHIND SEVERAL OPERATIONS IN HIS OWN COUNTRY AND SOME ABROAD.
WE SUSPECT HE HAS POWERS, POSSIBLY MYSTICAL. BUT HE HAS NOT DISPLAYED THEM IN PUBLIC.
STUPID CRIME LORDS, SPELLIN' NAMES ALL WEIRD...
I THINK HE'S GOT SOME KINDA MIND-LASER-BEAM-TRICK ACTION GOING ON. FIGURED WE COULD--
SO, WHAT'S THIS GUY LOOK LIKE?
THIS.
"SO IF THIS GUY'S GOT SOME KIND OF MIND TRICK, HERE'S MY IDEA:
"I'VE WHIPPED UP SOME HEADSETS AND A CENTRAL CONTROL UNIT THAT'LL INTERFERE WITH SEVERAL POSSIBLE MENTAL EMANATIONS ON A VARIETY OF WAVELENGTHS. I HOPE TO INTERCEPT AND DISTORT ANYTHING THIS JADE GUY MIGHT THROW OUR WAY."

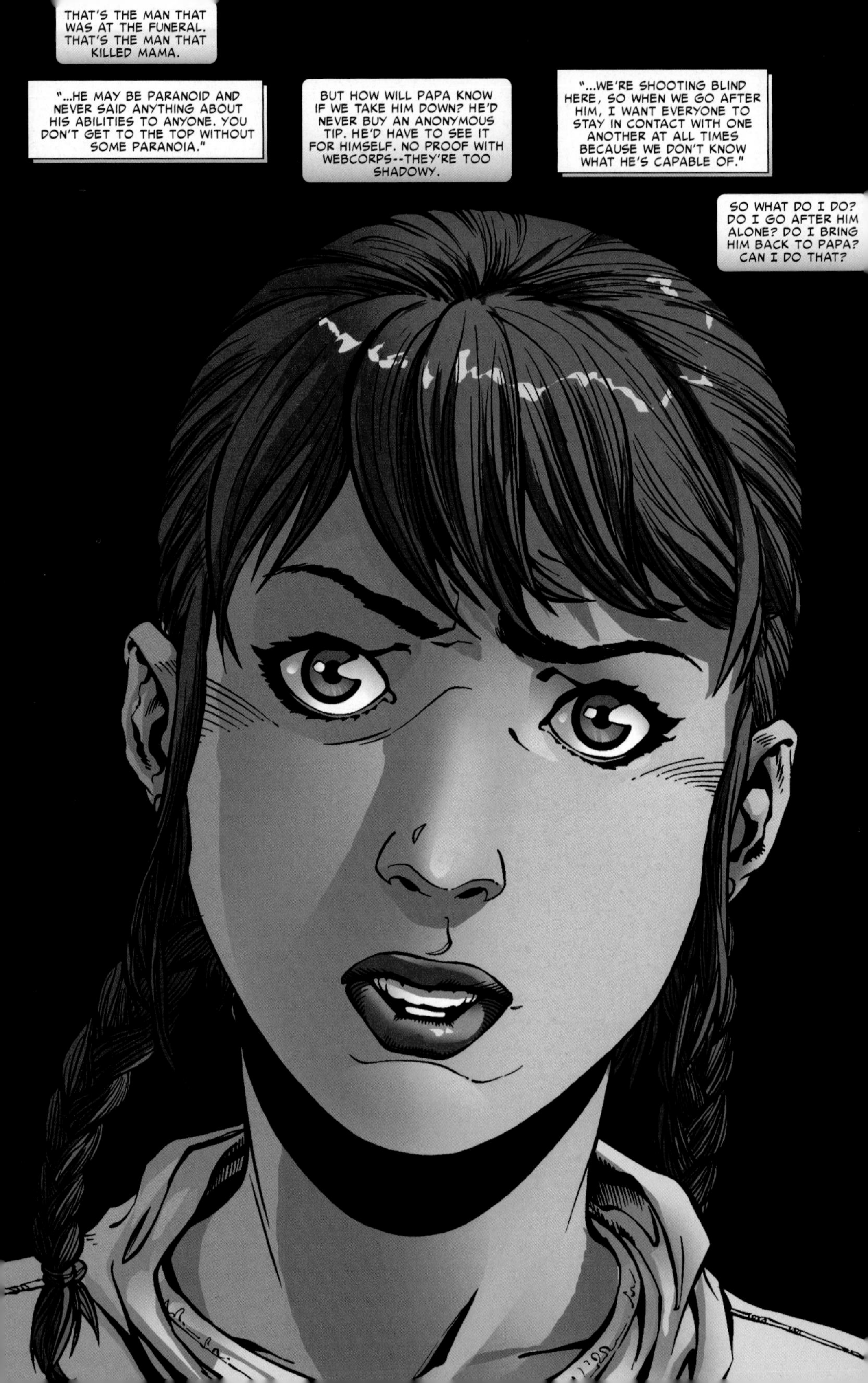
THAT'S THE MAN THAT WAS AT THE FUNERAL. THAT'S THE MAN THAT KILLED MAMA.
"...HE MAY BE PARANOID AND NEVER SAID ANYTHING ABOUT HIS ABILITIES TO ANYONE. YOU DON'T GET TO THE TOP WITHOUT SOME PARANOIA."
BUT HOW WILL PAPA KNOW IF WE TAKE HIM DOWN? HE'D NEVER BUY AN ANONYMOUS TIP. HE'D HAVE TO SEE IT FOR HIMSELF. NO PROOF WITH WEBCORPS--THEY'RE TOO SHADOWY.
"...WE'RE SHOOTING BLIND HERE, SO WHEN WE GO AFTER HIM, I WANT EVERYONE TO STAY IN CONTACT WITH ONE ANOTHER AT ALL TIMES BECAUSE WE DON'T KNOW WHAT HE'S CAPABLE OF."
SO WHAT DO I DO? DO I GO AFTER HIM ALONE? DO I BRING HIM BACK TO PAPA? CAN I DO THAT?

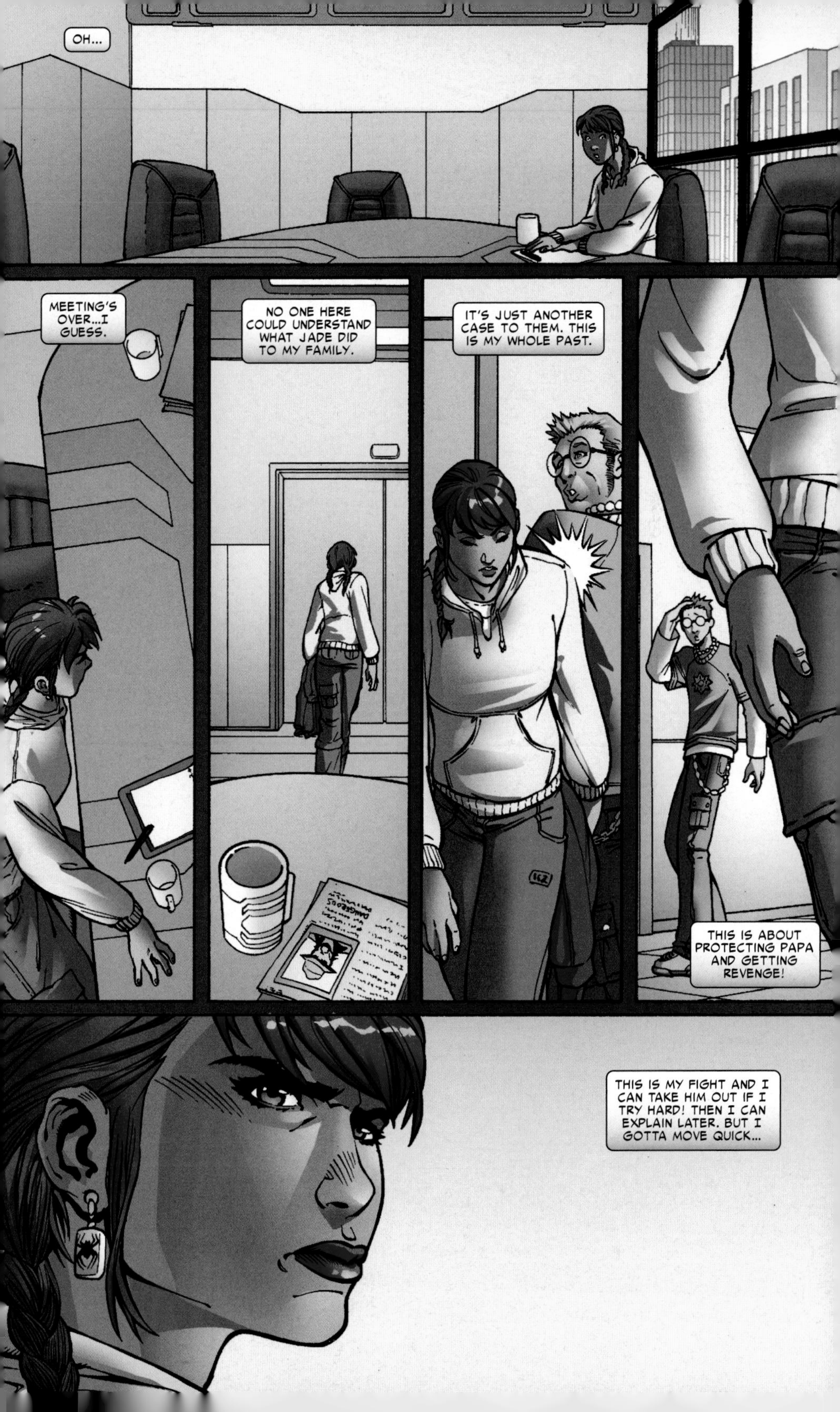
OH...
MEETING'S OVER...I GUESS.
NO ONE HERE COULD UNDERSTAND WHAT JADE DID TO MY FAMILY.
IT'S JUST ANOTHER CASE TO THEM. THIS IS MY WHOLE PAST.
THIS IS ABOUT PROTECTING PAPA AND GETTING REVENGE!
THIS IS MY FIGHT AND I CAN TAKE HIM OUT IF I TRY HARD! THEN I CAN EXPLAIN LATER. BUT I GOTTA MOVE QUICK...

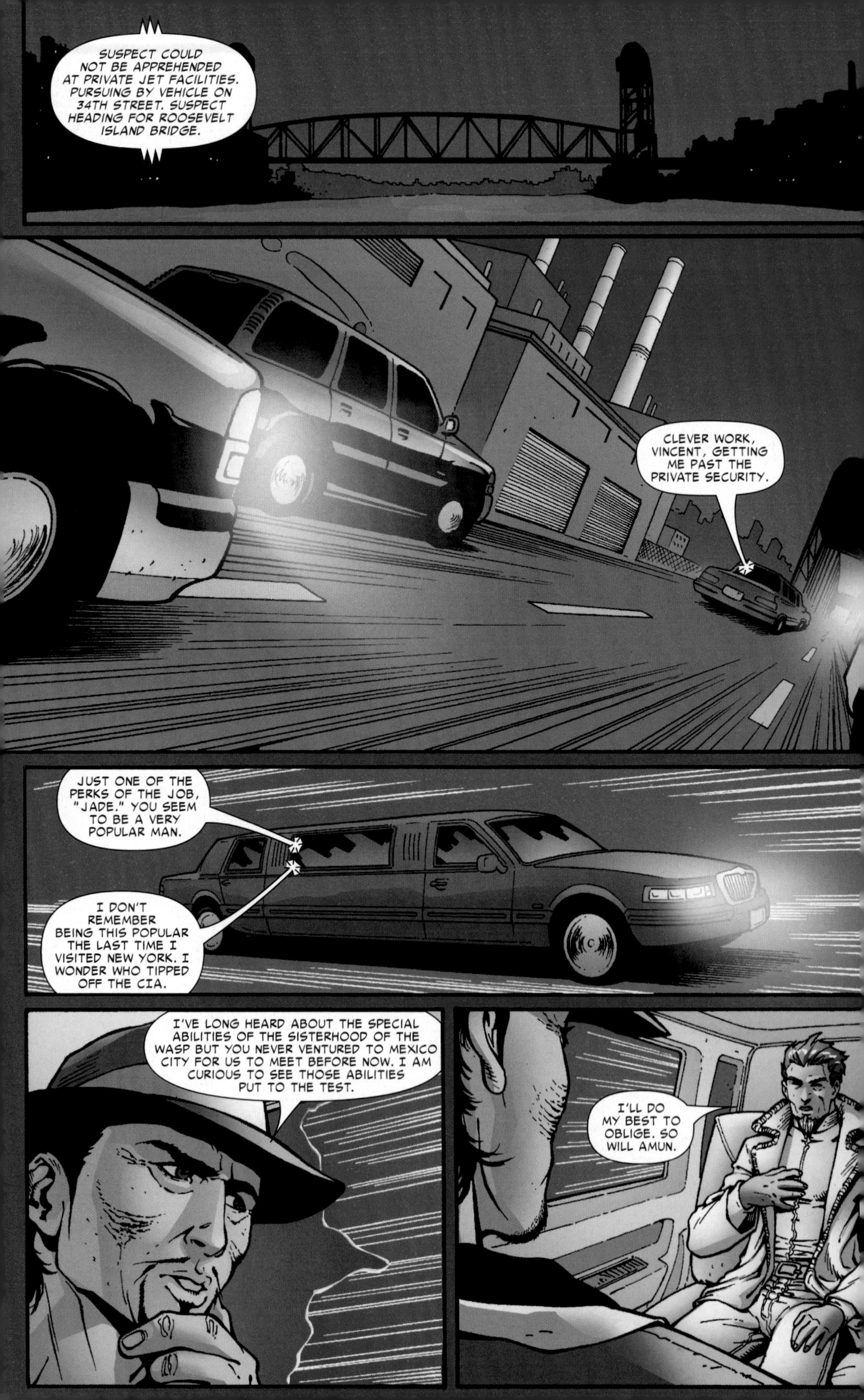
SUSPECT COULD NOT BE APPREHENDED AT PRIVATE JET FACILITIES. PURSUING BY VEHICLE ON 34TH STREET. SUSPECT HEADING FOR ROOSEVELT ISLAND BRIDGE.
CLEVER WORK, VINCENT, GETTING ME PAST THE PRIVATE SECURITY.
JUST ONE OF THE PERKS OF THE JOB, "JADE." YOU SEEM TO BE A VERY POPULAR MAN.
I DON'T REMEMBER BEING THIS POPULAR THE LAST TIME I VISITED NEW YORK. I WONDER WHO TIPPED OFF THE CIA.
I'VE LONG HEARD ABOUT THE SPECIAL ABILITIES OF THE SISTERHOOD OF THE WASP BUT YOU NEVER VENTURED TO MEXICO CITY FOR US TO MEET BEFORE NOW. I AM CURIOUS TO SEE THOSE ABILITIES PUT TO THE TEST.
I'LL DO MY BEST TO OBLIGE. SO WILL AMUN.

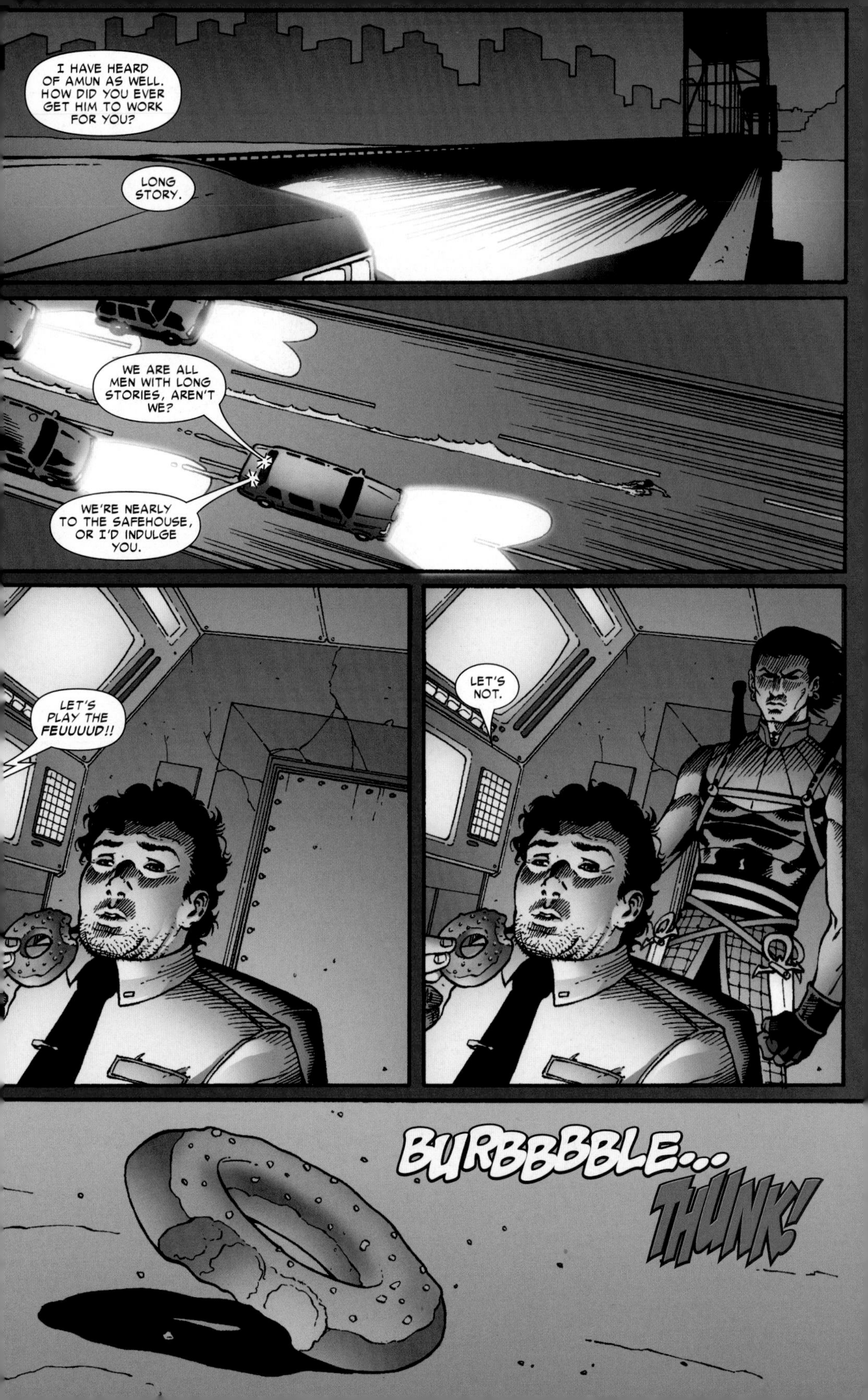
I HAVE HEARD OF AMUN AS WELL. HOW DID YOU EVER GET HIM TO WORK FOR YOU?
LONG STORY.
WE ARE ALL MEN WITH LONG STORIES, AREN'T WE?
WE'RE NEARLY TO THE SAFEHOUSE, OR I'D INDULGE YOU.
LET'S PLAY THE FEUUUUD!!
LET'S NOT.
BURBBBBLE...
THUNK!

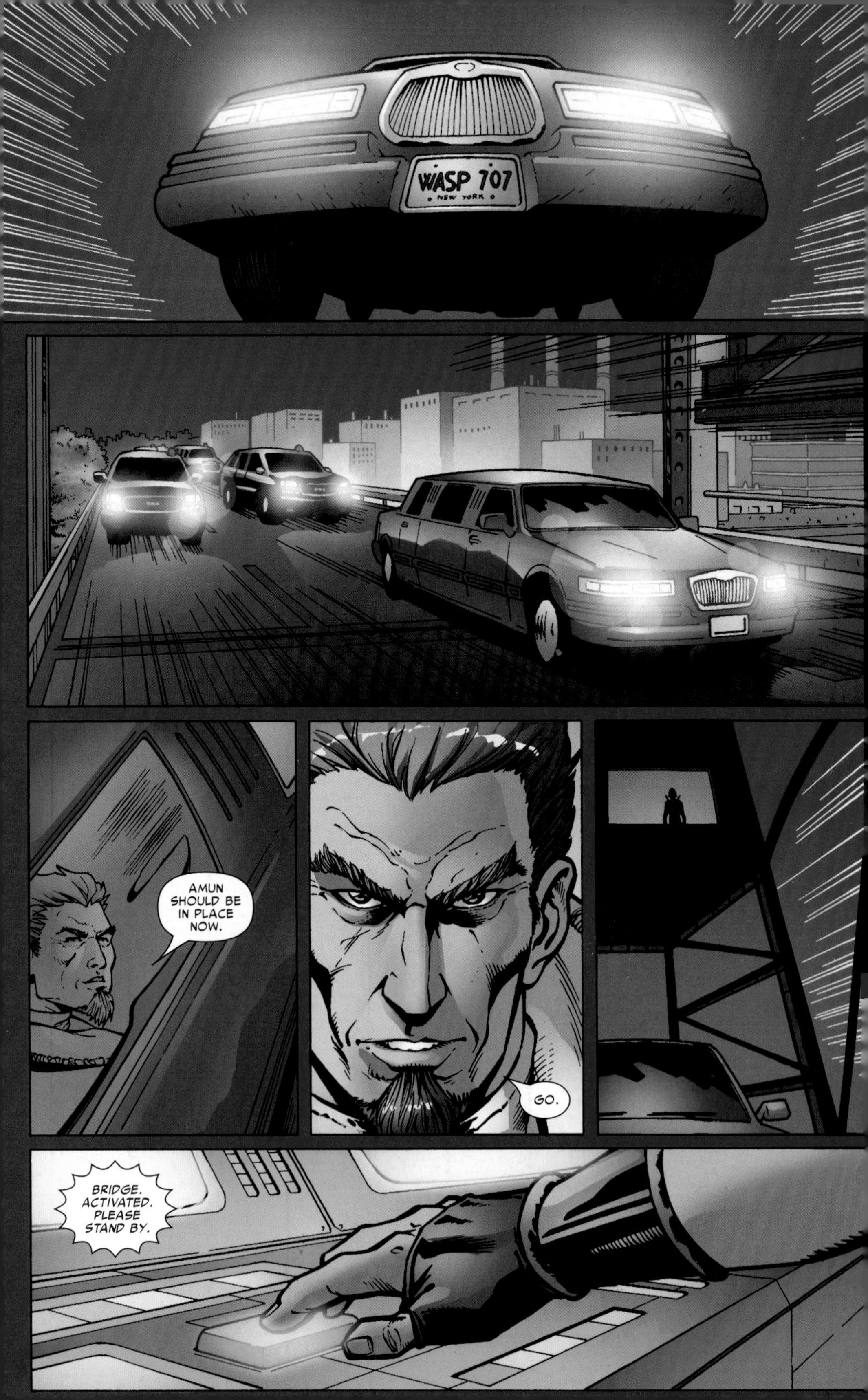
WASP 707
NEW YORK
AMUN SHOULD BE IN PLACE NOW.
GO.
BRIDGE. ACTIVATED. PLEASE STAND BY.

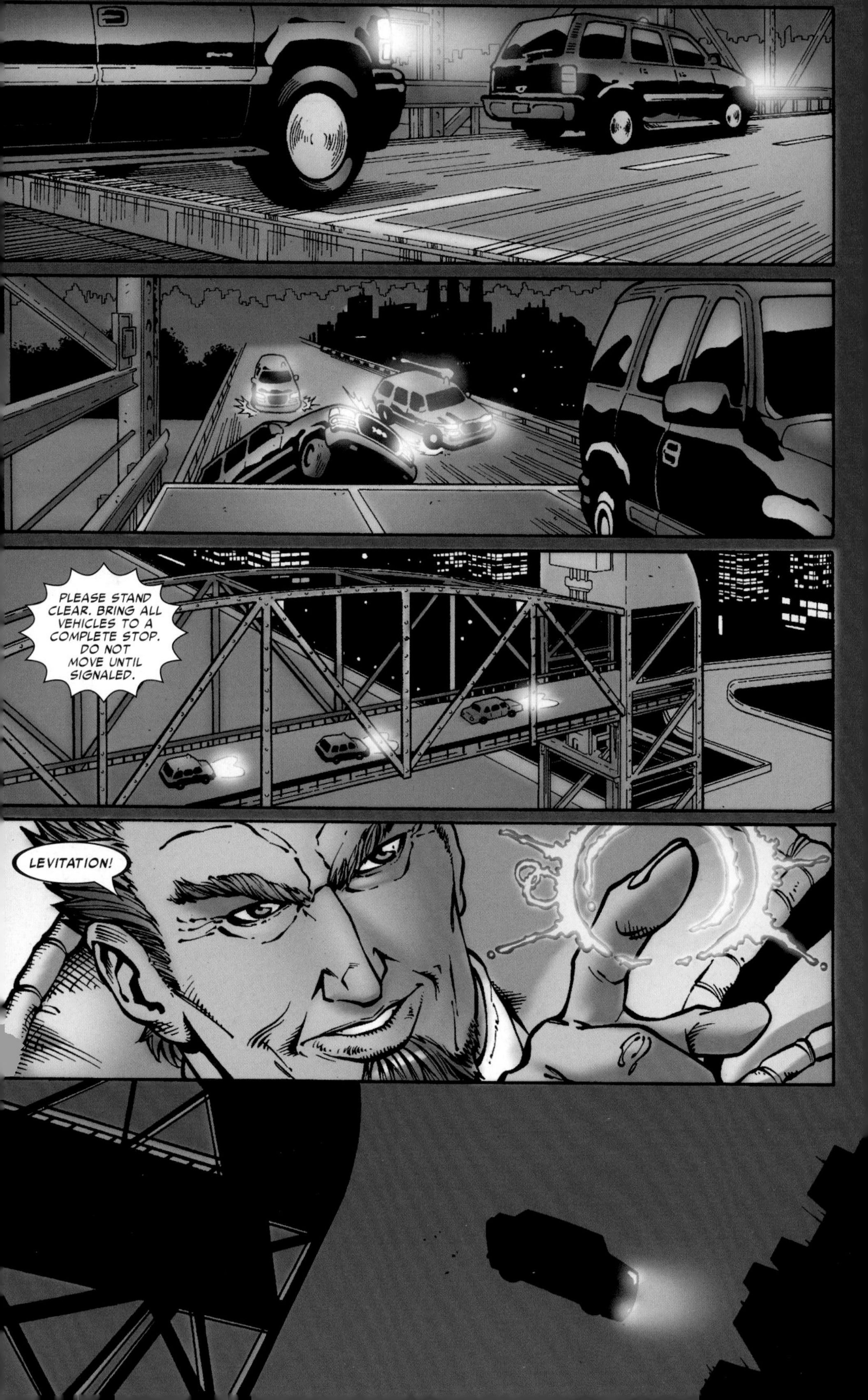
PLEASE STAND CLEAR. BRING ALL VEHICLES TO A COMPLETE STOP. DO NOT MOVE UNTIL SIGNALED.
LEVITATION!

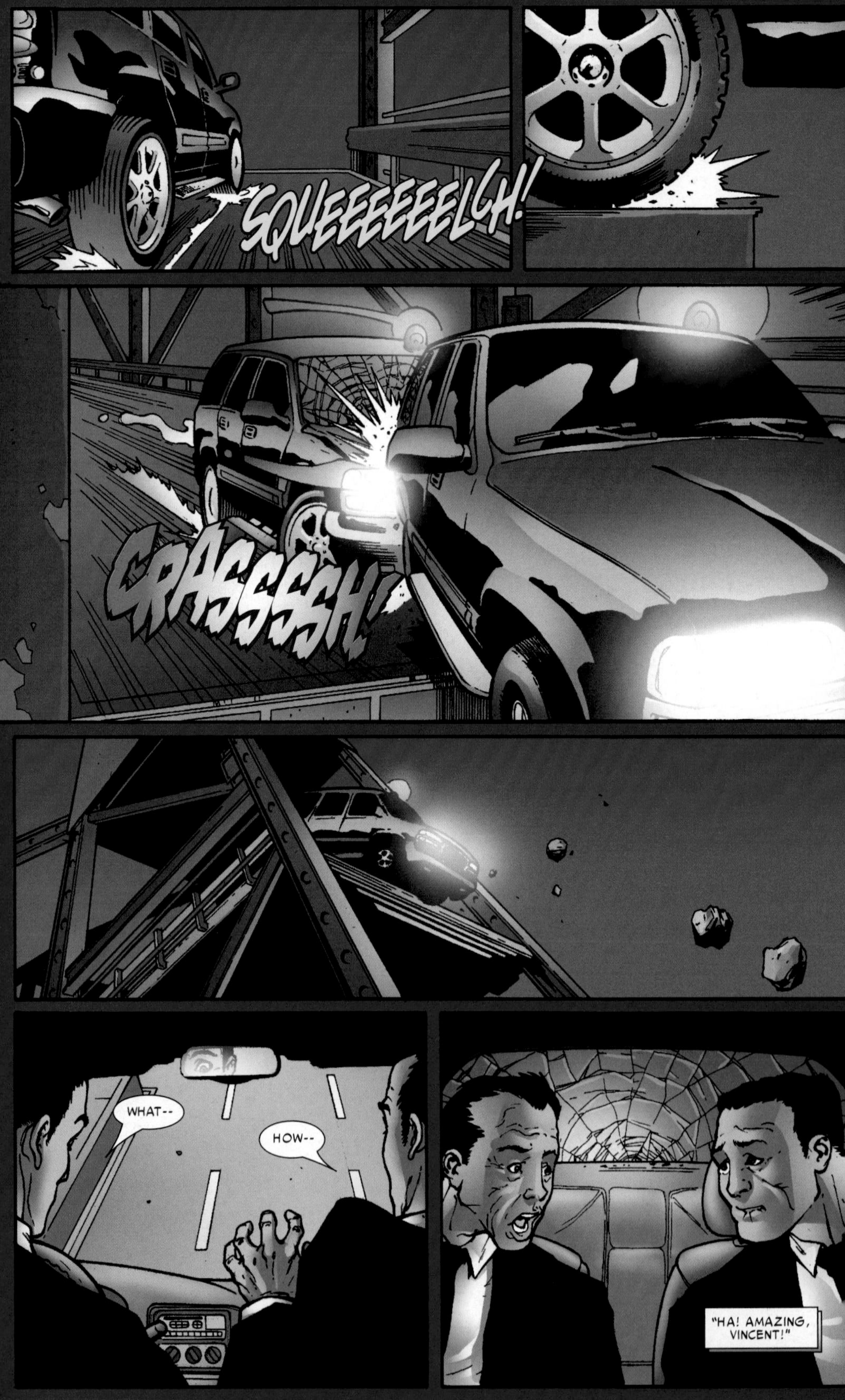
SQUEEEEEEELCH!
CRASSSSH!
WHAT--
HOW--
"HA! AMAZING, VINCENT!"

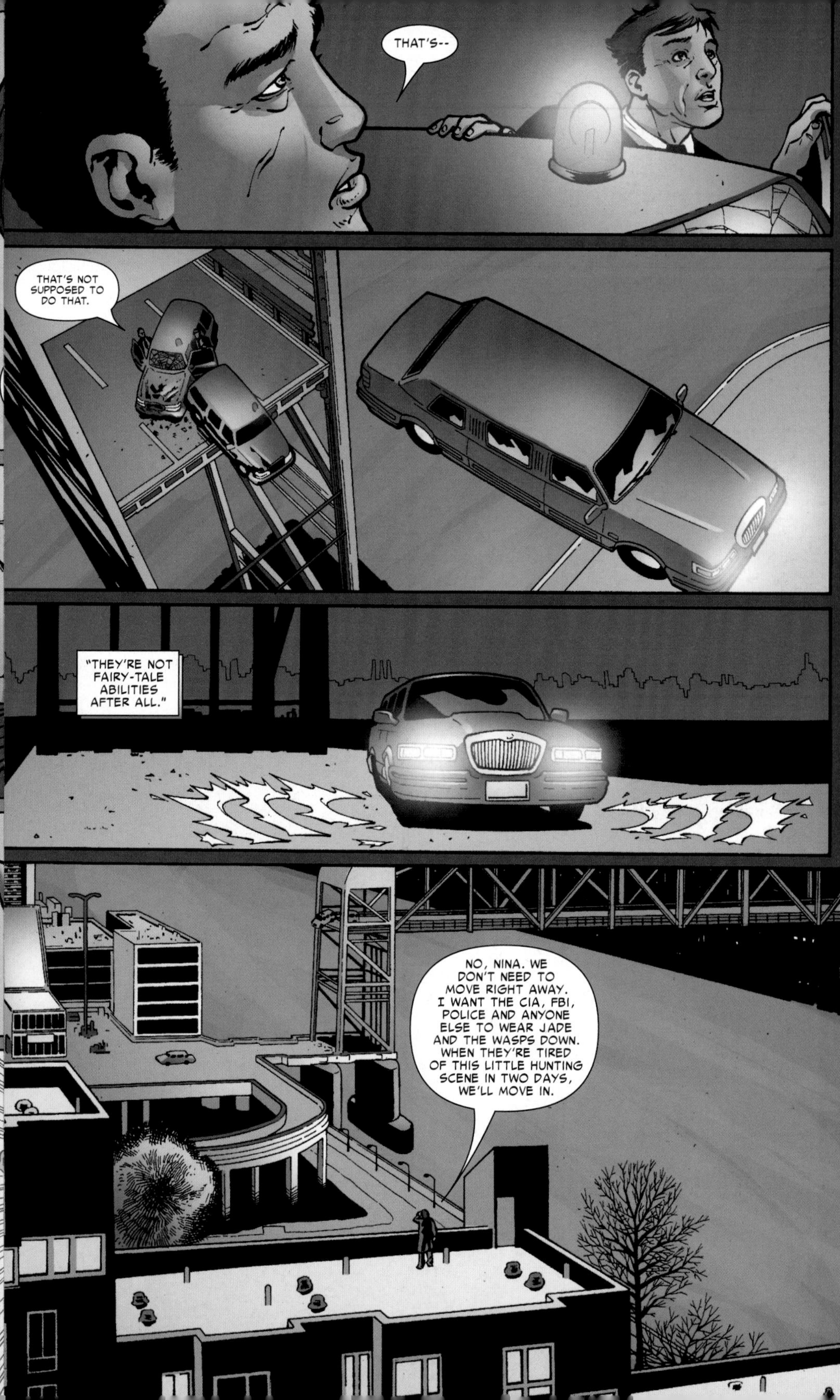
THAT'S--
THAT'S NOT SUPPOSED TO DO THAT.
"THEY'RE NOT FAIRY-TALE ABILITIES AFTER ALL."
NO, NINA. WE DON'T NEED TO MOVE RIGHT AWAY. I WANT THE CIA, FBI, POLICE AND ANYONE ELSE TO WEAR JADE AND THE WASPS DOWN. WHEN THEY'RE TIRED OF THIS LITTLE HUNTING SCENE IN TWO DAYS, WE'LL MOVE IN.

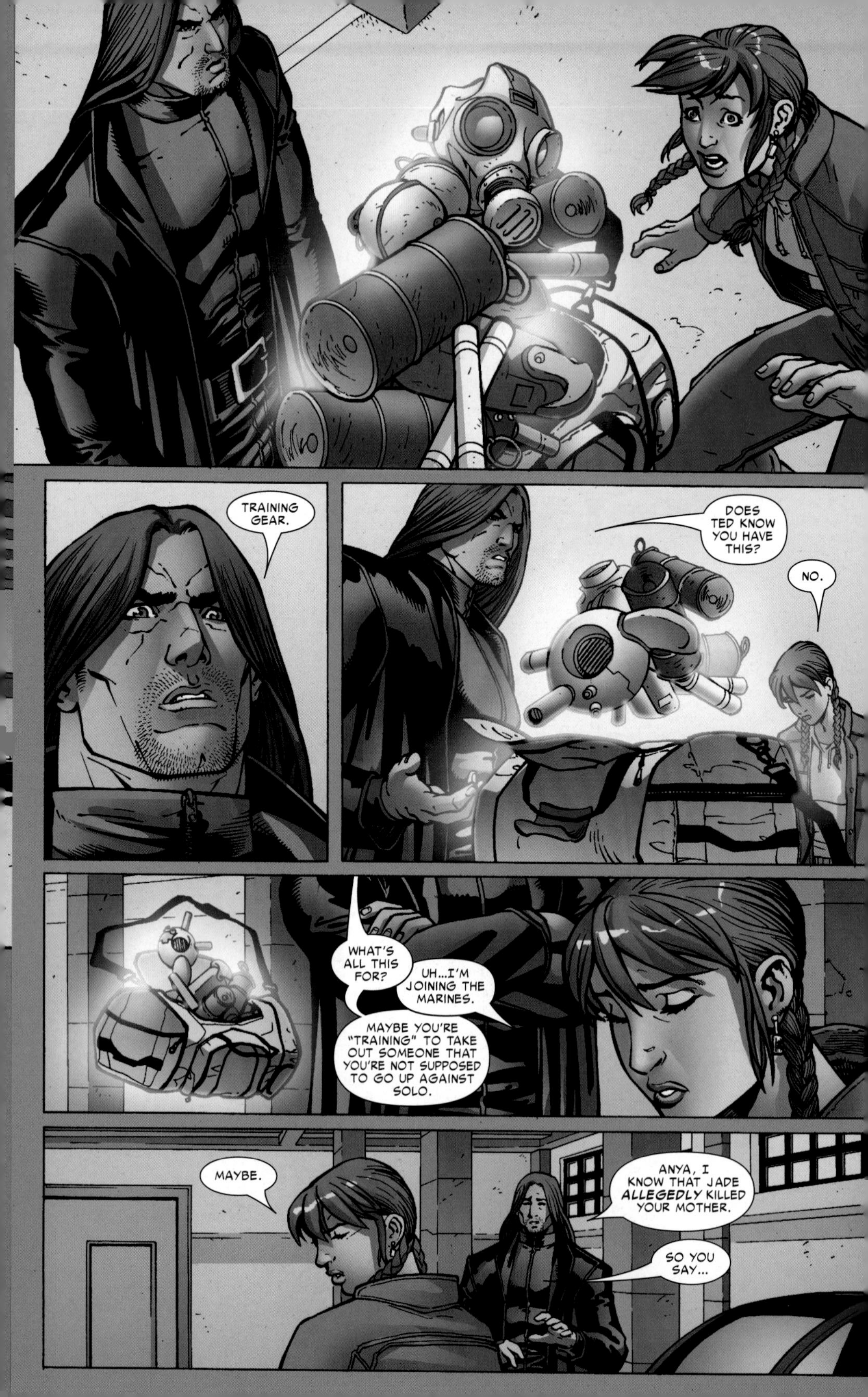
TRAINING GEAR.
DOES TED KNOW YOU HAVE THIS?
NO.
WHAT'S ALL THIS FOR?
UH...I'M JOINING THE MARINES.
MAYBE YOU'RE "TRAINING" TO TAKE OUT SOMEONE THAT YOU'RE NOT SUPPOSED TO GO UP AGAINST SOLO.
MAYBE.
ANYA, I KNOW THAT JADE *ALLEGEDLY* KILLED YOUR MOTHER.
SO YOU SAY...

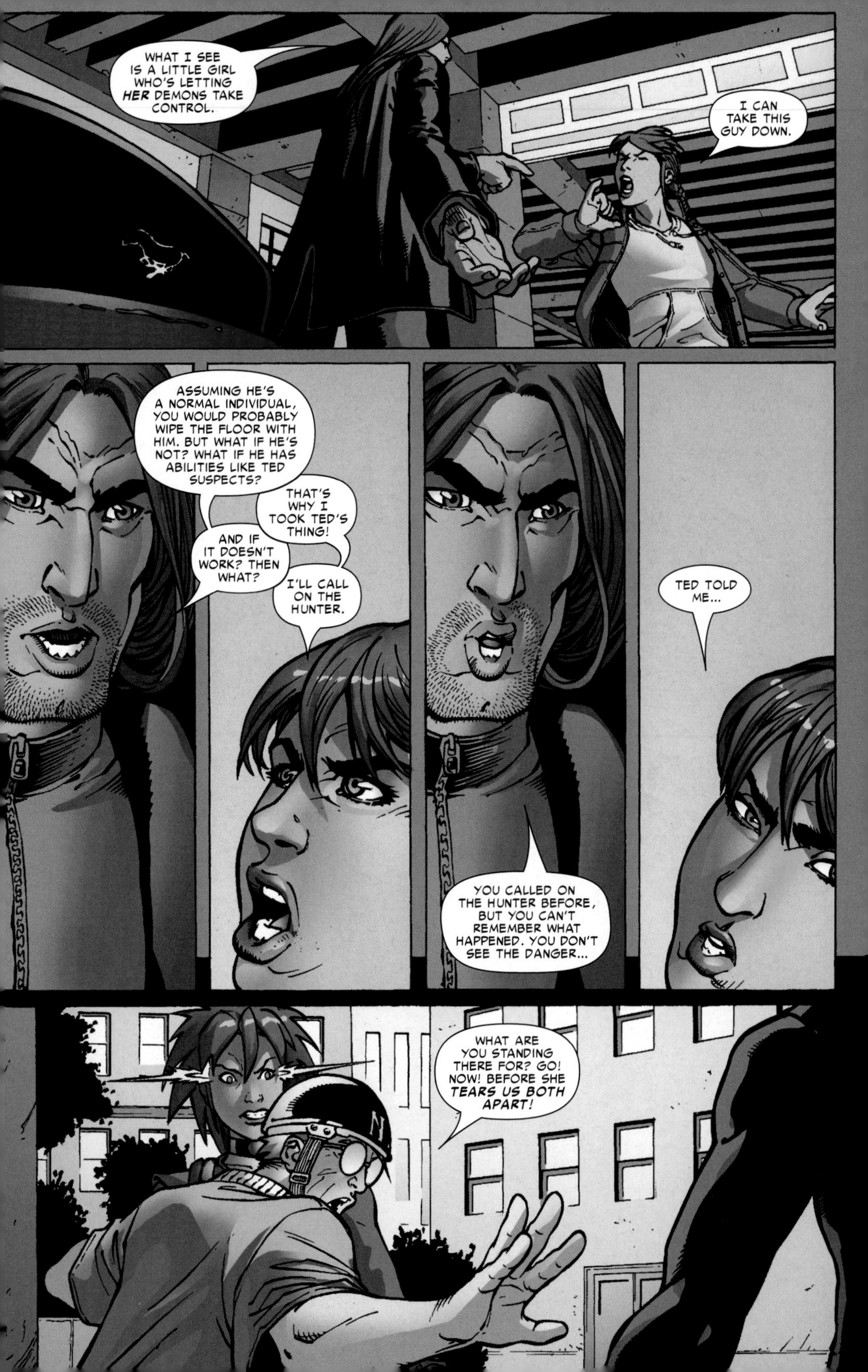
WHAT I SEE IS A LITTLE GIRL WHO'S LETTING *HER* DEMONS TAKE CONTROL.
I CAN TAKE THIS GUY DOWN.
ASSUMING HE'S A NORMAL INDIVIDUAL, YOU WOULD PROBABLY WIPE THE FLOOR WITH HIM. BUT WHAT IF HE'S NOT? WHAT IF HE HAS ABILITIES LIKE TED SUSPECTS?
THAT'S WHY I TOOK TED'S THING!
AND IF IT DOESN'T WORK? THEN WHAT?
I'LL CALL ON THE HUNTER.
YOU CALLED ON THE HUNTER BEFORE, BUT YOU CAN'T REMEMBER WHAT HAPPENED. YOU DON'T SEE THE DANGER...
TED TOLD ME...
WHAT ARE YOU STANDING THERE FOR? GO! NOW! BEFORE SHE *TEARS US BOTH APART!*

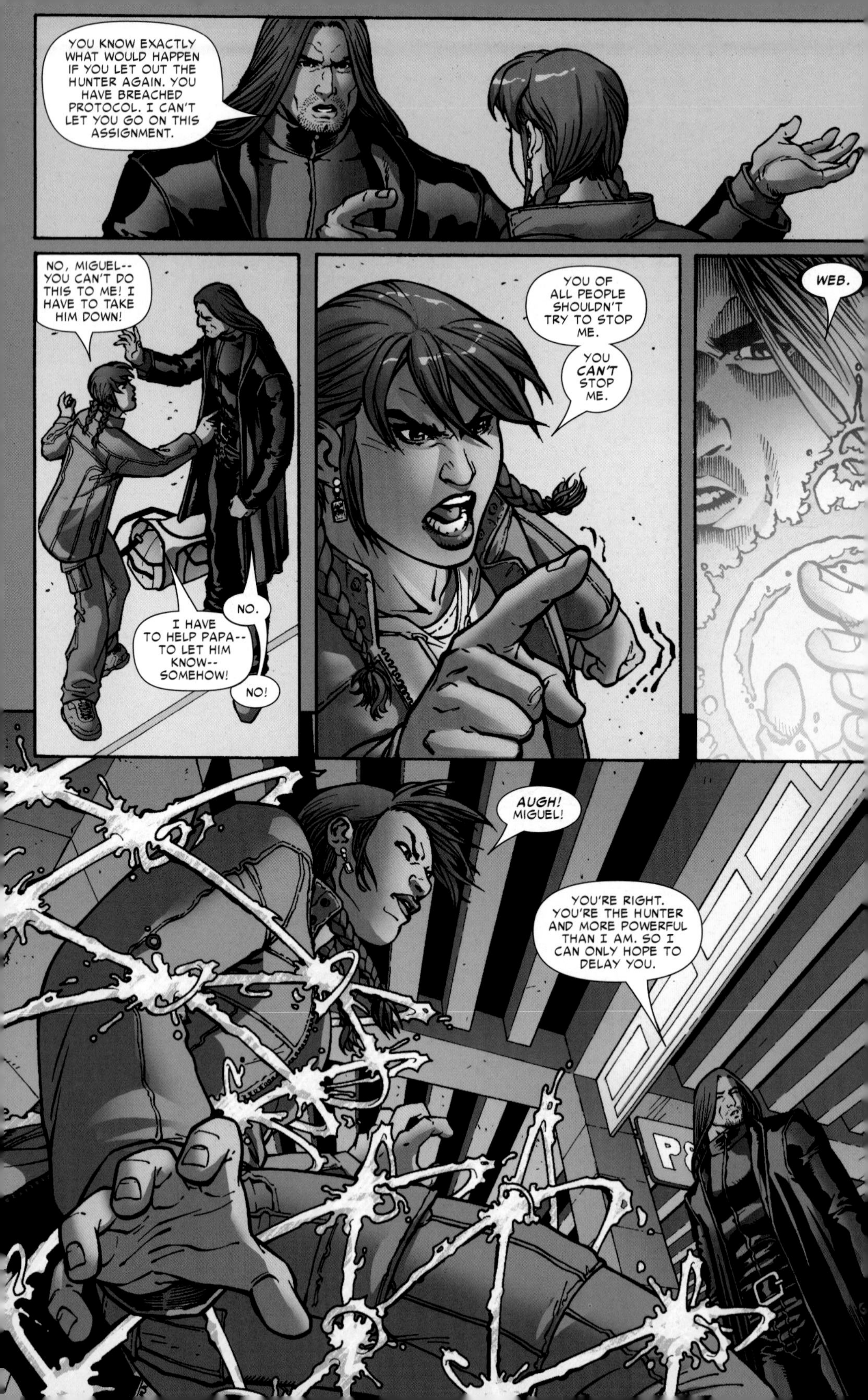
YOU KNOW EXACTLY WHAT WOULD HAPPEN IF YOU LET OUT THE HUNTER AGAIN. YOU HAVE BREACHED PROTOCOL. I CAN'T LET YOU GO ON THIS ASSIGNMENT.
NO, MIGUEL-- YOU CAN'T DO THIS TO ME! I HAVE TO TAKE HIM DOWN!
NO.
I HAVE TO HELP PAPA-- TO LET HIM KNOW-- SOMEHOW!
NO!
YOU OF ALL PEOPLE SHOULDN'T TRY TO STOP ME.
YOU CAN'T STOP ME.
WEB.
AUGH! MIGUEL!
YOU'RE RIGHT. YOU'RE THE HUNTER AND MORE POWERFUL THAN I AM. SO I CAN ONLY HOPE TO DELAY YOU.

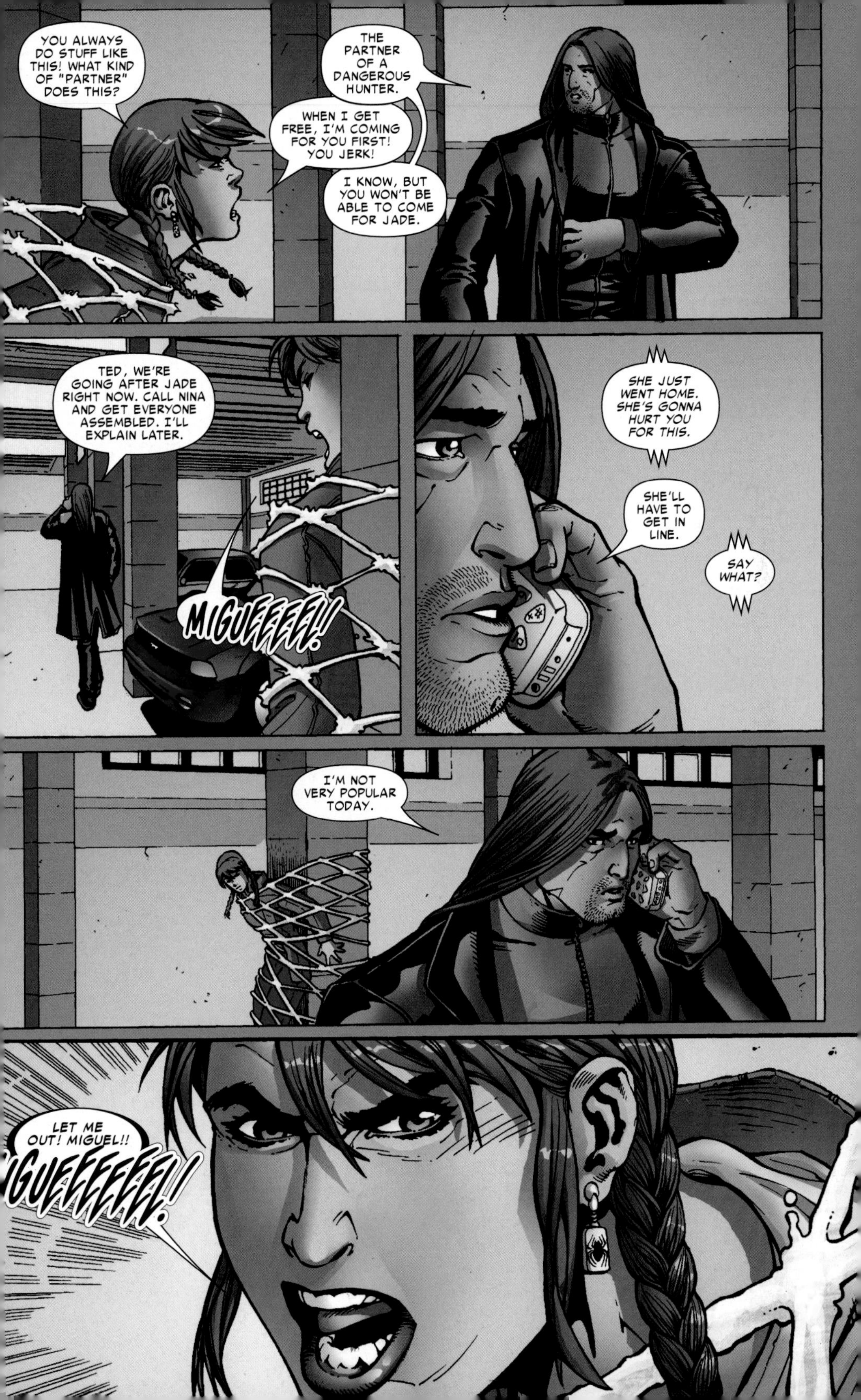
YOU ALWAYS DO STUFF LIKE THIS! WHAT KIND OF "PARTNER" DOES THIS?
THE PARTNER OF A DANGEROUS HUNTER.
WHEN I GET FREE, I'M COMING FOR YOU FIRST! YOU JERK!
I KNOW, BUT YOU WON'T BE ABLE TO COME FOR JADE.
TED, WE'RE GOING AFTER JADE RIGHT NOW. CALL NINA AND GET EVERYONE ASSEMBLED. I'LL EXPLAIN LATER.
MIGUEEEEL!
SHE JUST WENT HOME. SHE'S GONNA HURT YOU FOR THIS.
SHE'LL HAVE TO GET IN LINE.
SAY WHAT?
I'M NOT VERY POPULAR TODAY.
LET ME OUT! MIGUEL!!
...GUEEEEEL!

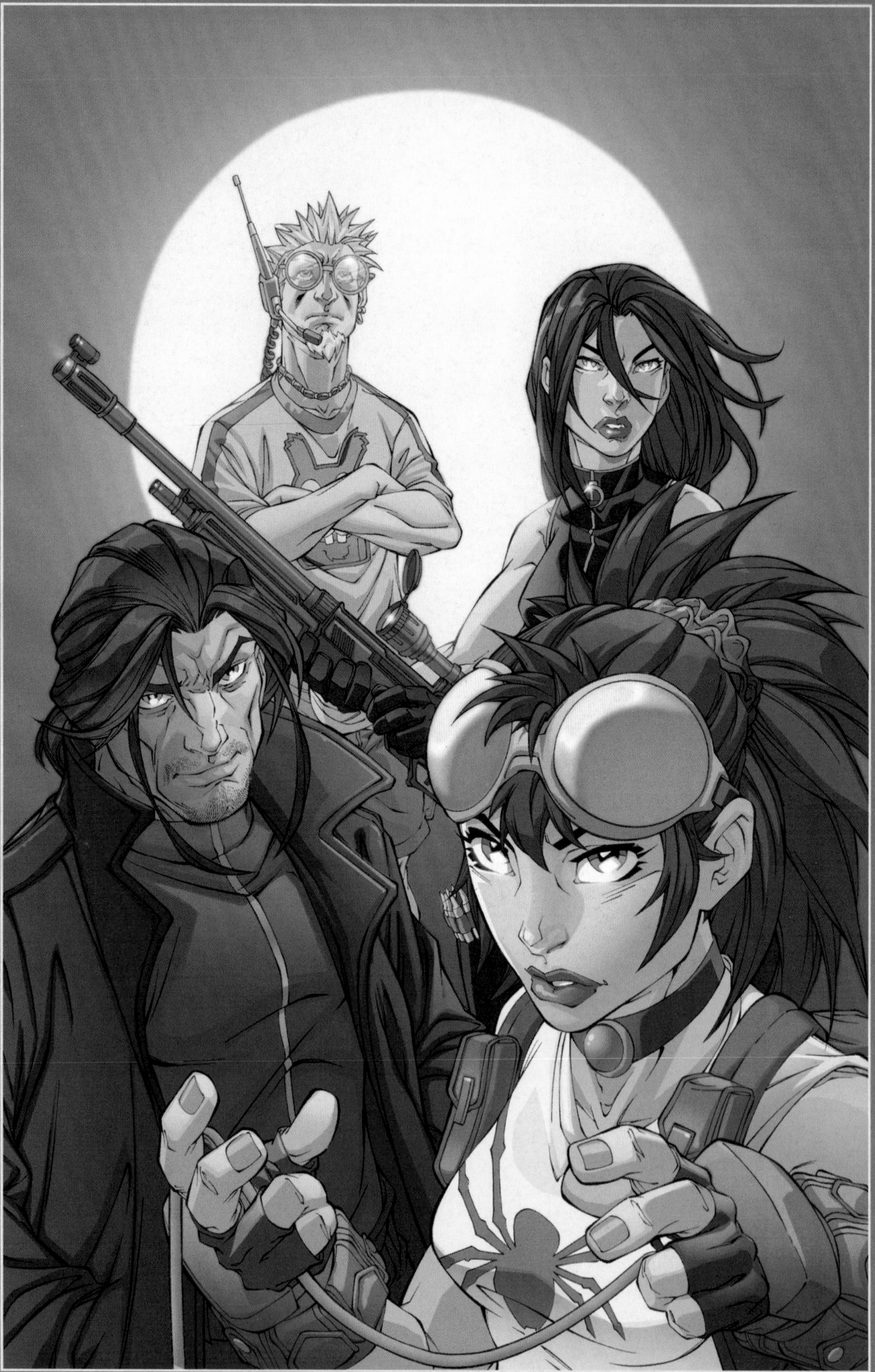

ARAÑA #9

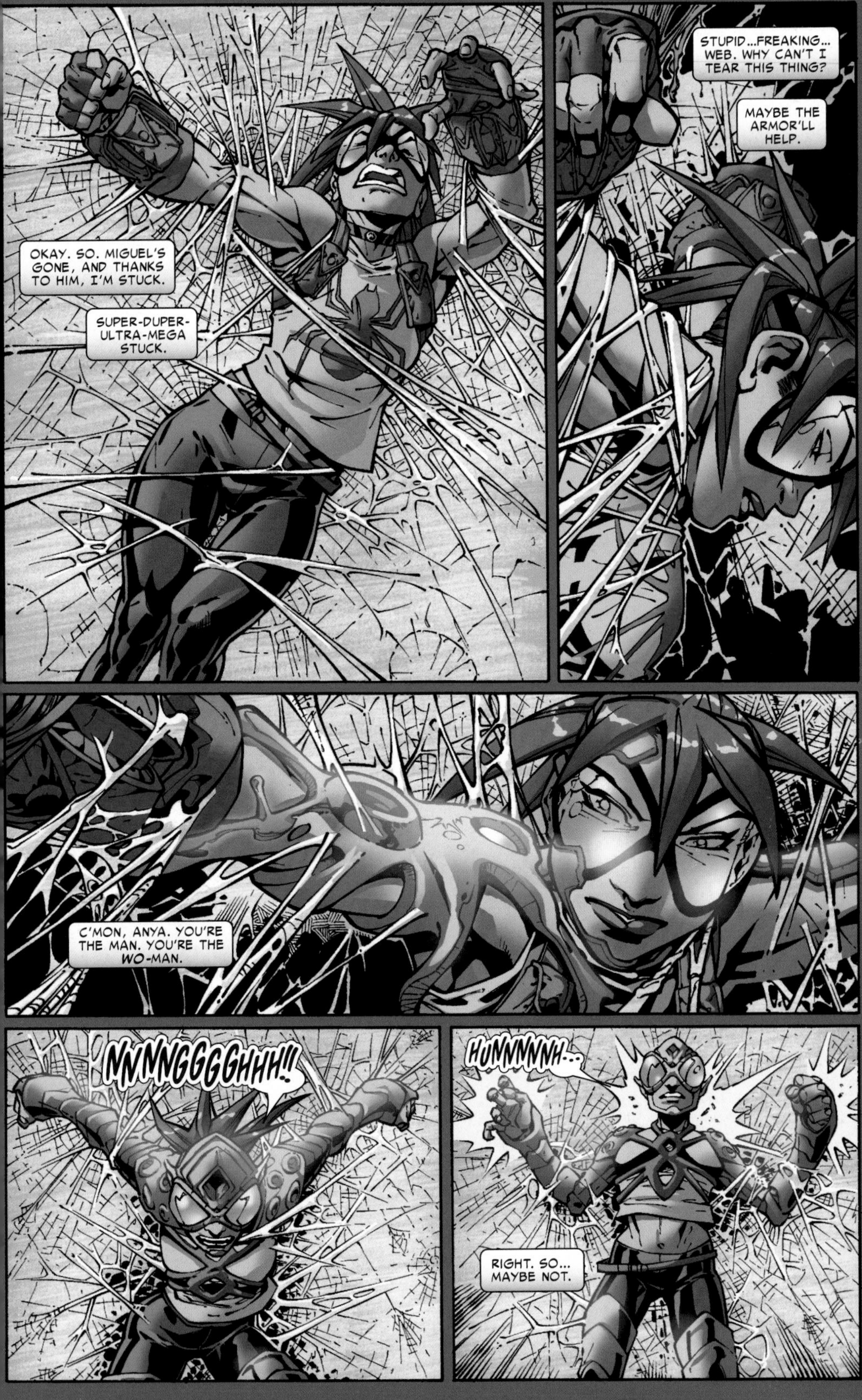
OKAY. SO. MIGUEL'S GONE, AND THANKS TO HIM, I'M STUCK.
SUPER-DUPER-ULTRA-MEGA STUCK.
STUPID...FREAKING... WEB. WHY CAN'T I TEAR THIS THING?
MAYBE THE ARMOR'LL HELP.
C'MON, ANYA. YOU'RE THE MAN. YOU'RE THE WO-MAN.
NNNNGGGGHHH!!
HUNNNNNH...
RIGHT. SO... MAYBE NOT.

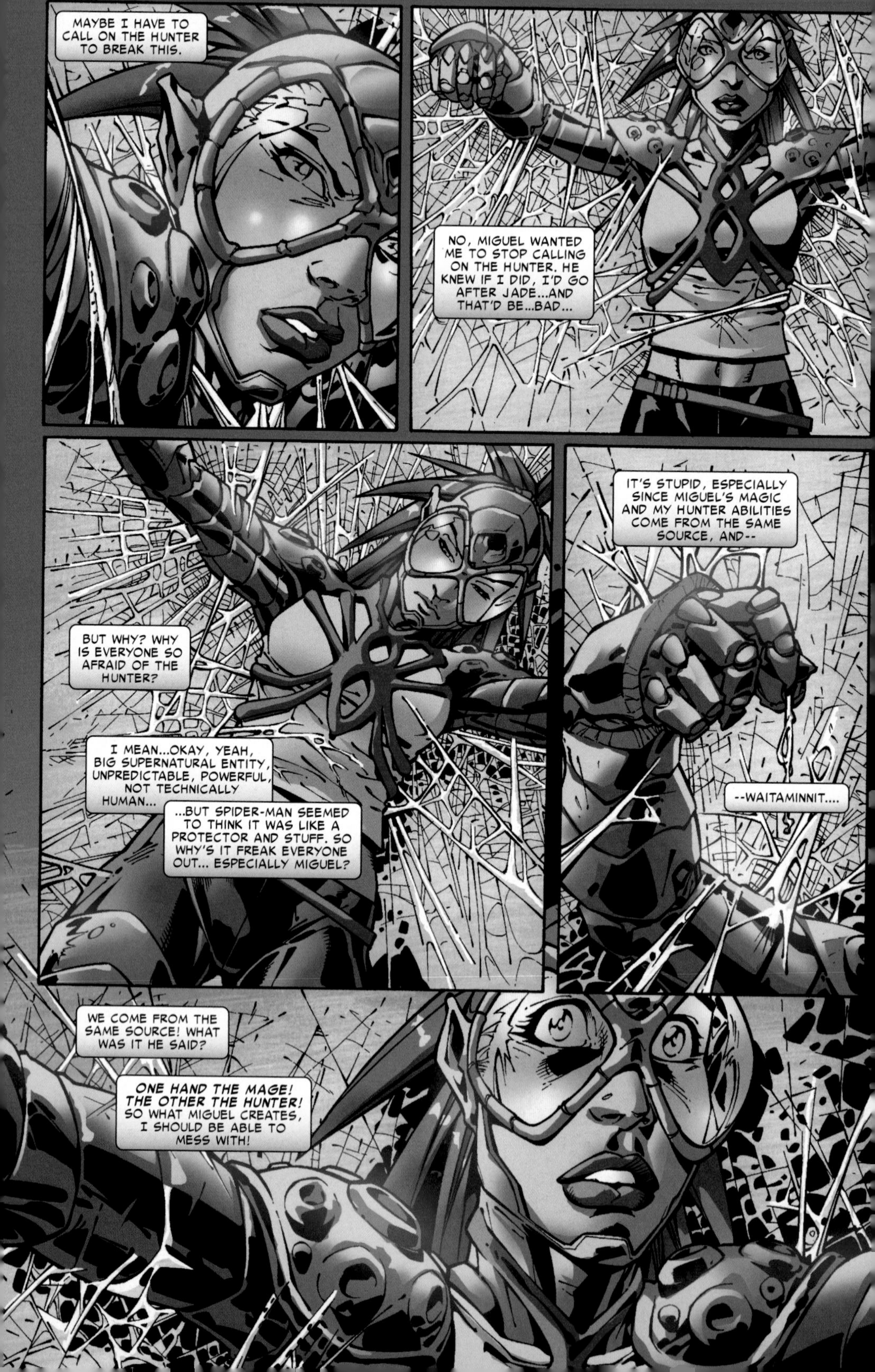
MAYBE I HAVE TO CALL ON THE HUNTER TO BREAK THIS.
NO, MIGUEL WANTED ME TO STOP CALLING ON THE HUNTER. HE KNEW IF I DID, I'D GO AFTER JADE...AND THAT'D BE...BAD...
BUT WHY? WHY IS EVERYONE SO AFRAID OF THE HUNTER?
I MEAN...OKAY, YEAH, BIG SUPERNATURAL ENTITY, UNPREDICTABLE, POWERFUL, NOT TECHNICALLY HUMAN...
...BUT SPIDER-MAN SEEMED TO THINK IT WAS LIKE A PROTECTOR AND STUFF. SO WHY'S IT FREAK EVERYONE OUT... ESPECIALLY MIGUEL?
IT'S STUPID, ESPECIALLY SINCE MIGUEL'S MAGIC AND MY HUNTER ABILITIES COME FROM THE SAME SOURCE, AND--
--WAITAMINNIT....
WE COME FROM THE SAME SOURCE! WHAT WAS IT HE SAID?
ONE HAND THE MAGE! THE OTHER THE HUNTER! SO WHAT MIGUEL CREATES, I SHOULD BE ABLE TO MESS WITH!

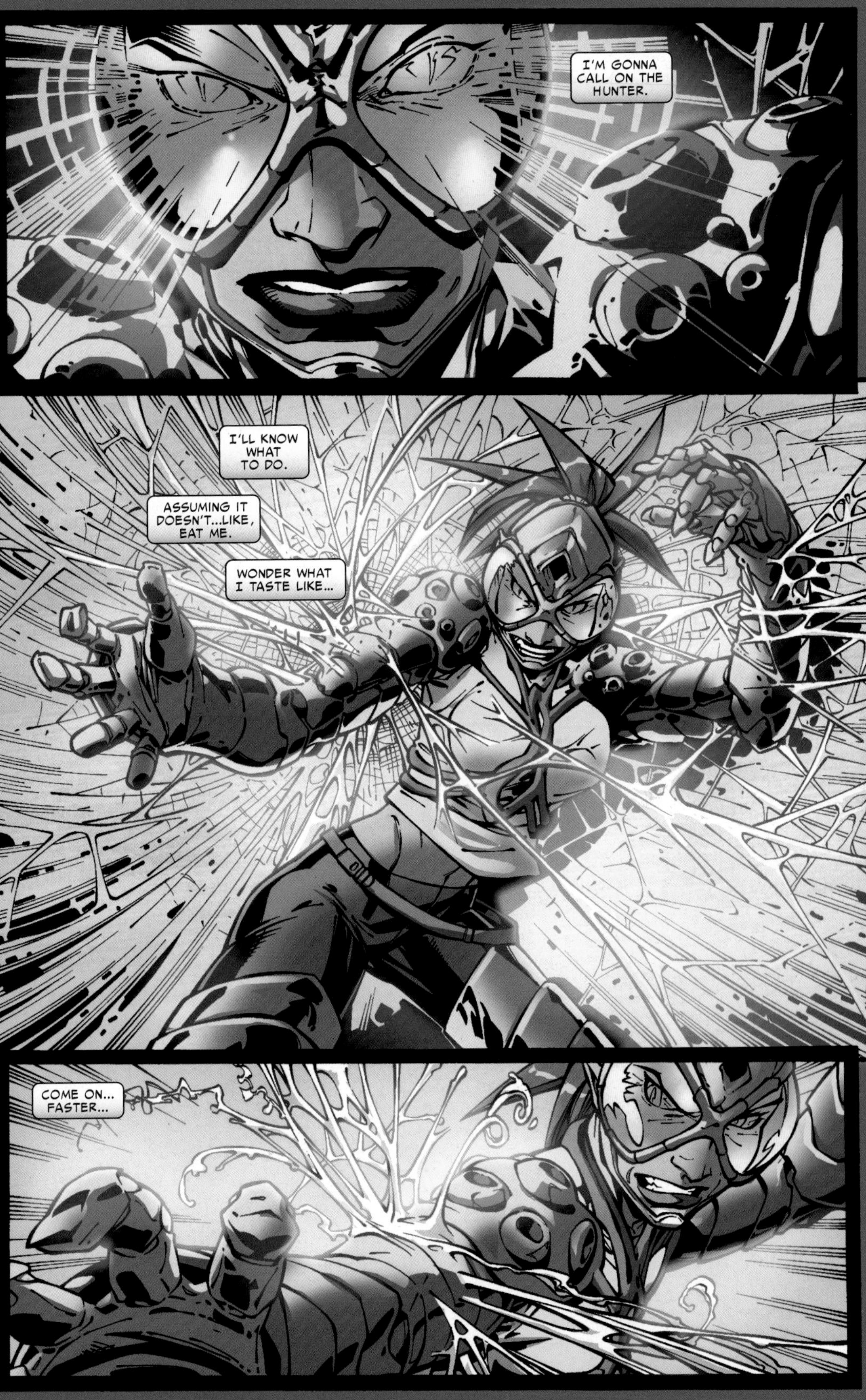
I'M GONNA CALL ON THE HUNTER.
I'LL KNOW WHAT TO DO.
ASSUMING IT DOESN'T...LIKE, EAT ME.
WONDER WHAT I TASTE LIKE...
COME ON... FASTER...

...NO TELLING WHAT I'M MISSING OUT THERE.

GO HOME, NINA. RELAX, NINA. TAKE A BUBBLE BATH, NINA...

DON'T EVEN HAVE DIRECTIONS...

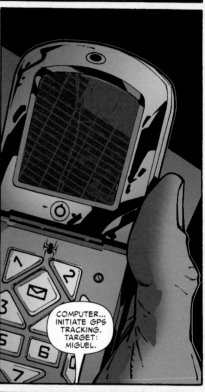

COMPUTER... INITIATE GPS TRACKING. TARGET: MIGUEL.

WHATEVER THIS IS, WHATEVER THE EMERGENCY...I JUST KNOW IT'S ARAÑA'S FAULT...

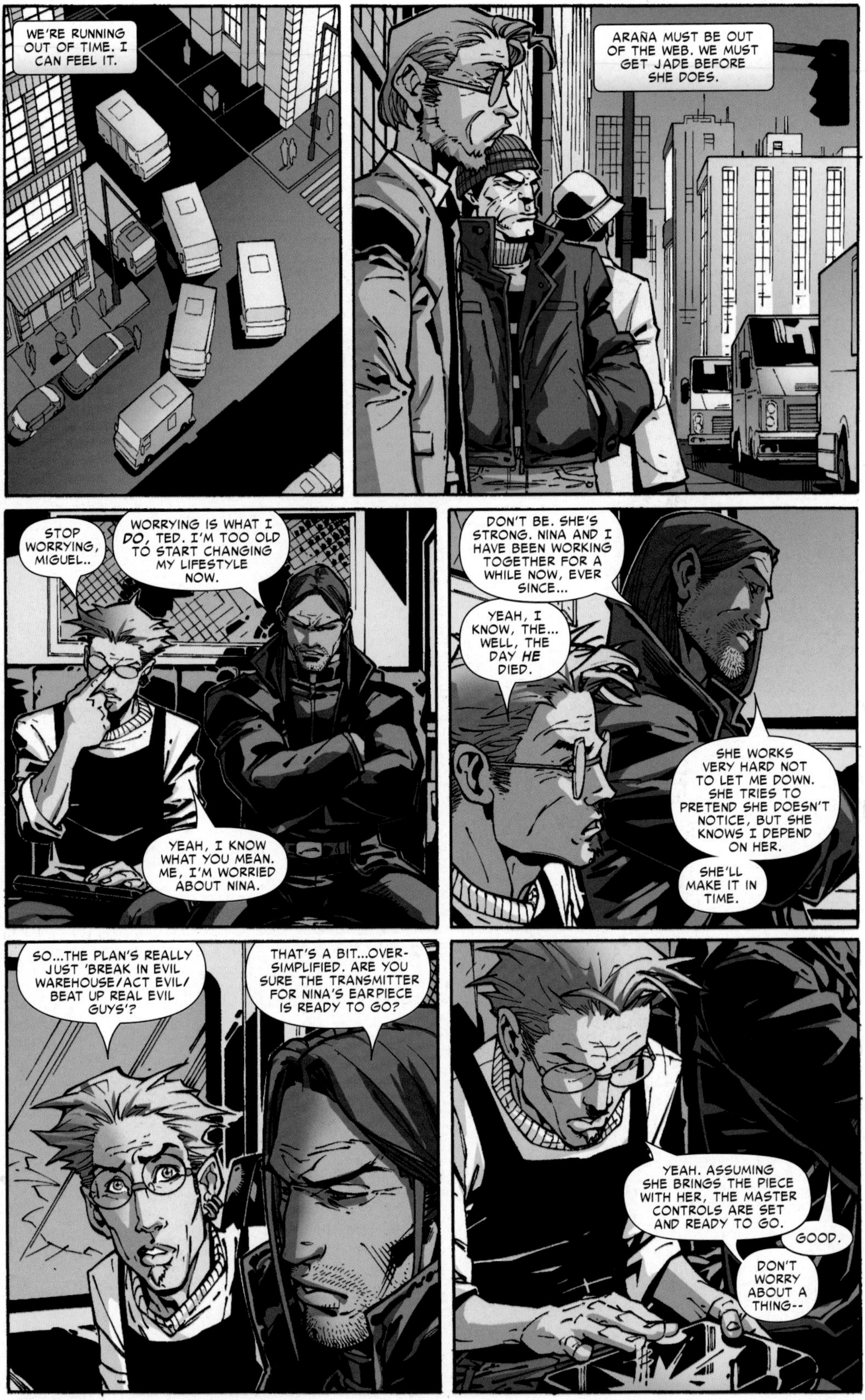
WE'RE RUNNING OUT OF TIME. I CAN FEEL IT.
ARAÑA MUST BE OUT OF THE WEB. WE MUST GET JADE BEFORE SHE DOES.
STOP WORRYING, MIGUEL..
WORRYING IS WHAT I DO, TED. I'M TOO OLD TO START CHANGING MY LIFESTYLE NOW.
YEAH, I KNOW WHAT YOU MEAN. ME, I'M WORRIED ABOUT NINA.
DON'T BE. SHE'S STRONG. NINA AND I HAVE BEEN WORKING TOGETHER FOR A WHILE NOW, EVER SINCE...
YEAH, I KNOW, THE... WELL, THE DAY HE DIED.
SHE WORKS VERY HARD NOT TO LET ME DOWN. SHE TRIES TO PRETEND SHE DOESN'T NOTICE, BUT SHE KNOWS I DEPEND ON HER.
SHE'LL MAKE IT IN TIME.
SO...THE PLAN'S REALLY JUST 'BREAK IN EVIL WAREHOUSE/ACT EVIL/ BEAT UP REAL EVIL GUYS'?
THAT'S A BIT...OVER-SIMPLIFIED. ARE YOU SURE THE TRANSMITTER FOR NINA'S EARPIECE IS READY TO GO?
YEAH. ASSUMING SHE BRINGS THE PIECE WITH HER, THE MASTER CONTROLS ARE SET AND READY TO GO.
GOOD.
DON'T WORRY ABOUT A THING--

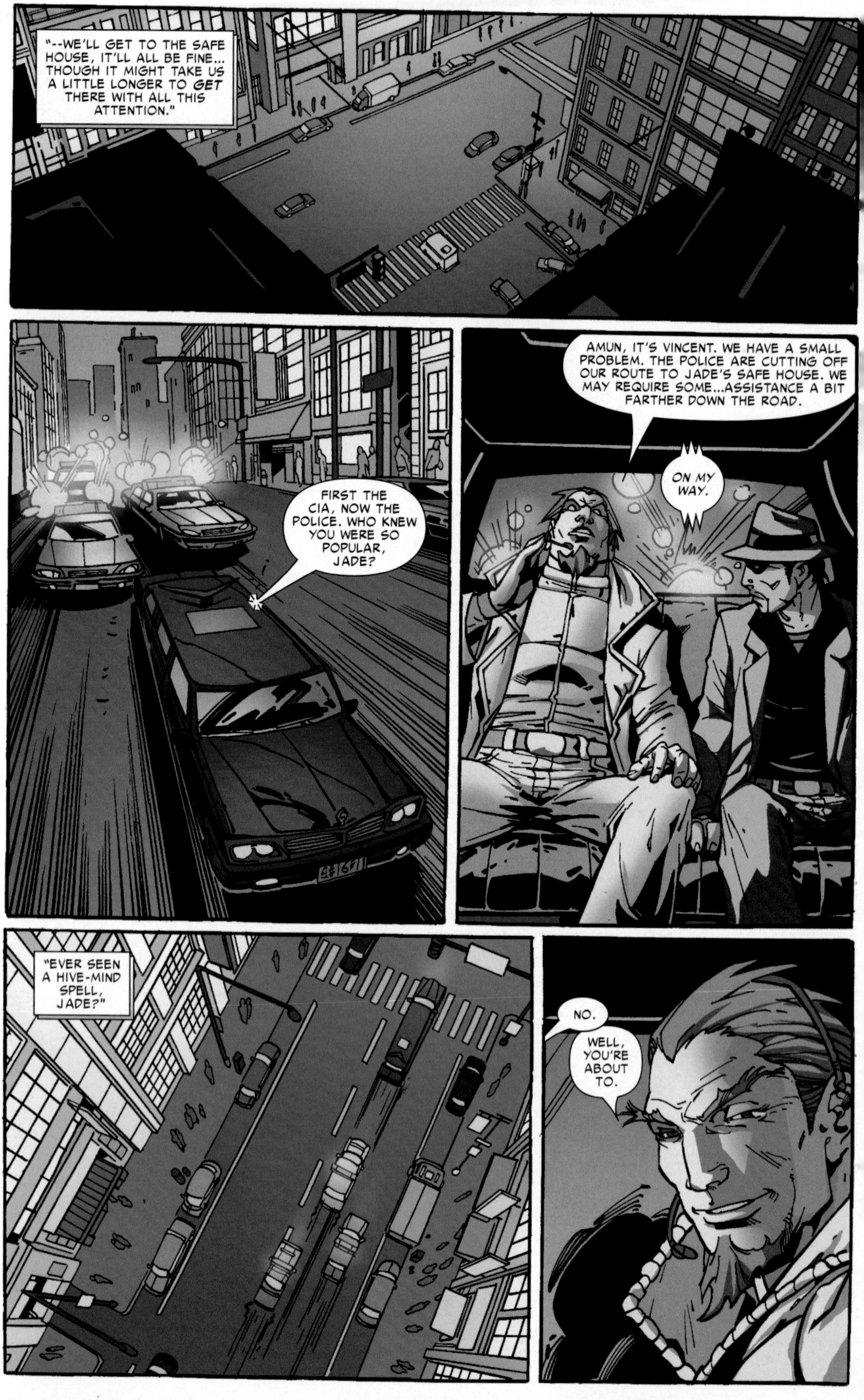
"--WE'LL GET TO THE SAFE HOUSE, IT'LL ALL BE FINE... THOUGH IT MIGHT TAKE US A LITTLE LONGER TO GET THERE WITH ALL THIS ATTENTION."
FIRST THE CIA, NOW THE POLICE. WHO KNEW YOU WERE SO POPULAR, JADE?
AMUN, IT'S VINCENT. WE HAVE A SMALL PROBLEM. THE POLICE ARE CUTTING OFF OUR ROUTE TO JADE'S SAFE HOUSE. WE MAY REQUIRE SOME...ASSISTANCE A BIT FARTHER DOWN THE ROAD.
ON MY WAY.
"EVER SEEN A HIVE-MIND SPELL, JADE?"
NO.
WELL, YOU'RE ABOUT TO.

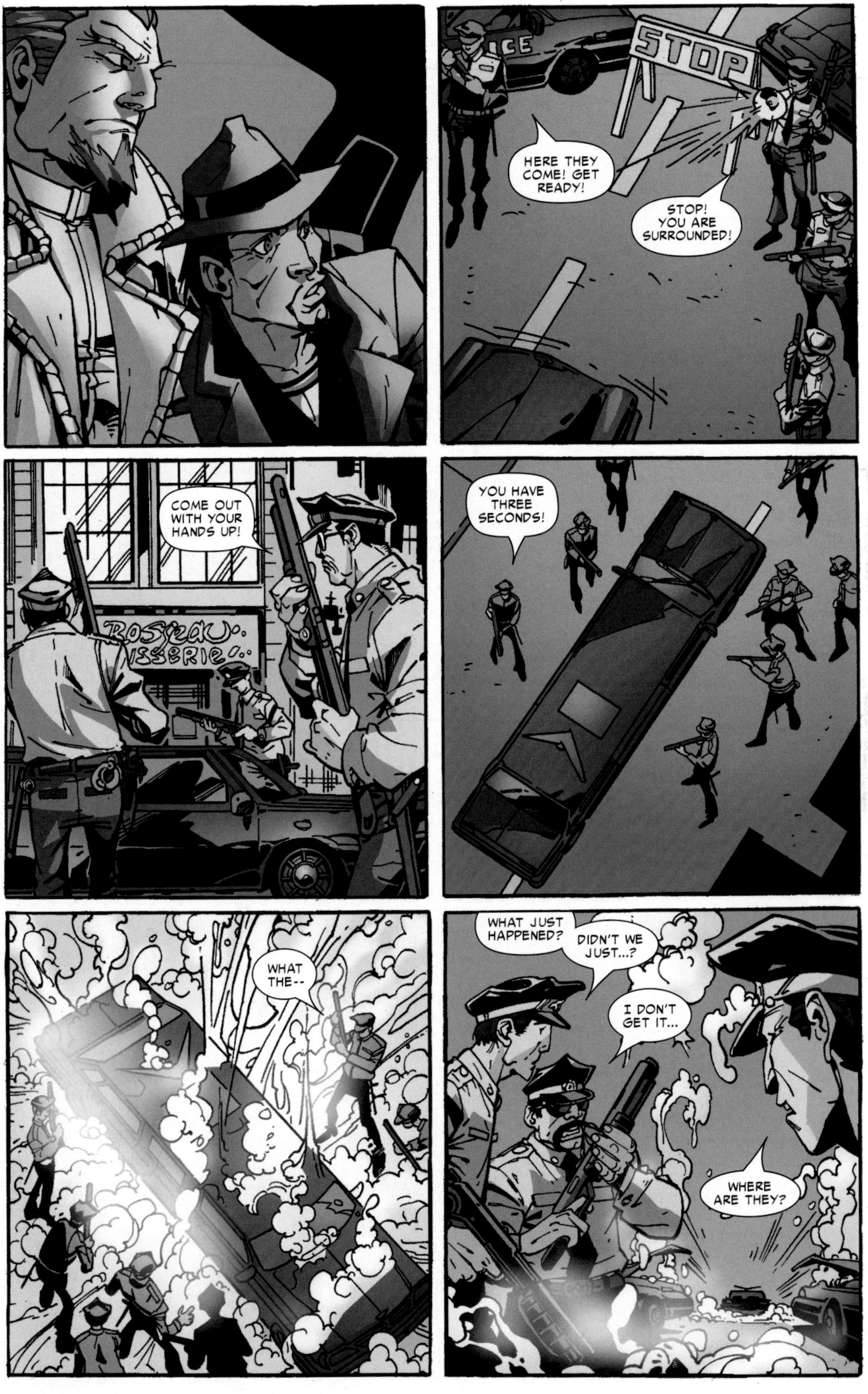
HERE THEY COME! GET READY!
STOP! YOU ARE SURROUNDED!
STOP
COME OUT WITH YOUR HANDS UP!
YOU HAVE THREE SECONDS!
WHAT THE--
WHAT JUST HAPPENED?
DIDN'T WE JUST...?
I DON'T GET IT...
WHERE ARE THEY?

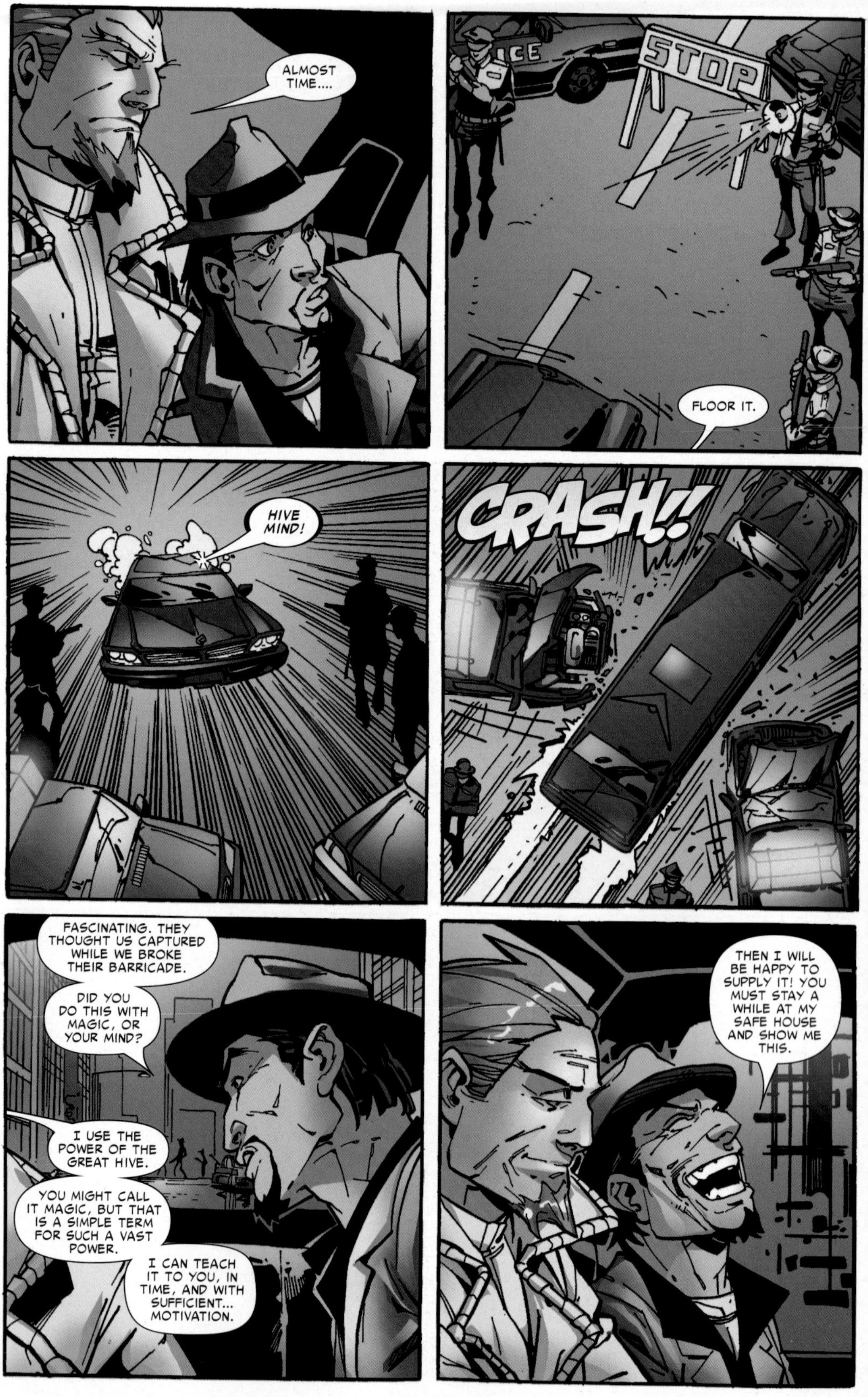
ALMOST TIME....
ICE
STOP
FLOOR IT.
HIVE MIND!
CRASH!!
FASCINATING. THEY THOUGHT US CAPTURED WHILE WE BROKE THEIR BARRICADE.
DID YOU DO THIS WITH MAGIC, OR YOUR MIND?
I USE THE POWER OF THE GREAT HIVE.
YOU MIGHT CALL IT MAGIC, BUT THAT IS A SIMPLE TERM FOR SUCH A VAST POWER.
I CAN TEACH IT TO YOU, IN TIME, AND WITH SUFFICIENT... MOTIVATION.
THEN I WILL BE HAPPY TO SUPPLY IT! YOU MUST STAY A WHILE AT MY SAFE HOUSE AND SHOW ME THIS.

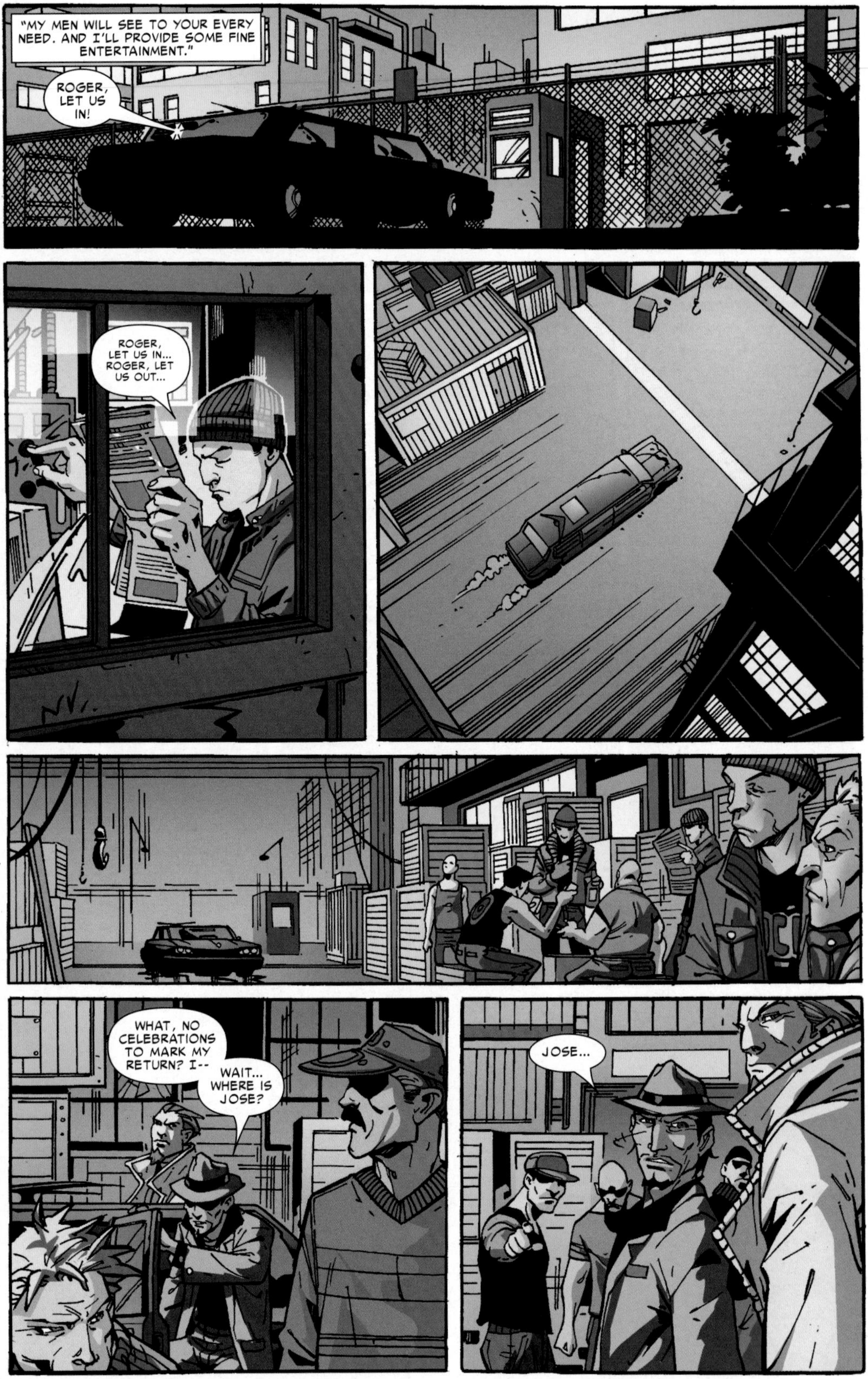
"MY MEN WILL SEE TO YOUR EVERY NEED. AND I'LL PROVIDE SOME FINE ENTERTAINMENT."
ROGER, LET US IN!
ROGER, LET US IN... ROGER, LET US OUT...
WHAT, NO CELEBRATIONS TO MARK MY RETURN? I--
WAIT... WHERE IS JOSE?
JOSE...

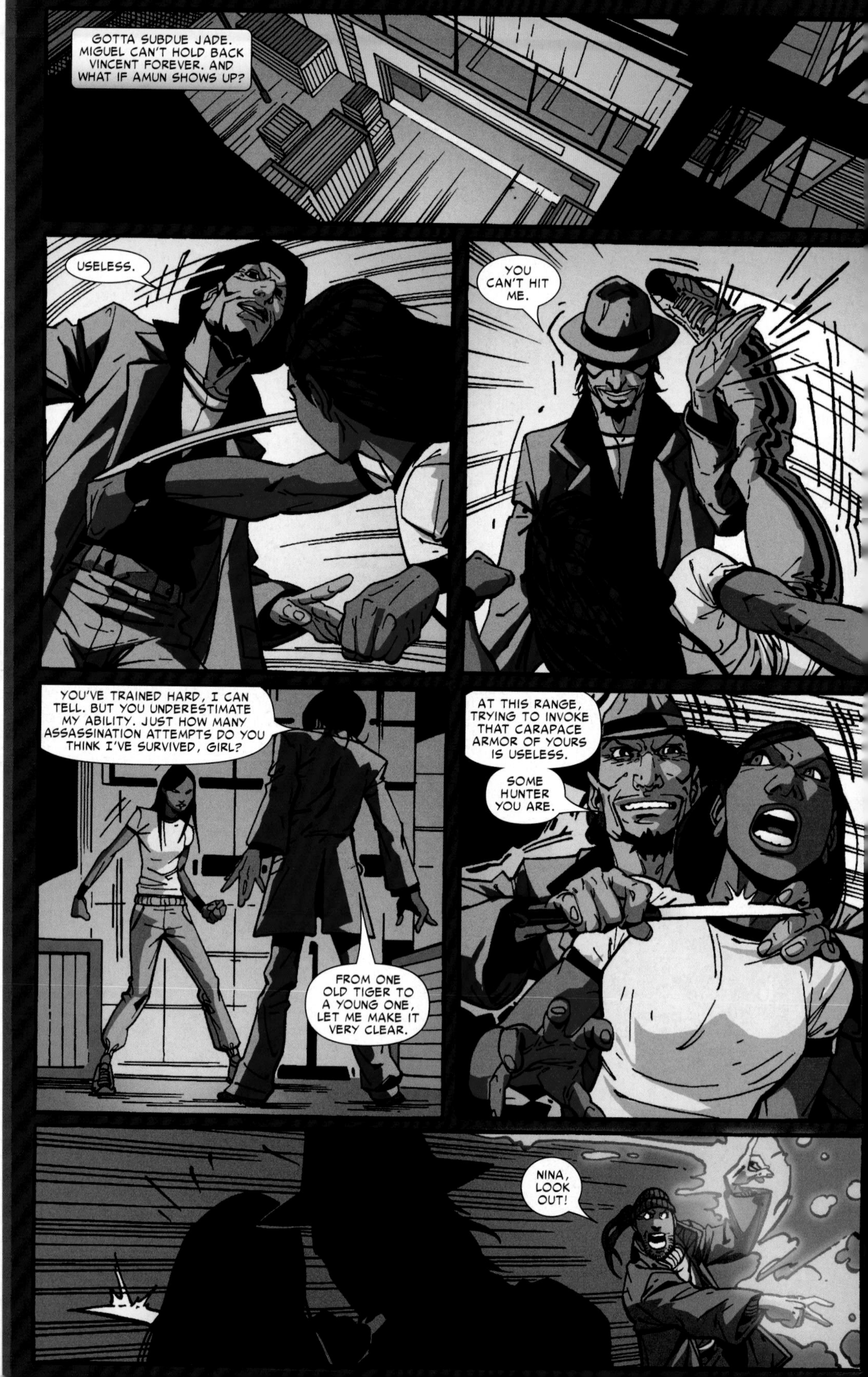
GOTTA SUBDUE JADE. MIGUEL CAN'T HOLD BACK VINCENT FOREVER. AND WHAT IF AMUN SHOWS UP?
USELESS.
YOU CAN'T HIT ME.
YOU'VE TRAINED HARD, I CAN TELL. BUT YOU UNDERESTIMATE MY ABILITY. JUST HOW MANY ASSASSINATION ATTEMPTS DO YOU THINK I'VE SURVIVED, GIRL?
FROM ONE OLD TIGER TO A YOUNG ONE, LET ME MAKE IT VERY CLEAR.
AT THIS RANGE, TRYING TO INVOKE THAT CARAPACE ARMOR OF YOURS IS USELESS.
SOME HUNTER YOU ARE.
NINA, LOOK OUT!

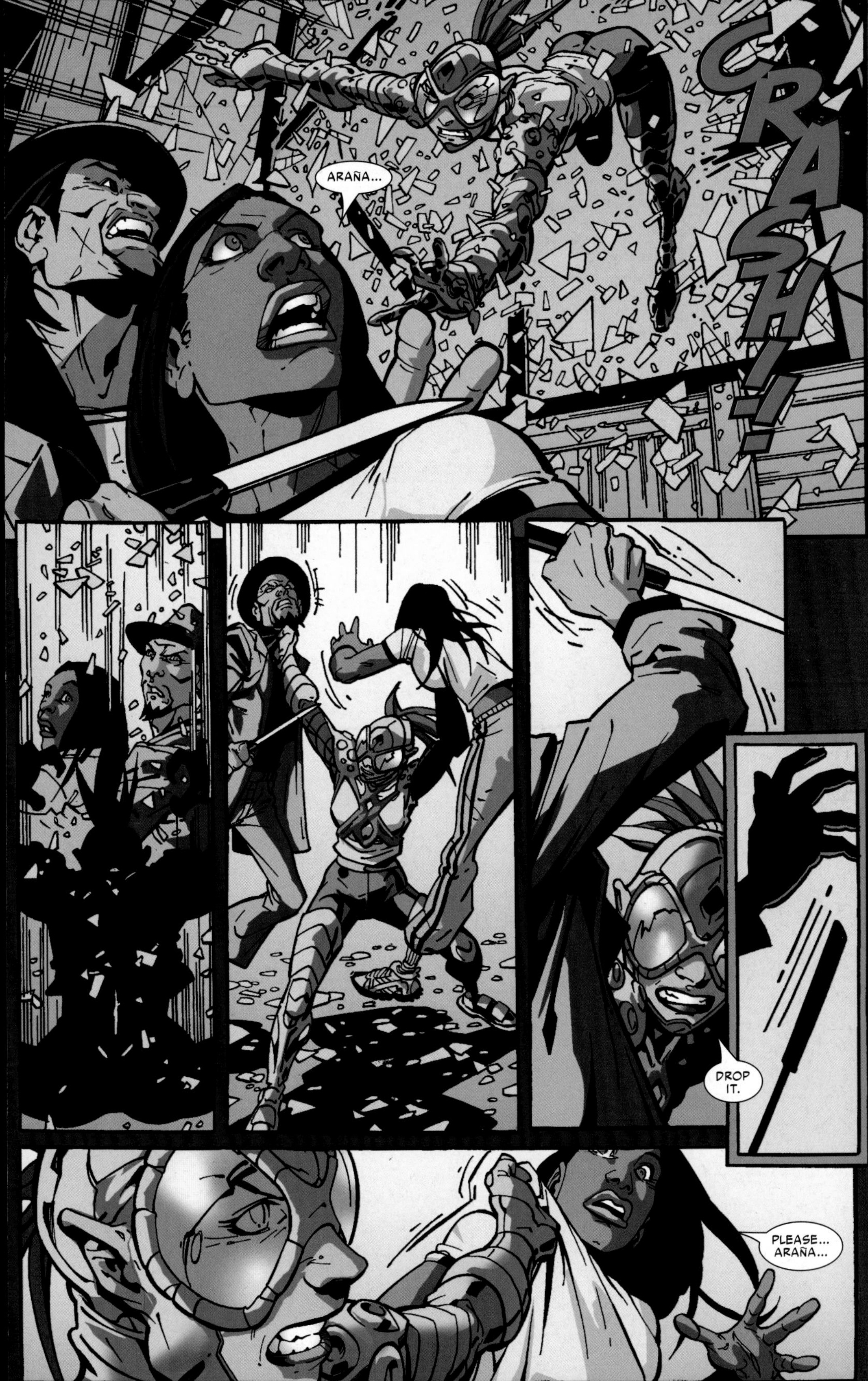
ARAÑA...
CRASH!!
DROP IT.
PLEASE... ARAÑA...

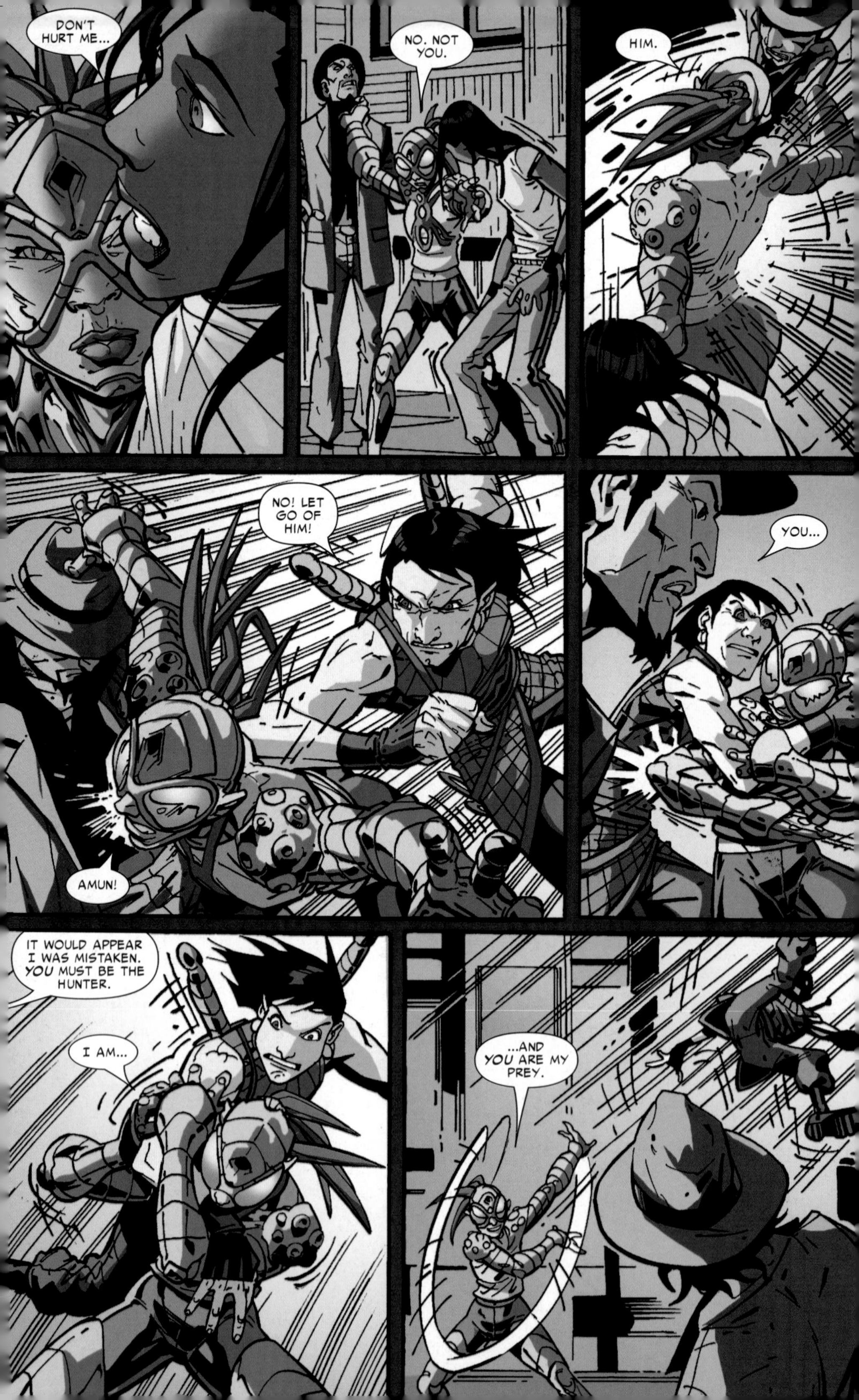
DON'T HURT ME...
NO. NOT YOU.
HIM.
NO! LET GO OF HIM!
AMUN!
YOU...
IT WOULD APPEAR I WAS MISTAKEN. YOU MUST BE THE HUNTER.
I AM...
...AND YOU ARE MY PREY.

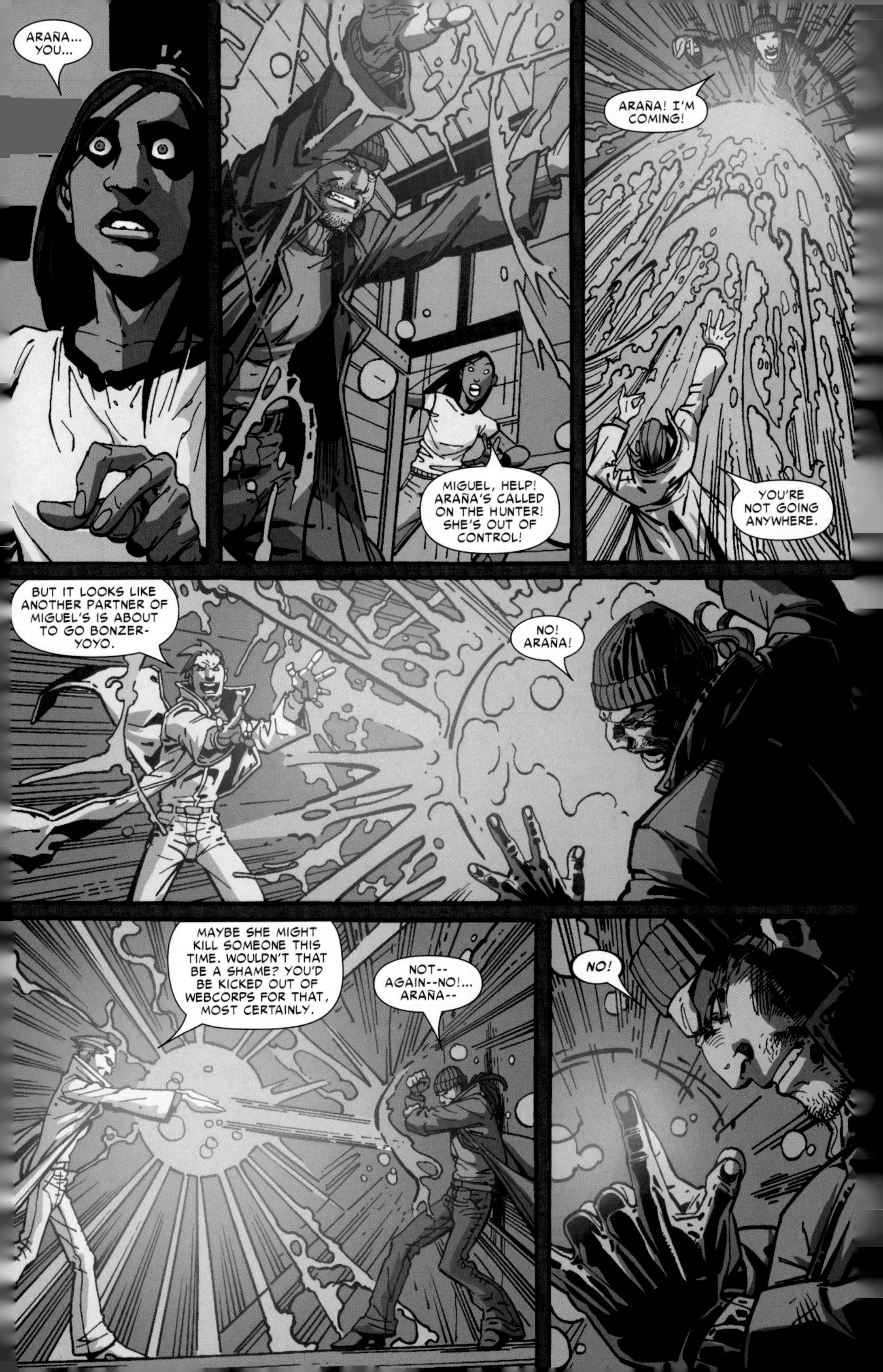
ARAÑA... YOU...
MIGUEL, HELP! ARAÑA'S CALLED ON THE HUNTER! SHE'S OUT OF CONTROL!
ARAÑA! I'M COMING!
YOU'RE NOT GOING ANYWHERE.
BUT IT LOOKS LIKE ANOTHER PARTNER OF MIGUEL'S IS ABOUT TO GO BONZER-YOYO.
NO! ARAÑA!
MAYBE SHE MIGHT KILL SOMEONE THIS TIME. WOULDN'T THAT BE A SHAME? YOU'D BE KICKED OUT OF WEBCORPS FOR THAT, MOST CERTAINLY.
NOT-- AGAIN--NO!... ARAÑA--
NO!

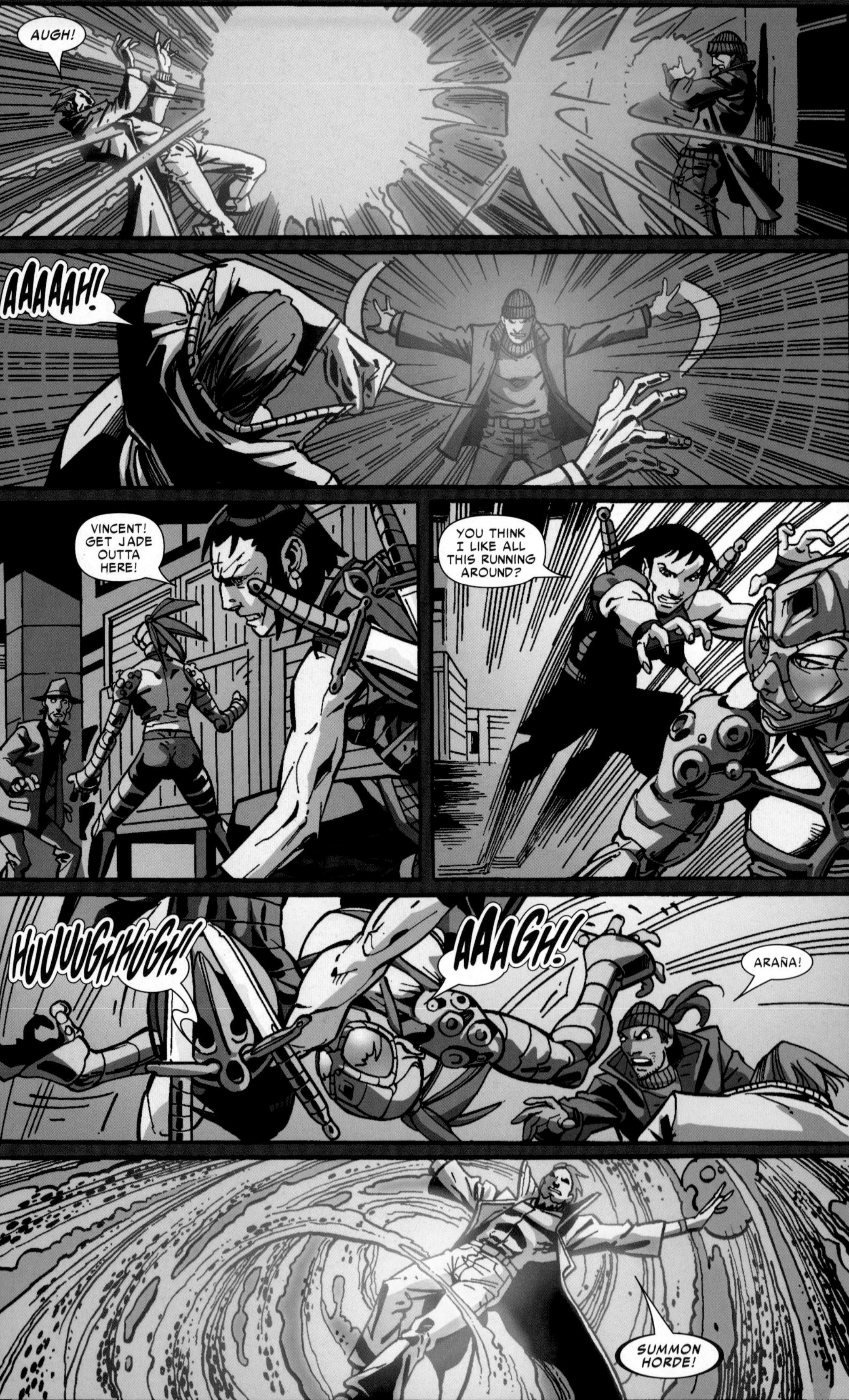
AUGH!
AAAAAH!
VINCENT! GET JADE OUTTA HERE!
YOU THINK I LIKE ALL THIS RUNNING AROUND?
HUUUUGHHUGH!
AAAGH!
ARAÑA!
SUMMON HORDE!

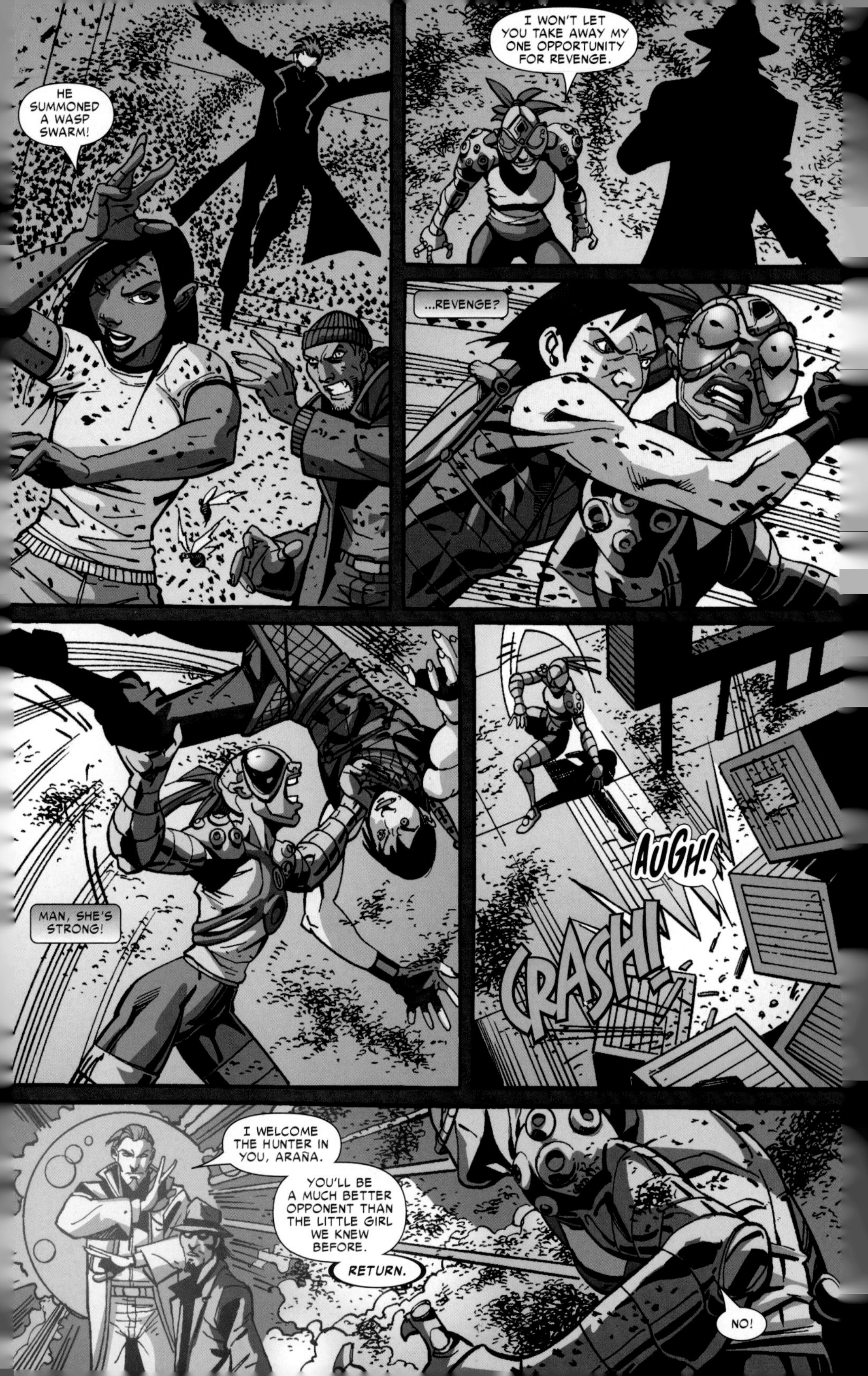
HE SUMMONED A WASP SWARM!
I WON'T LET YOU TAKE AWAY MY ONE OPPORTUNITY FOR REVENGE.
...REVENGE?
MAN, SHE'S STRONG!
AUGH!
CRASH!
I WELCOME THE HUNTER IN YOU, ARAÑA.
YOU'LL BE A MUCH BETTER OPPONENT THAN THE LITTLE GIRL WE KNEW BEFORE.
RETURN.
NO!

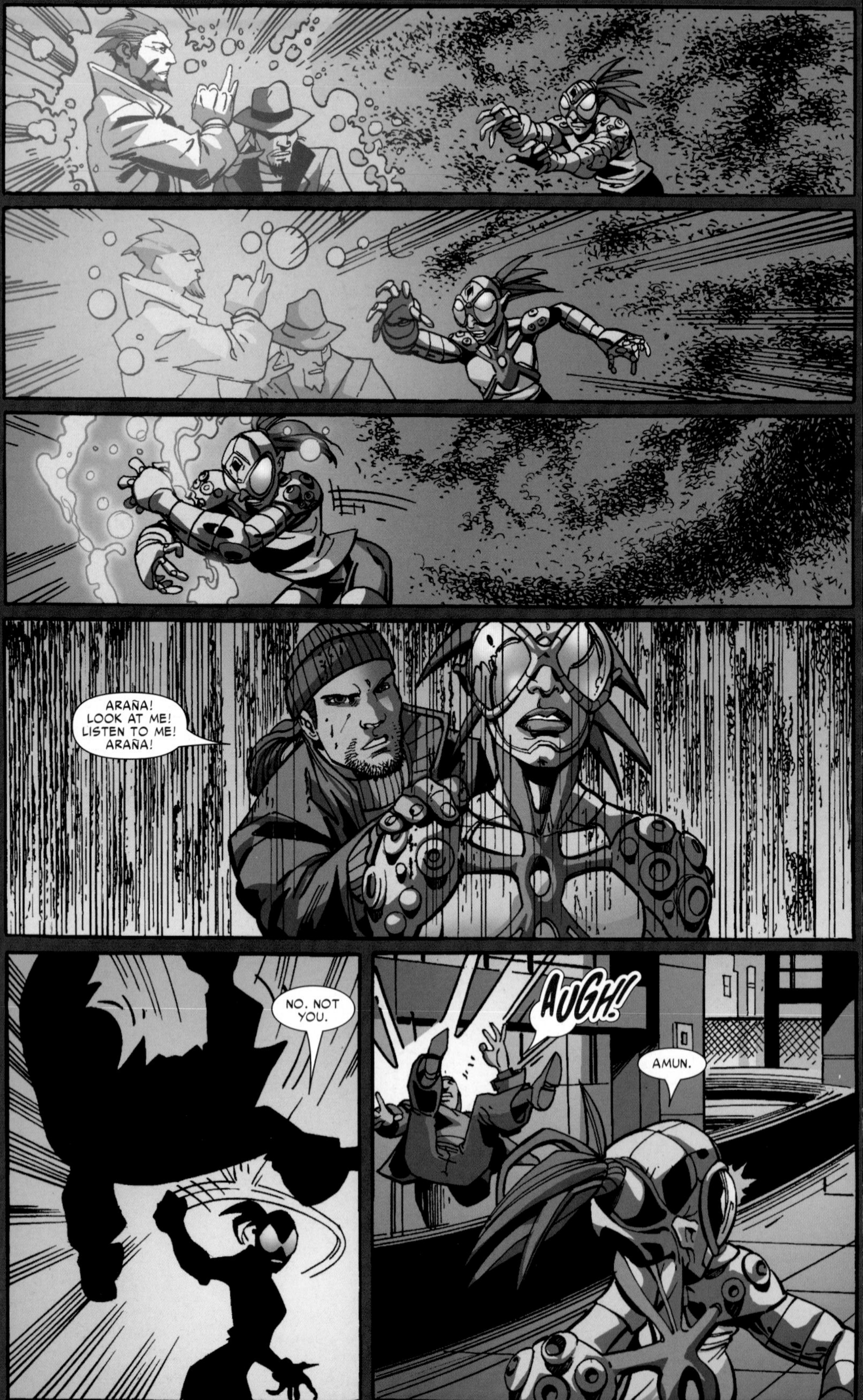
ARAÑA! LOOK AT ME! LISTEN TO ME! ARAÑA!
NO. NOT YOU.
AUGH!
AMUN.

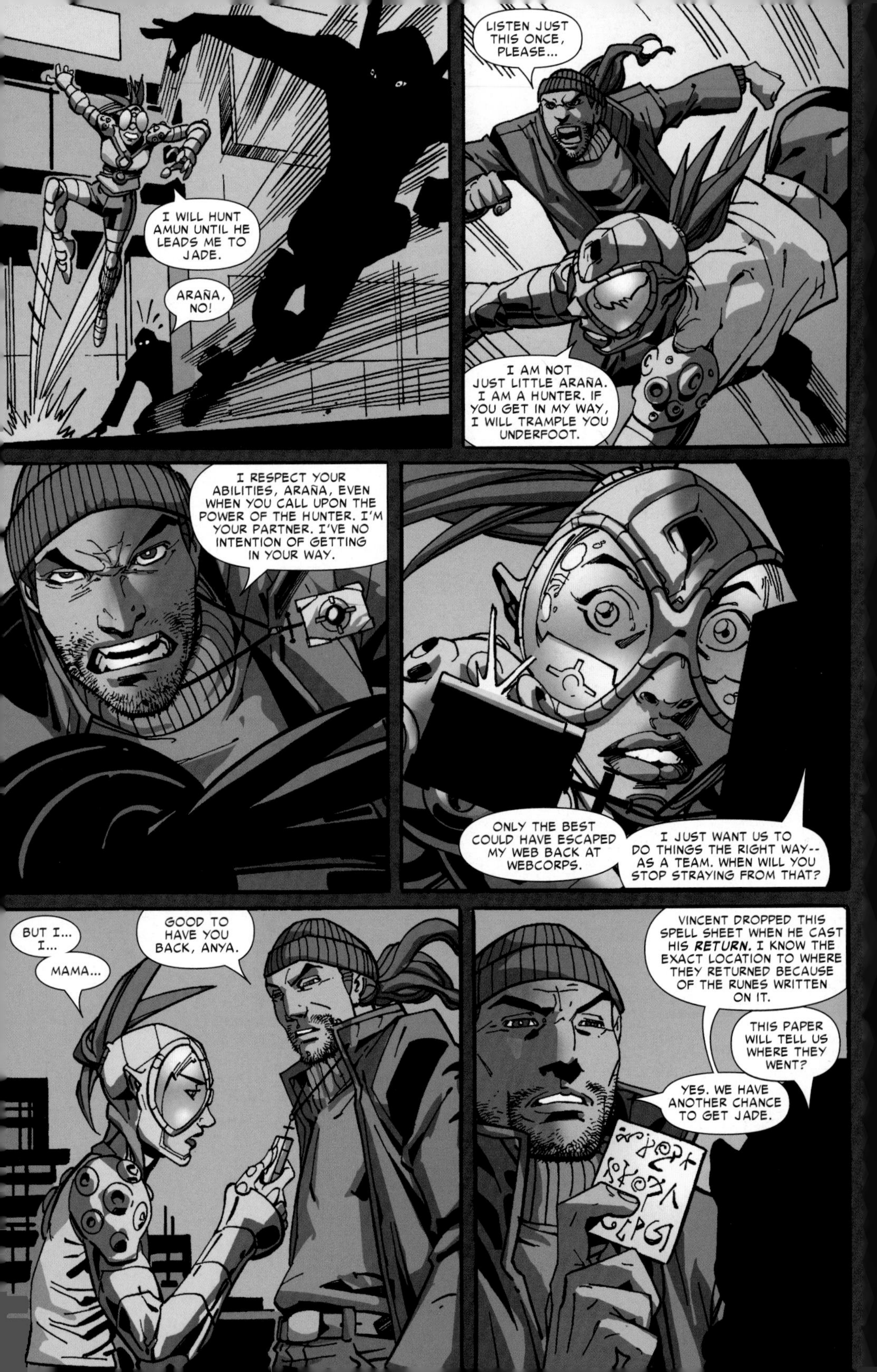
I WILL HUNT AMUN UNTIL HE LEADS ME TO JADE.
ARAÑA, NO!
LISTEN JUST THIS ONCE, PLEASE...
I AM NOT JUST LITTLE ARAÑA. I AM A HUNTER. IF YOU GET IN MY WAY, I WILL TRAMPLE YOU UNDERFOOT.
I RESPECT YOUR ABILITIES, ARAÑA, EVEN WHEN YOU CALL UPON THE POWER OF THE HUNTER. I'M YOUR PARTNER. I'VE NO INTENTION OF GETTING IN YOUR WAY.
ONLY THE BEST COULD HAVE ESCAPED MY WEB BACK AT WEBCORPS.
I JUST WANT US TO DO THINGS THE RIGHT WAY-- AS A TEAM. WHEN WILL YOU STOP STRAYING FROM THAT?
BUT I... I... MAMA...
GOOD TO HAVE YOU BACK, ANYA.
VINCENT DROPPED THIS SPELL SHEET WHEN HE CAST HIS ***RETURN.*** I KNOW THE EXACT LOCATION TO WHERE THEY RETURNED BECAUSE OF THE RUNES WRITTEN ON IT.
THIS PAPER WILL TELL US WHERE THEY WENT?
YES. WE HAVE ANOTHER CHANCE TO GET JADE.

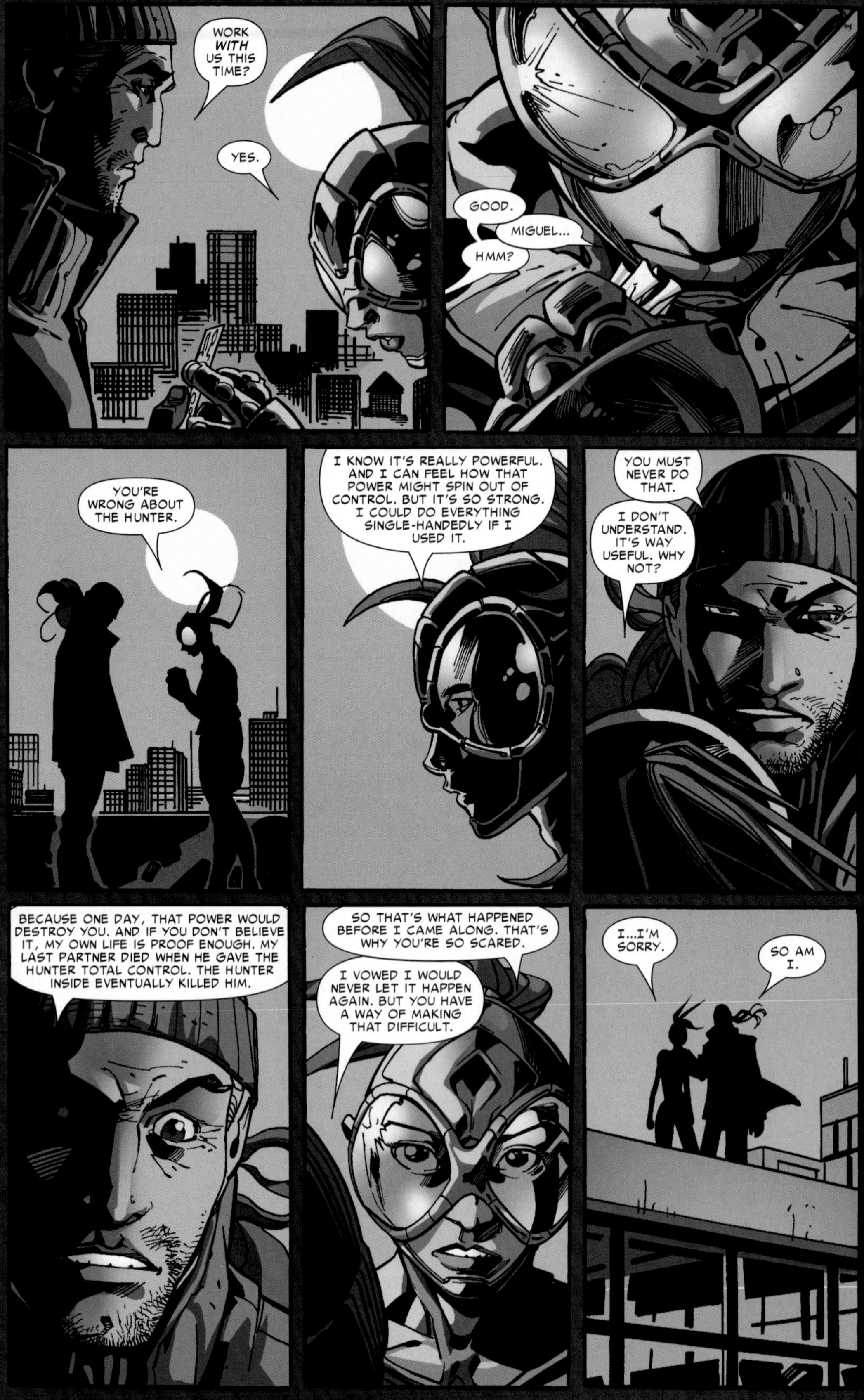
WORK WITH US THIS TIME?
YES.
GOOD.
MIGUEL...
HMM?
YOU'RE WRONG ABOUT THE HUNTER.
I KNOW IT'S REALLY POWERFUL. AND I CAN FEEL HOW THAT POWER MIGHT SPIN OUT OF CONTROL. BUT IT'S SO STRONG. I COULD DO EVERYTHING SINGLE-HANDEDLY IF I USED IT.
YOU MUST NEVER DO THAT.
I DON'T UNDERSTAND. IT'S WAY USEFUL. WHY NOT?
BECAUSE ONE DAY, THAT POWER WOULD DESTROY YOU. AND IF YOU DON'T BELIEVE IT, MY OWN LIFE IS PROOF ENOUGH. MY LAST PARTNER DIED WHEN HE GAVE THE HUNTER TOTAL CONTROL. THE HUNTER INSIDE EVENTUALLY KILLED HIM.
SO THAT'S WHAT HAPPENED BEFORE I CAME ALONG. THAT'S WHY YOU'RE SO SCARED.
I VOWED I WOULD NEVER LET IT HAPPEN AGAIN. BUT YOU HAVE A WAY OF MAKING THAT DIFFICULT.
I...I'M SORRY.
SO AM I.

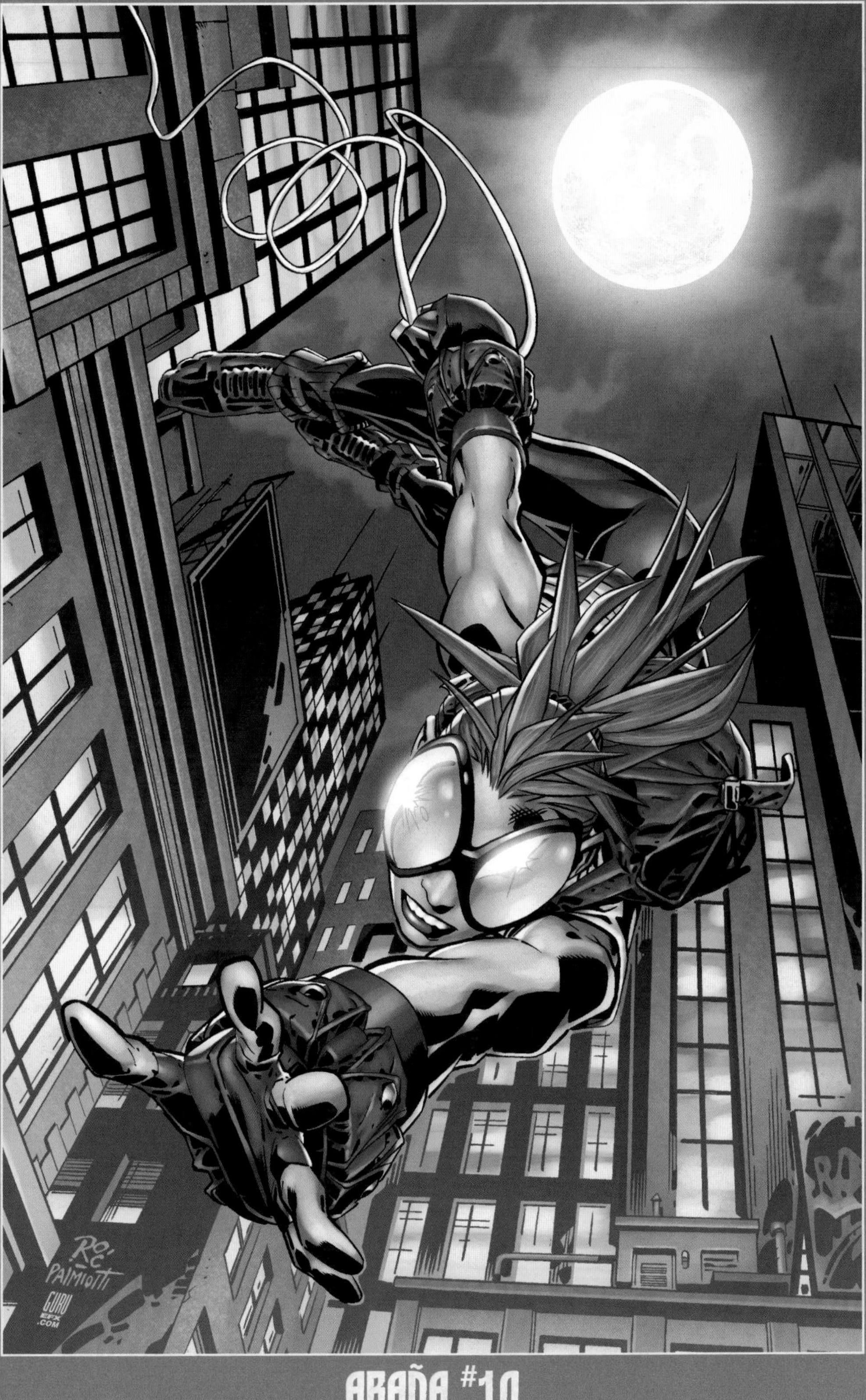
PAIMIOTTI
GURU EFX .COM

ARAÑA #10

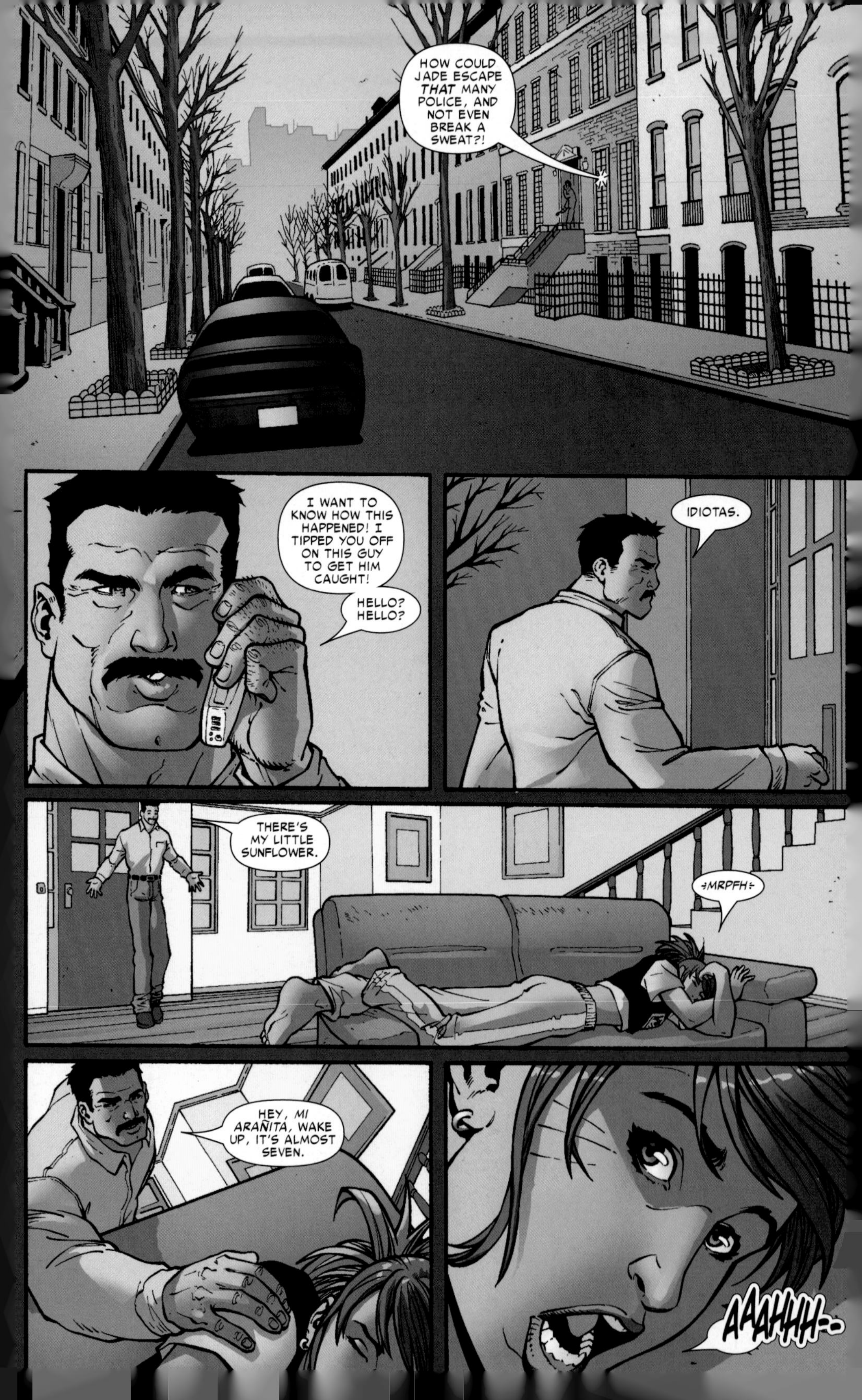

HOW COULD JADE ESCAPE *THAT* MANY POLICE, AND NOT EVEN BREAK A SWEAT?!
I WANT TO KNOW HOW THIS HAPPENED! I TIPPED YOU OFF ON THIS GUY TO GET HIM CAUGHT!
HELLO? HELLO?
IDIOTAS.
THERE'S MY LITTLE SUNFLOWER.
MRPFH
HEY, *MI ARAÑITA*, WAKE UP, IT'S ALMOST SEVEN.
AAAHHH-

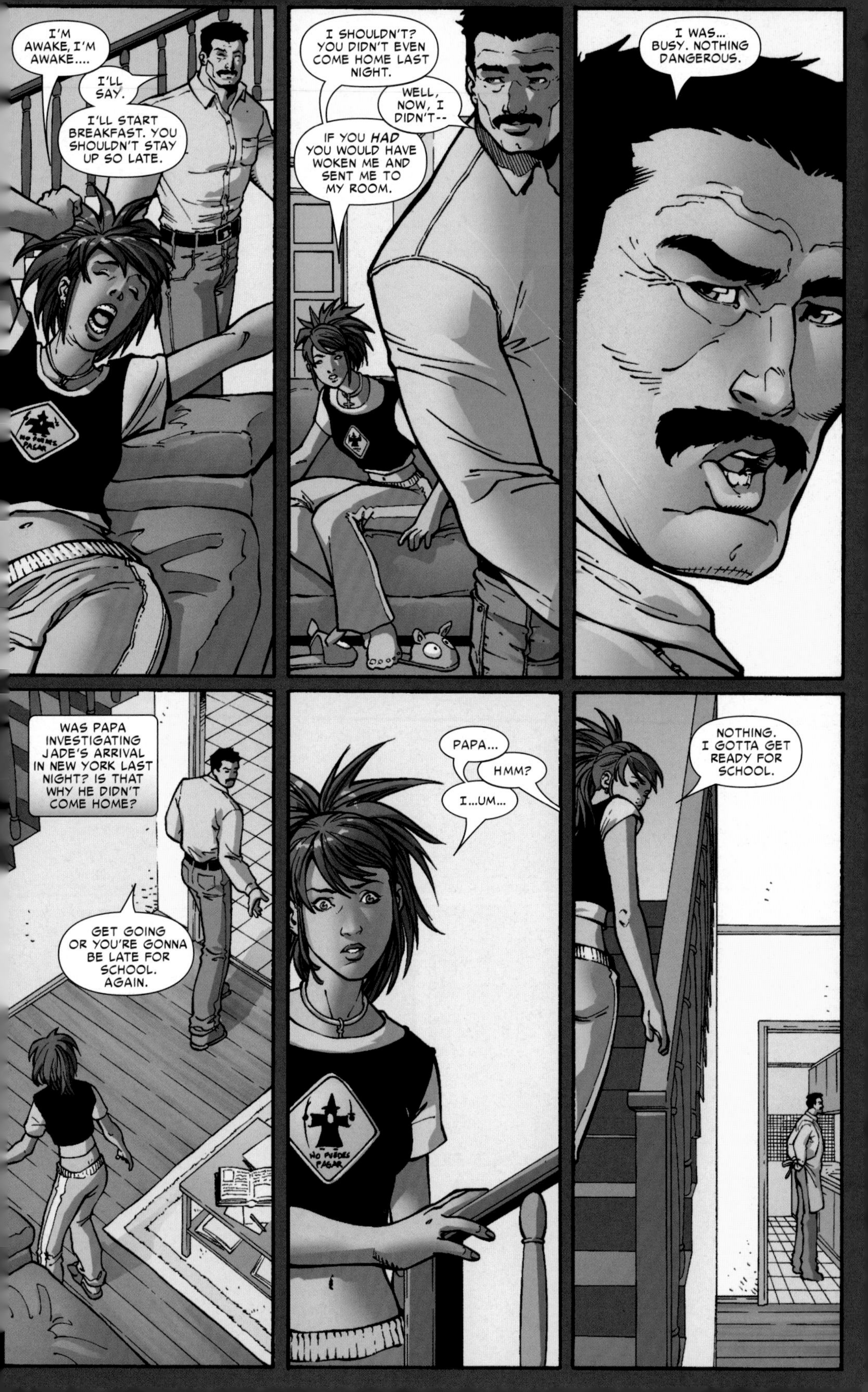
I'M AWAKE, I'M AWAKE....
I'LL SAY.
I'LL START BREAKFAST. YOU SHOULDN'T STAY UP SO LATE.
I SHOULDN'T? YOU DIDN'T EVEN COME HOME LAST NIGHT.
WELL, NOW, I DIDN'T--
IF YOU HAD YOU WOULD HAVE WOKEN ME AND SENT ME TO MY ROOM.
I WAS... BUSY. NOTHING DANGEROUS.
WAS PAPA INVESTIGATING JADE'S ARRIVAL IN NEW YORK LAST NIGHT? IS THAT WHY HE DIDN'T COME HOME?
GET GOING OR YOU'RE GONNA BE LATE FOR SCHOOL. AGAIN.
PAPA...
HMM?
I...UM...
NOTHING. I GOTTA GET READY FOR SCHOOL.

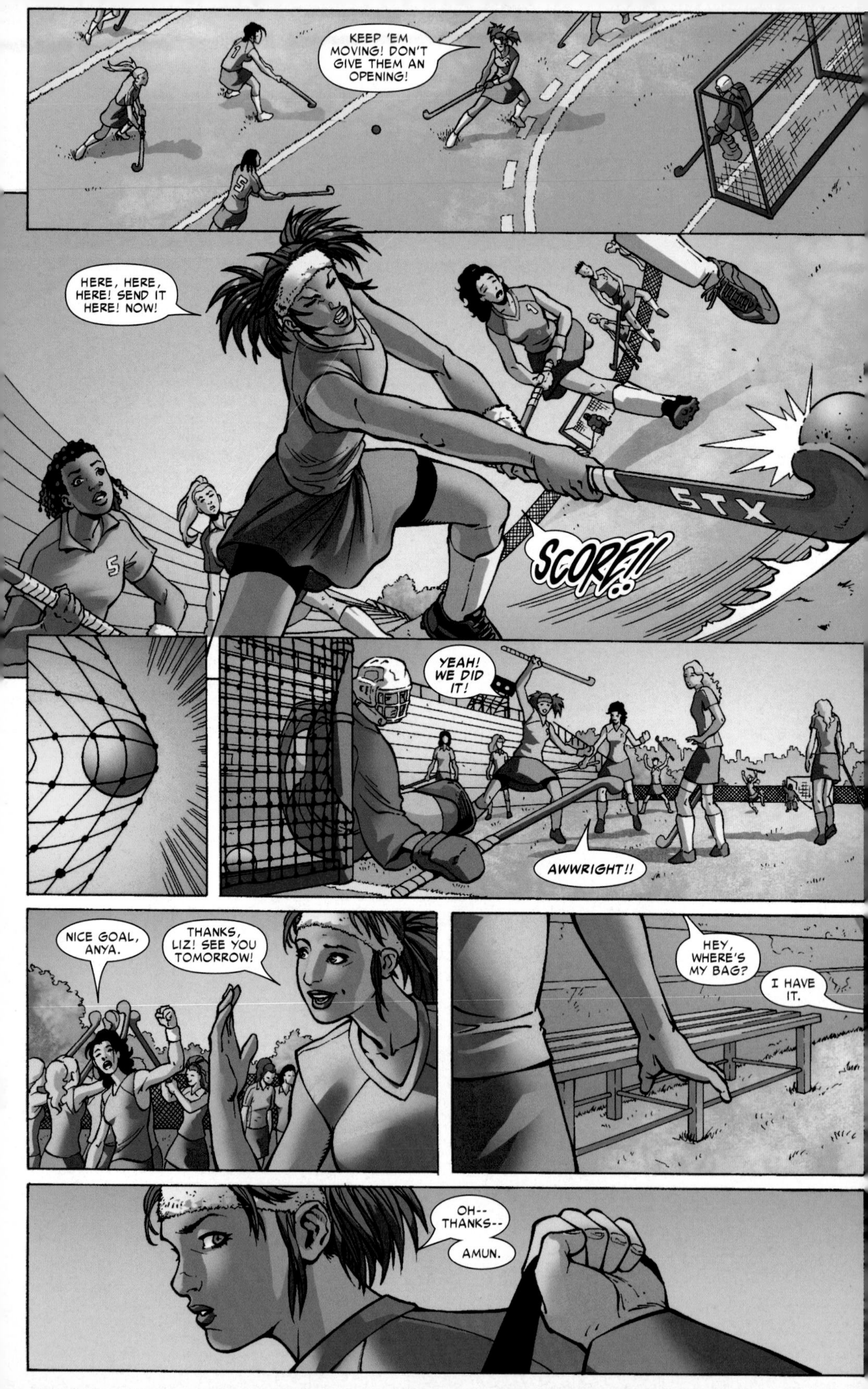
KEEP 'EM MOVING! DON'T GIVE THEM AN OPENING!
HERE, HERE, HERE! SEND IT HERE! NOW!
STX
SCORE!!
YEAH! WE DID IT!
AWWRIGHT!!
NICE GOAL, ANYA.
THANKS, LIZ! SEE YOU TOMORROW!
HEY, WHERE'S MY BAG?
I HAVE IT.
OH-- THANKS--
AMUN.

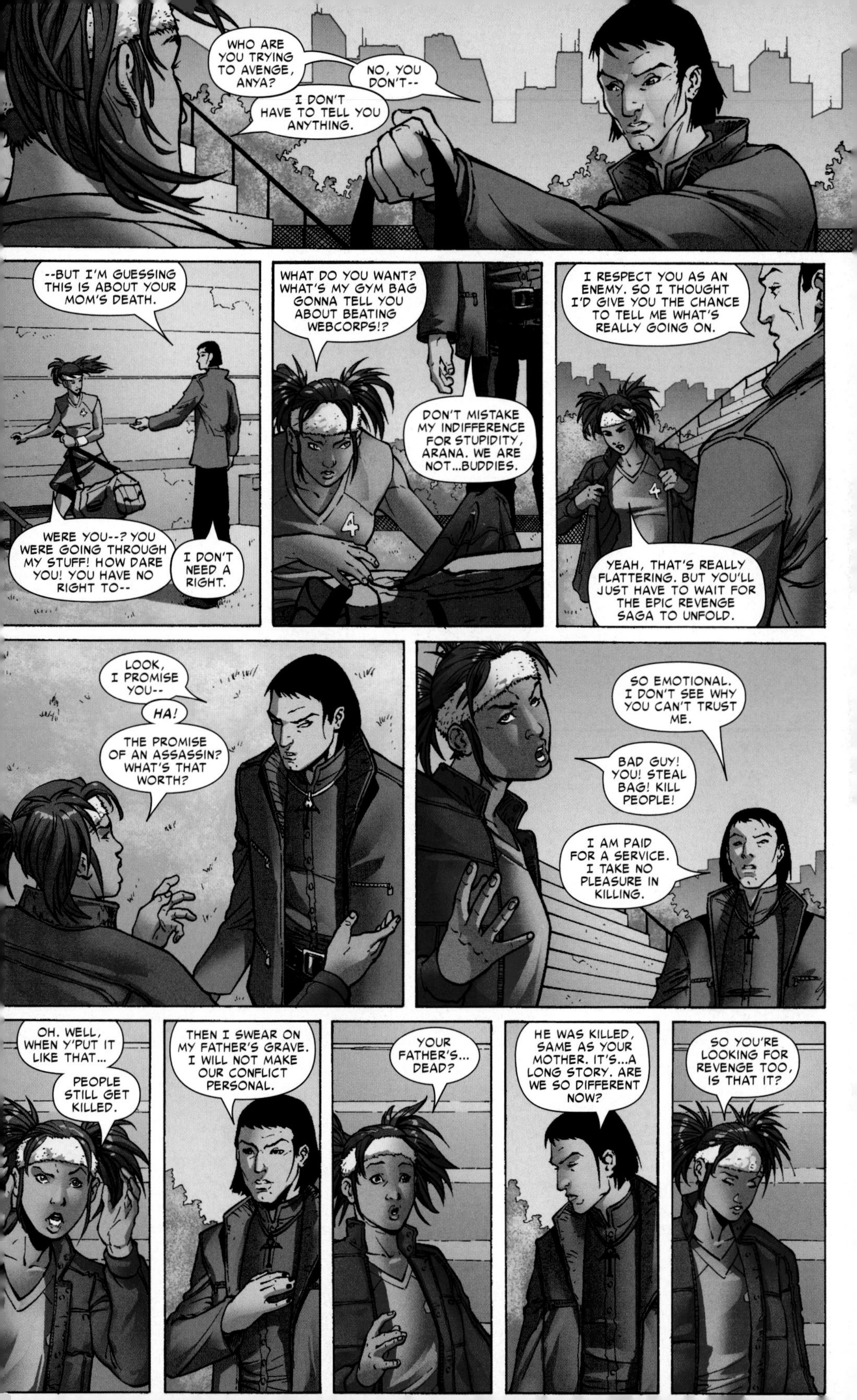
WHO ARE YOU TRYING TO AVENGE, ANYA?
NO, YOU DON'T--
I DON'T HAVE TO TELL YOU ANYTHING.
--BUT I'M GUESSING THIS IS ABOUT YOUR MOM'S DEATH.
WERE YOU--? YOU WERE GOING THROUGH MY STUFF! HOW DARE YOU! YOU HAVE NO RIGHT TO--
I DON'T NEED A RIGHT.
WHAT DO YOU WANT? WHAT'S MY GYM BAG GONNA TELL YOU ABOUT BEATING WEBCORPS!?
DON'T MISTAKE MY INDIFFERENCE FOR STUPIDITY, ARANA. WE ARE NOT...BUDDIES.
I RESPECT YOU AS AN ENEMY. SO I THOUGHT I'D GIVE YOU THE CHANCE TO TELL ME WHAT'S REALLY GOING ON.
YEAH, THAT'S REALLY FLATTERING. BUT YOU'LL JUST HAVE TO WAIT FOR THE EPIC REVENGE SAGA TO UNFOLD.
LOOK, I PROMISE YOU--
HA!
THE PROMISE OF AN ASSASSIN? WHAT'S THAT WORTH?
SO EMOTIONAL. I DON'T SEE WHY YOU CAN'T TRUST ME.
BAD GUY! YOU! STEAL BAG! KILL PEOPLE!
I AM PAID FOR A SERVICE. I TAKE NO PLEASURE IN KILLING.
OH. WELL, WHEN Y'PUT IT LIKE THAT...
PEOPLE STILL GET KILLED.
THEN I SWEAR ON MY FATHER'S GRAVE. I WILL NOT MAKE OUR CONFLICT PERSONAL.
YOUR FATHER'S... DEAD?
HE WAS KILLED, SAME AS YOUR MOTHER. IT'S...A LONG STORY. ARE WE SO DIFFERENT NOW?
SO YOU'RE LOOKING FOR REVENGE TOO, IS THAT IT?

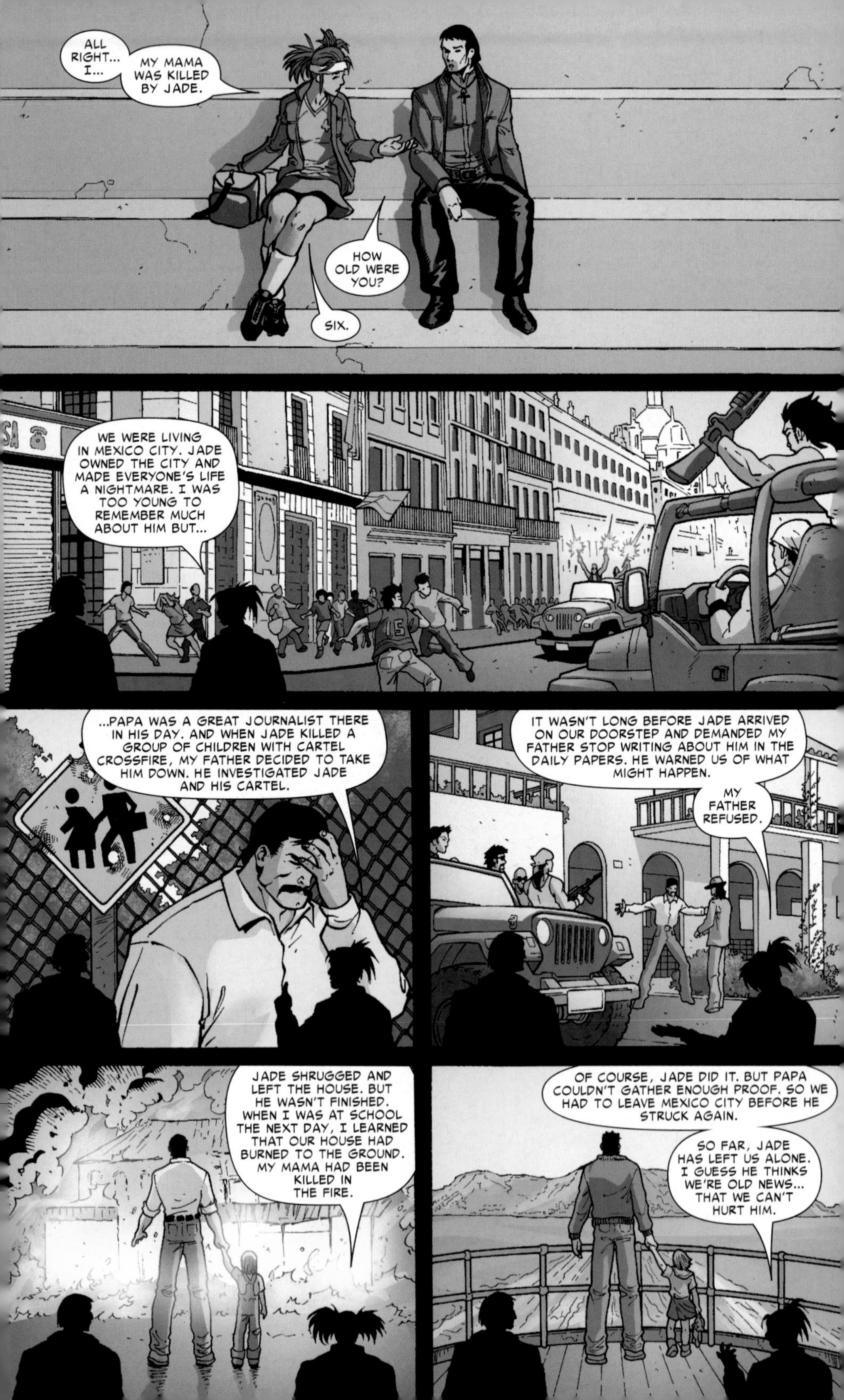
ALL RIGHT... I...
MY MAMA WAS KILLED BY JADE.
HOW OLD WERE YOU?
SIX.
WE WERE LIVING IN MEXICO CITY. JADE OWNED THE CITY AND MADE EVERYONE'S LIFE A NIGHTMARE. I WAS TOO YOUNG TO REMEMBER MUCH ABOUT HIM BUT...
...PAPA WAS A GREAT JOURNALIST THERE IN HIS DAY. AND WHEN JADE KILLED A GROUP OF CHILDREN WITH CARTEL CROSSFIRE, MY FATHER DECIDED TO TAKE HIM DOWN. HE INVESTIGATED JADE AND HIS CARTEL.
IT WASN'T LONG BEFORE JADE ARRIVED ON OUR DOORSTEP AND DEMANDED MY FATHER STOP WRITING ABOUT HIM IN THE DAILY PAPERS. HE WARNED US OF WHAT MIGHT HAPPEN.
MY FATHER REFUSED.
JADE SHRUGGED AND LEFT THE HOUSE. BUT HE WASN'T FINISHED. WHEN I WAS AT SCHOOL THE NEXT DAY, I LEARNED THAT OUR HOUSE HAD BURNED TO THE GROUND. MY MAMA HAD BEEN KILLED IN THE FIRE.
OF COURSE, JADE DID IT. BUT PAPA COULDN'T GATHER ENOUGH PROOF. SO WE HAD TO LEAVE MEXICO CITY BEFORE HE STRUCK AGAIN.
SO FAR, JADE HAS LEFT US ALONE. I GUESS HE THINKS WE'RE OLD NEWS... THAT WE CAN'T HURT HIM.

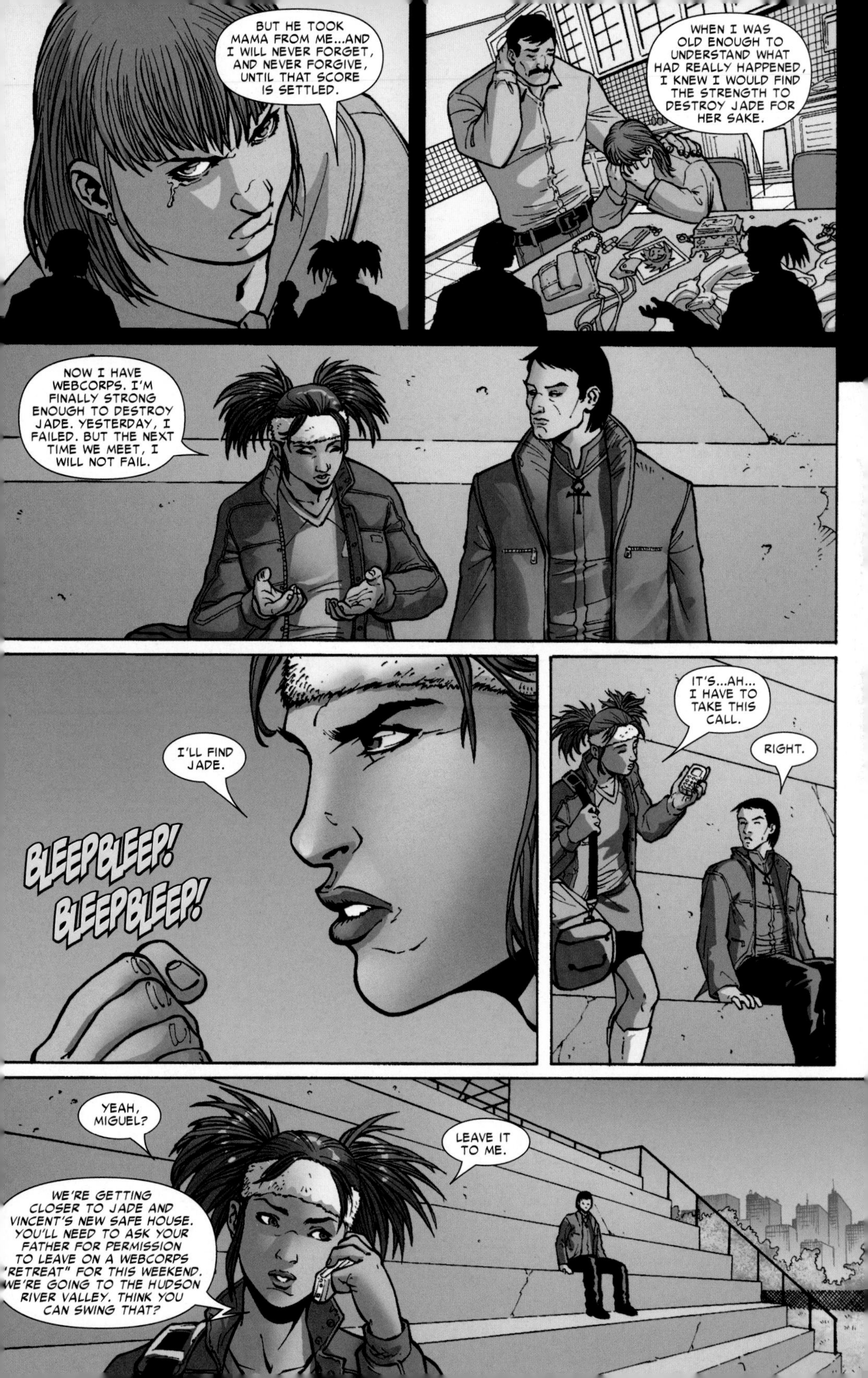
BUT HE TOOK MAMA FROM ME...AND I WILL NEVER FORGET, AND NEVER FORGIVE, UNTIL THAT SCORE IS SETTLED.
WHEN I WAS OLD ENOUGH TO UNDERSTAND WHAT HAD REALLY HAPPENED, I KNEW I WOULD FIND THE STRENGTH TO DESTROY JADE FOR HER SAKE.
NOW I HAVE WEBCORPS. I'M FINALLY STRONG ENOUGH TO DESTROY JADE. YESTERDAY, I FAILED. BUT THE NEXT TIME WE MEET, I WILL NOT FAIL.
I'LL FIND JADE.
BLEEPBLEEP! BLEEPBLEEP!
IT'S...AH... I HAVE TO TAKE THIS CALL.
RIGHT.
YEAH, MIGUEL?
WE'RE GETTING CLOSER TO JADE AND VINCENT'S NEW SAFE HOUSE. YOU'LL NEED TO ASK YOUR FATHER FOR PERMISSION TO LEAVE ON A WEBCORPS "RETREAT" FOR THIS WEEKEND. WE'RE GOING TO THE HUDSON RIVER VALLEY. THINK YOU CAN SWING THAT?
LEAVE IT TO ME.

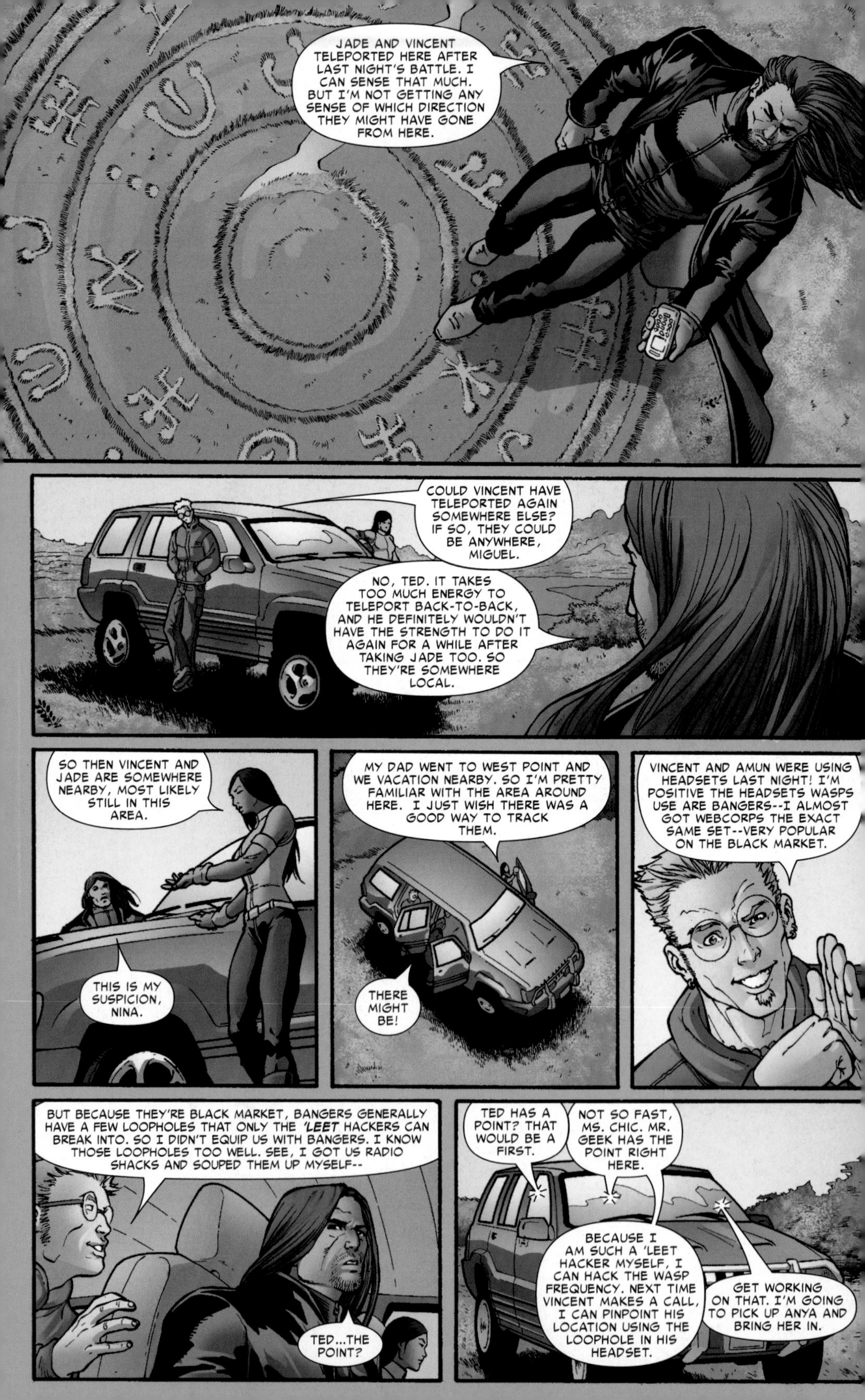

JADE AND VINCENT TELEPORTED HERE AFTER LAST NIGHT'S BATTLE. I CAN SENSE THAT MUCH. BUT I'M NOT GETTING ANY SENSE OF WHICH DIRECTION THEY MIGHT HAVE GONE FROM HERE.
COULD VINCENT HAVE TELEPORTED AGAIN SOMEWHERE ELSE? IF SO, THEY COULD BE ANYWHERE, MIGUEL.
NO, TED. IT TAKES TOO MUCH ENERGY TO TELEPORT BACK-TO-BACK, AND HE DEFINITELY WOULDN'T HAVE THE STRENGTH TO DO IT AGAIN FOR A WHILE AFTER TAKING JADE TOO. SO THEY'RE SOMEWHERE LOCAL.
SO THEN VINCENT AND JADE ARE SOMEWHERE NEARBY, MOST LIKELY STILL IN THIS AREA.
THIS IS MY SUSPICION, NINA.
MY DAD WENT TO WEST POINT AND WE VACATION NEARBY. SO I'M PRETTY FAMILIAR WITH THE AREA AROUND HERE. I JUST WISH THERE WAS A GOOD WAY TO TRACK THEM.
THERE MIGHT BE!
VINCENT AND AMUN WERE USING HEADSETS LAST NIGHT! I'M POSITIVE THE HEADSETS WASPS USE ARE BANGERS--I ALMOST GOT WEBCORPS THE EXACT SAME SET--VERY POPULAR ON THE BLACK MARKET.
BUT BECAUSE THEY'RE BLACK MARKET, BANGERS GENERALLY HAVE A FEW LOOPHOLES THAT ONLY THE *'LEET* HACKERS CAN BREAK INTO. SO I DIDN'T EQUIP US WITH BANGERS. I KNOW THOSE LOOPHOLES TOO WELL. SEE, I GOT US RADIO SHACKS AND SOUPED THEM UP MYSELF--
TED...THE POINT?
TED HAS A POINT? THAT WOULD BE A FIRST.
NOT SO FAST, MS. CHIC. MR. GEEK HAS THE POINT RIGHT HERE.
BECAUSE I AM SUCH A 'LEET HACKER MYSELF, I CAN HACK THE WASP FREQUENCY. NEXT TIME VINCENT MAKES A CALL, I CAN PINPOINT HIS LOCATION USING THE LOOPHOLE IN HIS HEADSET.
GET WORKING ON THAT. I'M GOING TO PICK UP ANYA AND BRING HER IN.

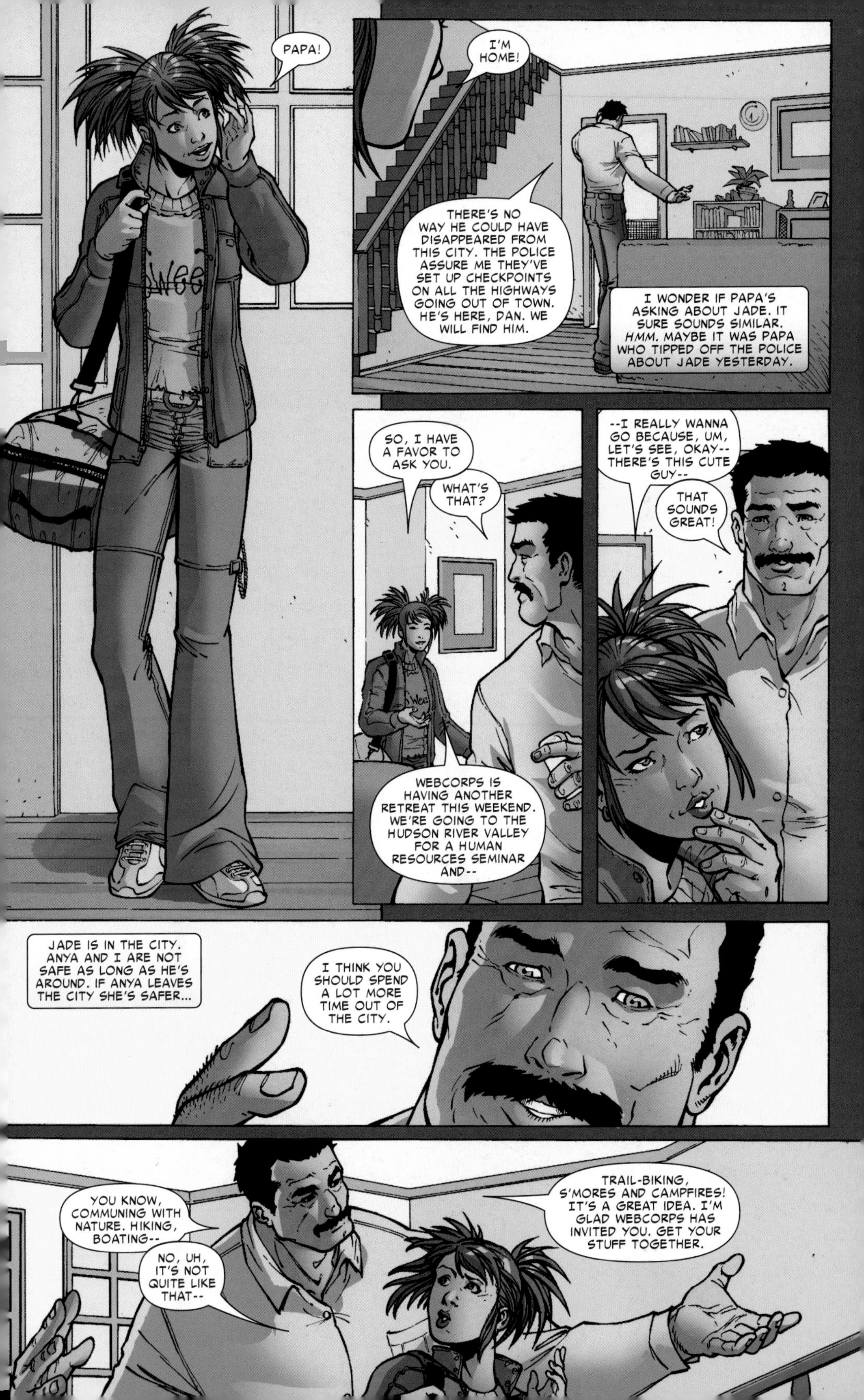
PAPA!
I'M HOME!
THERE'S NO WAY HE COULD HAVE DISAPPEARED FROM THIS CITY. THE POLICE ASSURE ME THEY'VE SET UP CHECKPOINTS ON ALL THE HIGHWAYS GOING OUT OF TOWN. HE'S HERE, DAN. WE WILL FIND HIM.
I WONDER IF PAPA'S ASKING ABOUT JADE. IT SURE SOUNDS SIMILAR. *HMM.* MAYBE IT WAS PAPA WHO TIPPED OFF THE POLICE ABOUT JADE YESTERDAY.
SO, I HAVE A FAVOR TO ASK YOU.
WHAT'S THAT?
WEBCORPS IS HAVING ANOTHER RETREAT THIS WEEKEND. WE'RE GOING TO THE HUDSON RIVER VALLEY FOR A HUMAN RESOURCES SEMINAR AND--
--I REALLY WANNA GO BECAUSE, UM, LET'S SEE, OKAY--THERE'S THIS CUTE GUY--
THAT SOUNDS GREAT!
JADE IS IN THE CITY. ANYA AND I ARE NOT SAFE AS LONG AS HE'S AROUND. IF ANYA LEAVES THE CITY SHE'S SAFER...
I THINK YOU SHOULD SPEND A LOT MORE TIME OUT OF THE CITY.
YOU KNOW, COMMUNING WITH NATURE. HIKING, BOATING--
NO, UH, IT'S NOT QUITE LIKE THAT--
TRAIL-BIKING, S'MORES AND CAMPFIRES! IT'S A GREAT IDEA. I'M GLAD WEBCORPS HAS INVITED YOU. GET YOUR STUFF TOGETHER.

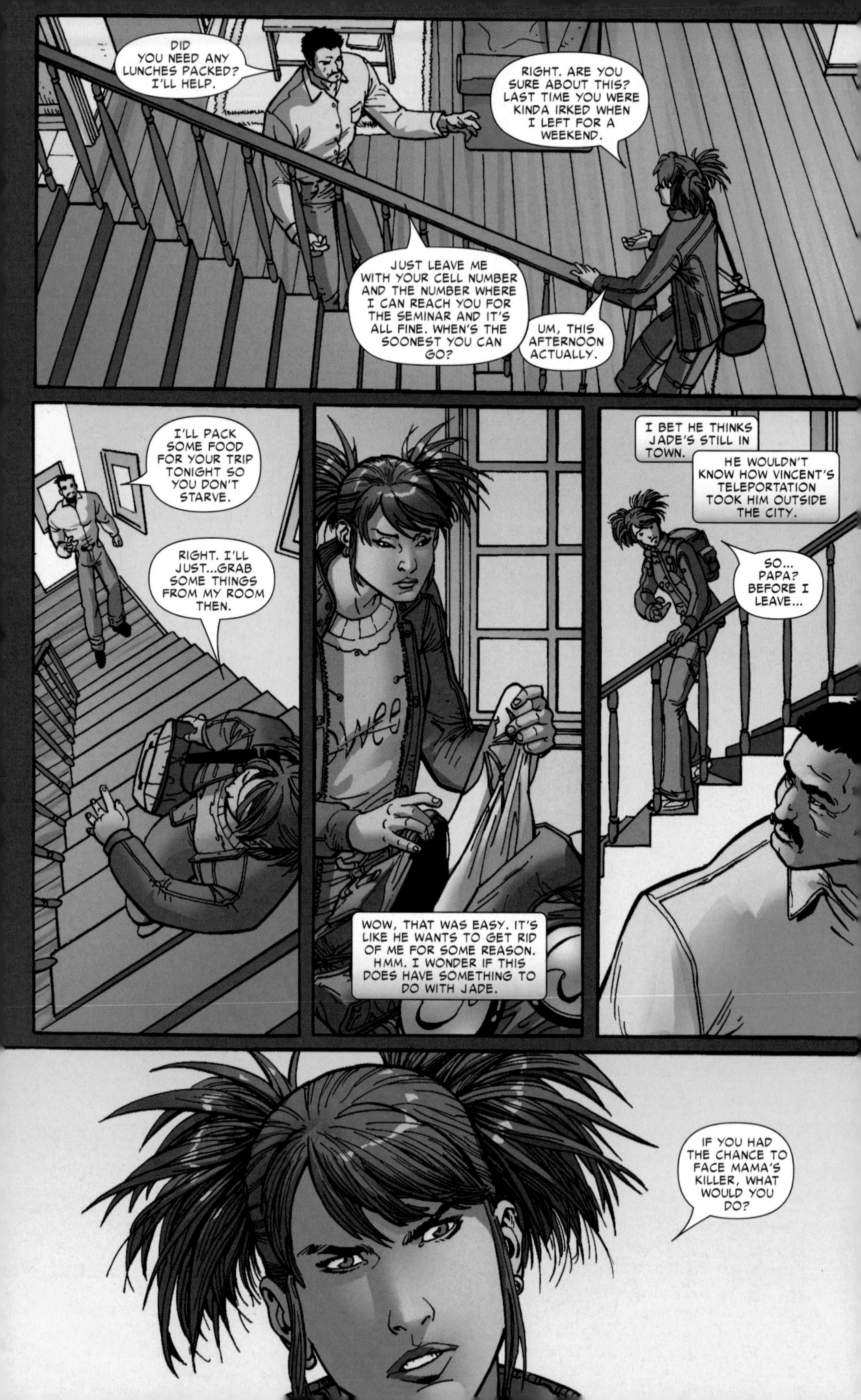
DID YOU NEED ANY LUNCHES PACKED? I'LL HELP.
RIGHT. ARE YOU SURE ABOUT THIS? LAST TIME YOU WERE KINDA IRKED WHEN I LEFT FOR A WEEKEND.
JUST LEAVE ME WITH YOUR CELL NUMBER AND THE NUMBER WHERE I CAN REACH YOU FOR THE SEMINAR AND IT'S ALL FINE. WHEN'S THE SOONEST YOU CAN GO?
UM, THIS AFTERNOON ACTUALLY.
I'LL PACK SOME FOOD FOR YOUR TRIP TONIGHT SO YOU DON'T STARVE.
RIGHT. I'LL JUST...GRAB SOME THINGS FROM MY ROOM THEN.
WOW, THAT WAS EASY. IT'S LIKE HE WANTS TO GET RID OF ME FOR SOME REASON. HMM. I WONDER IF THIS DOES HAVE SOMETHING TO DO WITH JADE.
I BET HE THINKS JADE'S STILL IN TOWN.
HE WOULDN'T KNOW HOW VINCENT'S TELEPORTATION TOOK HIM OUTSIDE THE CITY.
SO... PAPA? BEFORE I LEAVE...
IF YOU HAD THE CHANCE TO FACE MAMA'S KILLER, WHAT WOULD YOU DO?

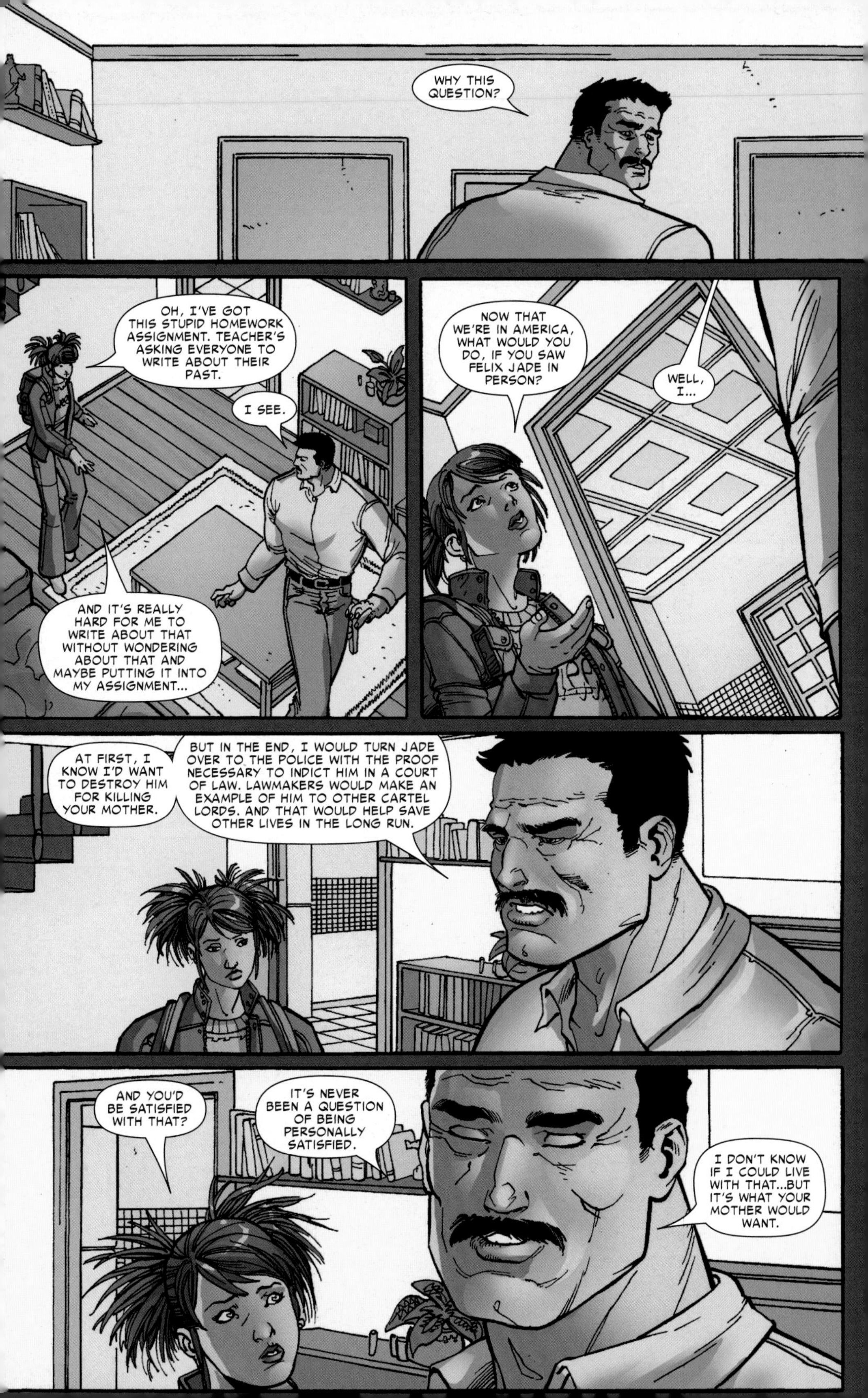
WHY THIS QUESTION?
OH, I'VE GOT THIS STUPID HOMEWORK ASSIGNMENT. TEACHER'S ASKING EVERYONE TO WRITE ABOUT THEIR PAST.
I SEE.
AND IT'S REALLY HARD FOR ME TO WRITE ABOUT THAT WITHOUT WONDERING ABOUT THAT AND MAYBE PUTTING IT INTO MY ASSIGNMENT...
NOW THAT WE'RE IN AMERICA, WHAT WOULD YOU DO, IF YOU SAW FELIX JADE IN PERSON?
WELL, I...
AT FIRST, I KNOW I'D WANT TO DESTROY HIM FOR KILLING YOUR MOTHER.
BUT IN THE END, I WOULD TURN JADE OVER TO THE POLICE WITH THE PROOF NECESSARY TO INDICT HIM IN A COURT OF LAW. LAWMAKERS WOULD MAKE AN EXAMPLE OF HIM TO OTHER CARTEL LORDS. AND THAT WOULD HELP SAVE OTHER LIVES IN THE LONG RUN.
AND YOU'D BE SATISFIED WITH THAT?
IT'S NEVER BEEN A QUESTION OF BEING PERSONALLY SATISFIED.
I DON'T KNOW IF I COULD LIVE WITH THAT...BUT IT'S WHAT YOUR MOTHER WOULD WANT.

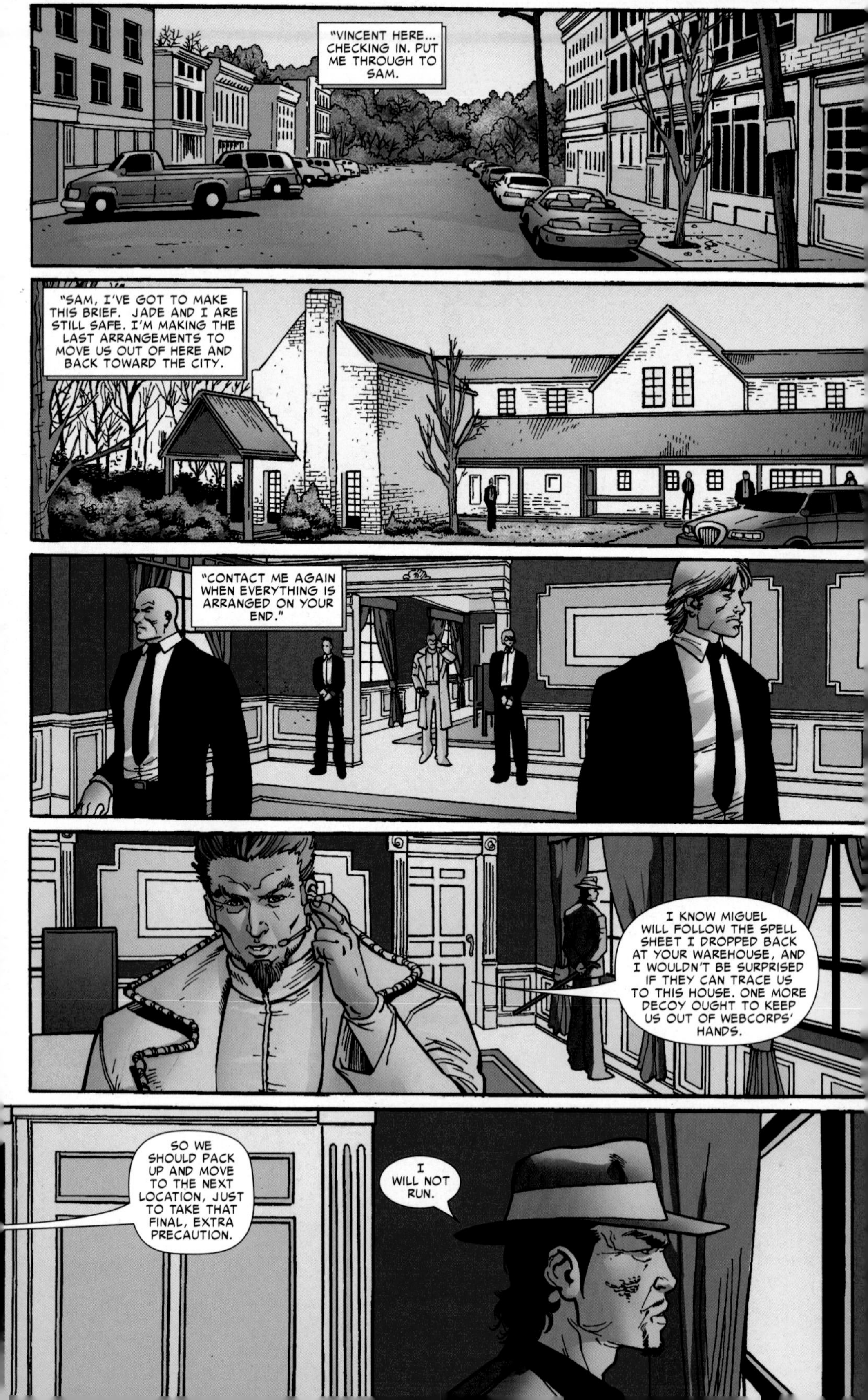

"VINCENT HERE... CHECKING IN. PUT ME THROUGH TO SAM.
"SAM, I'VE GOT TO MAKE THIS BRIEF. JADE AND I ARE STILL SAFE. I'M MAKING THE LAST ARRANGEMENTS TO MOVE US OUT OF HERE AND BACK TOWARD THE CITY.
"CONTACT ME AGAIN WHEN EVERYTHING IS ARRANGED ON YOUR END."
I KNOW MIGUEL WILL FOLLOW THE SPELL SHEET I DROPPED BACK AT YOUR WAREHOUSE, AND I WOULDN'T BE SURPRISED IF THEY CAN TRACE US TO THIS HOUSE. ONE MORE DECOY OUGHT TO KEEP US OUT OF WEBCORPS' HANDS.
SO WE SHOULD PACK UP AND MOVE TO THE NEXT LOCATION, JUST TO TAKE THAT FINAL, EXTRA PRECAUTION.
I WILL NOT RUN.

THAT'S HARDLY PRUDENT.

...I TELEPORTED YOU...

I NEVER AGREED TO YOUR-- WHATEVER YOU DID TO BRING ME HERE.

I PREFER TO STAND AND FIGHT. I DON'T KNOW WHO WEBCORPS IS TO TRY AND INTERFERE WITH ME, BUT I WILL NOW CRUSH THEM.

THEY ARE ALMOST AS POWERFUL AS THE WASPS. I THINK IT WOULD BE UNWISE FOR YOU TO TRY AND STAND UP TO THEM WITHOUT SOME UNDERSTANDING.

YOU MAY FEAR THEM BUT I DON'T RUN WHENEVER YOU LIKE. I AM STAYING RIGHT HERE AND IF THEY COME, I WILL DEAL WITH THEM.

HOW? THEY'LL MOW YOU OVER. THIS IS JUST YOUR PRIDE TALKING.

IF THAT'S HOW YOU FEEL, THEN YOU WILL LEAVE. I WILL NOT HUMOR SOMEONE SO WEAK IN THE KNEES. YOU'RE FREE TO GO.

SORRY, I CAN'T DO THAT EITHER. I WAS ORDERED BY THE WASPS TO PROTECT YOU. AND I NEVER DISOBEY ORDERS.

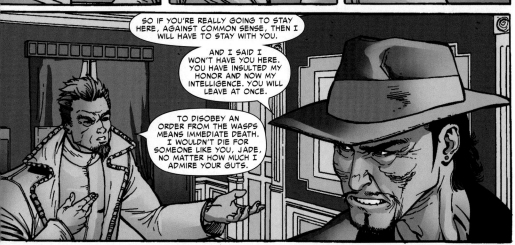

SO IF YOU'RE REALLY GOING TO STAY HERE, AGAINST COMMON SENSE, THEN I WILL HAVE TO STAY WITH YOU.

AND I SAID I WON'T HAVE YOU HERE. YOU HAVE INSULTED MY HONOR AND NOW MY INTELLIGENCE. YOU WILL LEAVE AT ONCE.

TO DISOBEY AN ORDER FROM THE WASPS MEANS IMMEDIATE DEATH. I WOULDN'T DIE FOR SOMEONE LIKE YOU, JADE, NO MATTER HOW MUCH I ADMIRE YOUR GUTS.

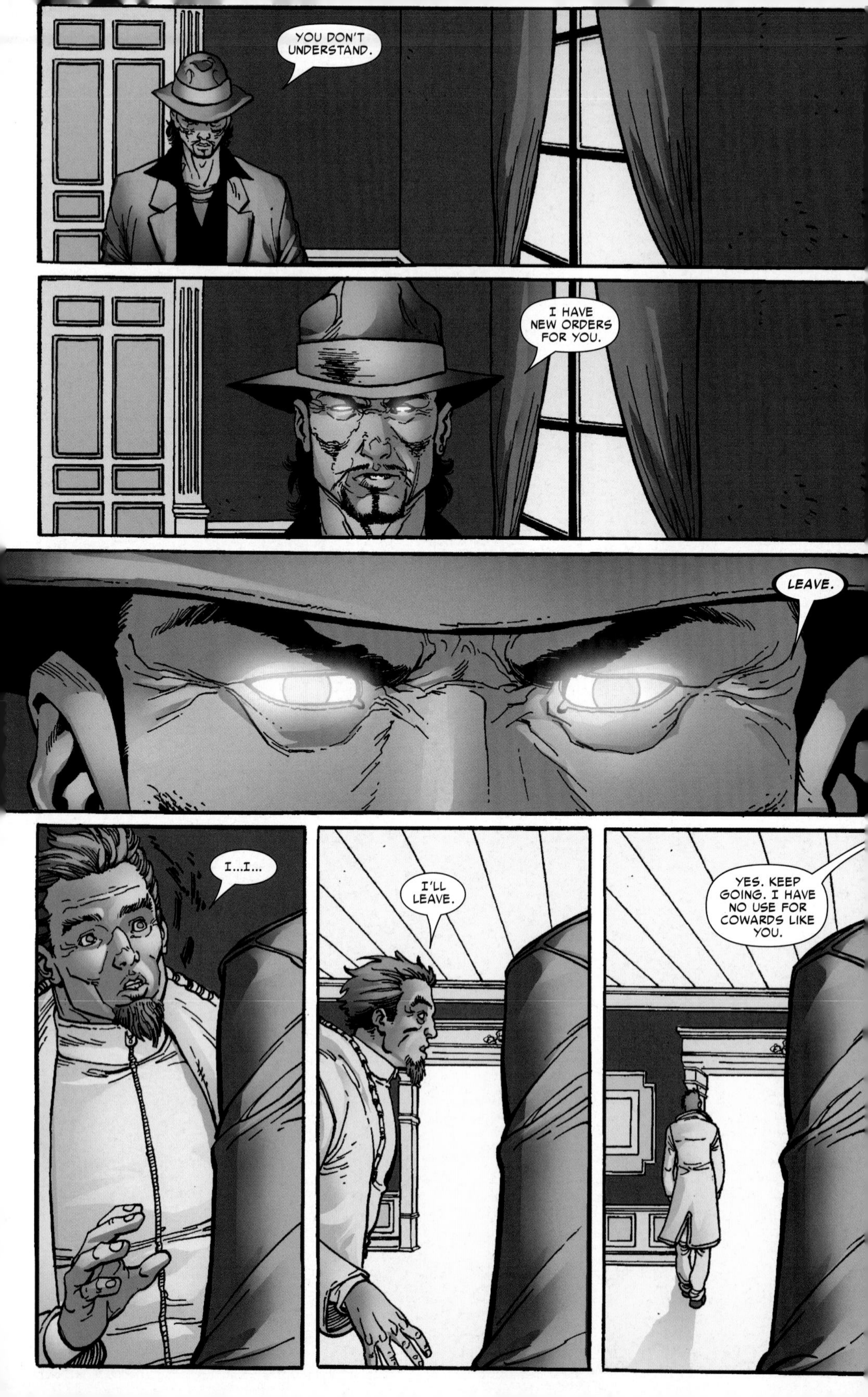
YOU DON'T UNDERSTAND.
I HAVE NEW ORDERS FOR YOU.
LEAVE.
I...I...
I'LL LEAVE.
YES. KEEP GOING. I HAVE NO USE FOR COWARDS LIKE YOU.

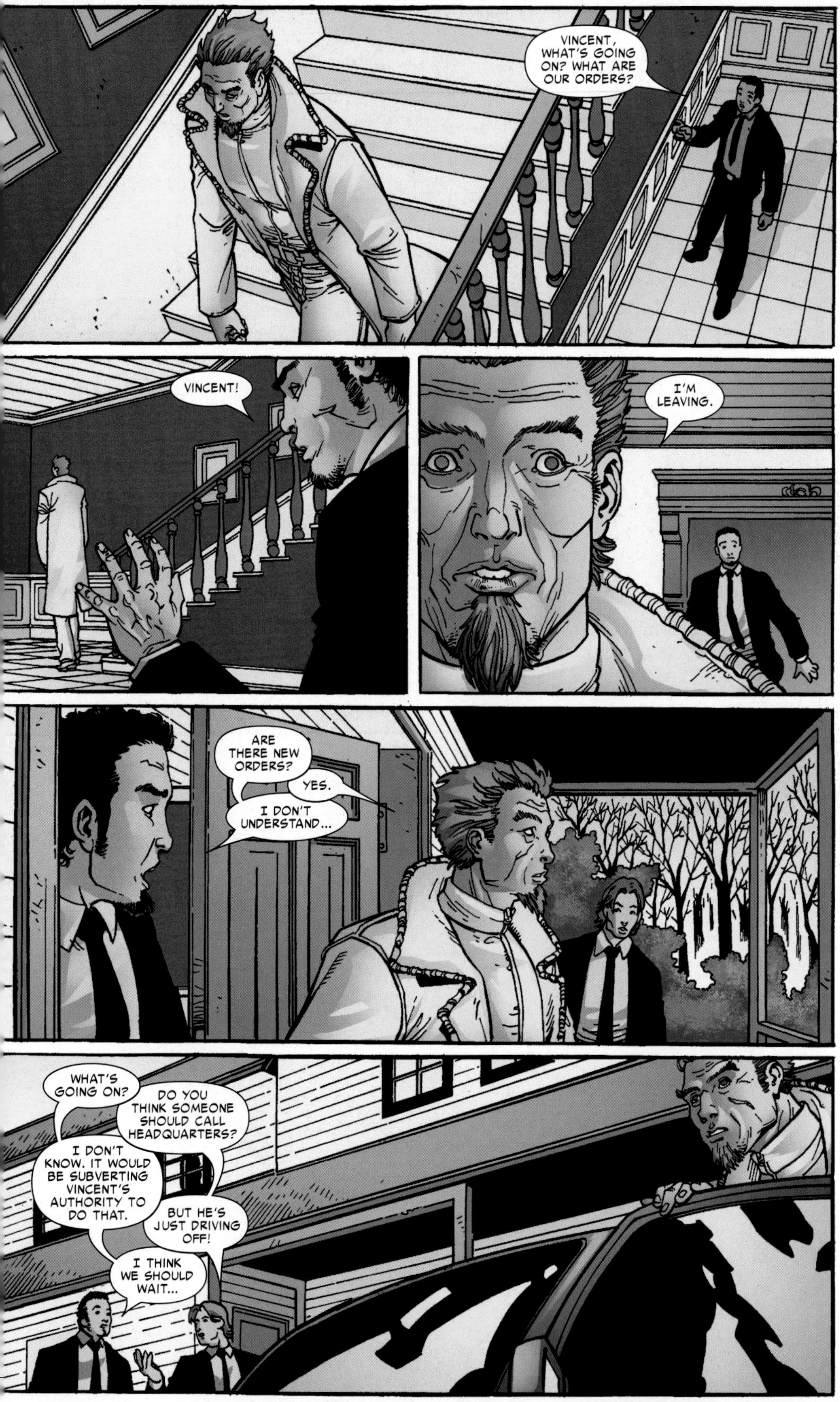
VINCENT, WHAT'S GOING ON? WHAT ARE OUR ORDERS?
VINCENT!
I'M LEAVING.
ARE THERE NEW ORDERS?
YES.
I DON'T UNDERSTAND...
WHAT'S GOING ON?
DO YOU THINK SOMEONE SHOULD CALL HEADQUARTERS?
I DON'T KNOW. IT WOULD BE SUBVERTING VINCENT'S AUTHORITY TO DO THAT.
BUT HE'S JUST DRIVING OFF!
I THINK WE SHOULD WAIT...

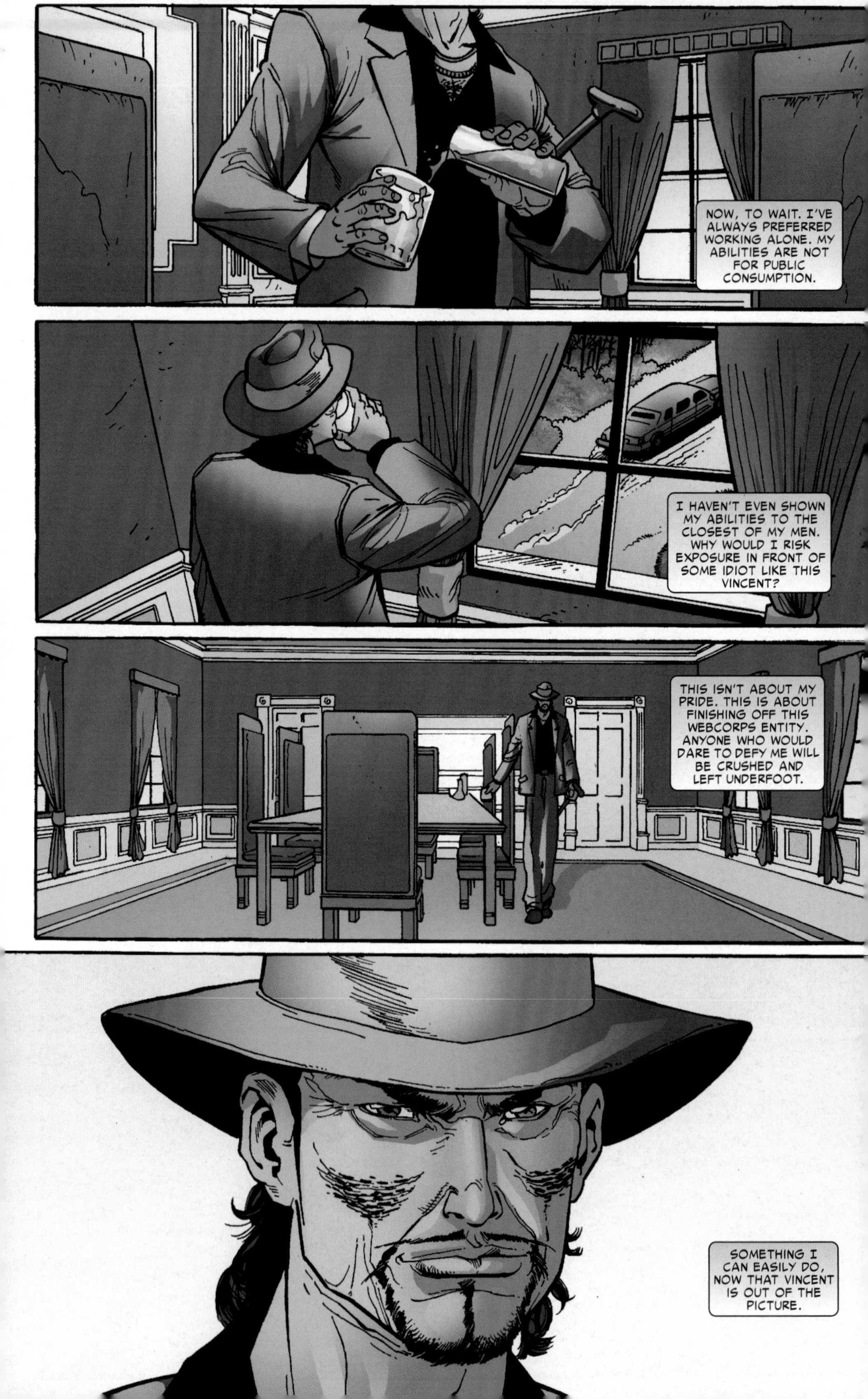
NOW, TO WAIT. I'VE ALWAYS PREFERRED WORKING ALONE. MY ABILITIES ARE NOT FOR PUBLIC CONSUMPTION.
I HAVEN'T EVEN SHOWN MY ABILITIES TO THE CLOSEST OF MY MEN. WHY WOULD I RISK EXPOSURE IN FRONT OF SOME IDIOT LIKE THIS VINCENT?
THIS ISN'T ABOUT MY PRIDE. THIS IS ABOUT FINISHING OFF THIS WEBCORPS ENTITY. ANYONE WHO WOULD DARE TO DEFY ME WILL BE CRUSHED AND LEFT UNDERFOOT.
SOMETHING I CAN EASILY DO, NOW THAT VINCENT IS OUT OF THE PICTURE.

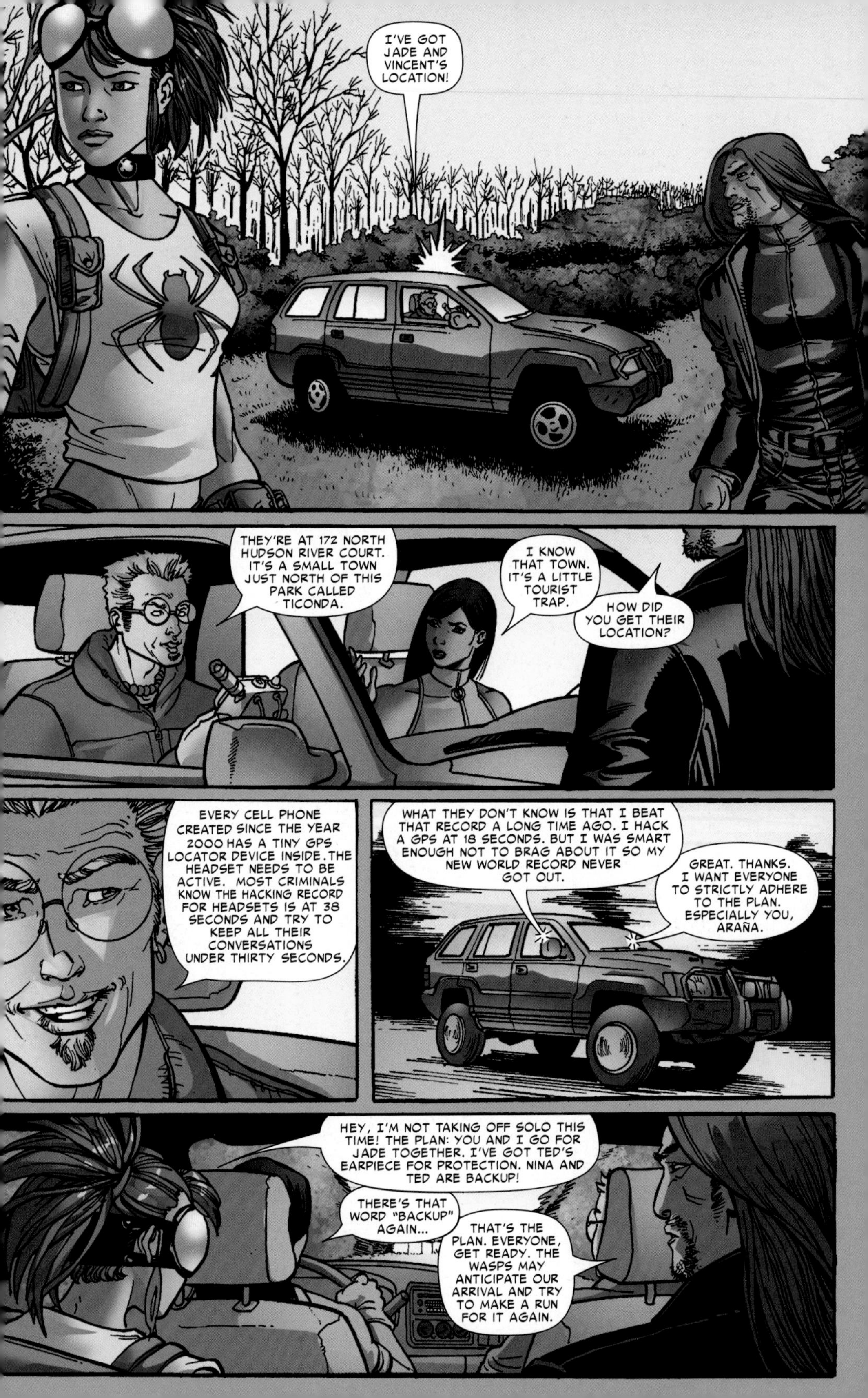

I'VE GOT JADE AND VINCENT'S LOCATION!
THEY'RE AT 172 NORTH HUDSON RIVER COURT. IT'S A SMALL TOWN JUST NORTH OF THIS PARK CALLED TICONDA.
I KNOW THAT TOWN. IT'S A LITTLE TOURIST TRAP.
HOW DID YOU GET THEIR LOCATION?
EVERY CELL PHONE CREATED SINCE THE YEAR 2000 HAS A TINY GPS LOCATOR DEVICE INSIDE. THE HEADSET NEEDS TO BE ACTIVE. MOST CRIMINALS KNOW THE HACKING RECORD FOR HEADSETS IS AT 38 SECONDS AND TRY TO KEEP ALL THEIR CONVERSATIONS UNDER THIRTY SECONDS.
WHAT THEY DON'T KNOW IS THAT I BEAT THAT RECORD A LONG TIME AGO. I HACK A GPS AT 18 SECONDS. BUT I WAS SMART ENOUGH NOT TO BRAG ABOUT IT SO MY NEW WORLD RECORD NEVER GOT OUT.
GREAT. THANKS. I WANT EVERYONE TO STRICTLY ADHERE TO THE PLAN. ESPECIALLY YOU, ARAÑA.
HEY, I'M NOT TAKING OFF SOLO THIS TIME! THE PLAN: YOU AND I GO FOR JADE TOGETHER. I'VE GOT TED'S EARPIECE FOR PROTECTION. NINA AND TED ARE BACKUP!
THERE'S THAT WORD "BACKUP" AGAIN...
THAT'S THE PLAN. EVERYONE, GET READY. THE WASPS MAY ANTICIPATE OUR ARRIVAL AND TRY TO MAKE A RUN FOR IT AGAIN.

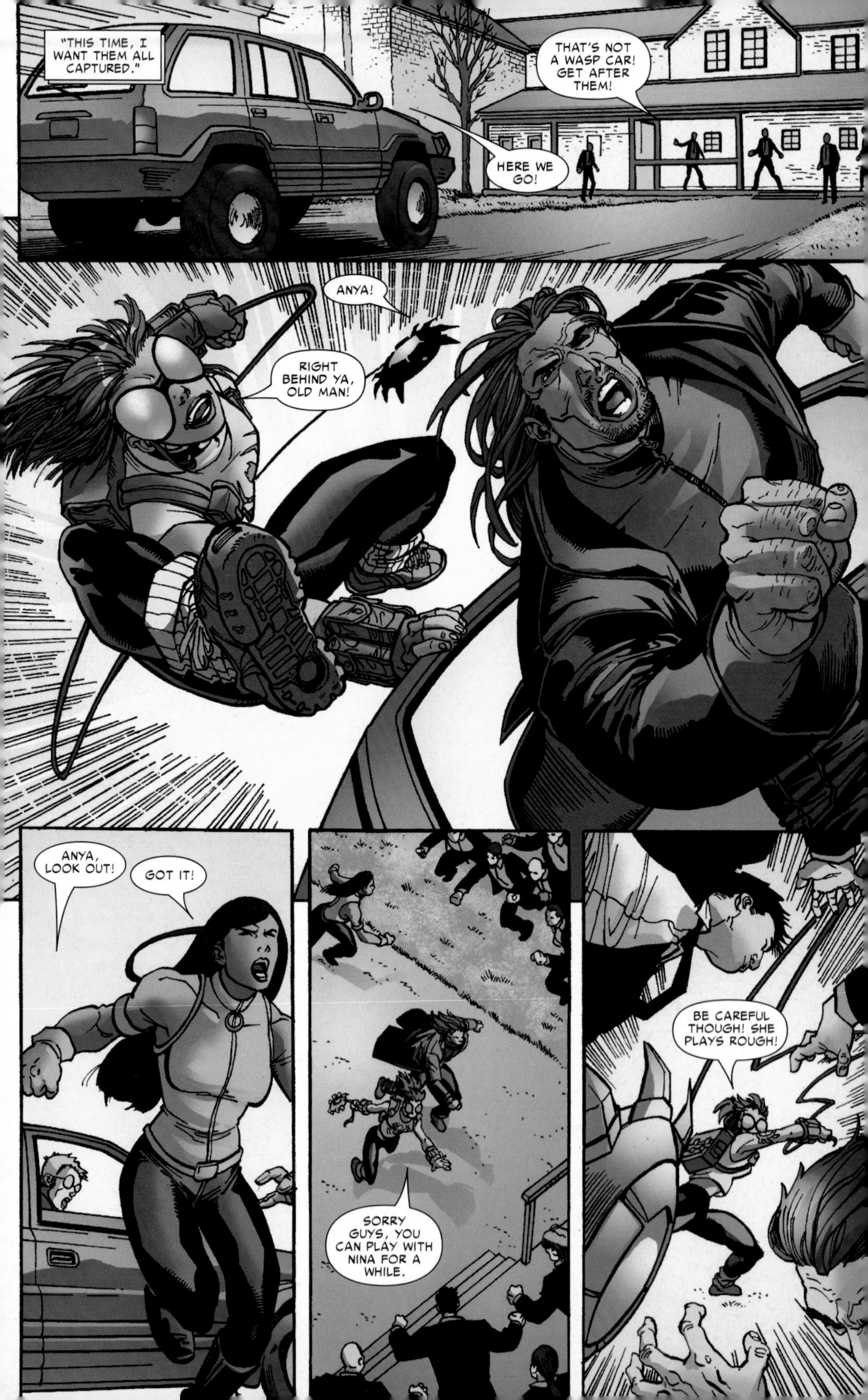
"THIS TIME, I WANT THEM ALL CAPTURED."
THAT'S NOT A WASP CAR! GET AFTER THEM!
HERE WE GO!
ANYA!
RIGHT BEHIND YA, OLD MAN!
ANYA, LOOK OUT!
GOT IT!
SORRY GUYS, YOU CAN PLAY WITH NINA FOR A WHILE.
BE CAREFUL THOUGH! SHE PLAYS ROUGH!

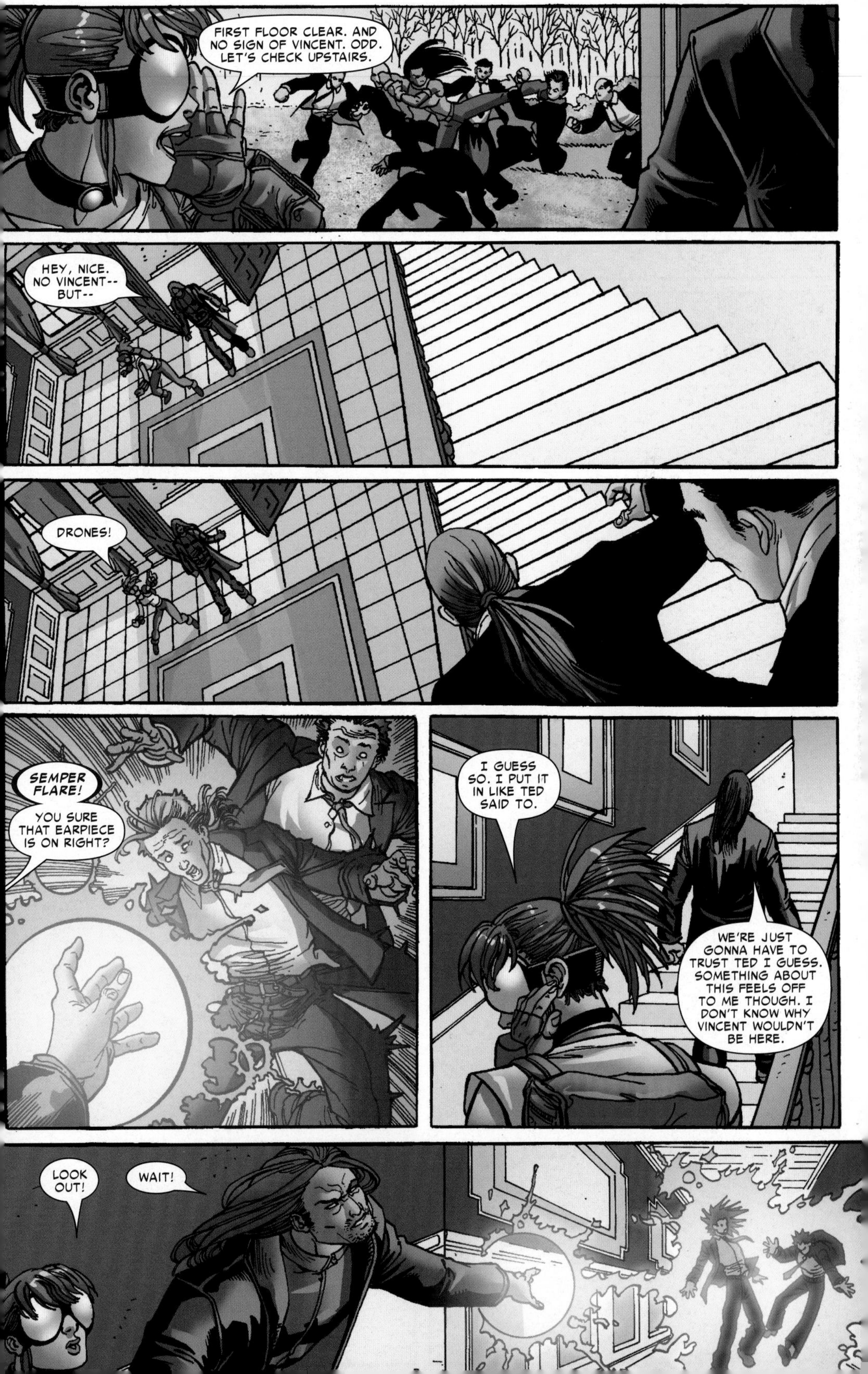
FIRST FLOOR CLEAR. AND NO SIGN OF VINCENT. ODD. LET'S CHECK UPSTAIRS.
HEY, NICE. NO VINCENT-- BUT--
DRONES!
SEMPER FLARE!
YOU SURE THAT EARPIECE IS ON RIGHT?
I GUESS SO. I PUT IT IN LIKE TED SAID TO.
WE'RE JUST GONNA HAVE TO TRUST TED I GUESS. SOMETHING ABOUT THIS FEELS OFF TO ME THOUGH. I DON'T KNOW WHY VINCENT WOULDN'T BE HERE.
LOOK OUT!
WAIT!

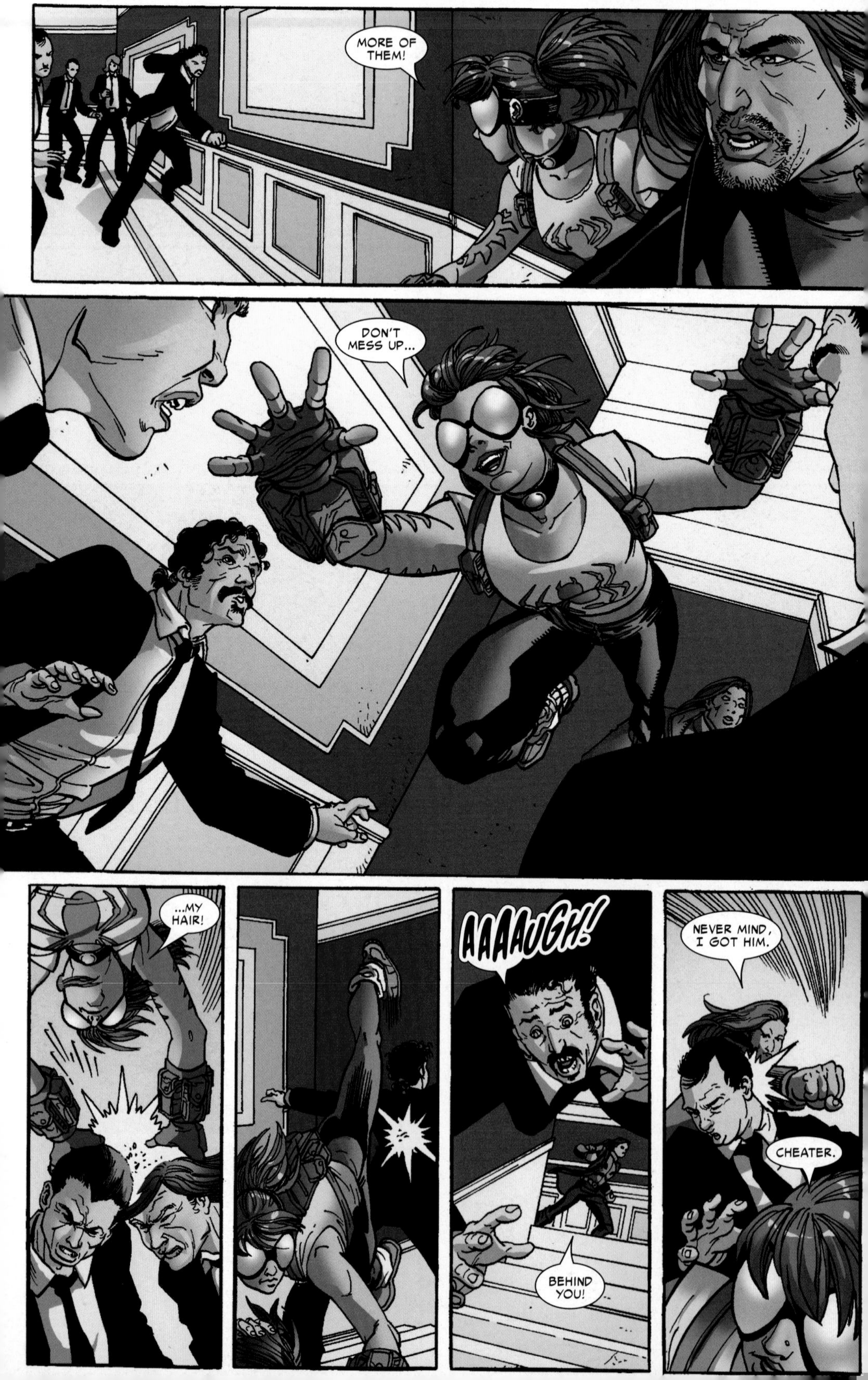
MORE OF THEM!
DON'T MESS UP...
...MY HAIR!
AAAAUGH!
BEHIND YOU!
NEVER MIND, I GOT HIM.
CHEATER.

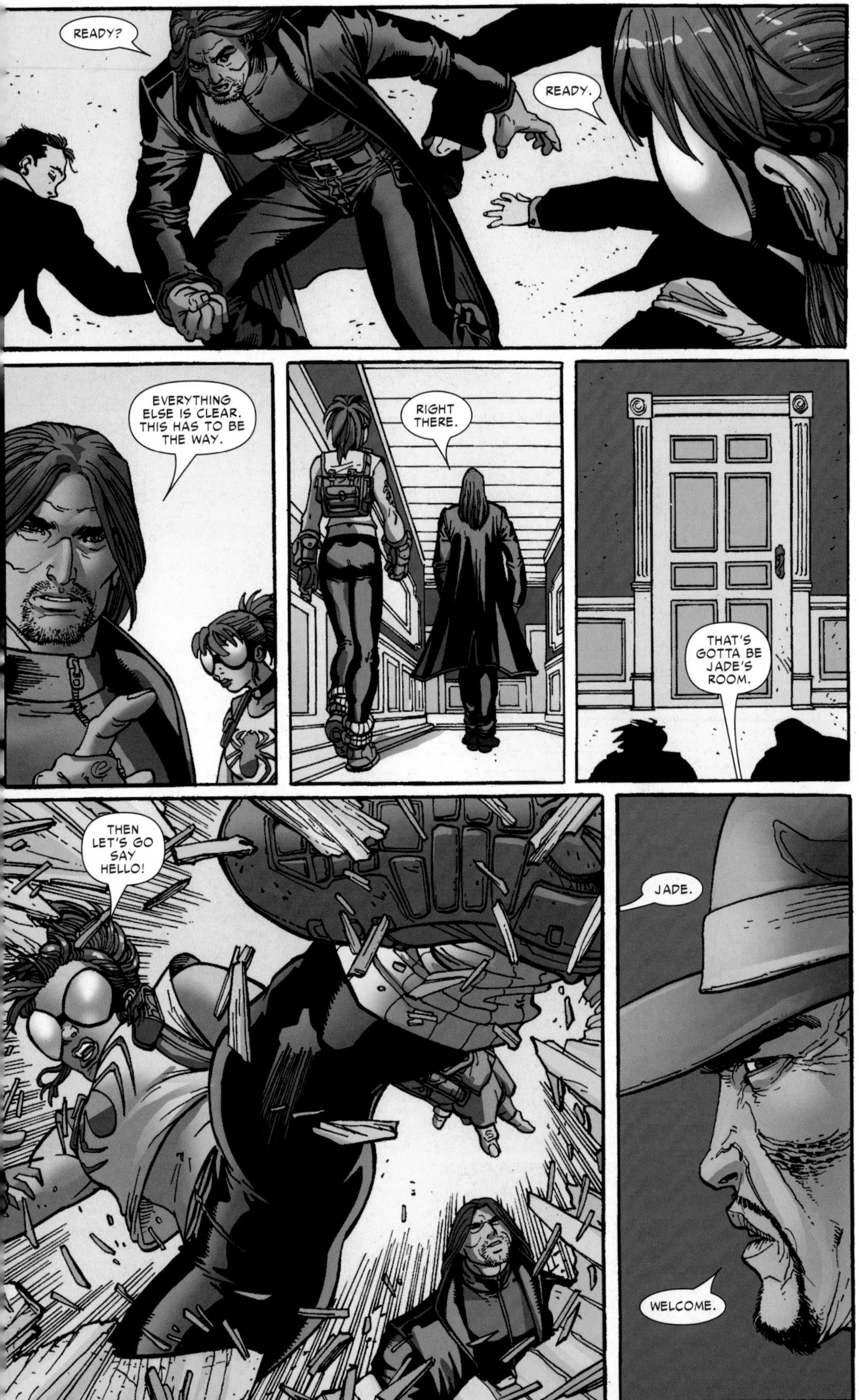
READY?
READY.
EVERYTHING ELSE IS CLEAR. THIS HAS TO BE THE WAY.
RIGHT THERE.
THAT'S GOTTA BE JADE'S ROOM.
THEN LET'S GO SAY HELLO!
JADE.
WELCOME.

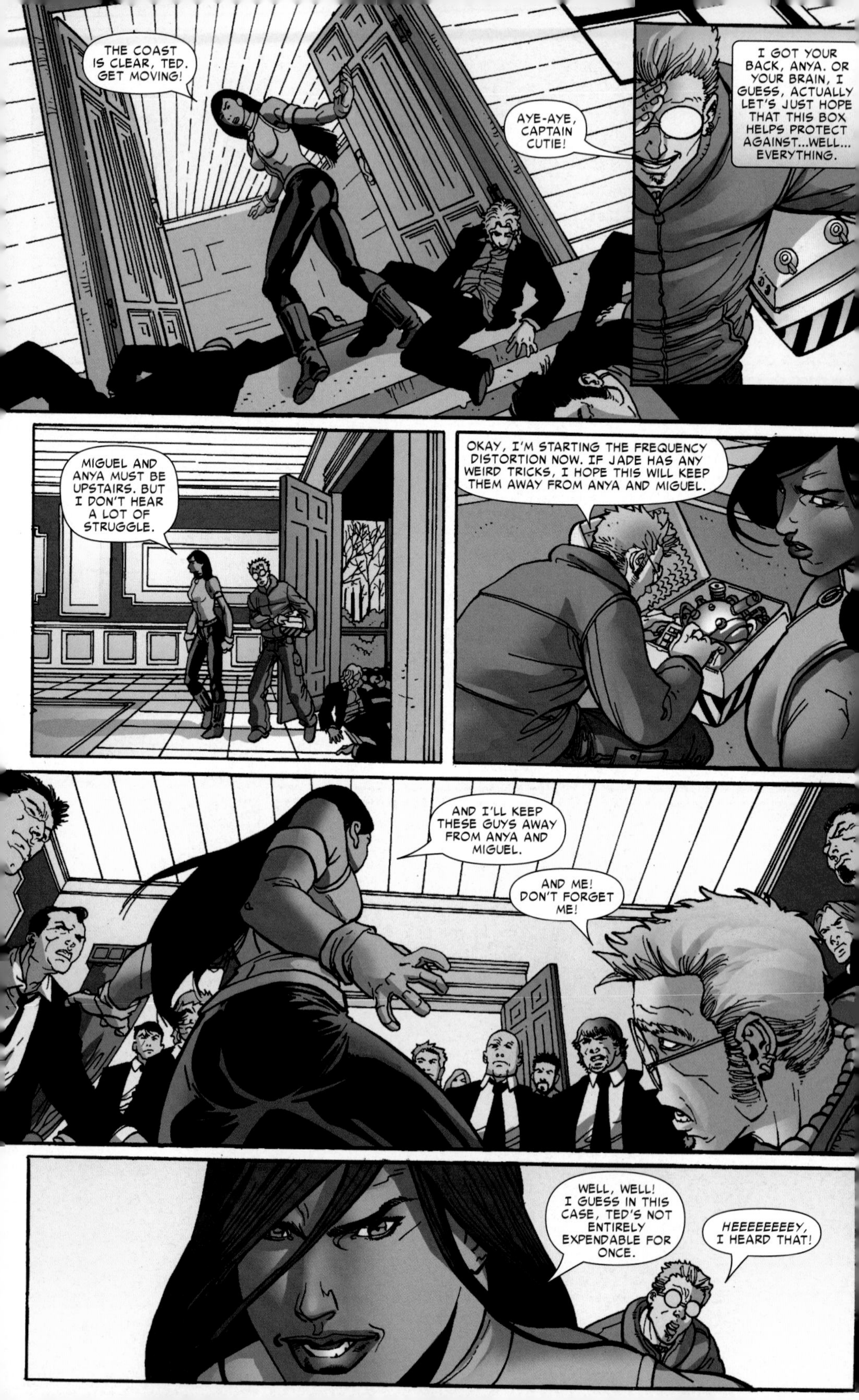
THE COAST IS CLEAR, TED. GET MOVING!
AYE-AYE, CAPTAIN CUTIE!
I GOT YOUR BACK, ANYA. OR YOUR BRAIN, I GUESS, ACTUALLY LET'S JUST HOPE THAT THIS BOX HELPS PROTECT AGAINST...WELL... EVERYTHING.
MIGUEL AND ANYA MUST BE UPSTAIRS. BUT I DON'T HEAR A LOT OF STRUGGLE.
OKAY, I'M STARTING THE FREQUENCY DISTORTION NOW. IF JADE HAS ANY WEIRD TRICKS, I HOPE THIS WILL KEEP THEM AWAY FROM ANYA AND MIGUEL.
AND I'LL KEEP THESE GUYS AWAY FROM ANYA AND MIGUEL.
AND ME! DON'T FORGET ME!
WELL, WELL! I GUESS IN THIS CASE, TED'S NOT ENTIRELY EXPENDABLE FOR ONCE.
HEEEEEEEEY, I HEARD THAT!

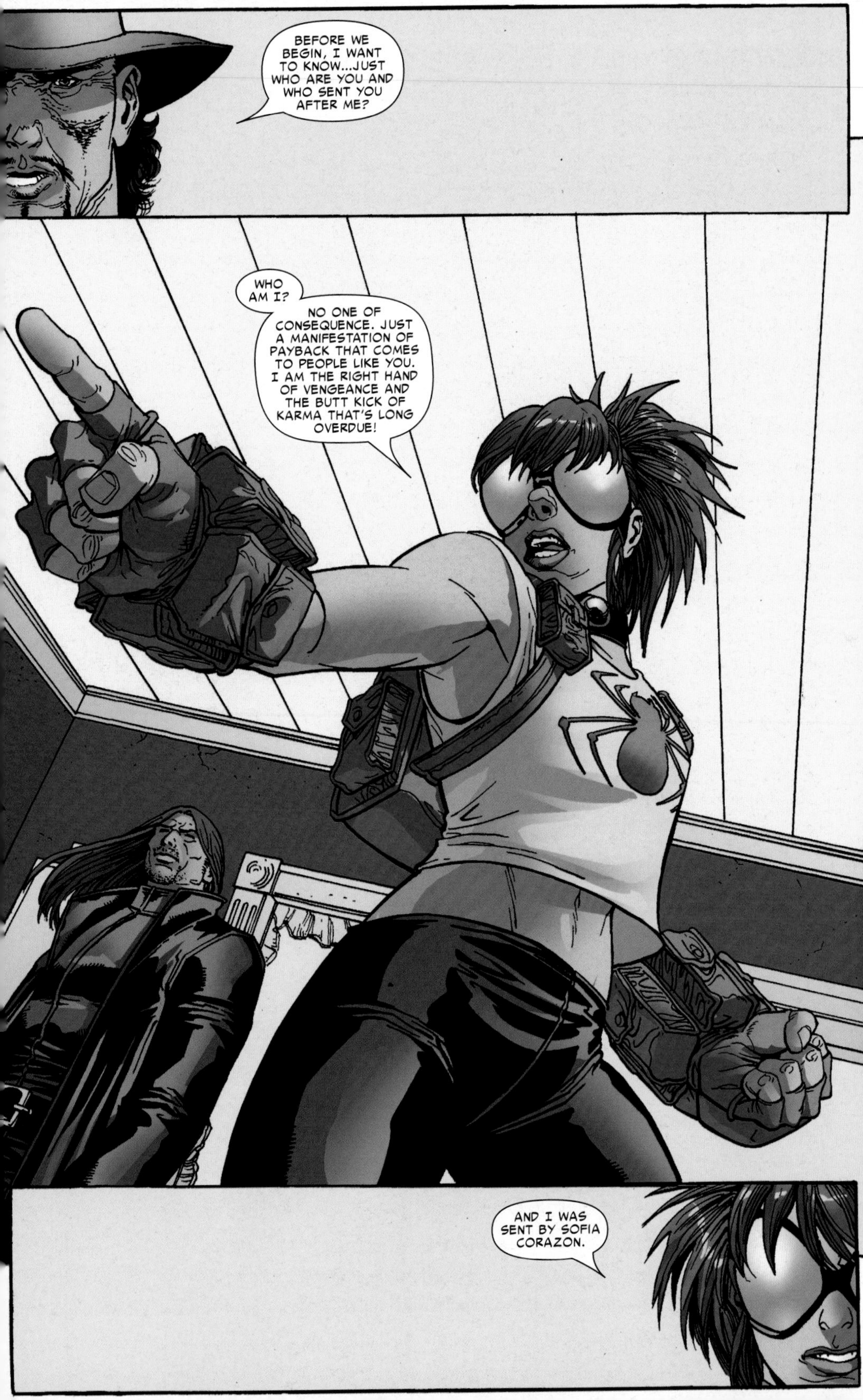
BEFORE WE BEGIN, I WANT TO KNOW...JUST WHO ARE YOU AND WHO SENT YOU AFTER ME?
WHO AM I?
NO ONE OF CONSEQUENCE. JUST A MANIFESTATION OF PAYBACK THAT COMES TO PEOPLE LIKE YOU. I AM THE RIGHT HAND OF VENGEANCE AND THE BUTT KICK OF KARMA THAT'S LONG OVERDUE!
AND I WAS SENT BY SOFIA CORAZON.

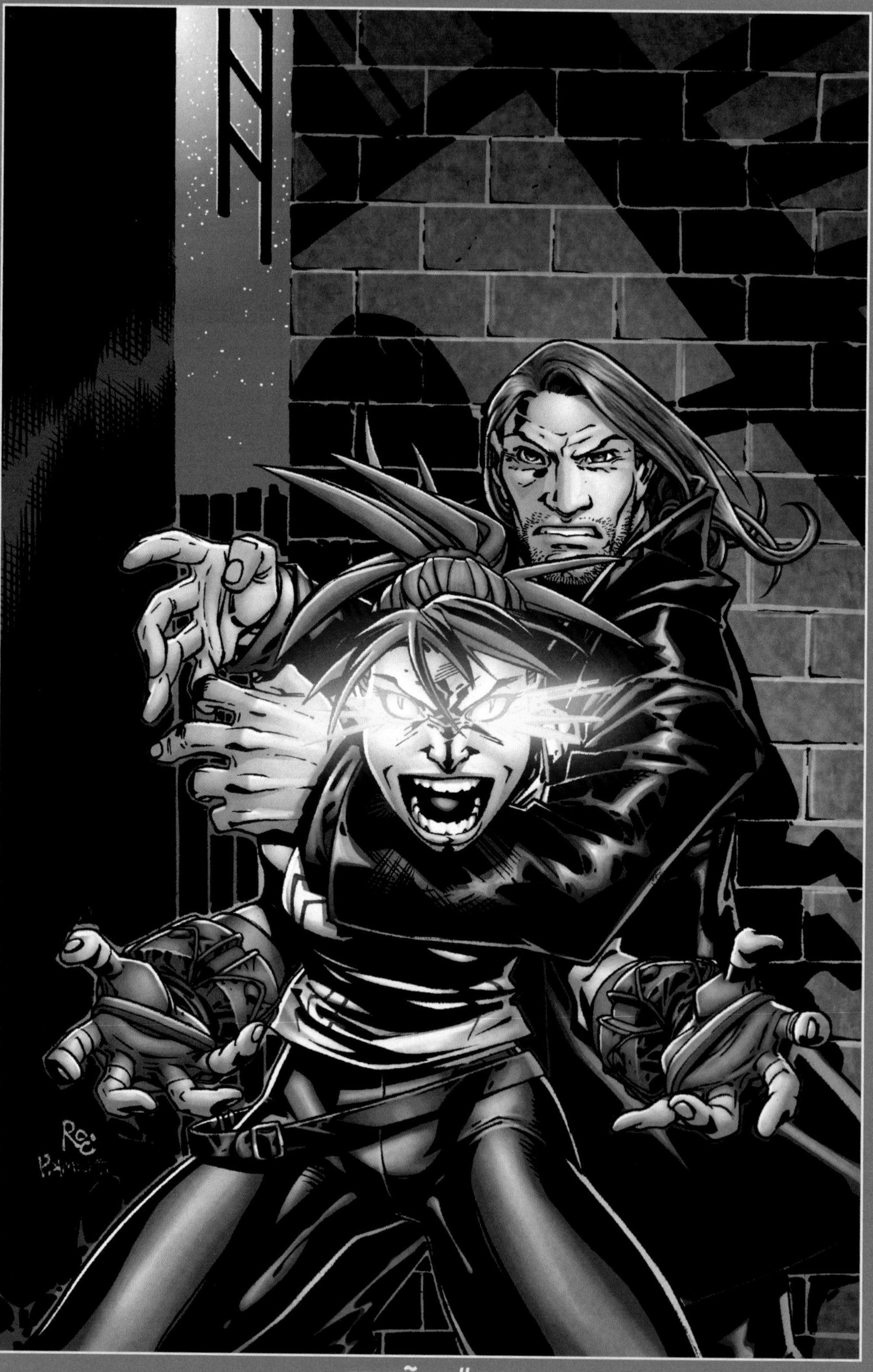

ARAÑA #11

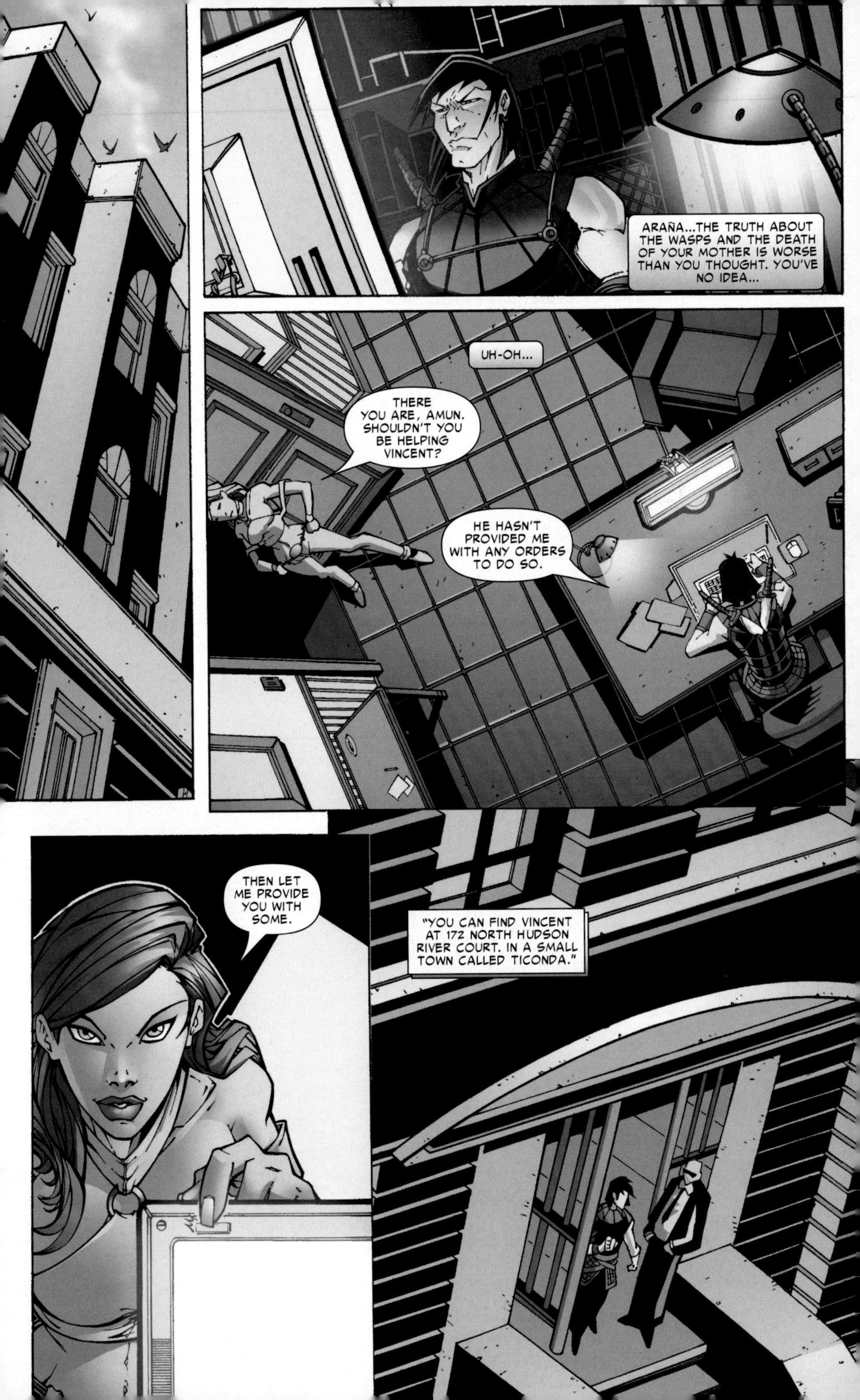
ARAÑA...THE TRUTH ABOUT THE WASPS AND THE DEATH OF YOUR MOTHER IS WORSE THAN YOU THOUGHT. YOU'VE NO IDEA...
UH-OH...
THERE YOU ARE, AMUN. SHOULDN'T YOU BE HELPING VINCENT?
HE HASN'T PROVIDED ME WITH ANY ORDERS TO DO SO.
THEN LET ME PROVIDE YOU WITH SOME.
"YOU CAN FIND VINCENT AT 172 NORTH HUDSON RIVER COURT. IN A SMALL TOWN CALLED TICONDA."

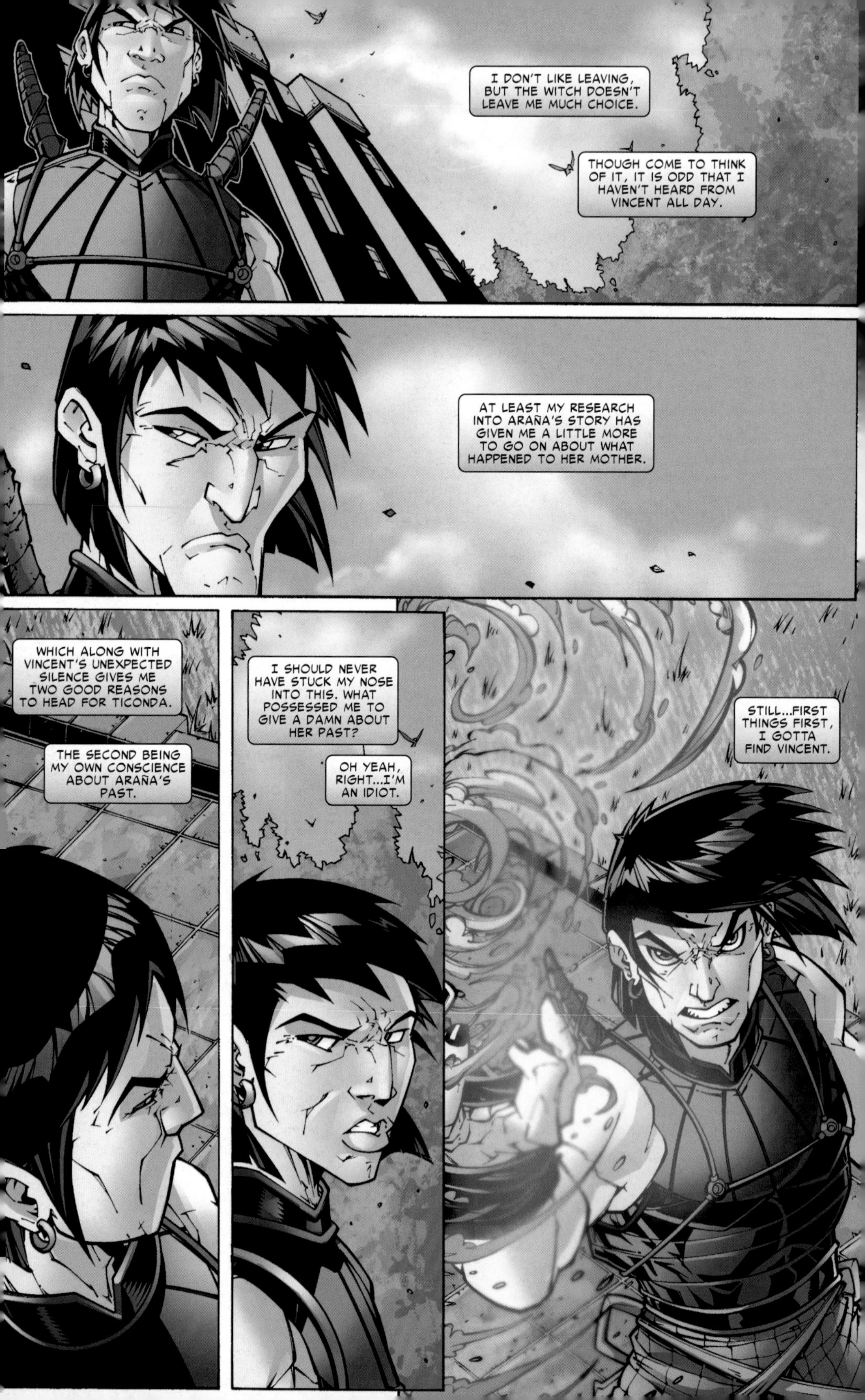
I DON'T LIKE LEAVING, BUT THE WITCH DOESN'T LEAVE ME MUCH CHOICE.
THOUGH COME TO THINK OF IT, IT IS ODD THAT I HAVEN'T HEARD FROM VINCENT ALL DAY.
AT LEAST MY RESEARCH INTO ARAÑA'S STORY HAS GIVEN ME A LITTLE MORE TO GO ON ABOUT WHAT HAPPENED TO HER MOTHER.
WHICH ALONG WITH VINCENT'S UNEXPECTED SILENCE GIVES ME TWO GOOD REASONS TO HEAD FOR TICONDA.
THE SECOND BEING MY OWN CONSCIENCE ABOUT ARAÑA'S PAST.
I SHOULD NEVER HAVE STUCK MY NOSE INTO THIS. WHAT POSSESSED ME TO GIVE A DAMN ABOUT HER PAST?
OH YEAH, RIGHT...I'M AN IDIOT.
STILL...FIRST THINGS FIRST, I GOTTA FIND VINCENT.

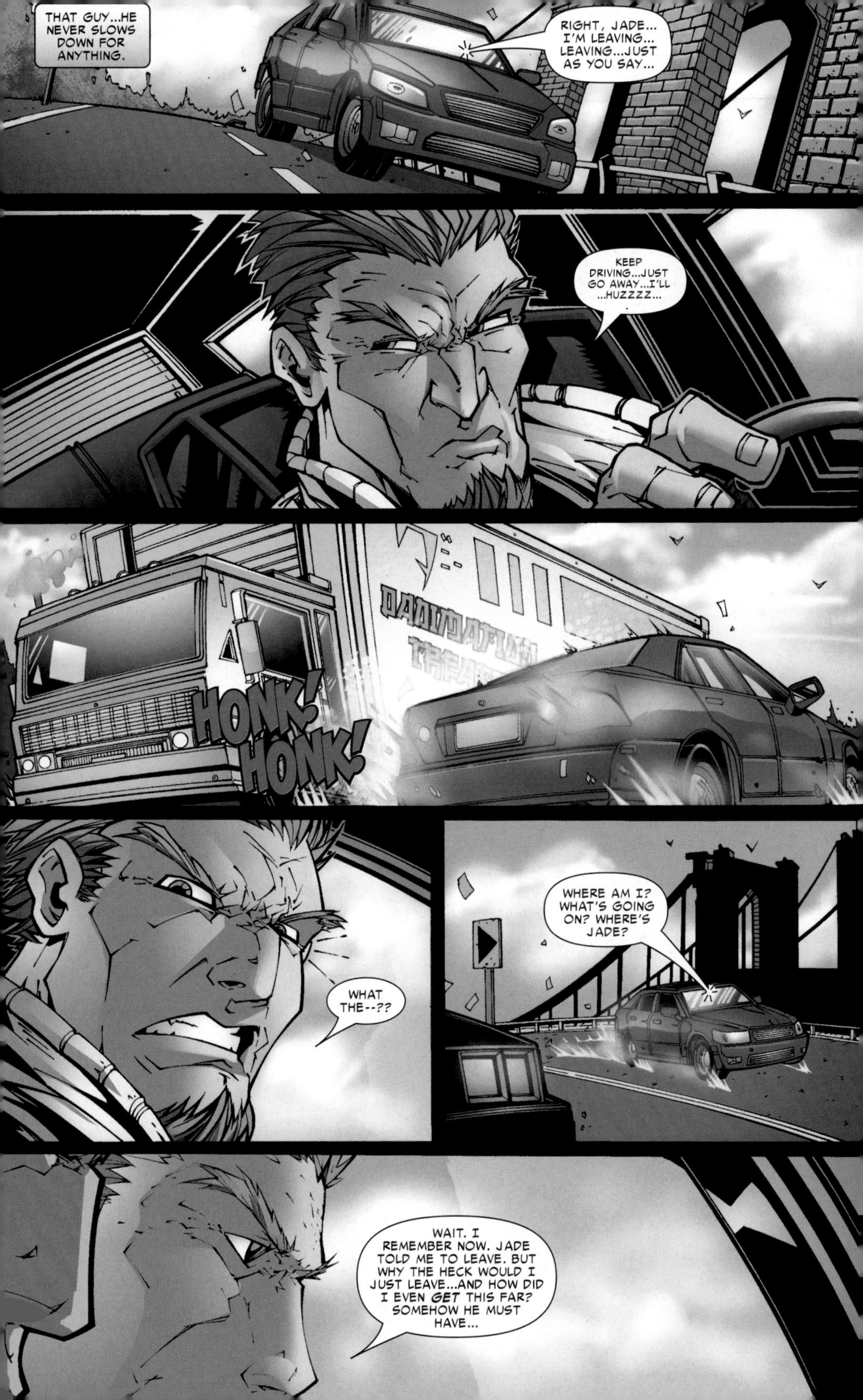
THAT GUY...HE NEVER SLOWS DOWN FOR ANYTHING.
RIGHT, JADE... I'M LEAVING... LEAVING...JUST AS YOU SAY...
KEEP DRIVING...JUST GO AWAY...I'LL ...HUZZZZ...
HONK! HONK!
WHAT THE--??
WHERE AM I? WHAT'S GOING ON? WHERE'S JADE?
WAIT. I REMEMBER NOW. JADE TOLD ME TO LEAVE. BUT WHY THE HECK WOULD I JUST LEAVE...AND HOW DID I EVEN GET THIS FAR? SOMEHOW HE MUST HAVE...

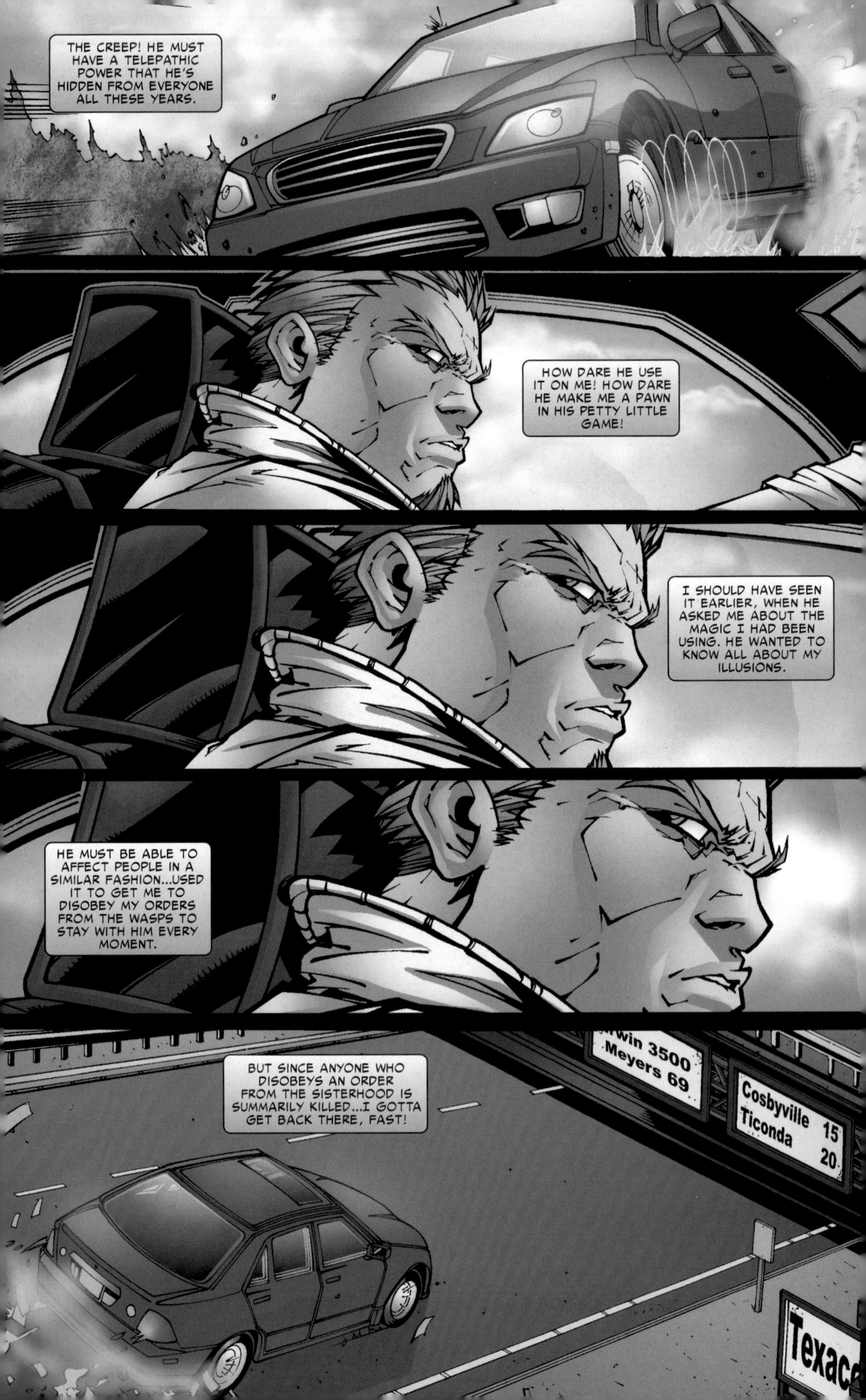
THE CREEP! HE MUST HAVE A TELEPATHIC POWER THAT HE'S HIDDEN FROM EVERYONE ALL THESE YEARS.
HOW DARE HE USE IT ON ME! HOW DARE HE MAKE ME A PAWN IN HIS PETTY LITTLE GAME!
I SHOULD HAVE SEEN IT EARLIER, WHEN HE ASKED ME ABOUT THE MAGIC I HAD BEEN USING. HE WANTED TO KNOW ALL ABOUT MY ILLUSIONS.
HE MUST BE ABLE TO AFFECT PEOPLE IN A SIMILAR FASHION...USED IT TO GET ME TO DISOBEY MY ORDERS FROM THE WASPS TO STAY WITH HIM EVERY MOMENT.
BUT SINCE ANYONE WHO DISOBEYS AN ORDER FROM THE SISTERHOOD IS SUMMARILY KILLED...I GOTTA GET BACK THERE, FAST!
Twin 3500
Meyers 69
Cosbyville 15
Ticonda 20
Texac

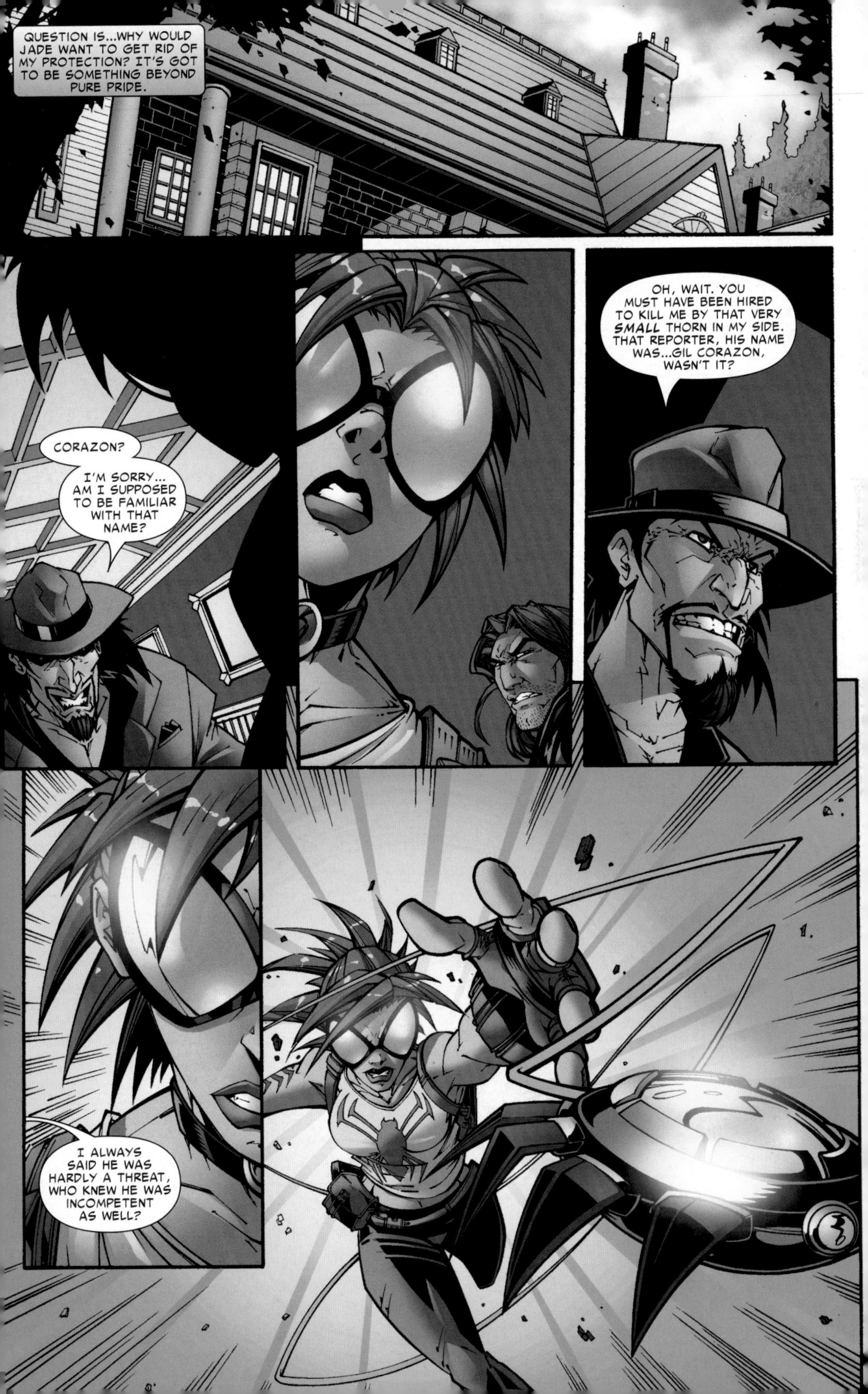
QUESTION IS...WHY WOULD JADE WANT TO GET RID OF MY PROTECTION? IT'S GOT TO BE SOMETHING BEYOND PURE PRIDE.
CORAZON?
I'M SORRY... AM I SUPPOSED TO BE FAMILIAR WITH THAT NAME?
OH, WAIT. YOU MUST HAVE BEEN HIRED TO KILL ME BY THAT VERY SMALL THORN IN MY SIDE. THAT REPORTER, HIS NAME WAS...GIL CORAZON, WASN'T IT?
I ALWAYS SAID HE WAS HARDLY A THREAT, WHO KNEW HE WAS INCOMPETENT AS WELL?

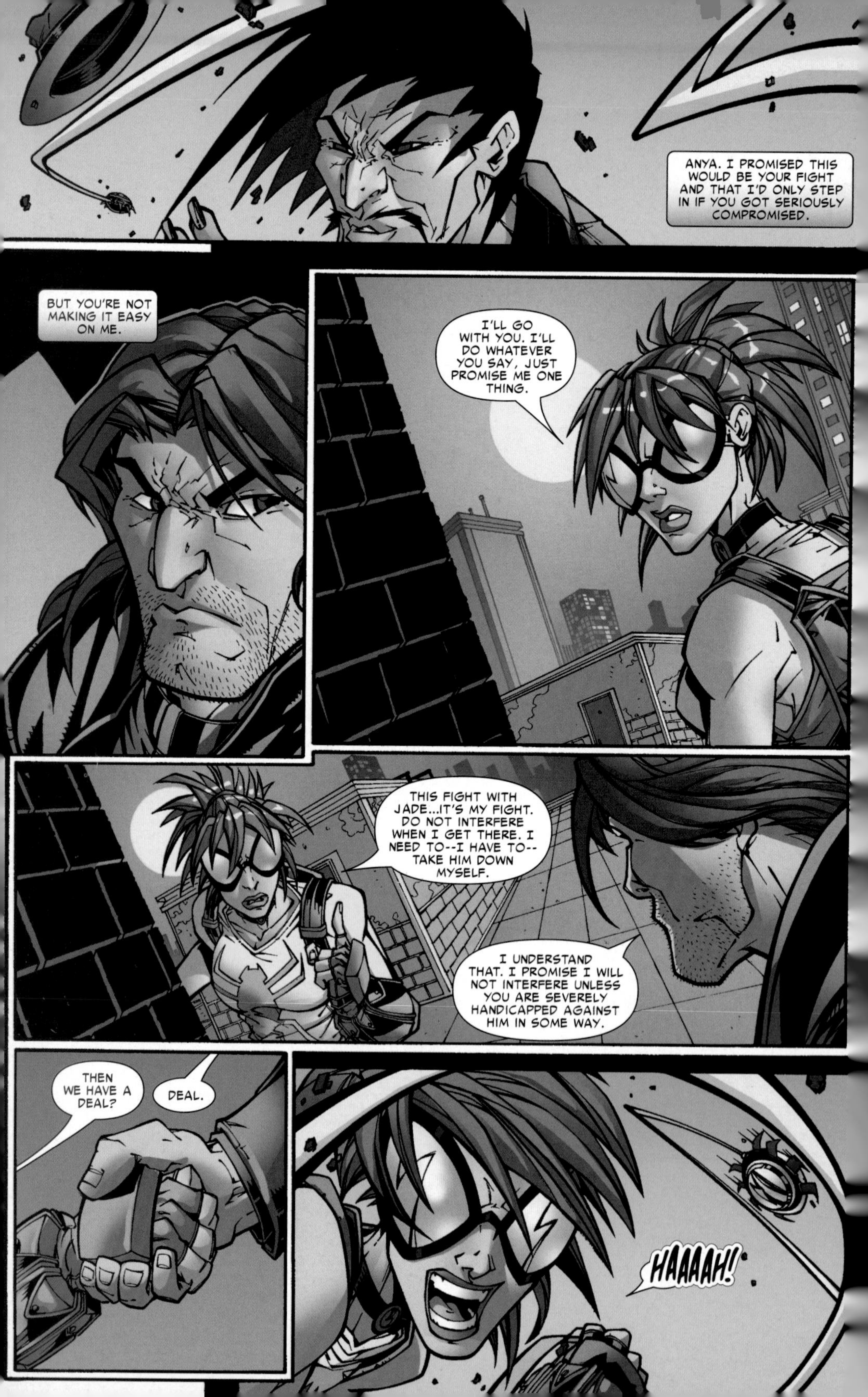
ANYA. I PROMISED THIS WOULD BE YOUR FIGHT AND THAT I'D ONLY STEP IN IF YOU GOT SERIOUSLY COMPROMISED.
BUT YOU'RE NOT MAKING IT EASY ON ME.
I'LL GO WITH YOU. I'LL DO WHATEVER YOU SAY, JUST PROMISE ME ONE THING.
THIS FIGHT WITH JADE...IT'S MY FIGHT. DO NOT INTERFERE WHEN I GET THERE. I NEED TO--I HAVE TO--TAKE HIM DOWN MYSELF.
I UNDERSTAND THAT. I PROMISE I WILL NOT INTERFERE UNLESS YOU ARE SEVERELY HANDICAPPED AGAINST HIM IN SOME WAY.
THEN WE HAVE A DEAL?
DEAL.
HAAAAH!

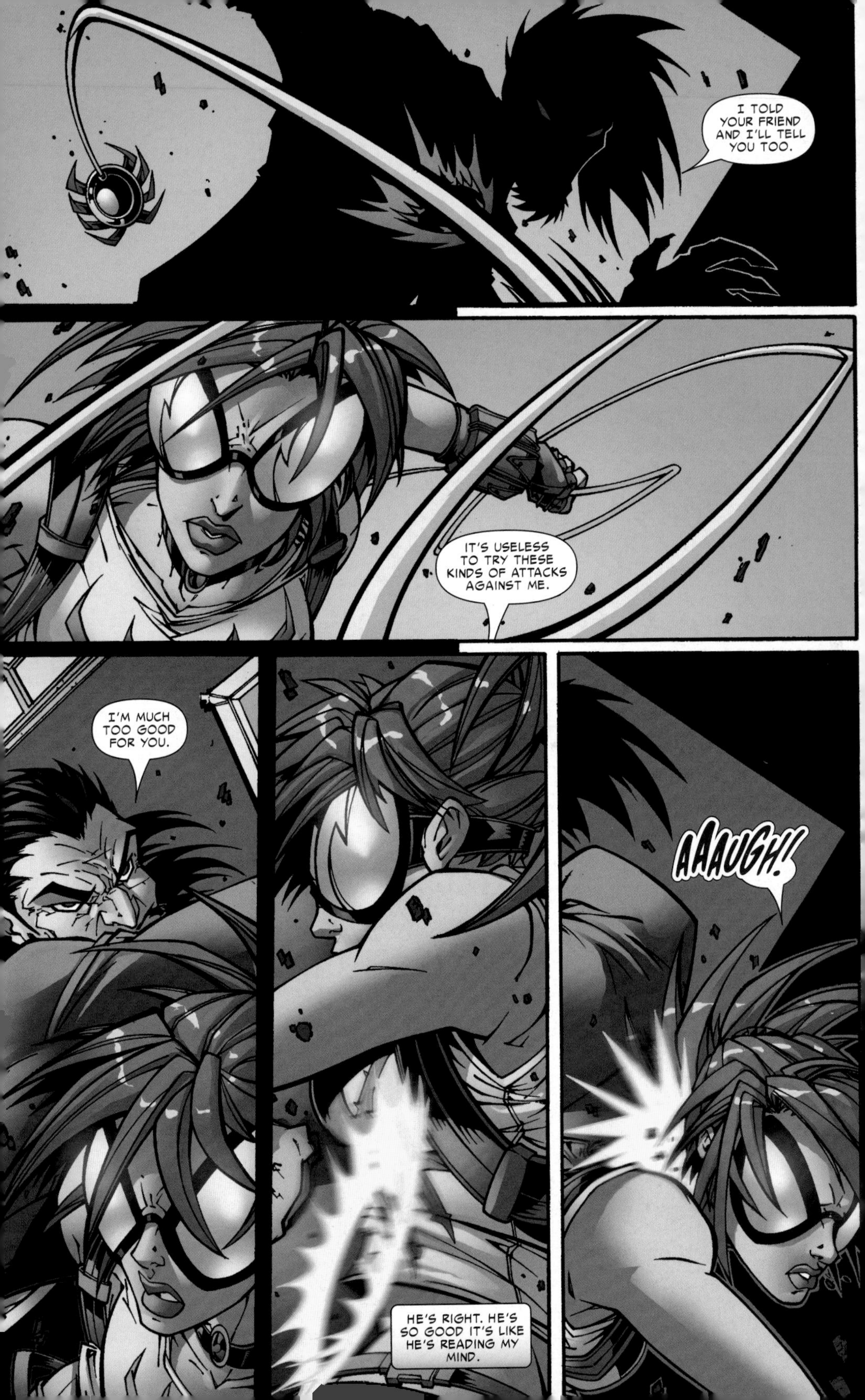
I TOLD YOUR FRIEND AND I'LL TELL YOU TOO.
IT'S USELESS TO TRY THESE KINDS OF ATTACKS AGAINST ME.
I'M MUCH TOO GOOD FOR YOU.
HE'S RIGHT. HE'S SO GOOD IT'S LIKE HE'S READING MY MIND.
AAAUGH!

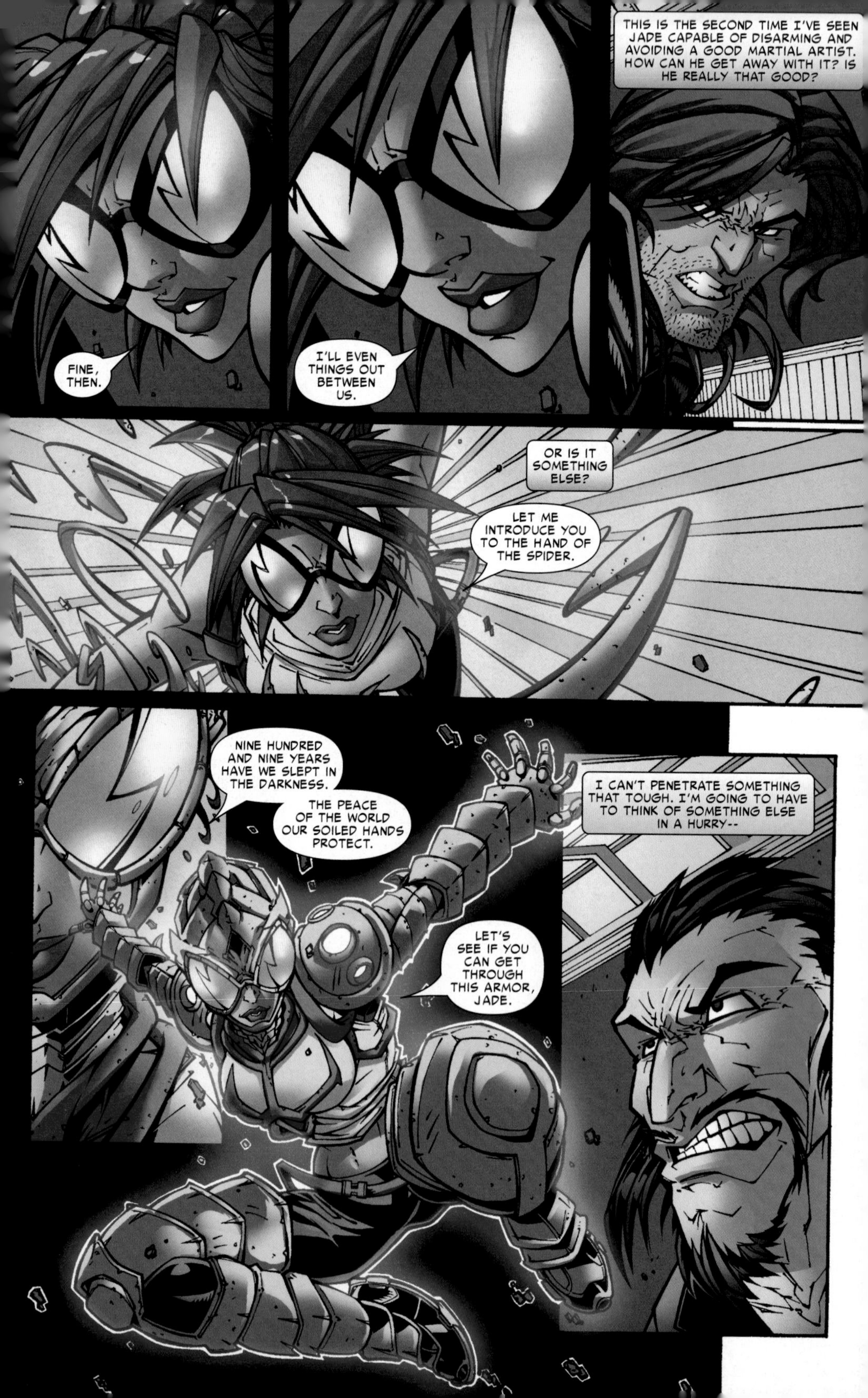
FINE, THEN.
I'LL EVEN THINGS OUT BETWEEN US.
THIS IS THE SECOND TIME I'VE SEEN JADE CAPABLE OF DISARMING AND AVOIDING A GOOD MARTIAL ARTIST. HOW CAN HE GET AWAY WITH IT? IS HE REALLY THAT GOOD?
OR IS IT SOMETHING ELSE?
LET ME INTRODUCE YOU TO THE HAND OF THE SPIDER.
NINE HUNDRED AND NINE YEARS HAVE WE SLEPT IN THE DARKNESS.
THE PEACE OF THE WORLD OUR SOILED HANDS PROTECT.
I CAN'T PENETRATE SOMETHING THAT TOUGH. I'M GOING TO HAVE TO THINK OF SOMETHING ELSE IN A HURRY--
LET'S SEE IF YOU CAN GET THROUGH THIS ARMOR, JADE.

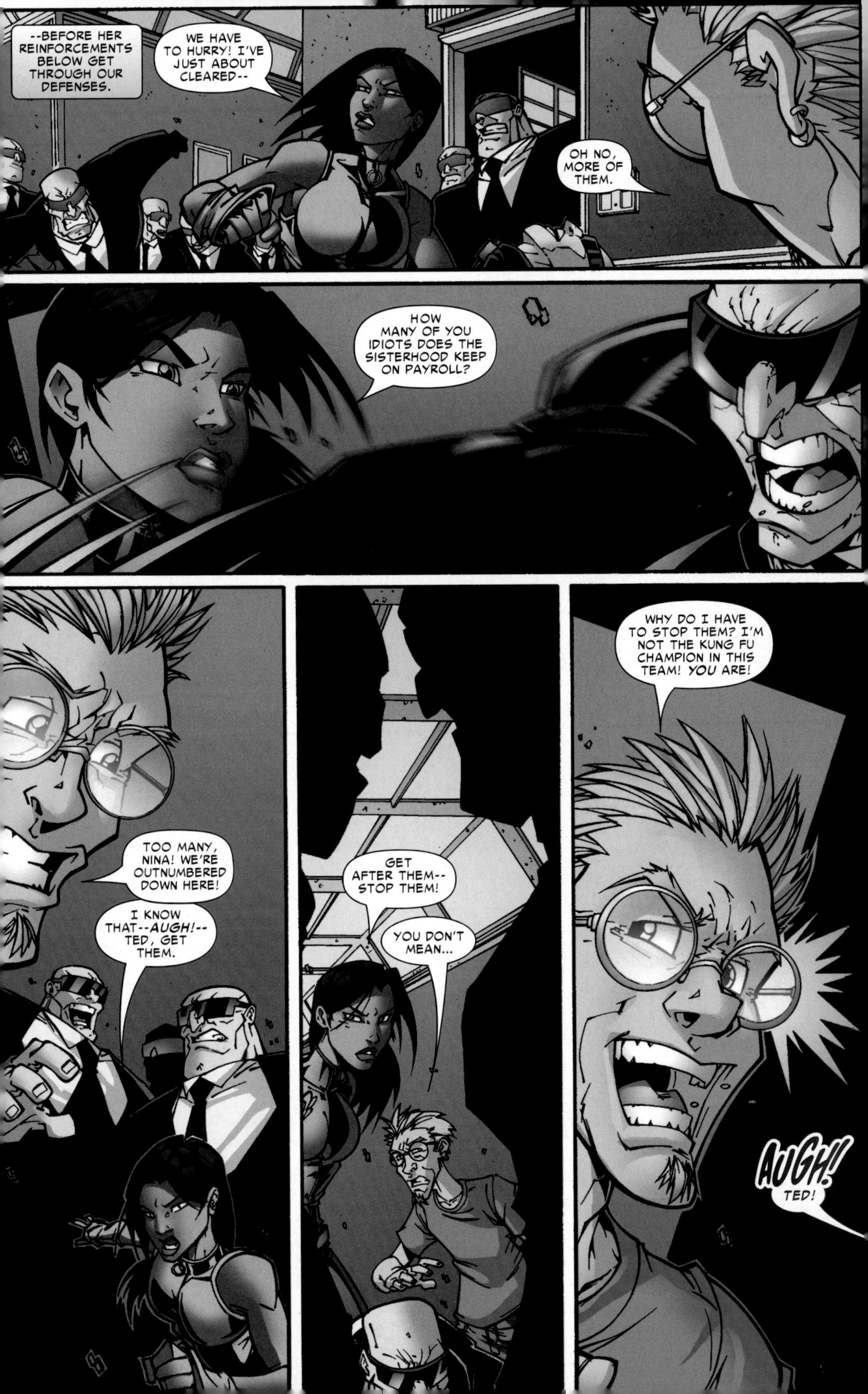
--BEFORE HER REINFORCEMENTS BELOW GET THROUGH OUR DEFENSES.
WE HAVE TO HURRY! I'VE JUST ABOUT CLEARED--
OH NO, MORE OF THEM.
HOW MANY OF YOU IDIOTS DOES THE SISTERHOOD KEEP ON PAYROLL?
TOO MANY, NINA! WE'RE OUTNUMBERED DOWN HERE!
I KNOW THAT--*AUGH!*--TED, GET THEM.
GET AFTER THEM--STOP THEM!
YOU DON'T MEAN...
WHY DO I HAVE TO STOP THEM? I'M NOT THE KUNG FU CHAMPION IN THIS TEAM! *YOU* ARE!
AUGH!
TED!

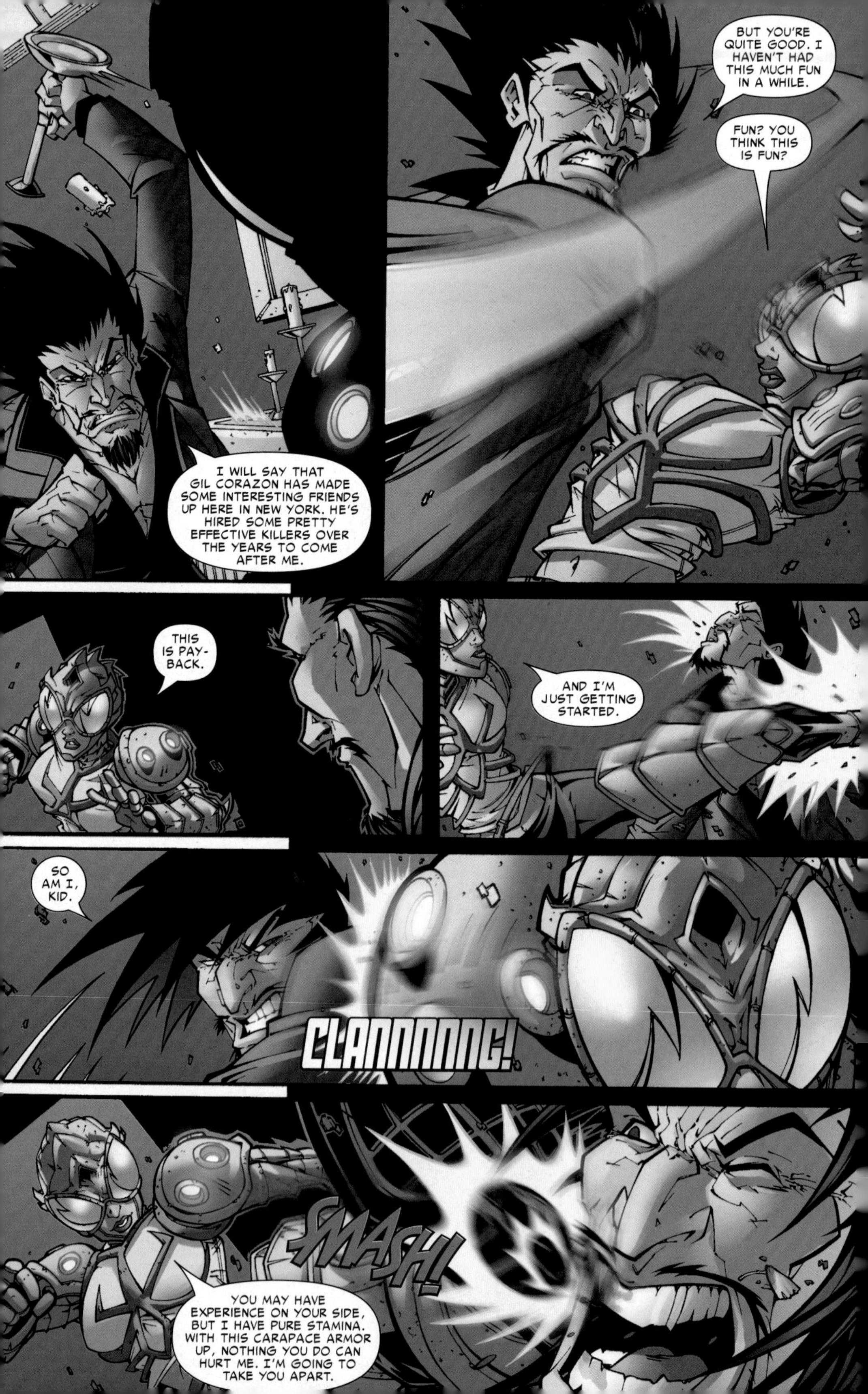
I WILL SAY THAT GIL CORAZON HAS MADE SOME INTERESTING FRIENDS UP HERE IN NEW YORK. HE'S HIRED SOME PRETTY EFFECTIVE KILLERS OVER THE YEARS TO COME AFTER ME.
BUT YOU'RE QUITE GOOD. I HAVEN'T HAD THIS MUCH FUN IN A WHILE.
FUN? YOU THINK THIS IS FUN?
THIS IS PAY-BACK.
AND I'M JUST GETTING STARTED.
SO AM I, KID.
CLANNNNNG!
SMASH!
YOU MAY HAVE EXPERIENCE ON YOUR SIDE, BUT I HAVE PURE STAMINA. WITH THIS CARAPACE ARMOR UP, NOTHING YOU DO CAN HURT ME. I'M GOING TO TAKE YOU APART.

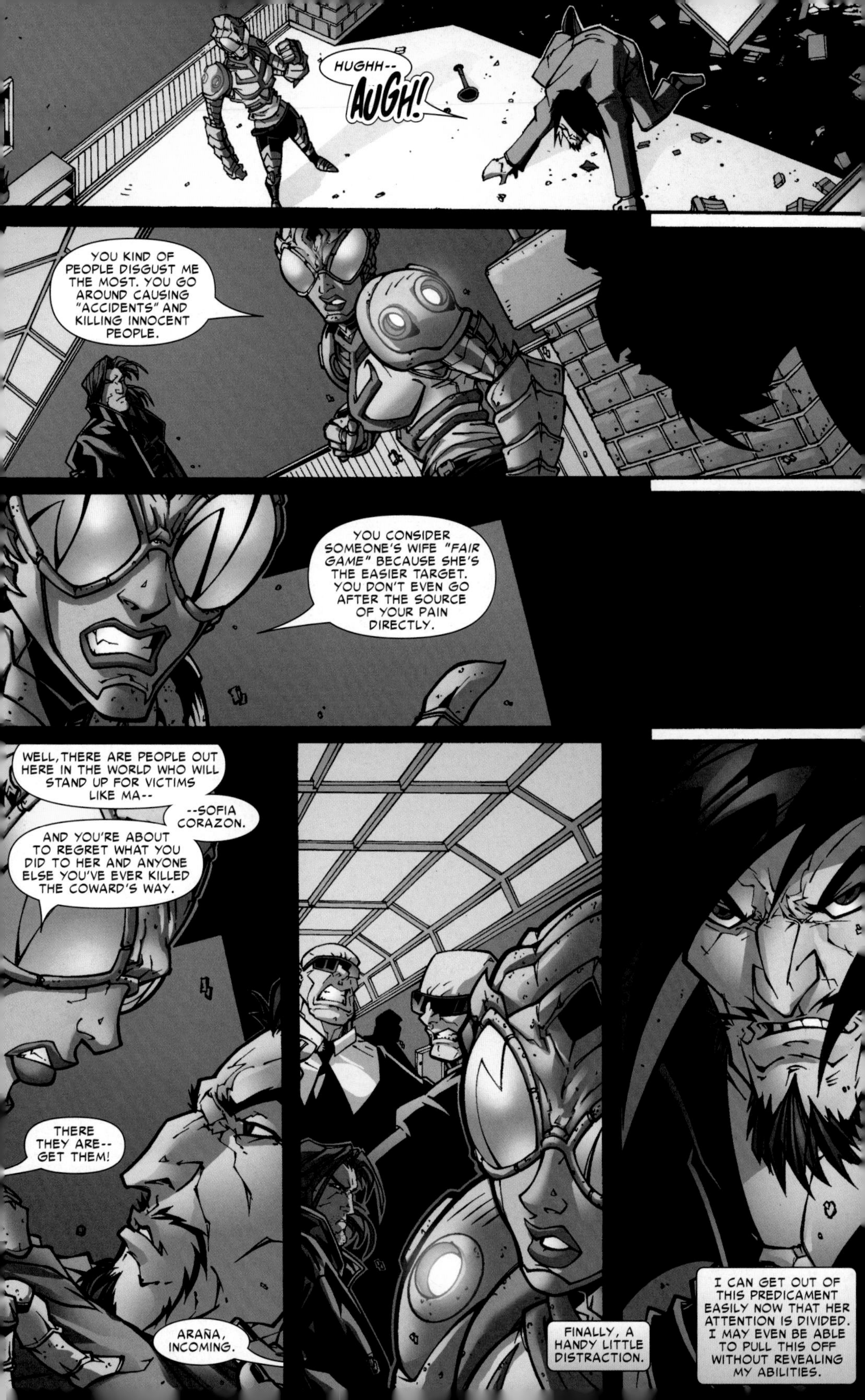
HUGHH--
AUGH!
YOU KIND OF PEOPLE DISGUST ME THE MOST. YOU GO AROUND CAUSING "ACCIDENTS" AND KILLING INNOCENT PEOPLE.
YOU CONSIDER SOMEONE'S WIFE "FAIR GAME" BECAUSE SHE'S THE EASIER TARGET. YOU DON'T EVEN GO AFTER THE SOURCE OF YOUR PAIN DIRECTLY.
WELL, THERE ARE PEOPLE OUT HERE IN THE WORLD WHO WILL STAND UP FOR VICTIMS LIKE MA--
--SOFIA CORAZON.
AND YOU'RE ABOUT TO REGRET WHAT YOU DID TO HER AND ANYONE ELSE YOU'VE EVER KILLED THE COWARD'S WAY.
THERE THEY ARE-- GET THEM!
ARAÑA, INCOMING.
FINALLY, A HANDY LITTLE DISTRACTION.
I CAN GET OUT OF THIS PREDICAMENT EASILY NOW THAT HER ATTENTION IS DIVIDED. I MAY EVEN BE ABLE TO PULL THIS OFF WITHOUT REVEALING MY ABILITIES.

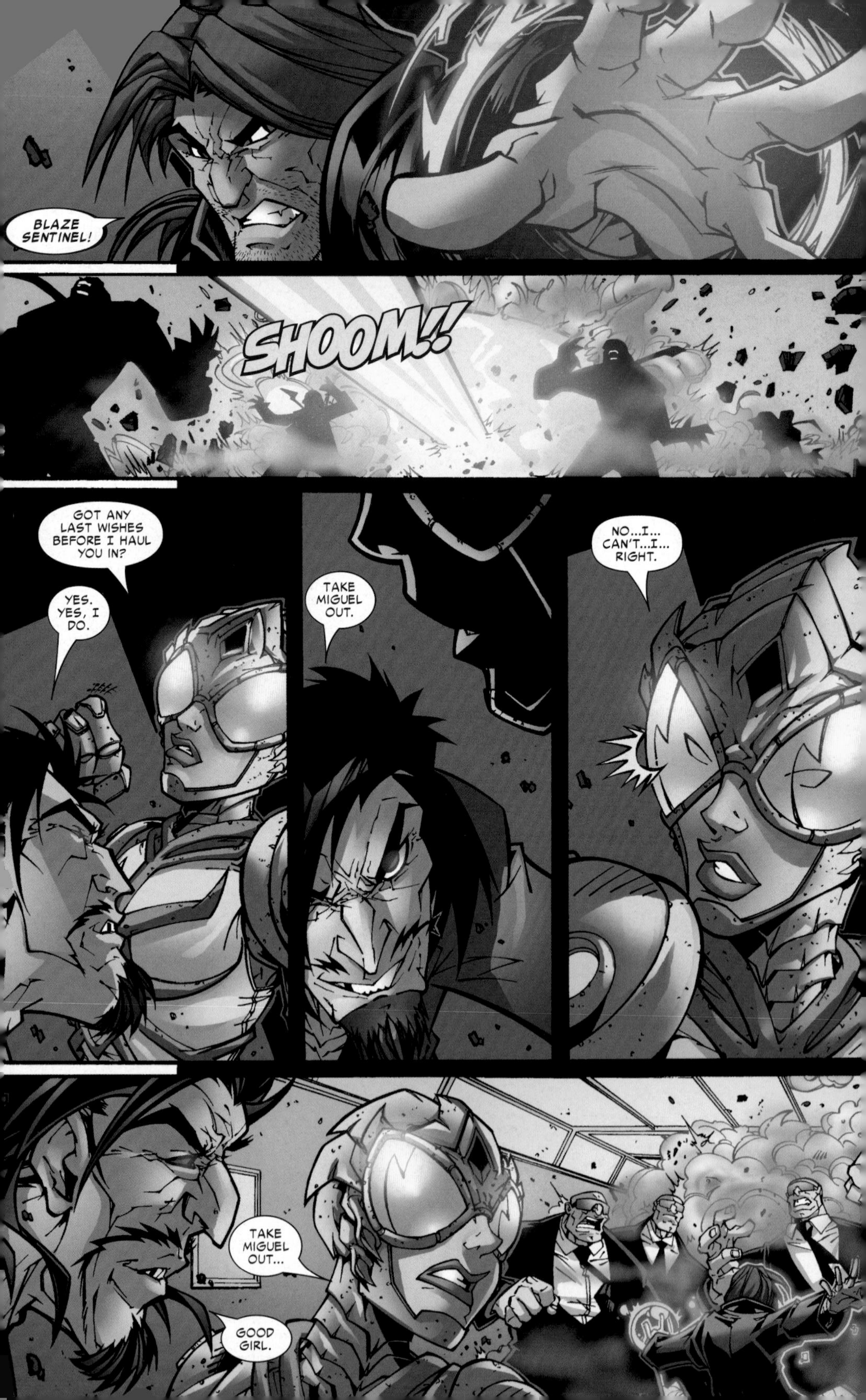
BLAZE SENTINEL!
SHOOM!!
GOT ANY LAST WISHES BEFORE I HAUL YOU IN?
YES. YES, I DO.
TAKE MIGUEL OUT.
NO...I... CAN'T...I... RIGHT.
TAKE MIGUEL OUT...
GOOD GIRL.

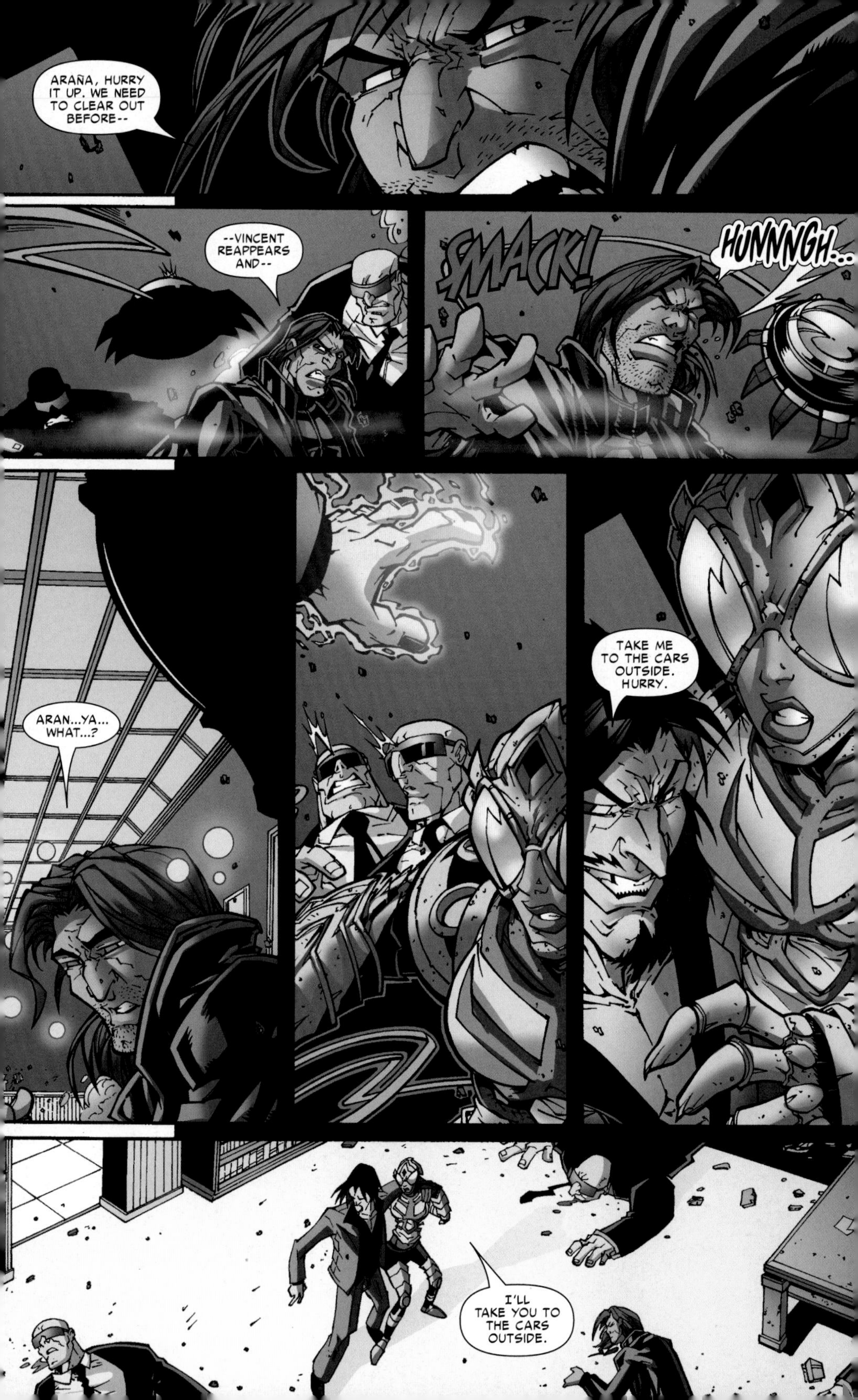
ARAÑA, HURRY IT UP. WE NEED TO CLEAR OUT BEFORE--
--VINCENT REAPPEARS AND--
SMACK!
HUNNNGH...
ARAN...YA... WHAT...?
TAKE ME TO THE CARS OUTSIDE. HURRY.
I'LL TAKE YOU TO THE CARS OUTSIDE.

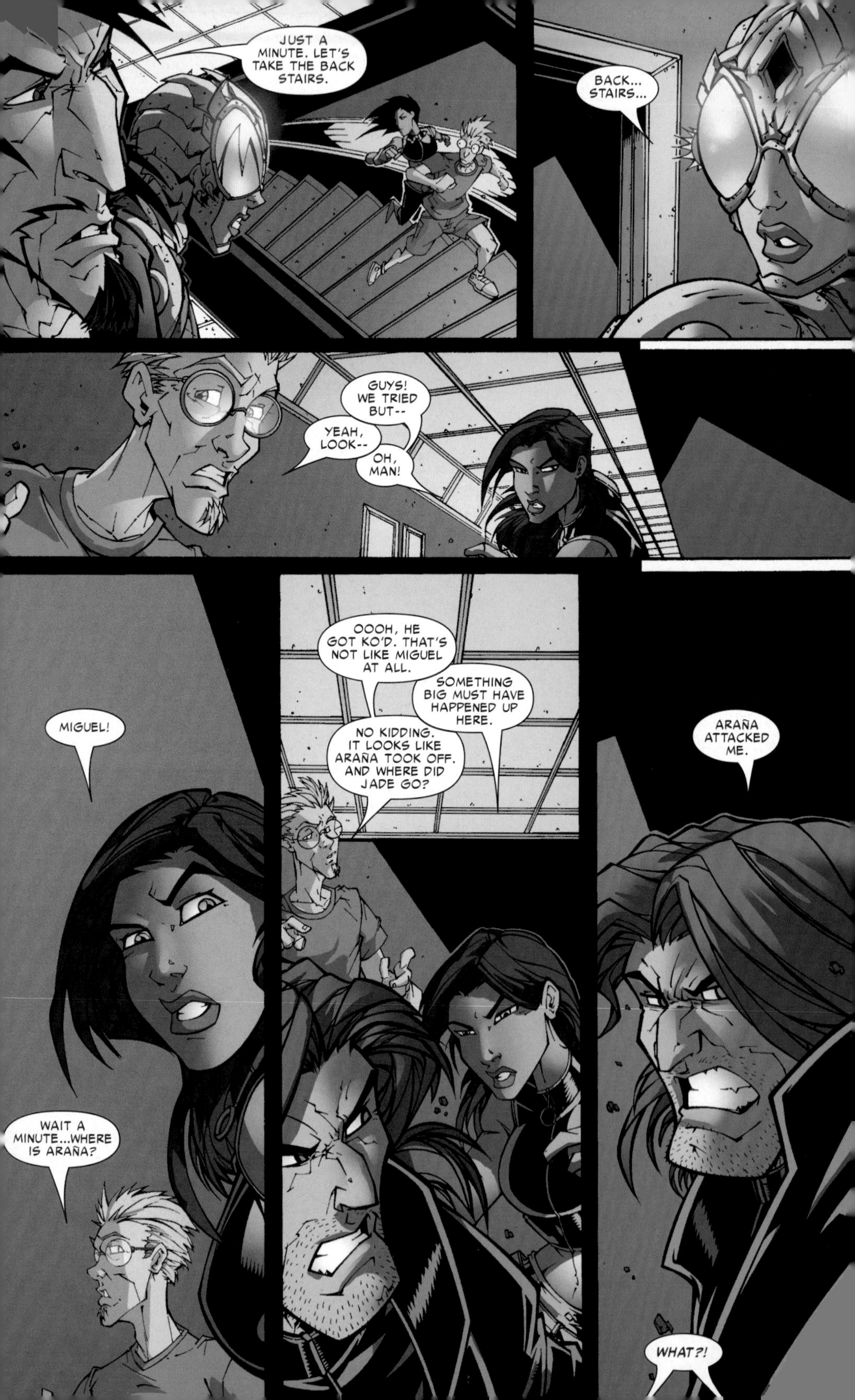
JUST A MINUTE. LET'S TAKE THE BACK STAIRS.
BACK... STAIRS...
GUYS! WE TRIED BUT--
YEAH, LOOK--
OH, MAN!
MIGUEL!
WAIT A MINUTE...WHERE IS ARAÑA?
OOOH, HE GOT KO'D. THAT'S NOT LIKE MIGUEL AT ALL.
SOMETHING BIG MUST HAVE HAPPENED UP HERE.
NO KIDDING. IT LOOKS LIKE ARAÑA TOOK OFF. AND WHERE DID JADE GO?
ARAÑA ATTACKED ME.
WHAT?!

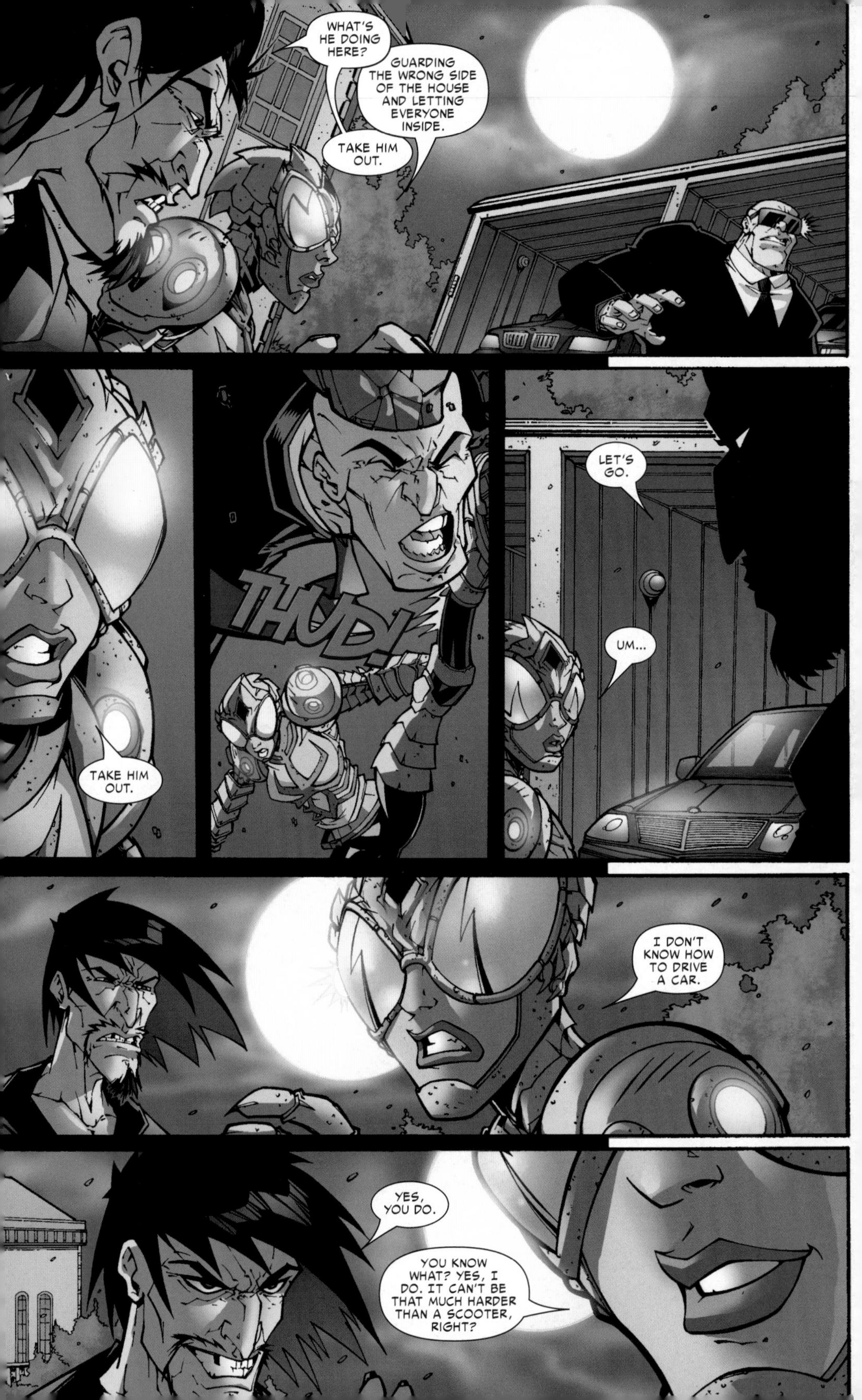
WHAT'S HE DOING HERE?
GUARDING THE WRONG SIDE OF THE HOUSE AND LETTING EVERYONE INSIDE.
TAKE HIM OUT.
TAKE HIM OUT.
THUD!
LET'S GO.
UM...
I DON'T KNOW HOW TO DRIVE A CAR.
YES, YOU DO.
YOU KNOW WHAT? YES, I DO. IT CAN'T BE THAT MUCH HARDER THAN A SCOOTER, RIGHT?

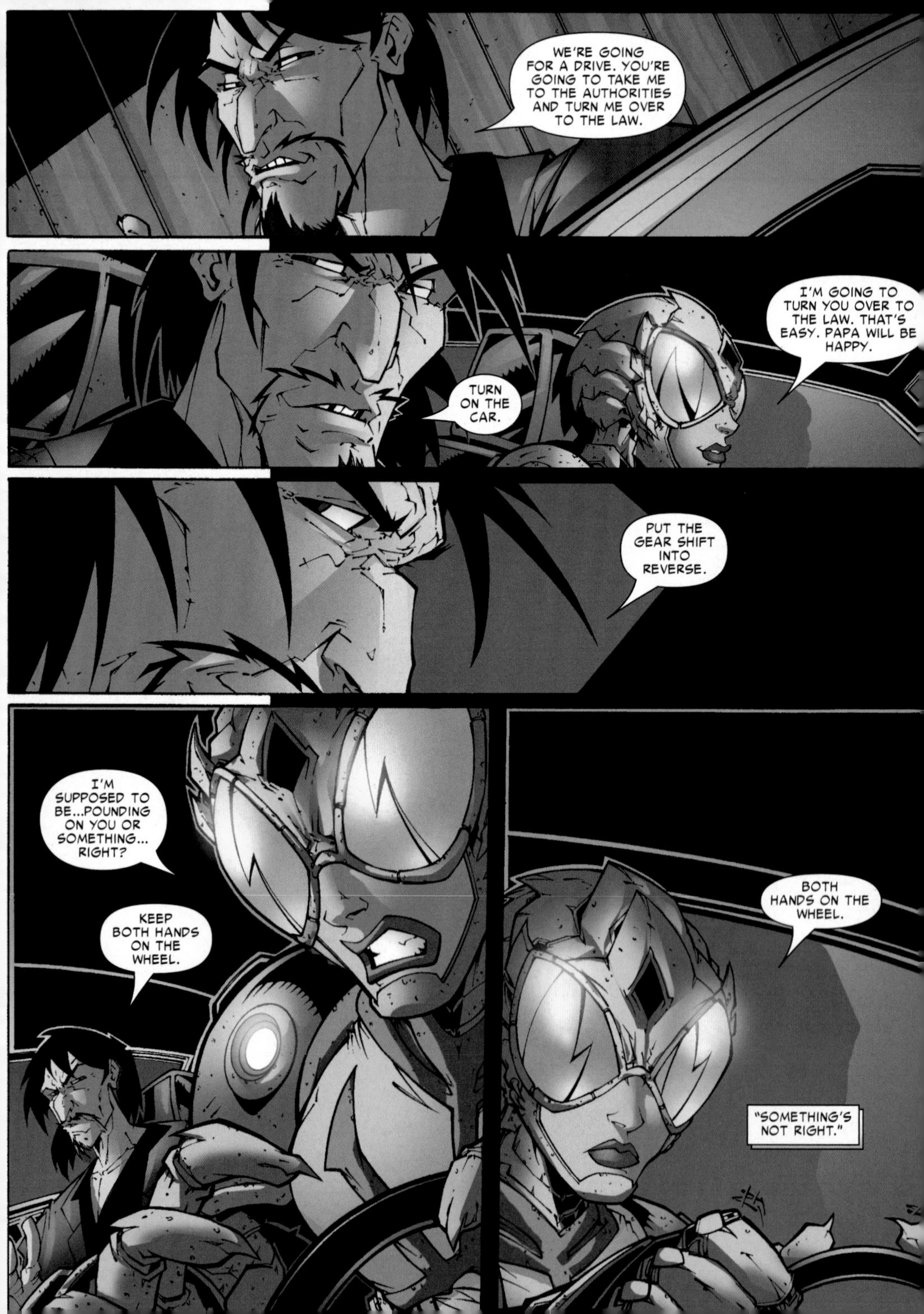
WE'RE GOING FOR A DRIVE. YOU'RE GOING TO TAKE ME TO THE AUTHORITIES AND TURN ME OVER TO THE LAW.
I'M GOING TO TURN YOU OVER TO THE LAW. THAT'S EASY. PAPA WILL BE HAPPY.
TURN ON THE CAR.
PUT THE GEAR SHIFT INTO REVERSE.
I'M SUPPOSED TO BE...POUNDING ON YOU OR SOMETHING... RIGHT?
KEEP BOTH HANDS ON THE WHEEL.
BOTH HANDS ON THE WHEEL.
"SOMETHING'S NOT RIGHT."

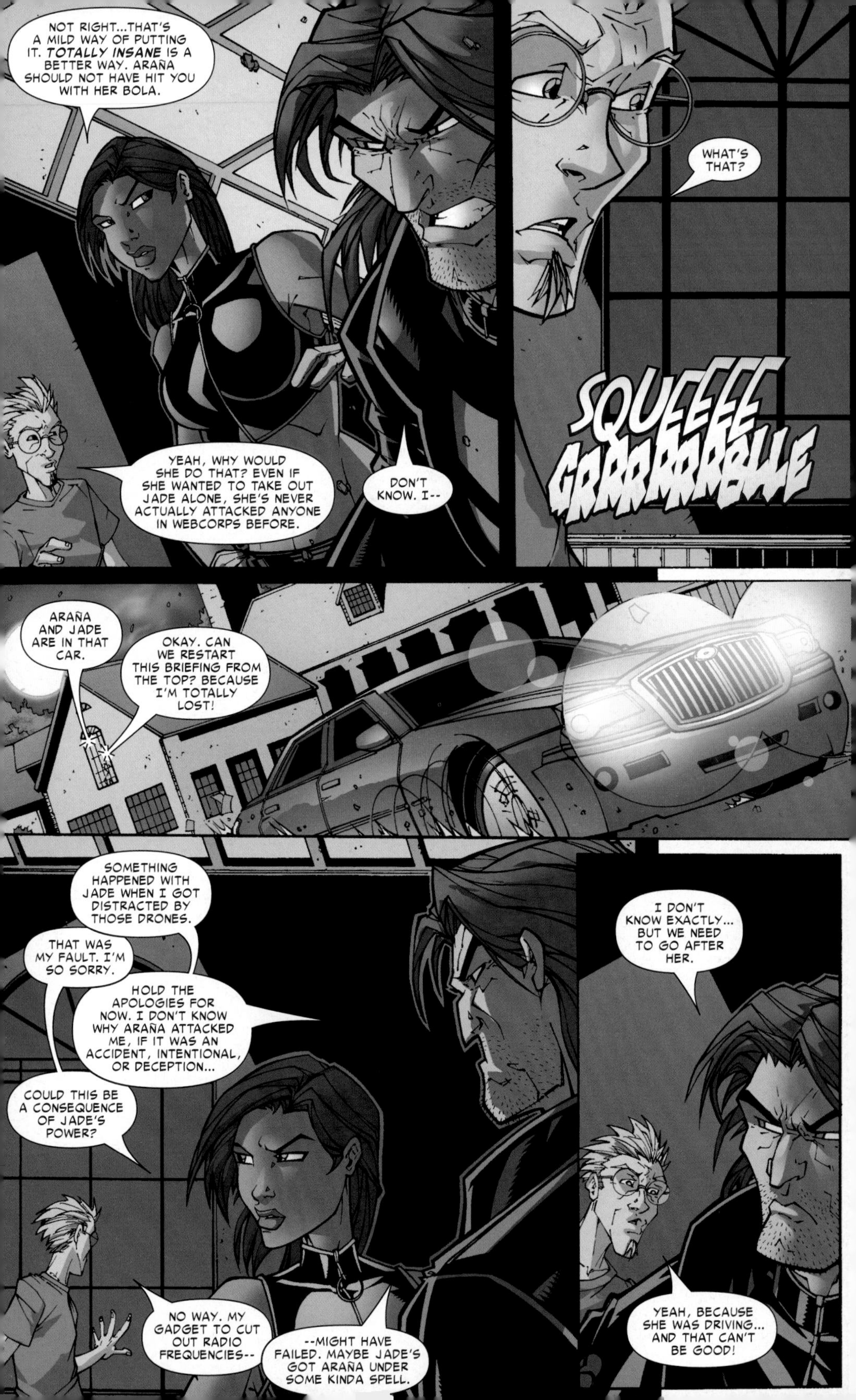

NOT RIGHT...THAT'S A MILD WAY OF PUTTING IT. *TOTALLY INSANE* IS A BETTER WAY. ARAÑA SHOULD NOT HAVE HIT YOU WITH HER BOLA.
YEAH, WHY WOULD SHE DO THAT? EVEN IF SHE WANTED TO TAKE OUT JADE ALONE, SHE'S NEVER ACTUALLY ATTACKED ANYONE IN WEBCORPS BEFORE.
DON'T KNOW. I--
WHAT'S THAT?
SQUEEEE
GRRRRRRBLLE
ARAÑA AND JADE ARE IN THAT CAR.
OKAY. CAN WE RESTART THIS BRIEFING FROM THE TOP? BECAUSE I'M TOTALLY LOST!
SOMETHING HAPPENED WITH JADE WHEN I GOT DISTRACTED BY THOSE DRONES.
THAT WAS MY FAULT. I'M SO SORRY.
HOLD THE APOLOGIES FOR NOW. I DON'T KNOW WHY ARAÑA ATTACKED ME, IF IT WAS AN ACCIDENT, INTENTIONAL, OR DECEPTION...
COULD THIS BE A CONSEQUENCE OF JADE'S POWER?
NO WAY. MY GADGET TO CUT OUT RADIO FREQUENCIES--
--MIGHT HAVE FAILED. MAYBE JADE'S GOT ARAÑA UNDER SOME KINDA SPELL.
I DON'T KNOW EXACTLY... BUT WE NEED TO GO AFTER HER.
YEAH, BECAUSE SHE WAS DRIVING... AND THAT CAN'T BE GOOD!

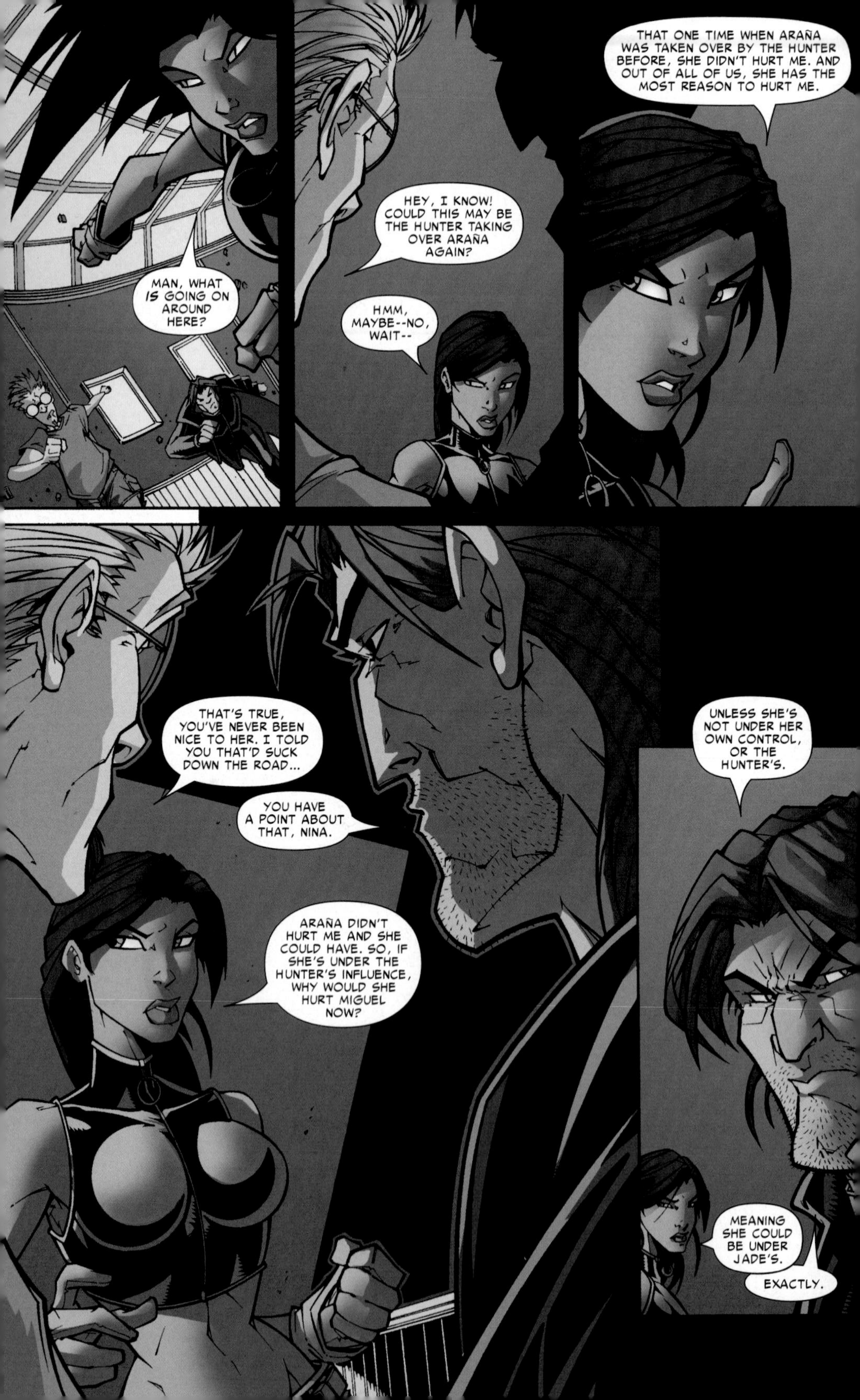
MAN, WHAT IS GOING ON AROUND HERE?
HEY, I KNOW! COULD THIS MAY BE THE HUNTER TAKING OVER ARAÑA AGAIN?
HMM, MAYBE--NO, WAIT--
THAT ONE TIME WHEN ARAÑA WAS TAKEN OVER BY THE HUNTER BEFORE, SHE DIDN'T HURT ME. AND OUT OF ALL OF US, SHE HAS THE MOST REASON TO HURT ME.
THAT'S TRUE, YOU'VE NEVER BEEN NICE TO HER. I TOLD YOU THAT'D SUCK DOWN THE ROAD...
YOU HAVE A POINT ABOUT THAT, NINA.
ARAÑA DIDN'T HURT ME AND SHE COULD HAVE. SO, IF SHE'S UNDER THE HUNTER'S INFLUENCE, WHY WOULD SHE HURT MIGUEL NOW?
UNLESS SHE'S NOT UNDER HER OWN CONTROL, OR THE HUNTER'S.
MEANING SHE COULD BE UNDER JADE'S.
EXACTLY.

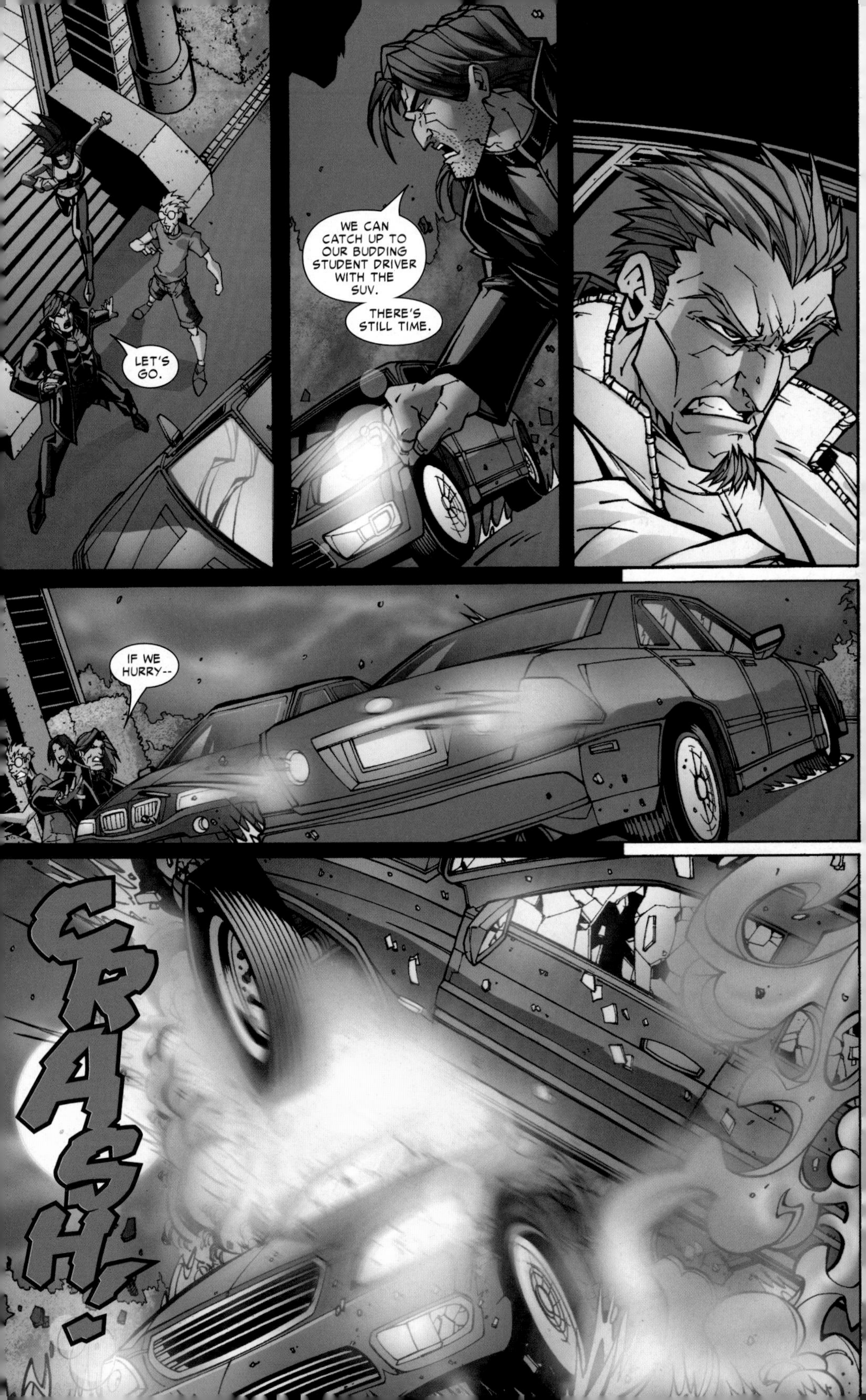
LET'S GO.
WE CAN CATCH UP TO OUR BUDDING STUDENT DRIVER WITH THE SUV.
THERE'S STILL TIME.
IF WE HURRY--
CRASH!

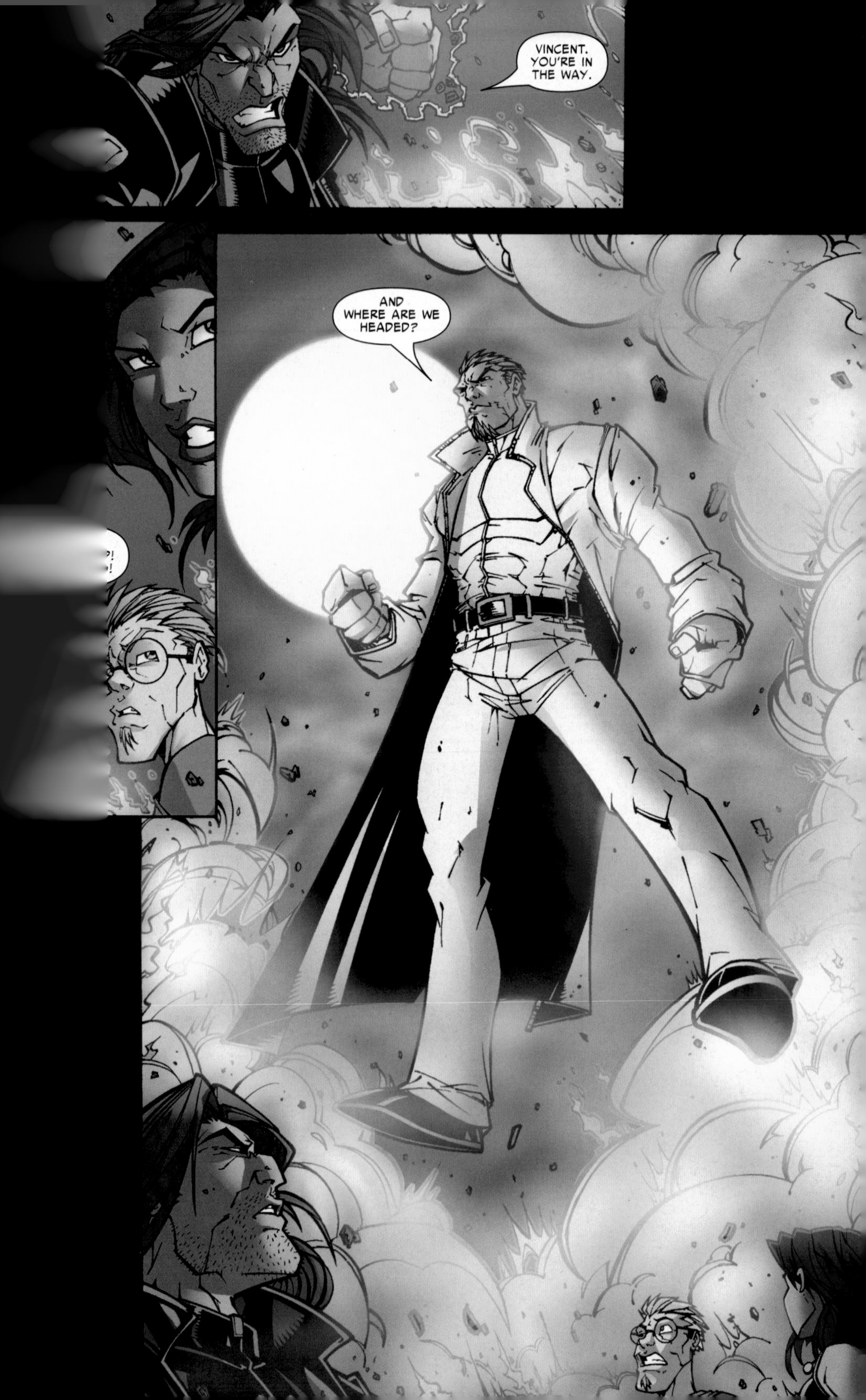
VINCENT. YOU'RE IN THE WAY.
AND WHERE ARE WE HEADED?

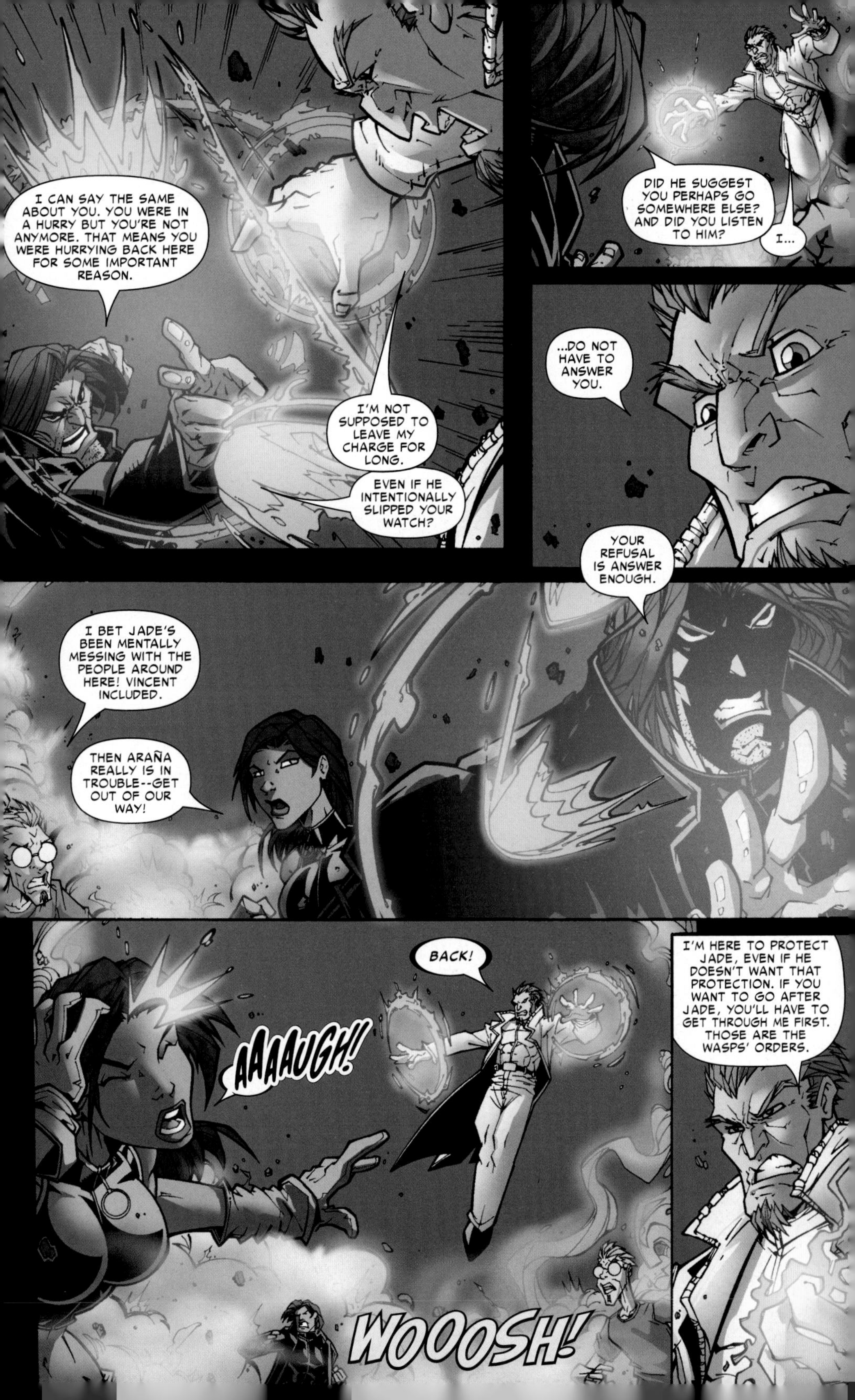
I CAN SAY THE SAME ABOUT YOU. YOU WERE IN A HURRY BUT YOU'RE NOT ANYMORE. THAT MEANS YOU WERE HURRYING BACK HERE FOR SOME IMPORTANT REASON.
I'M NOT SUPPOSED TO LEAVE MY CHARGE FOR LONG.
EVEN IF HE INTENTIONALLY SLIPPED YOUR WATCH?
DID HE SUGGEST YOU PERHAPS GO SOMEWHERE ELSE? AND DID YOU LISTEN TO HIM?
I...
...DO NOT HAVE TO ANSWER YOU.
YOUR REFUSAL IS ANSWER ENOUGH.
I BET JADE'S BEEN MENTALLY MESSING WITH THE PEOPLE AROUND HERE! VINCENT INCLUDED.
THEN ARAÑA REALLY IS IN TROUBLE--GET OUT OF OUR WAY!
AAAAUGH!
BACK!
I'M HERE TO PROTECT JADE, EVEN IF HE DOESN'T WANT THAT PROTECTION. IF YOU WANT TO GO AFTER JADE, YOU'LL HAVE TO GET THROUGH ME FIRST. THOSE ARE THE WASPS' ORDERS.
WOOOSH!

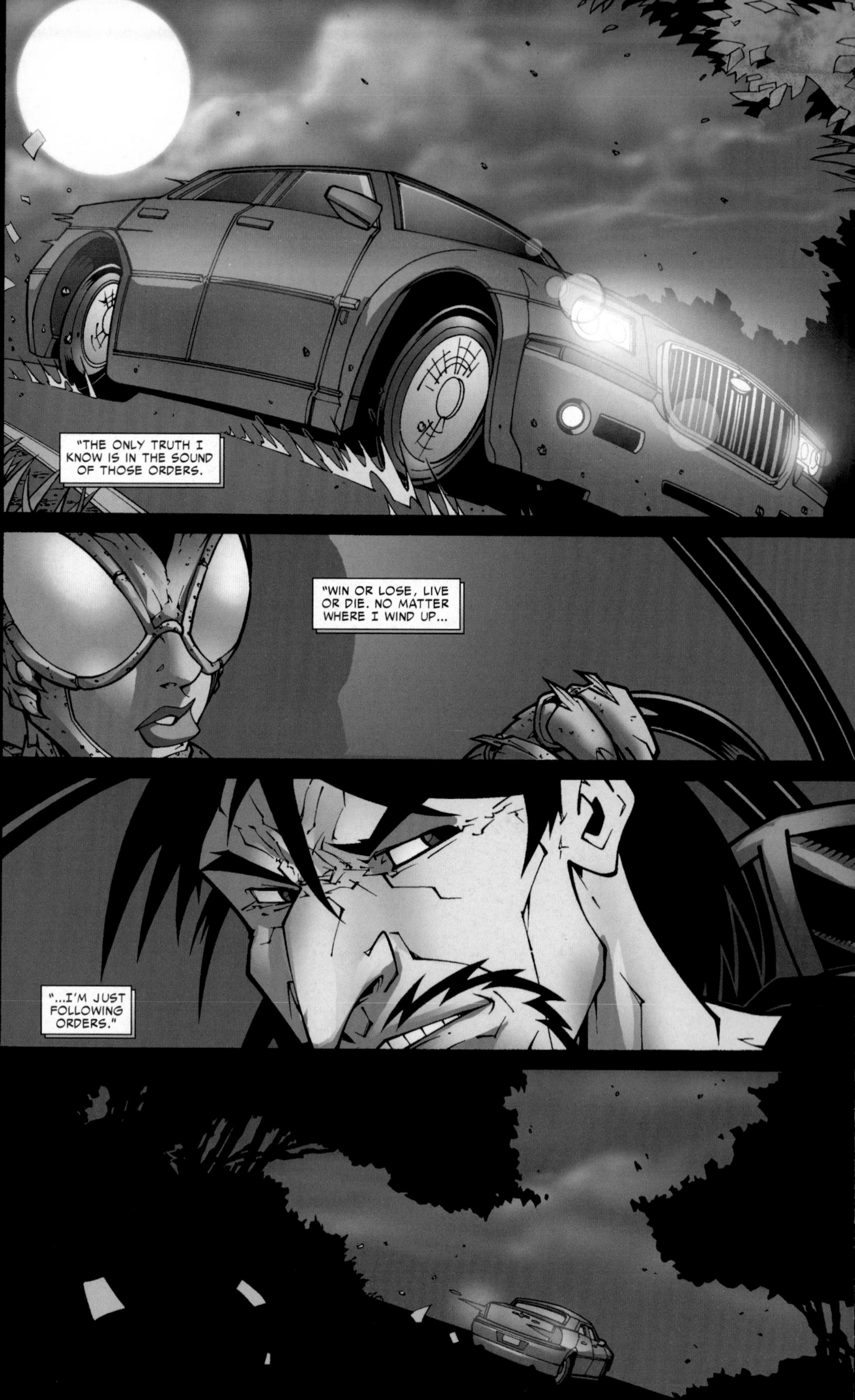
"THE ONLY TRUTH I KNOW IS IN THE SOUND OF THOSE ORDERS.
"WIN OR LOSE, LIVE OR DIE. NO MATTER WHERE I WIND UP...
"...I'M JUST FOLLOWING ORDERS."

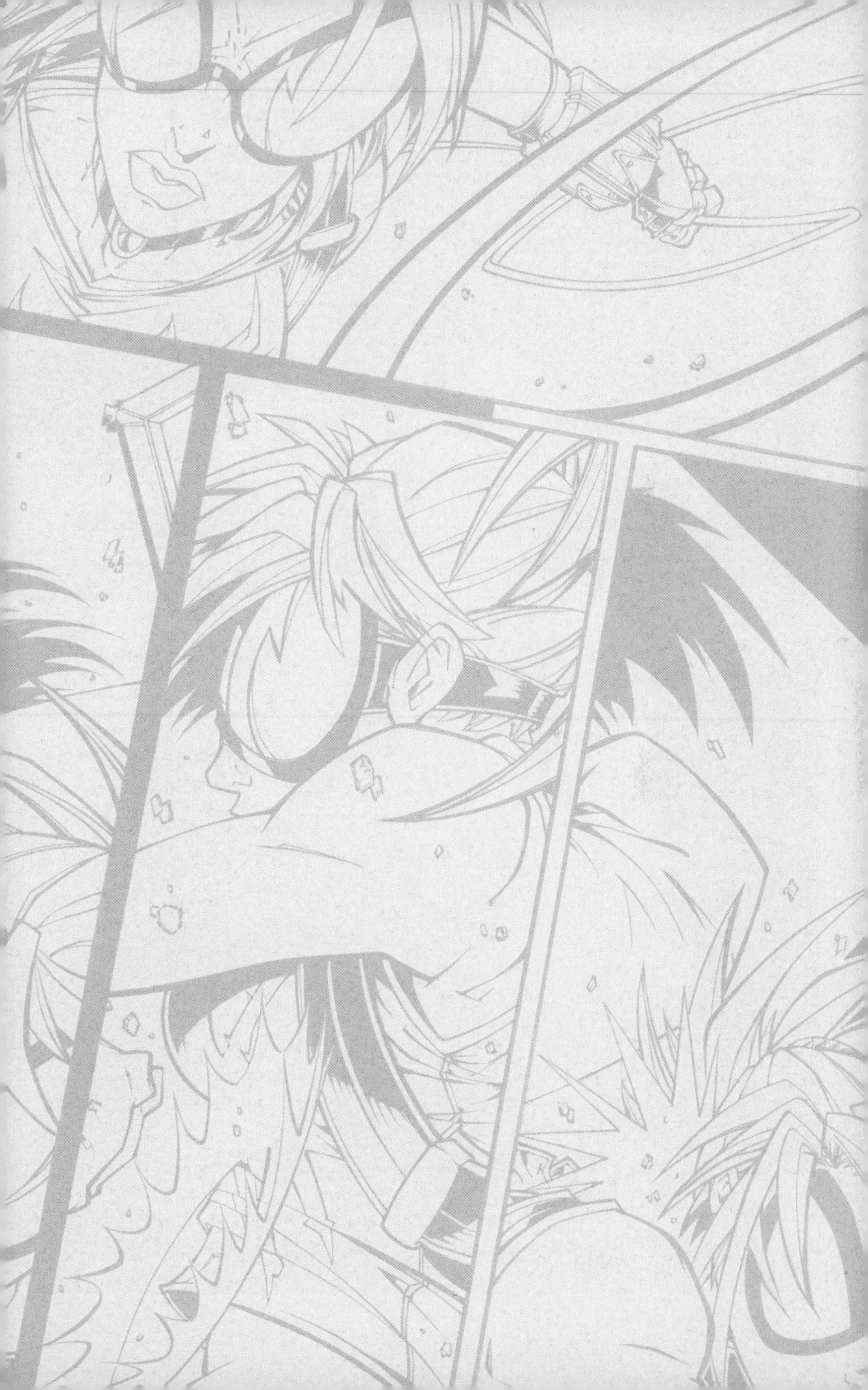

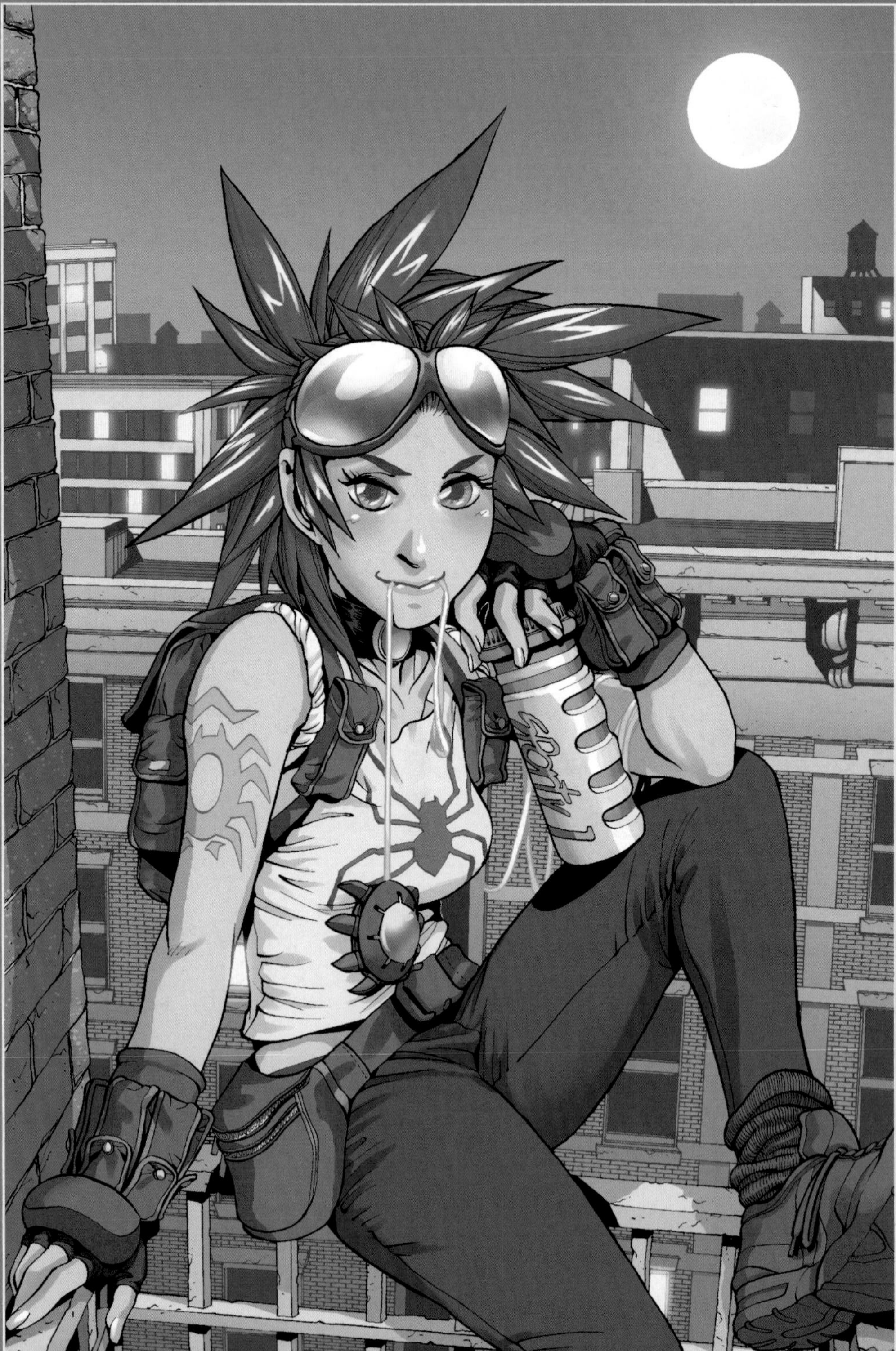
Sporty

ARAÑA #12

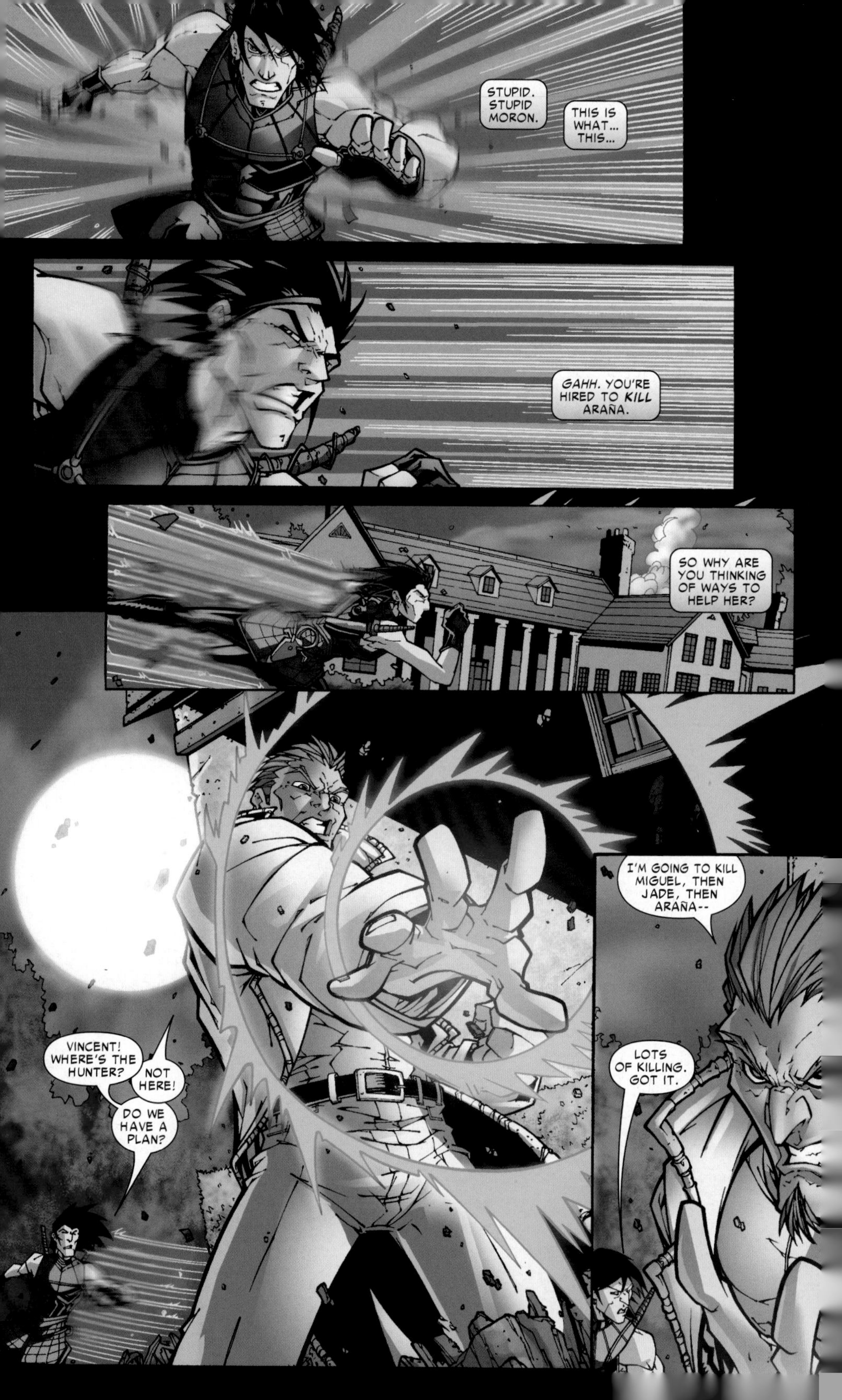
STUPID. STUPID MORON.
THIS IS WHAT... THIS...
GAHH. YOU'RE HIRED TO KILL ARAÑA.
SO WHY ARE YOU THINKING OF WAYS TO HELP HER?
VINCENT! WHERE'S THE HUNTER?
NOT HERE!
DO WE HAVE A PLAN?
I'M GOING TO KILL MIGUEL, THEN JADE, THEN ARAÑA--
LOTS OF KILLING. GOT IT.

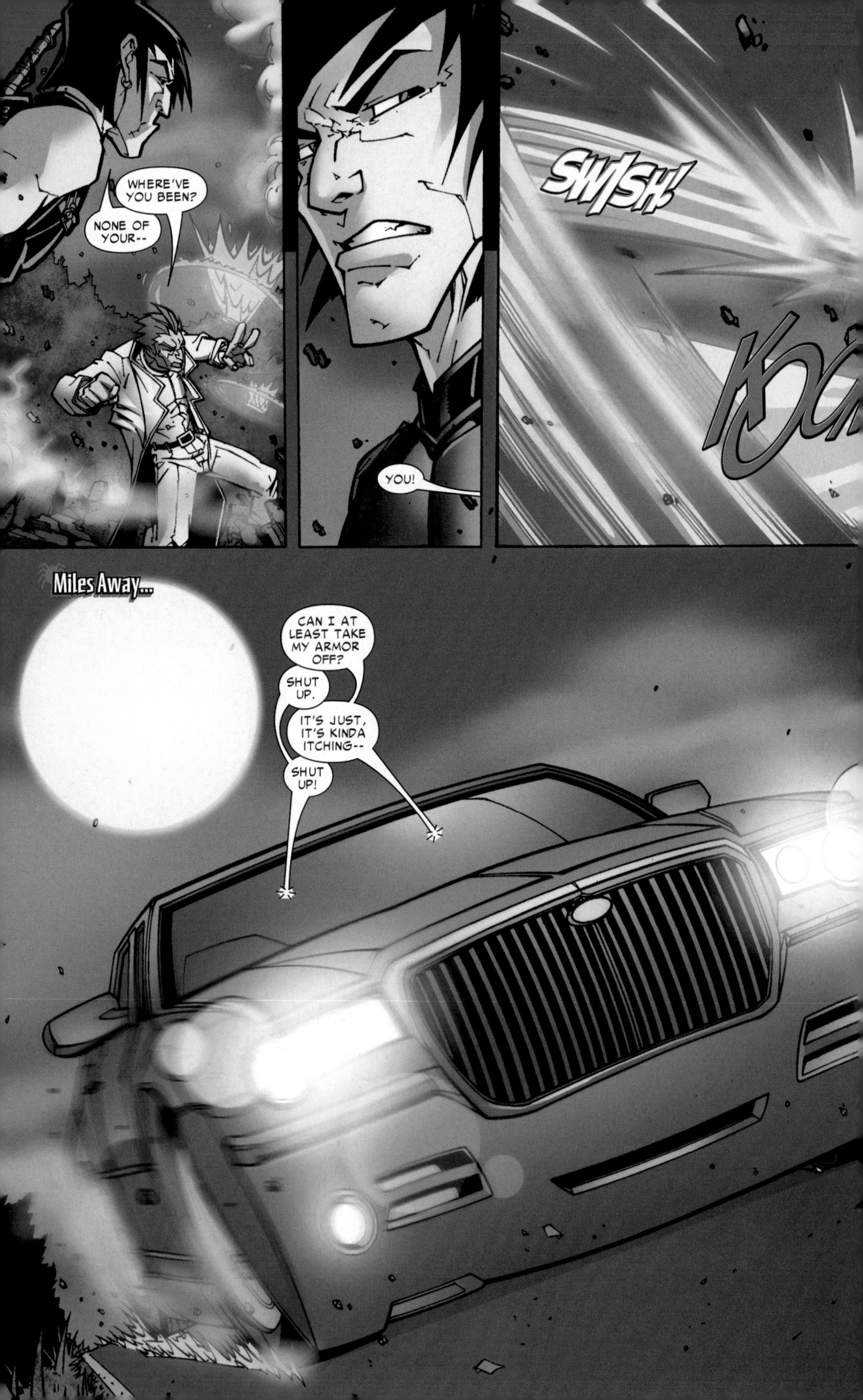
WHERE'VE YOU BEEN?
NONE OF YOUR--
YOU!
SWISH!
Miles Away...
CAN I AT LEAST TAKE MY ARMOR OFF?
SHUT UP.
IT'S JUST, IT'S KINDA ITCHING--
SHUT UP!

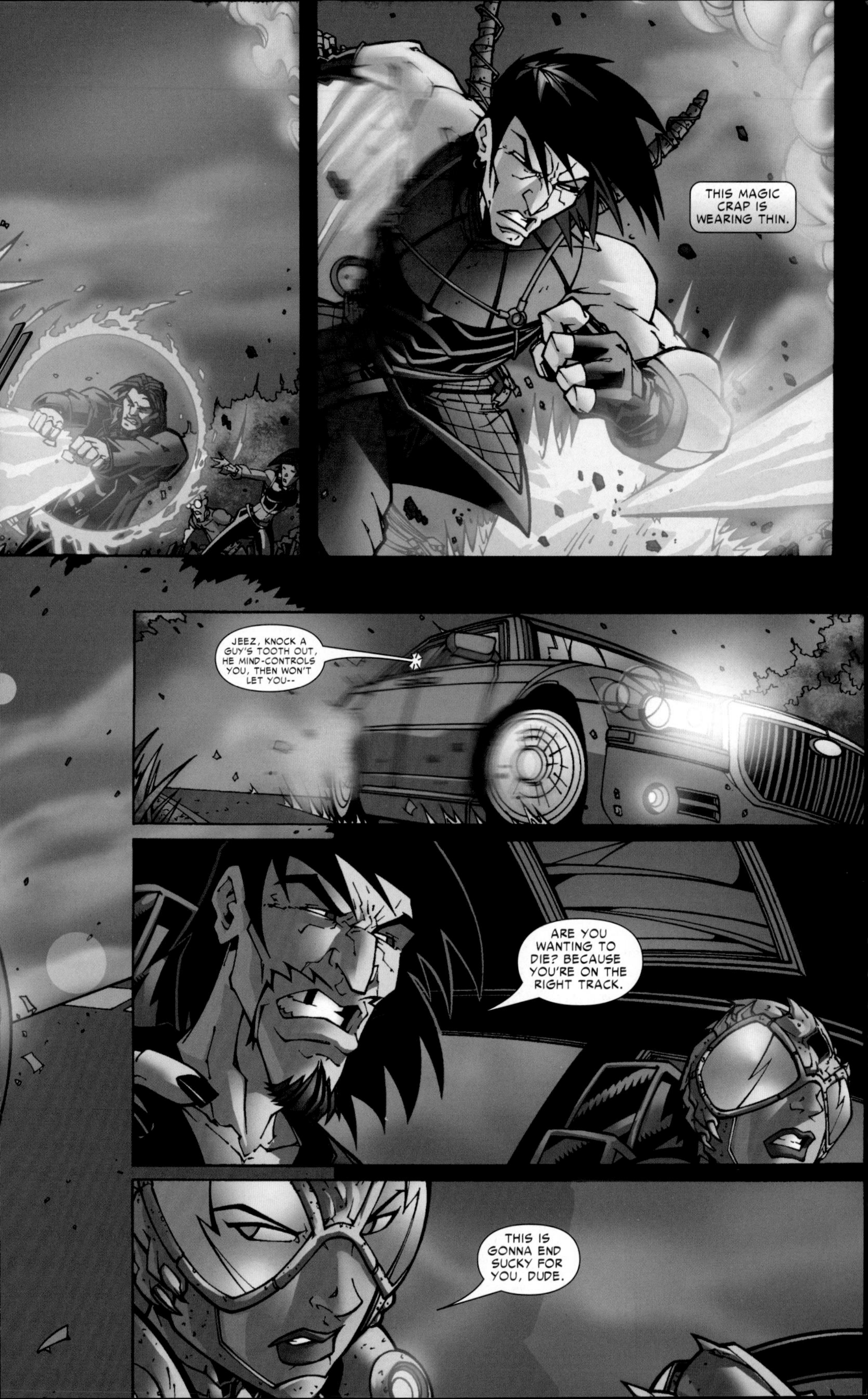
THIS MAGIC CRAP IS WEARING THIN.
JEEZ, KNOCK A GUY'S TOOTH OUT, HE MIND-CONTROLS YOU, THEN WON'T LET YOU--
ARE YOU WANTING TO DIE? BECAUSE YOU'RE ON THE RIGHT TRACK.
THIS IS GONNA END SUCKY FOR YOU, DUDE.

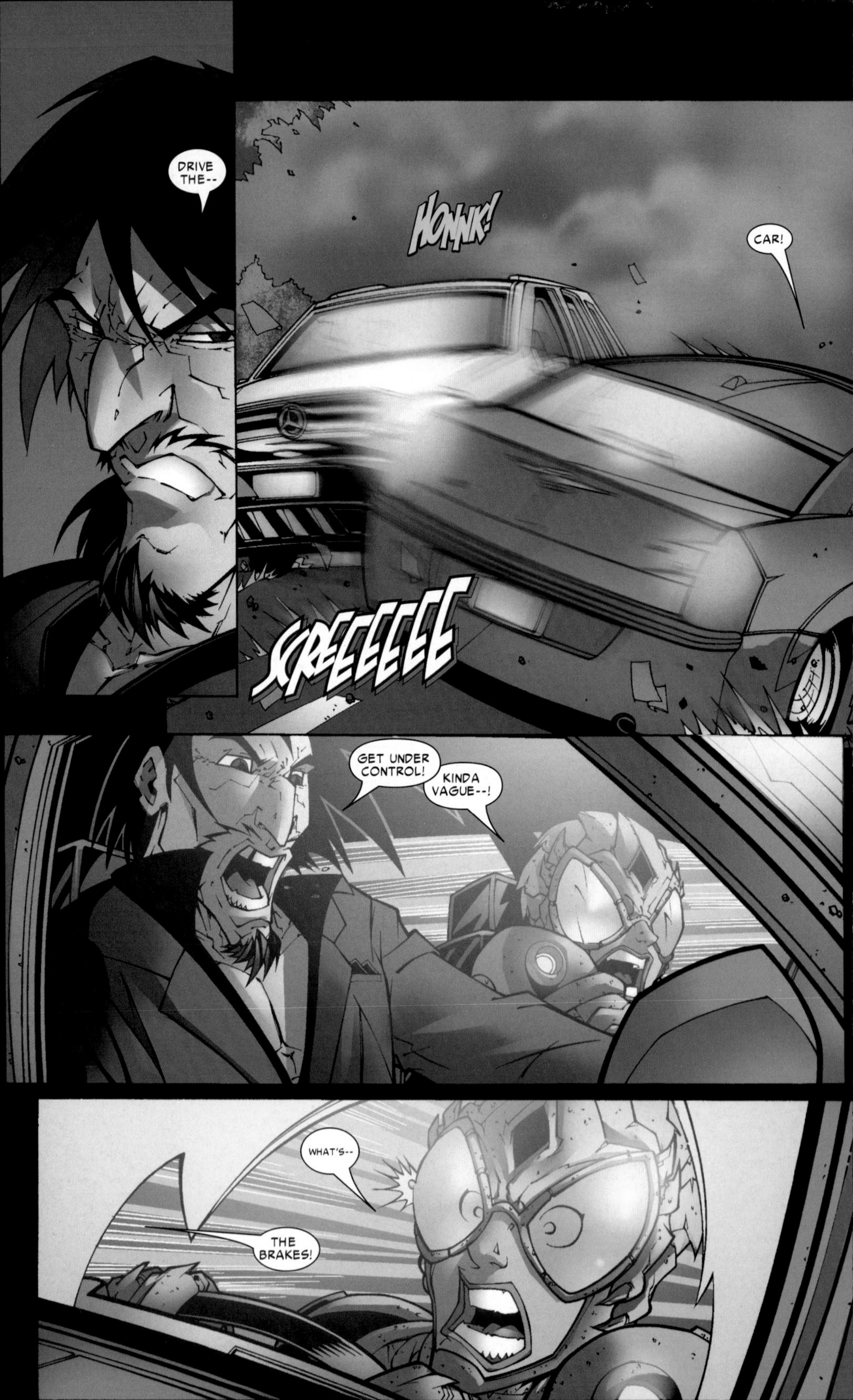
DRIVE THE--
HONNK!
CAR!
SCREEEEEEE
GET UNDER CONTROL!
KINDA VAGUE--!
WHAT'S--
THE BRAKES!

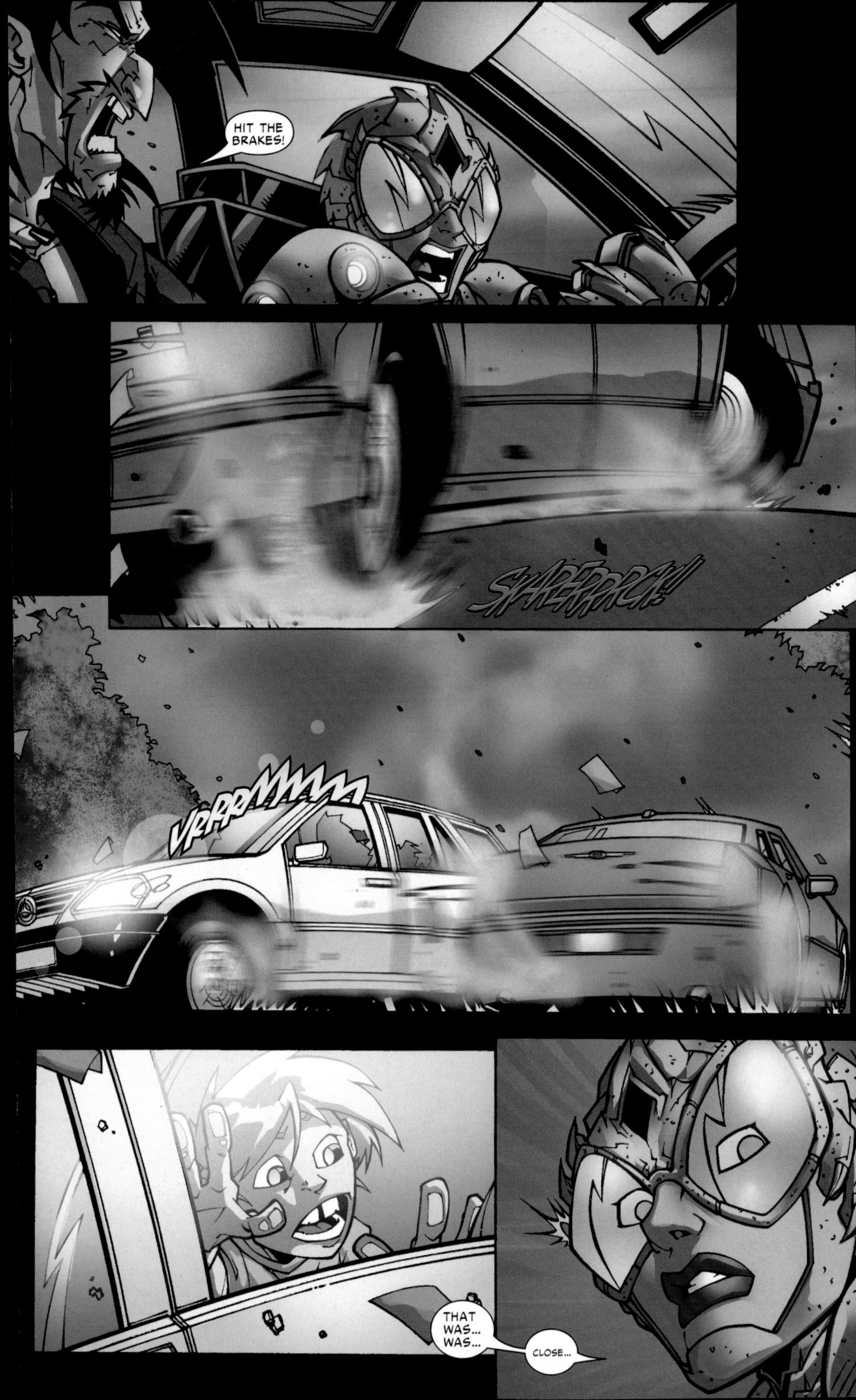
HIT THE BRAKES!
SKREEEEEEK!!
VRRRMMMM
THAT WAS... WAS...
CLOSE...

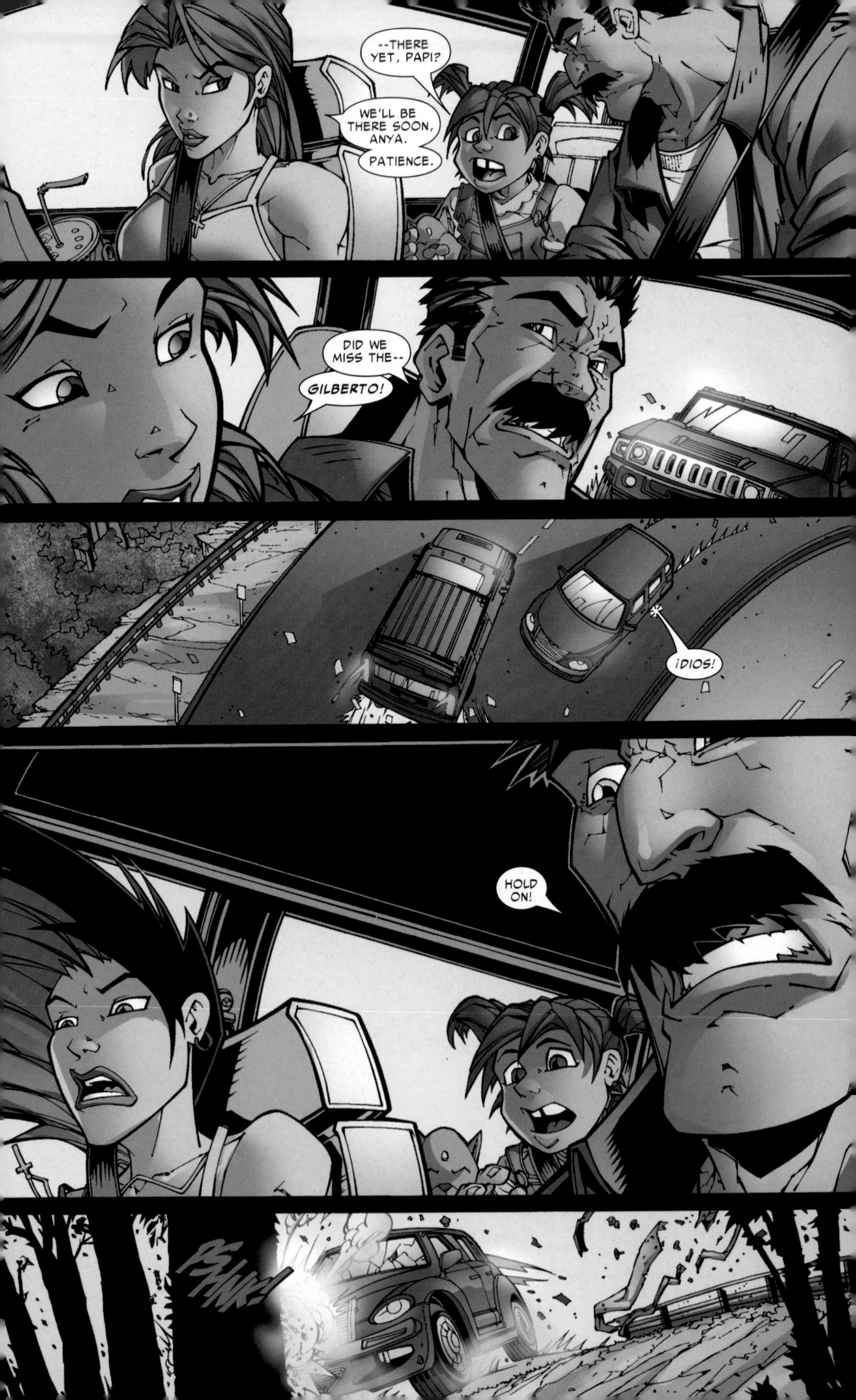
--THERE YET, PAPI?
WE'LL BE THERE SOON, ANYA.
PATIENCE.
DID WE MISS THE--
GILBERTO!
¡DIOS!
HOLD ON!
PSHNK!

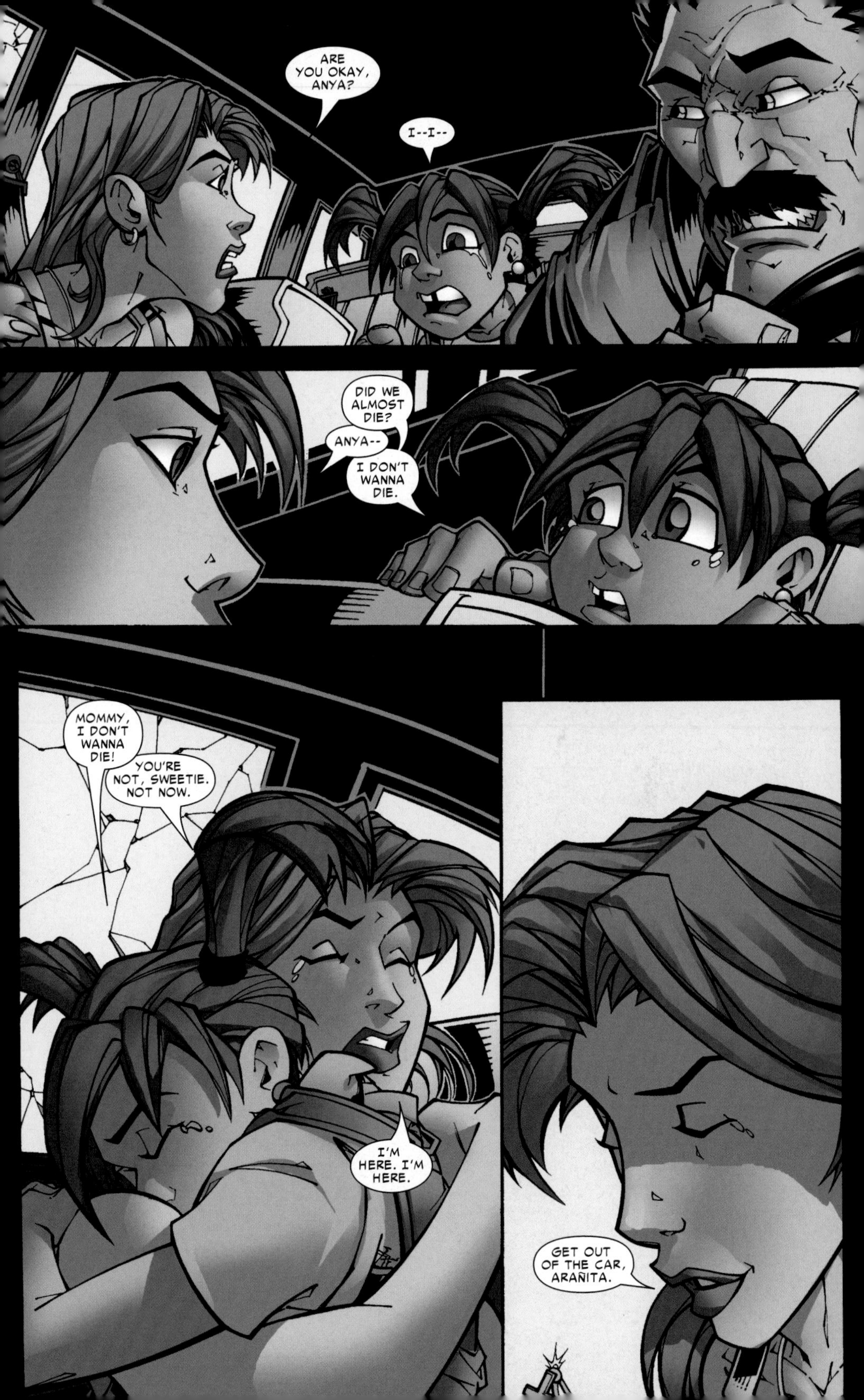
ARE YOU OKAY, ANYA?
I--I--
DID WE ALMOST DIE?
ANYA--
I DON'T WANNA DIE.
MOMMY, I DON'T WANNA DIE!
YOU'RE NOT, SWEETIE. NOT NOW.
I'M HERE. I'M HERE.
GET OUT OF THE CAR, ARAÑITA.

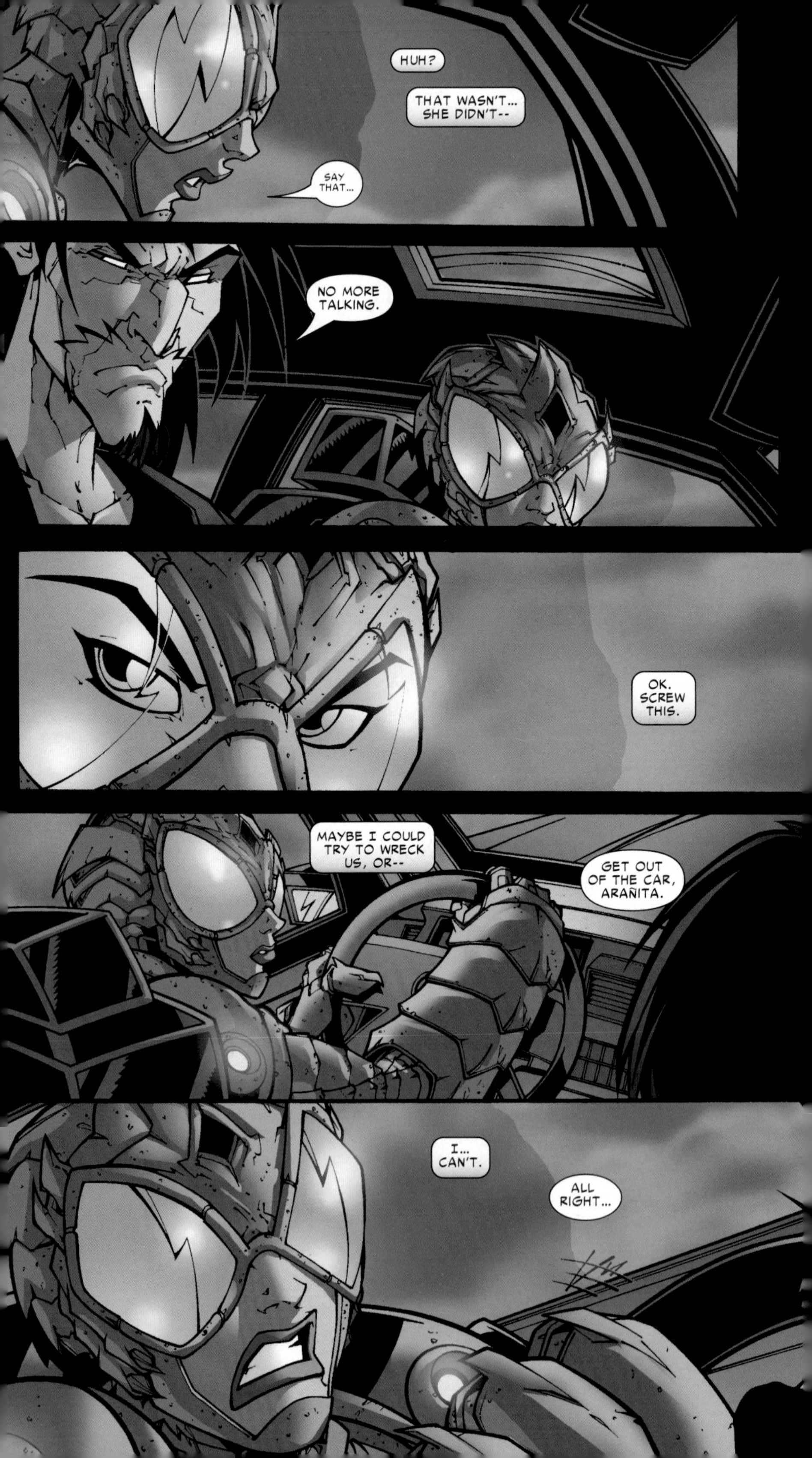
HUH?
THAT WASN'T... SHE DIDN'T--
SAY THAT...
NO MORE TALKING.
OK. SCREW THIS.
MAYBE I COULD TRY TO WRECK US, OR--
GET OUT OF THE CAR, ARAÑITA.
I... CAN'T.
ALL RIGHT...

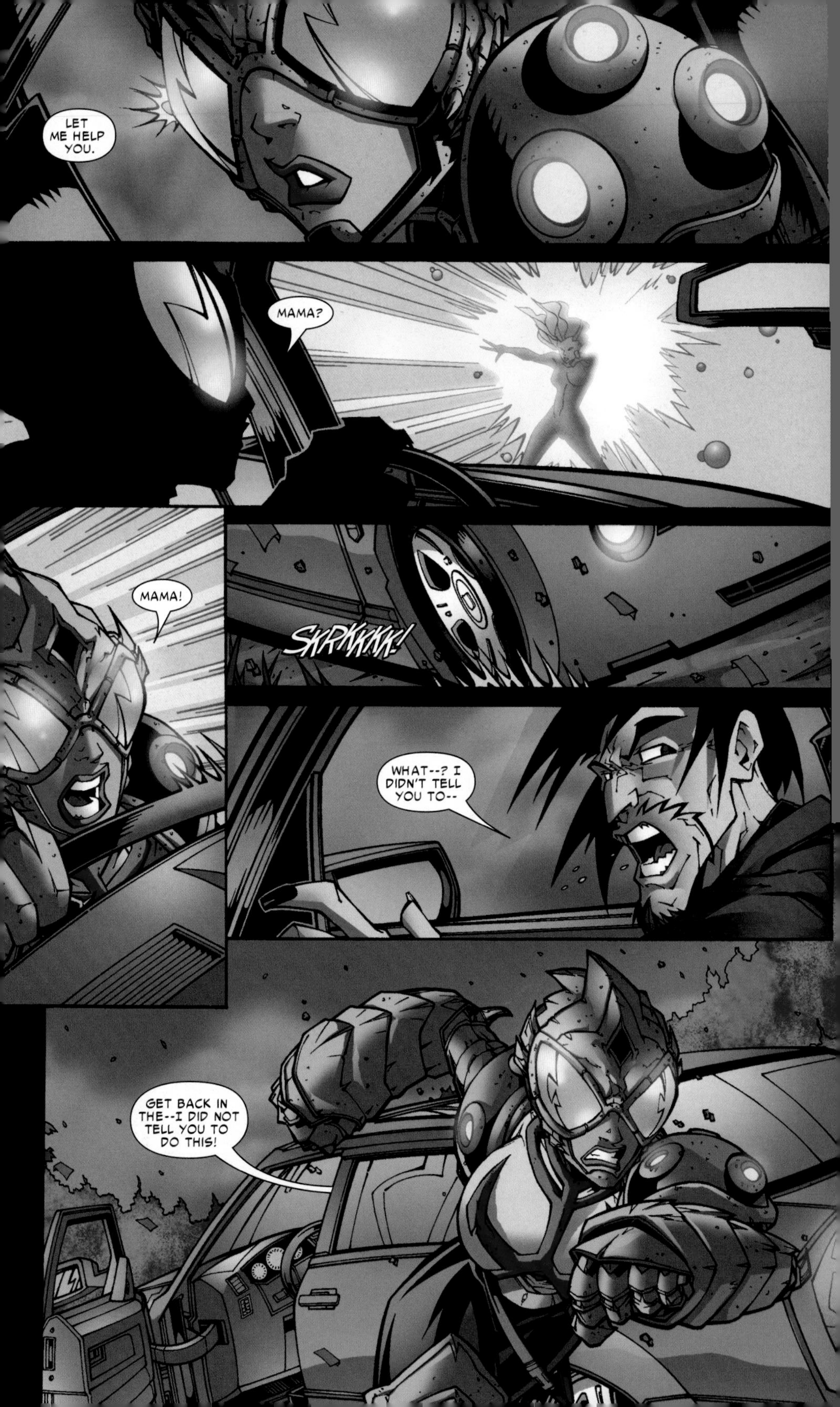
LET ME HELP YOU.
MAMA?
MAMA!
SKRKKKK!
WHAT--? I DIDN'T TELL YOU TO--
GET BACK IN THE--I DID NOT TELL YOU TO DO THIS!

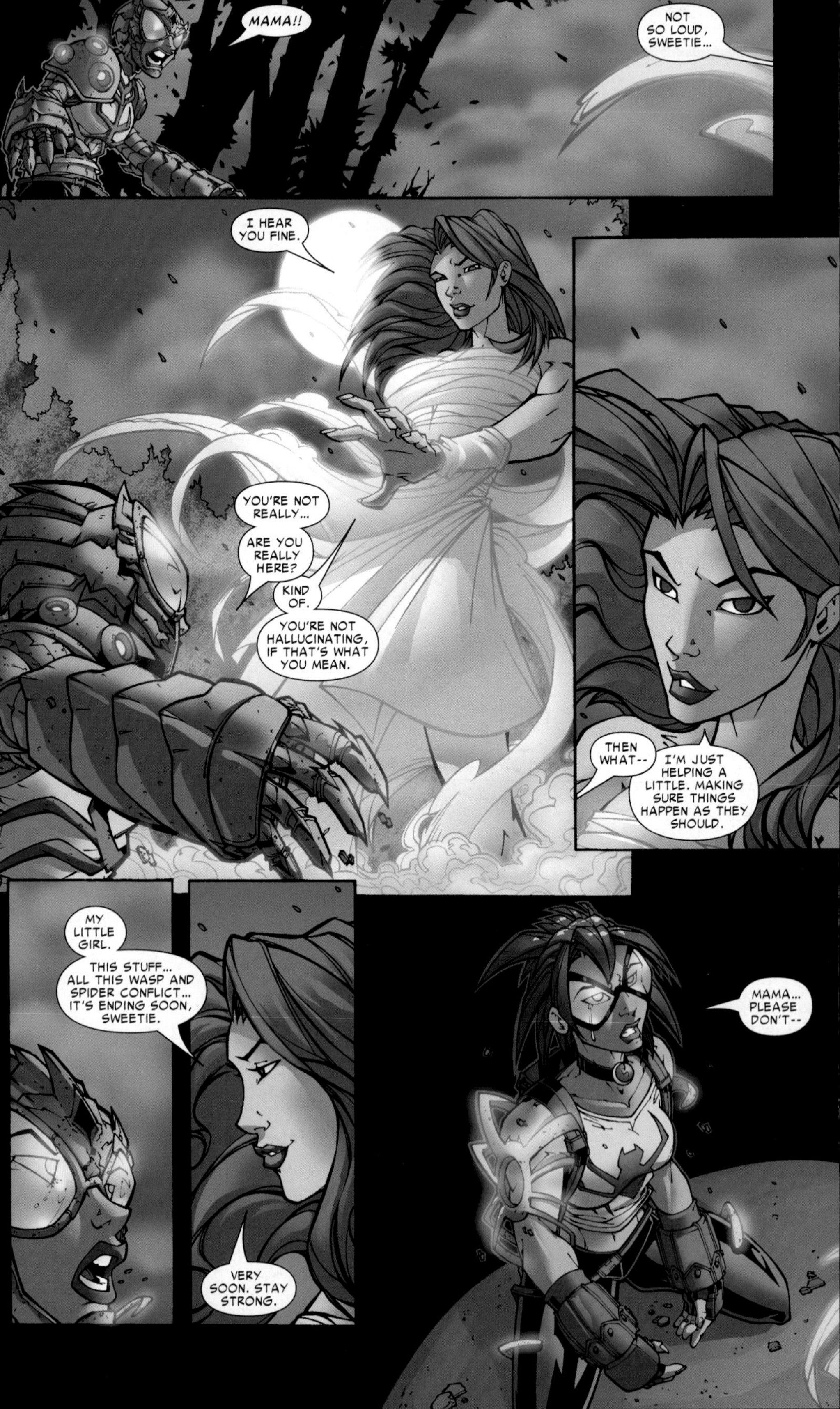
MAMA!!
NOT SO LOUD, SWEETIE...
I HEAR YOU FINE.
YOU'RE NOT REALLY...
ARE YOU REALLY HERE?
KIND OF.
YOU'RE NOT HALLUCINATING, IF THAT'S WHAT YOU MEAN.
THEN WHAT--
I'M JUST HELPING A LITTLE. MAKING SURE THINGS HAPPEN AS THEY SHOULD.
MY LITTLE GIRL.
THIS STUFF... ALL THIS WASP AND SPIDER CONFLICT... IT'S ENDING SOON, SWEETIE.
VERY SOON. STAY STRONG.
MAMA... PLEASE DON'T--

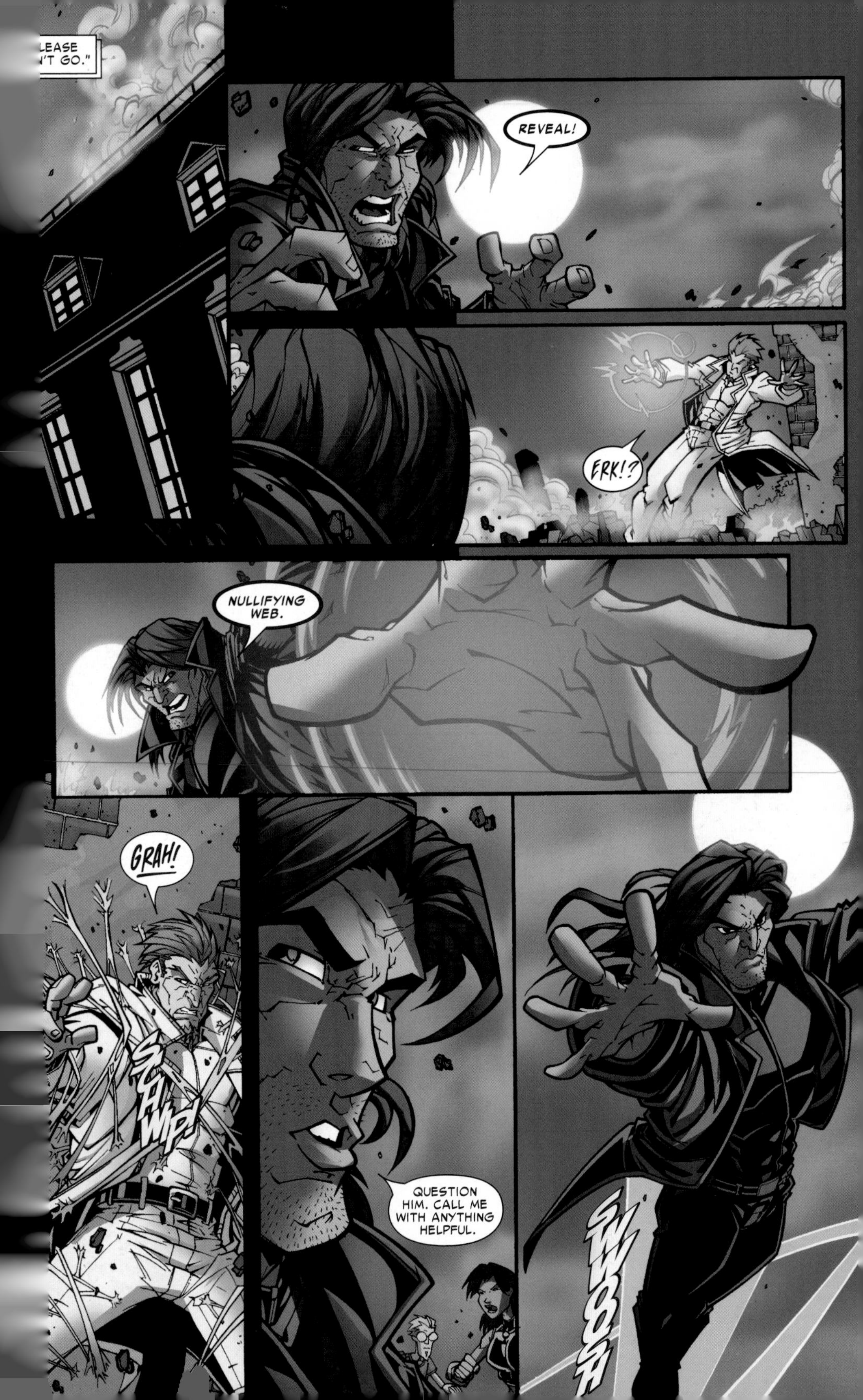

LEASE
N'T GO."
REVEAL!
ERK!?
NULLIFYING WEB.
GRAH!
SHWIP!
QUESTION HIM. CALL ME WITH ANYTHING HELPFUL.
SWOOSH

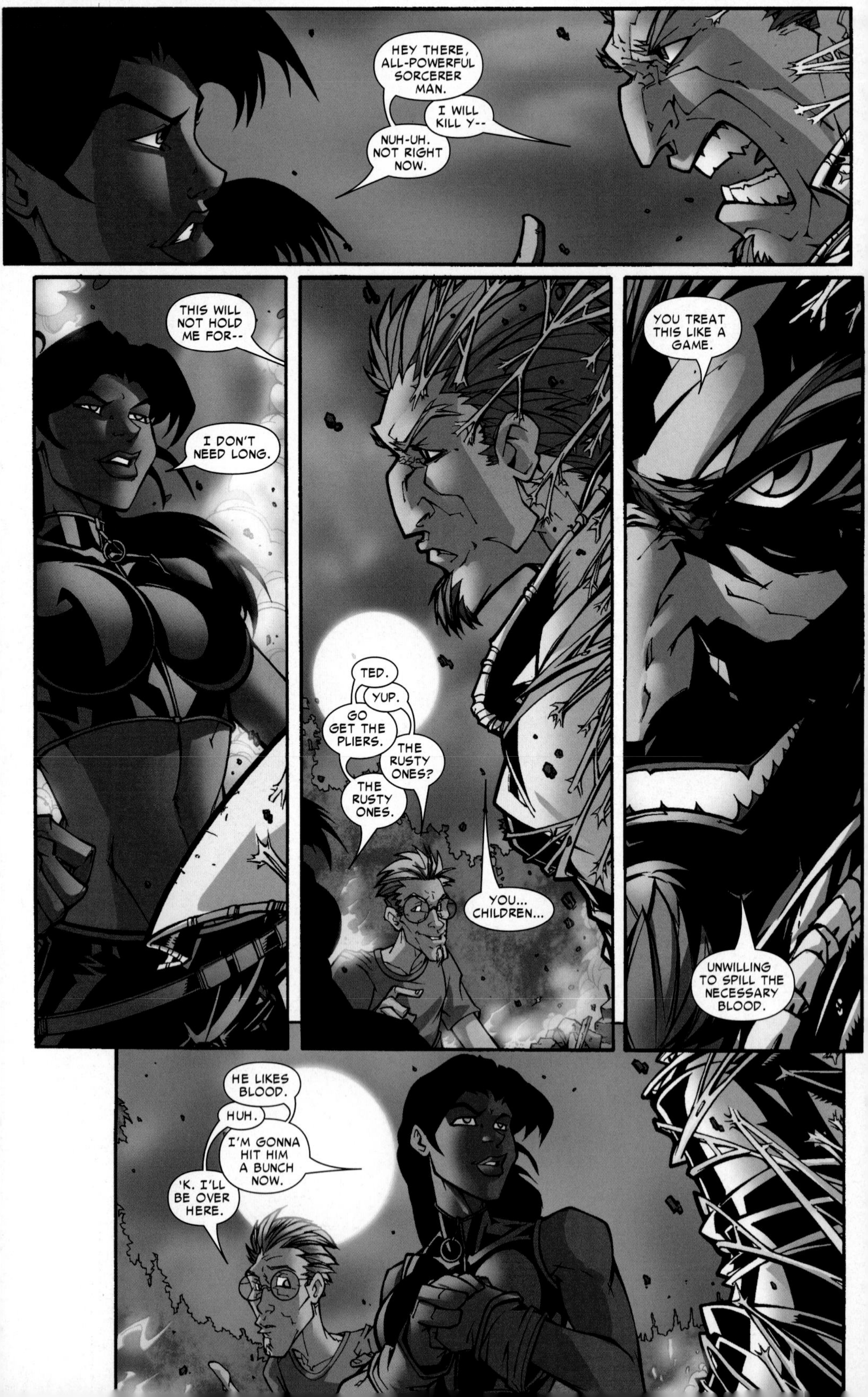
HEY THERE, ALL-POWERFUL SORCERER MAN.
I WILL KILL Y--
NUH-UH. NOT RIGHT NOW.
THIS WILL NOT HOLD ME FOR--
I DON'T NEED LONG.
TED.
YUP.
GO GET THE PLIERS.
THE RUSTY ONES?
THE RUSTY ONES.
YOU... CHILDREN...
YOU TREAT THIS LIKE A GAME.
UNWILLING TO SPILL THE NECESSARY BLOOD.
HE LIKES BLOOD.
HUH.
I'M GONNA HIT HIM A BUNCH NOW.
'K. I'LL BE OVER HERE.

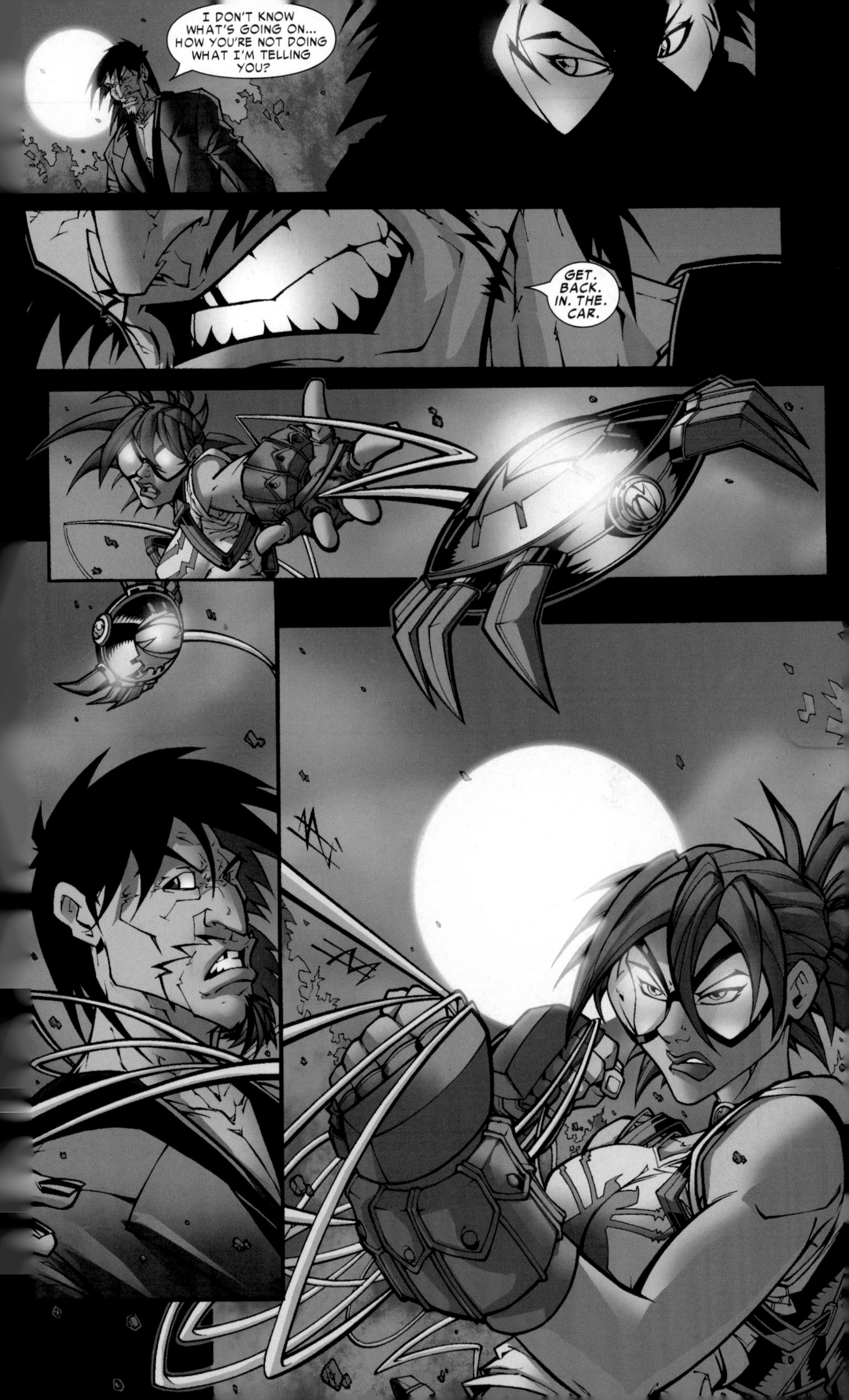
I DON'T KNOW WHAT'S GOING ON... HOW YOU'RE NOT DOING WHAT I'M TELLING YOU?
GET. BACK. IN. THE. CAR.

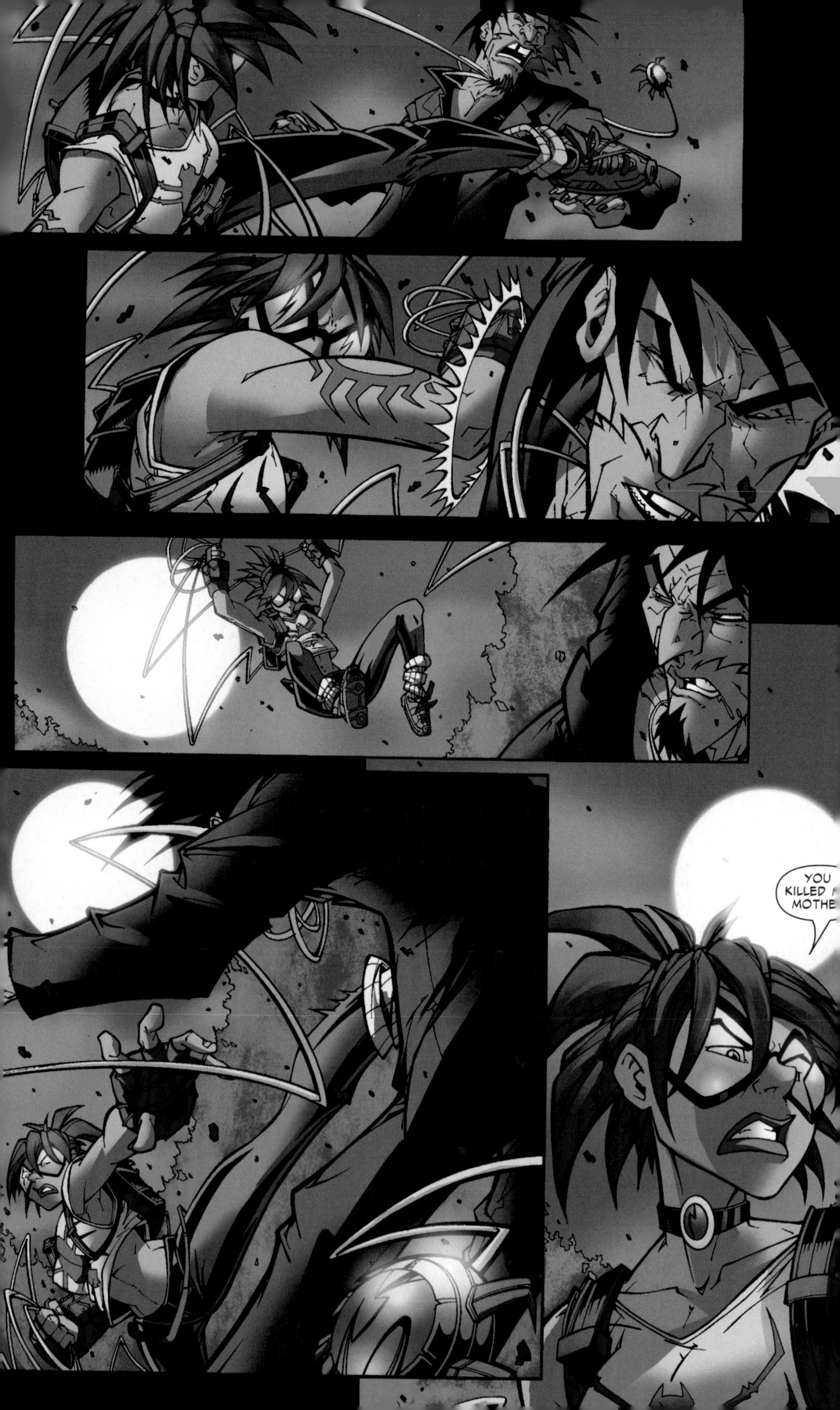
YOU KILLED MOTHE

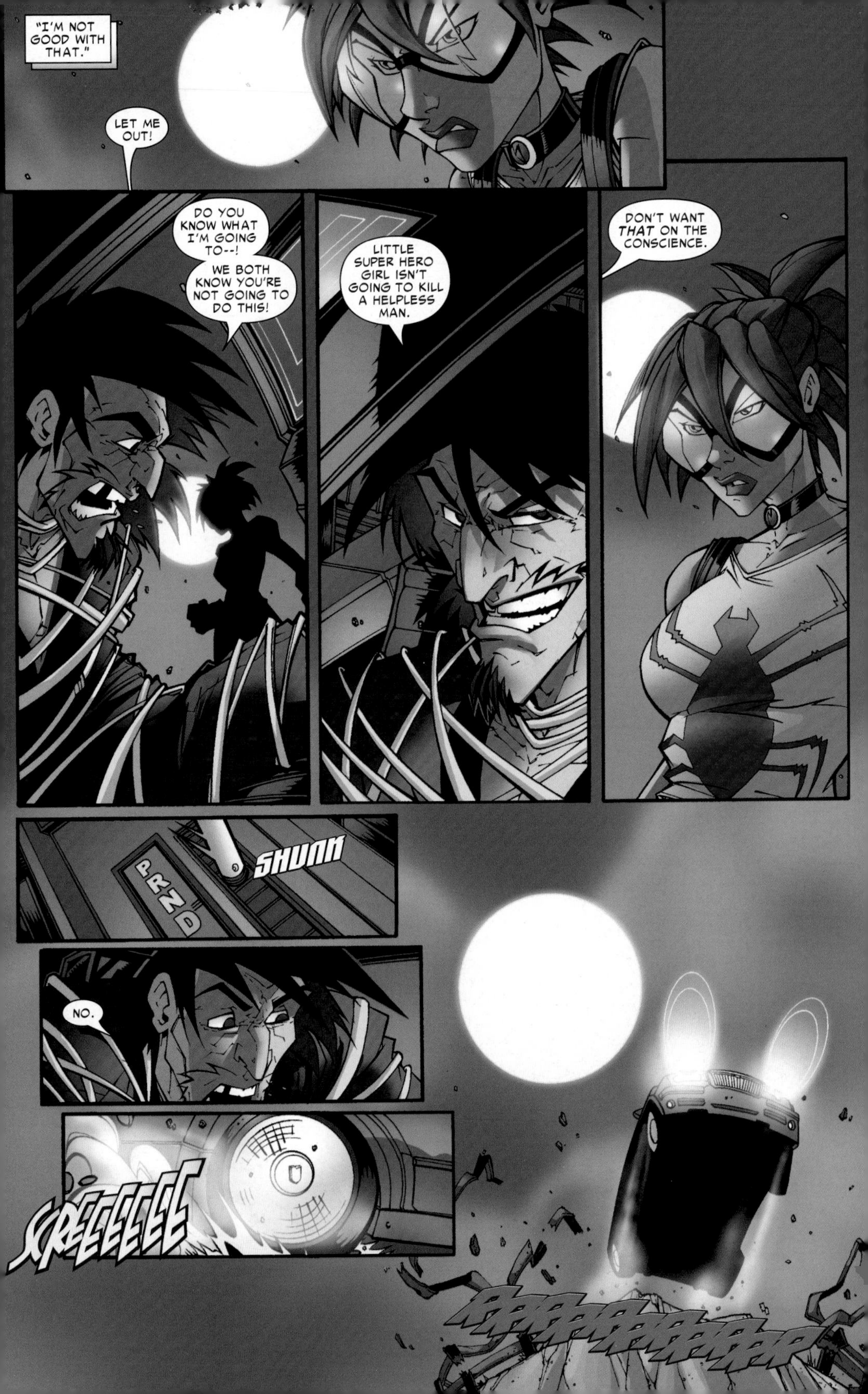
"I'M NOT GOOD WITH THAT."
LET ME OUT!
DO YOU KNOW WHAT I'M GOING TO--!
WE BOTH KNOW YOU'RE NOT GOING TO DO THIS!
LITTLE SUPER HERO GIRL ISN'T GOING TO KILL A HELPLESS MAN.
DON'T WANT *THAT* ON THE CONSCIENCE.
PRND
SHUNK
NO.
SCREEEEEEE

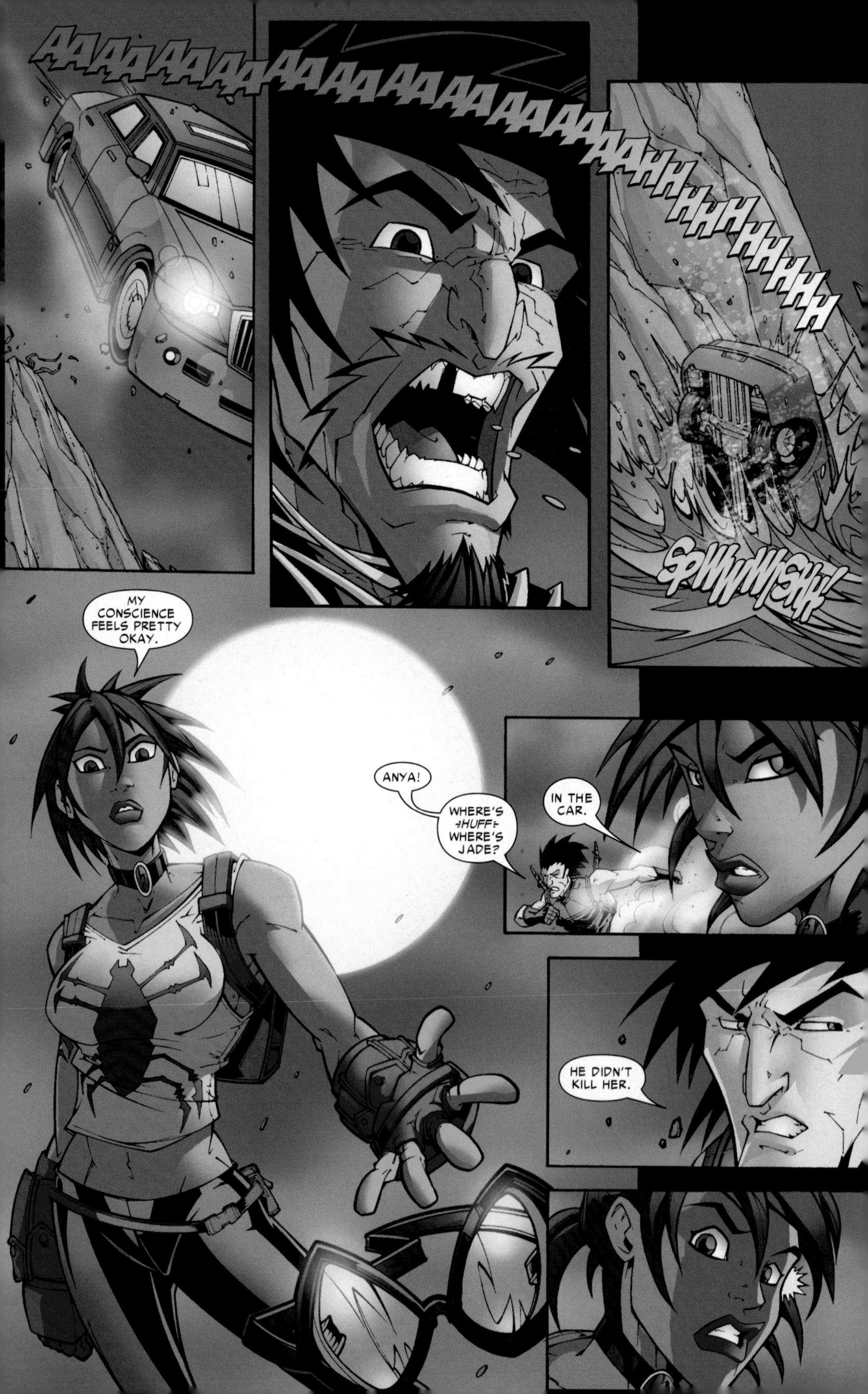
AAAAAAAAAAAAAAAAAAAAAAAAAAAAAHHHHHHHHHH
SPWWWISHH!
MY CONSCIENCE FEELS PRETTY OKAY.
ANYA!
WHERE'S -HUFF- WHERE'S JADE?
IN THE CAR.
HE DIDN'T KILL HER.

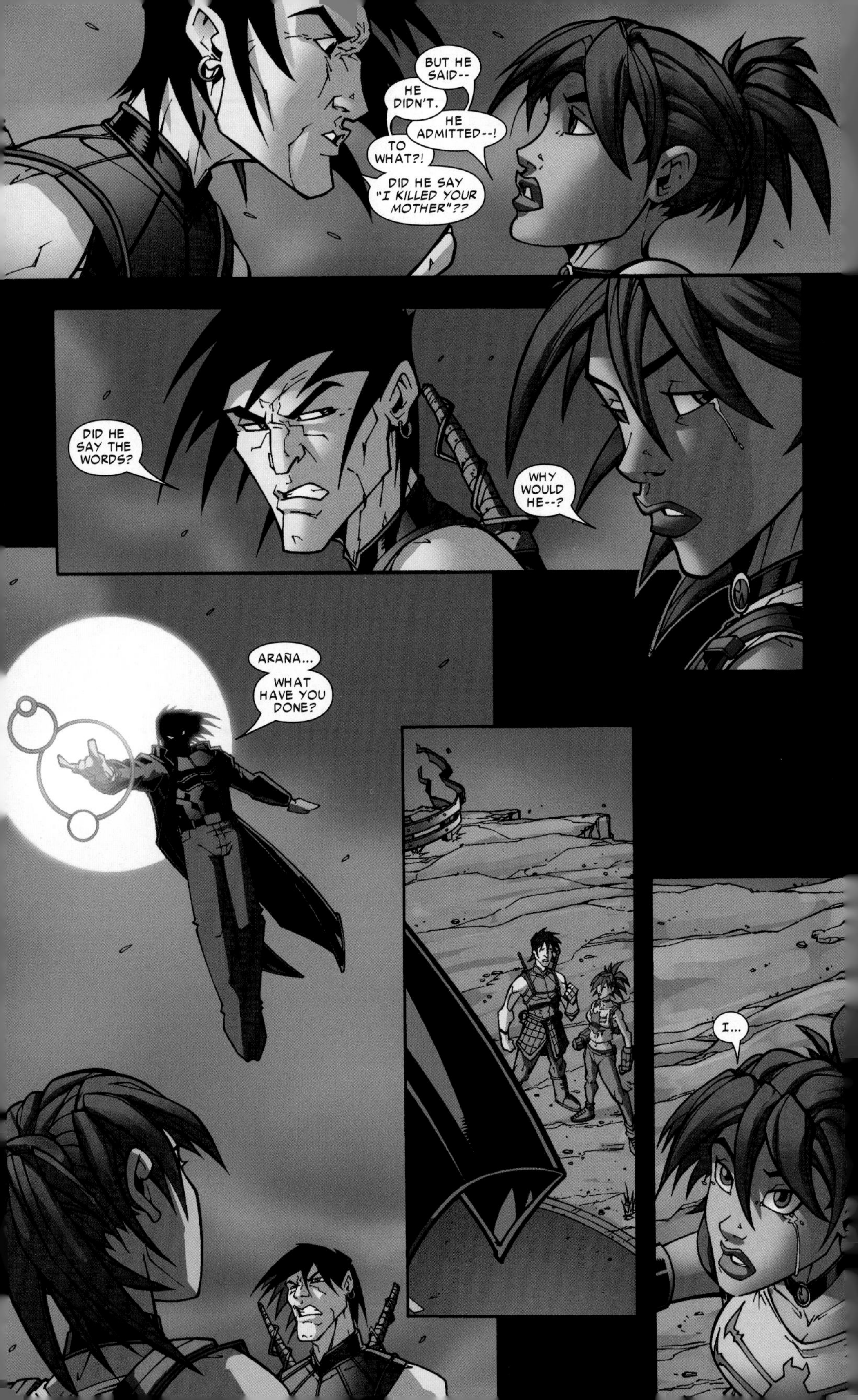
BUT HE SAID--
HE DIDN'T.
HE ADMITTED--!
TO WHAT?!
DID HE SAY "I KILLED YOUR MOTHER"??
DID HE SAY THE WORDS?
WHY WOULD HE--?
ARAÑA...
WHAT HAVE YOU DONE?
I...

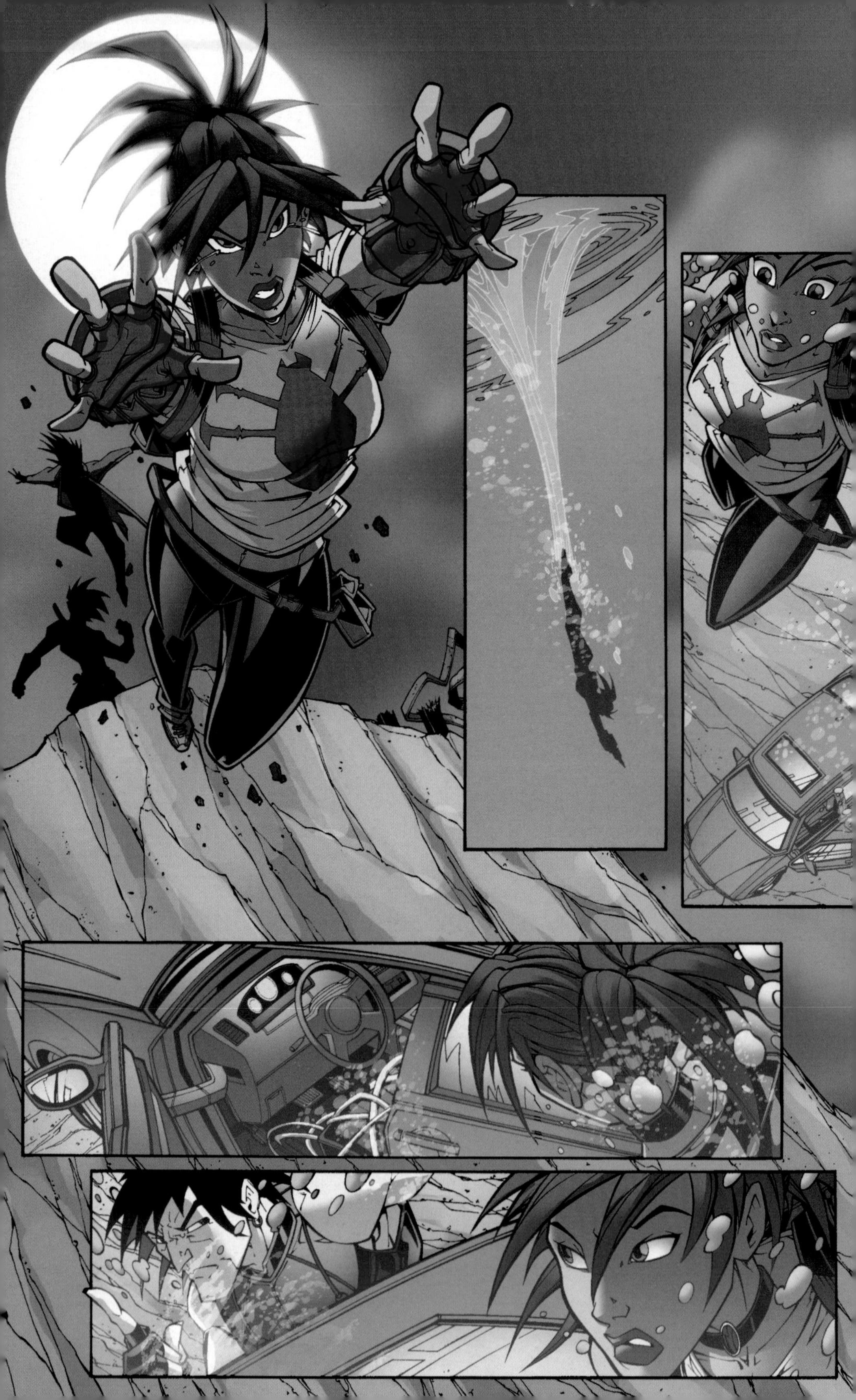

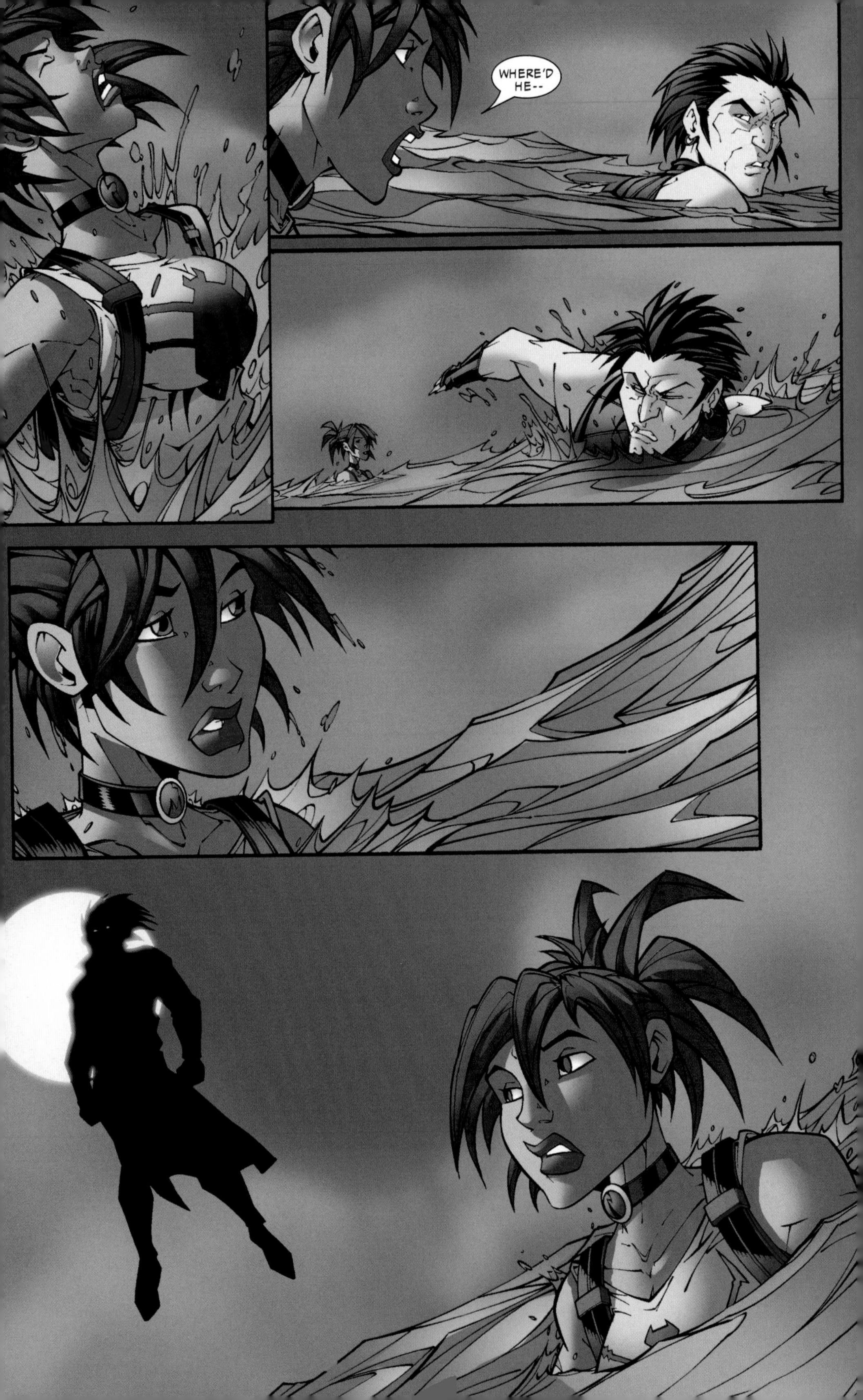
WHERE'D HE--

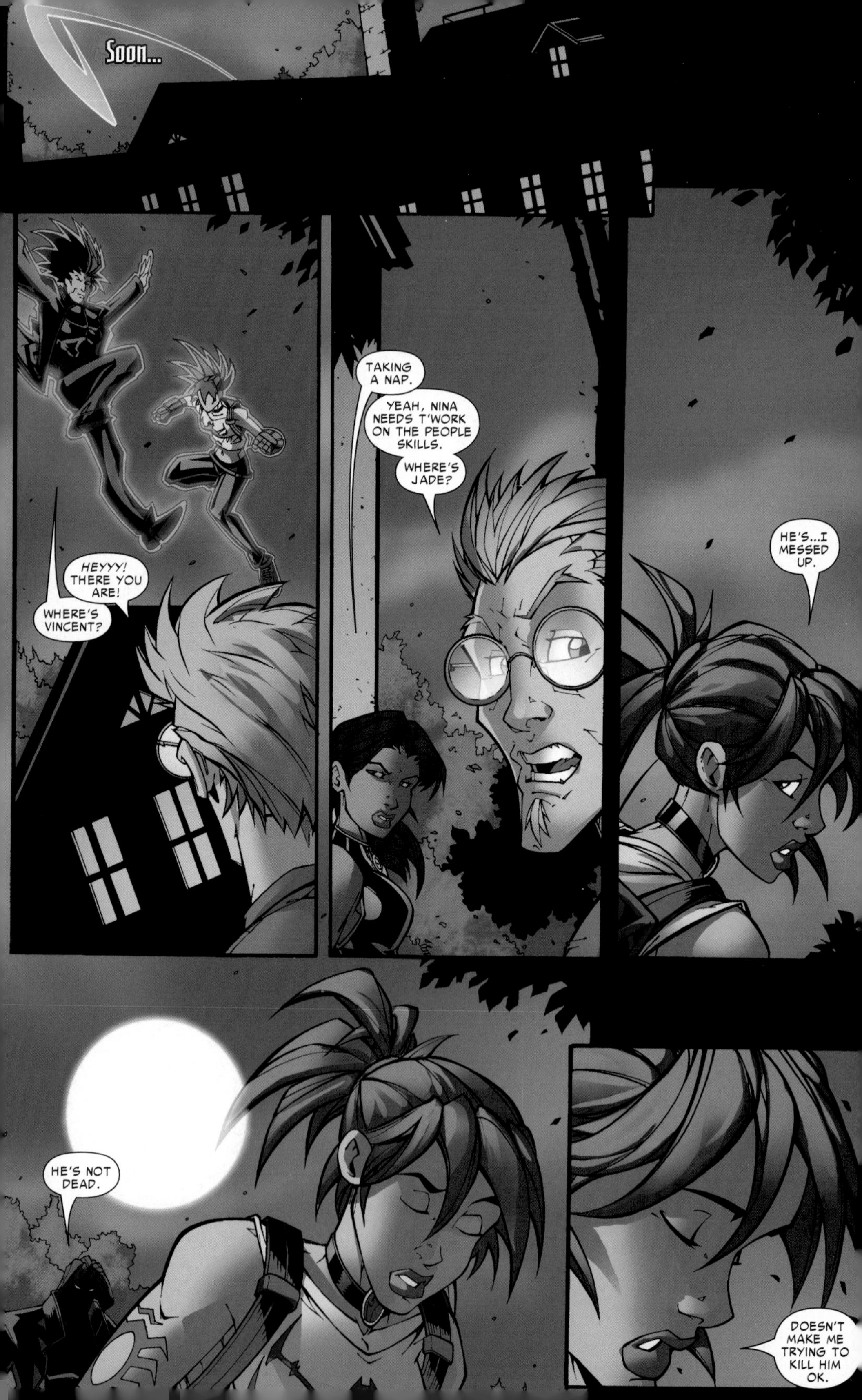
Soon...
HEYYY! THERE YOU ARE!
WHERE'S VINCENT?
TAKING A NAP.
YEAH, NINA NEEDS T'WORK ON THE PEOPLE SKILLS.
WHERE'S JADE?
HE'S...I MESSED UP.
HE'S NOT DEAD.
DOESN'T MAKE ME TRYING TO KILL HIM OK.

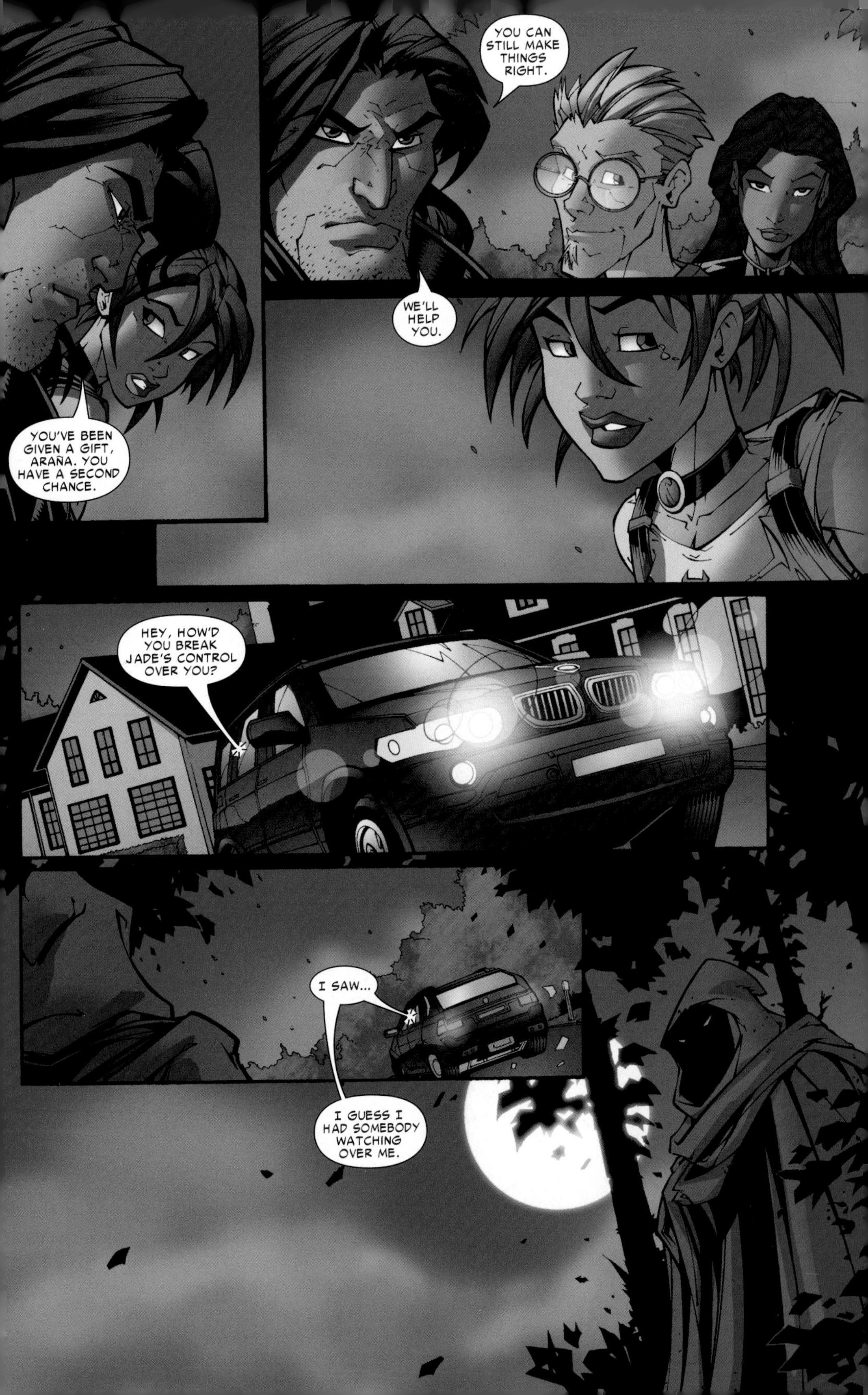
YOU'VE BEEN GIVEN A GIFT, ARAÑA. YOU HAVE A SECOND CHANCE.
YOU CAN STILL MAKE THINGS RIGHT.
WE'LL HELP YOU.
HEY, HOW'D YOU BREAK JADE'S CONTROL OVER YOU?
I SAW...
I GUESS I HAD SOMEBODY WATCHING OVER ME.

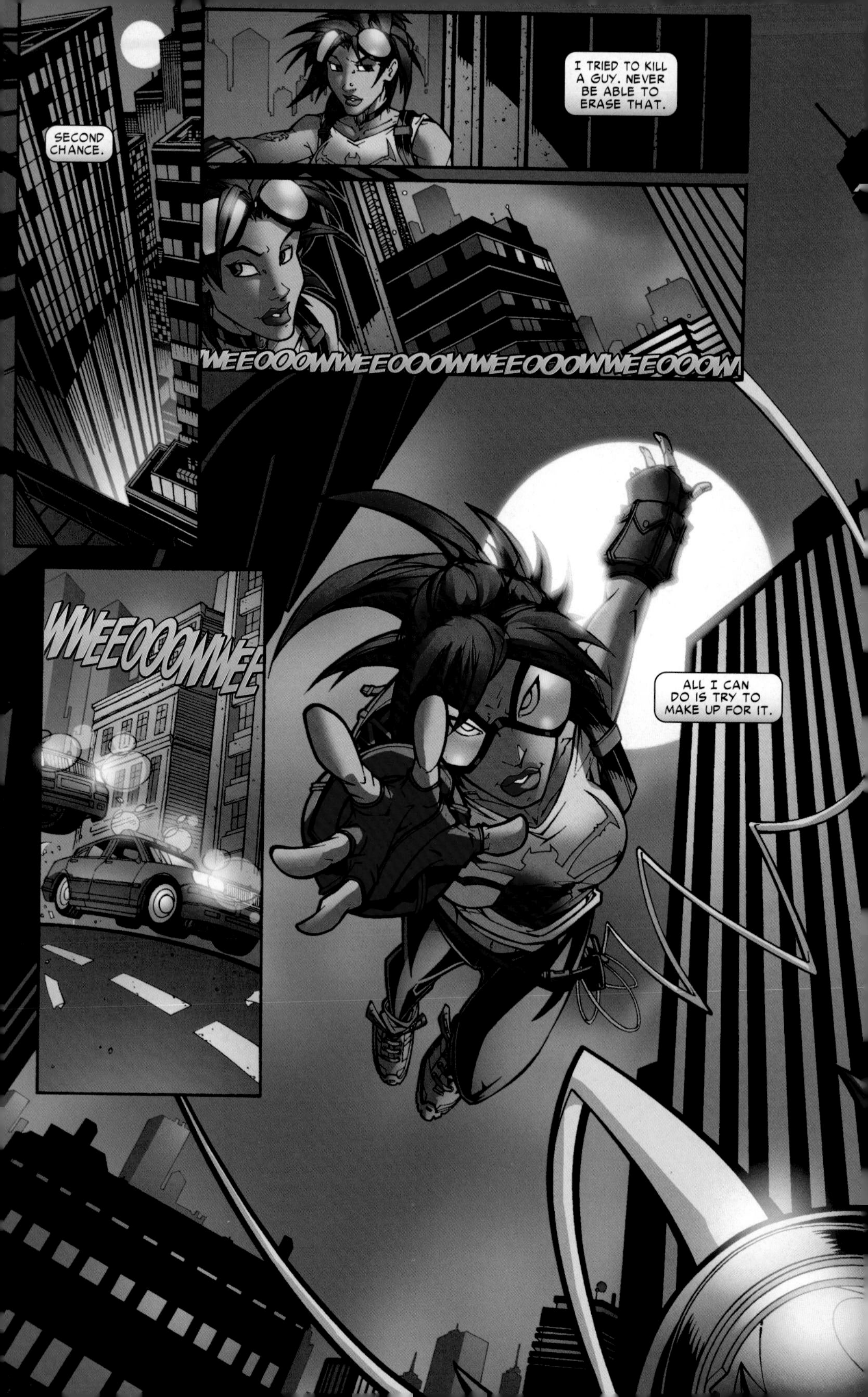
SECOND CHANCE.
I TRIED TO KILL A GUY. NEVER BE ABLE TO ERASE THAT.
WEEOOOWWEEOOOWWEEOOOWWEEOOOW
WWEEOOOWWEE
ALL I CAN DO IS TRY TO MAKE UP FOR IT.

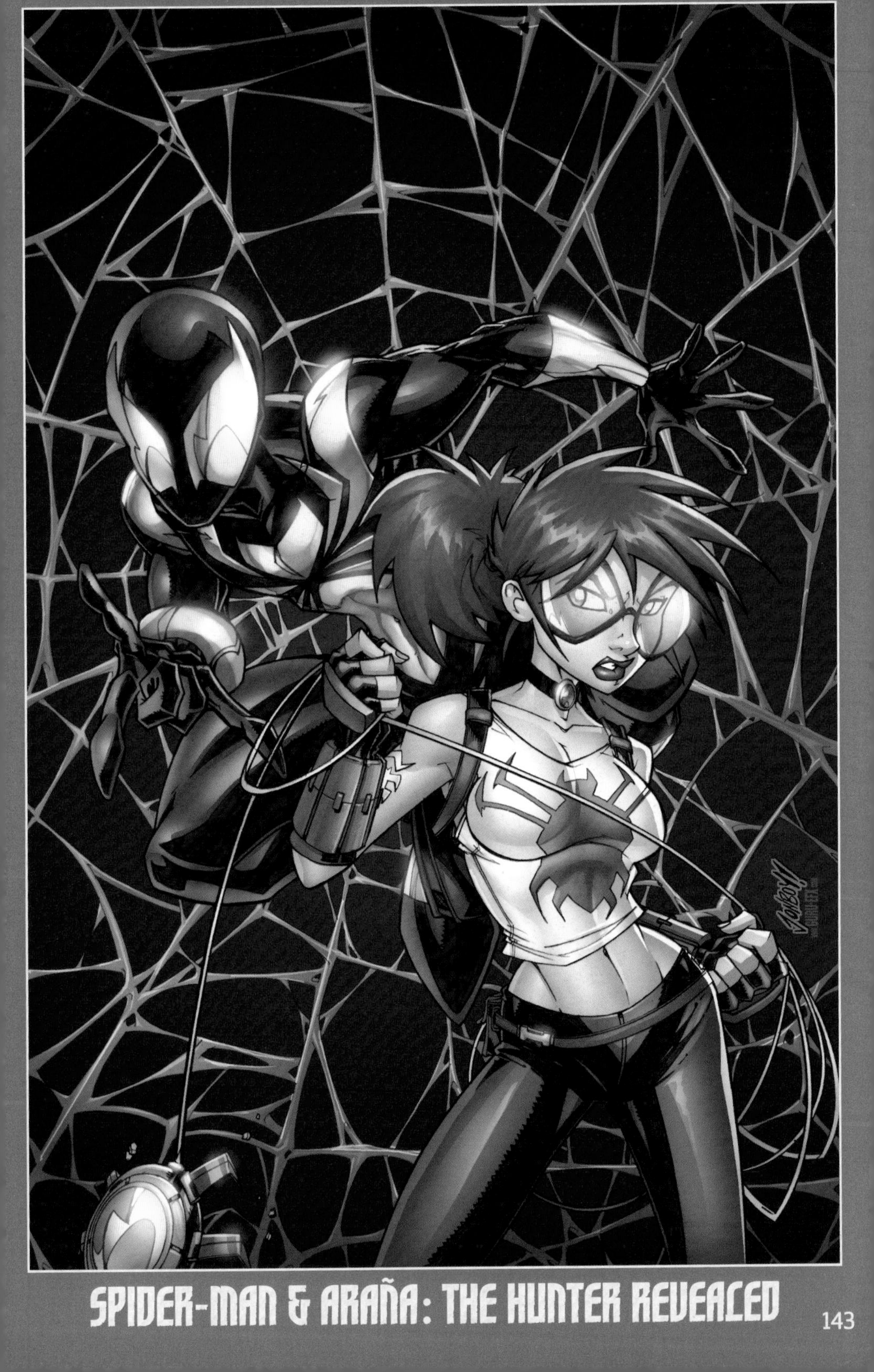

SPIDER-MAN & ARAÑA: THE HUNTER REVEALED

SPIDER-MAN & ARAÑA
THE HUNTER REVEALED

Tania Del Rio Writer
Jonboy Meyers Artist, pages 1-7, 16-38
Tania Del Rio Artist, pages 8-15
Jim Royal & Mark Irwin Inkers, pages 1-7, 16-38
Impacto Studios' Debora Carita Color Artist, pages 1-7, 16-38
Guru eFx Color, pages 8-15
VC's Randy Gentile Letterer
Jonboy Meyers & Guru eFx Cover
Byron Penaranda Title Page Art
Jacob Chabot Production
Nathan Cosby Assistant Editor
Mark Paniccia Editor
Joe Quesada Editor in Chief
Dan Buckley Publisher

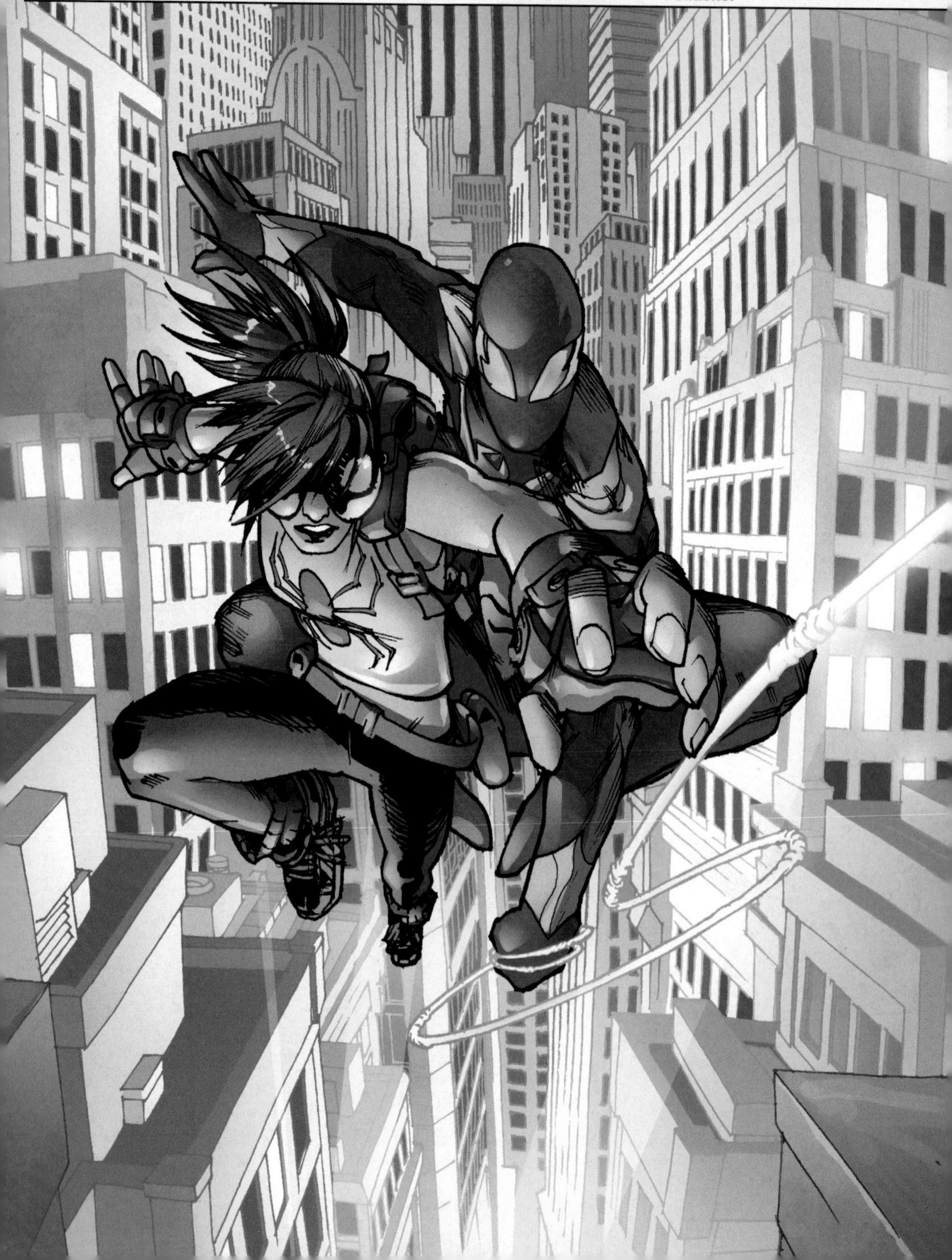

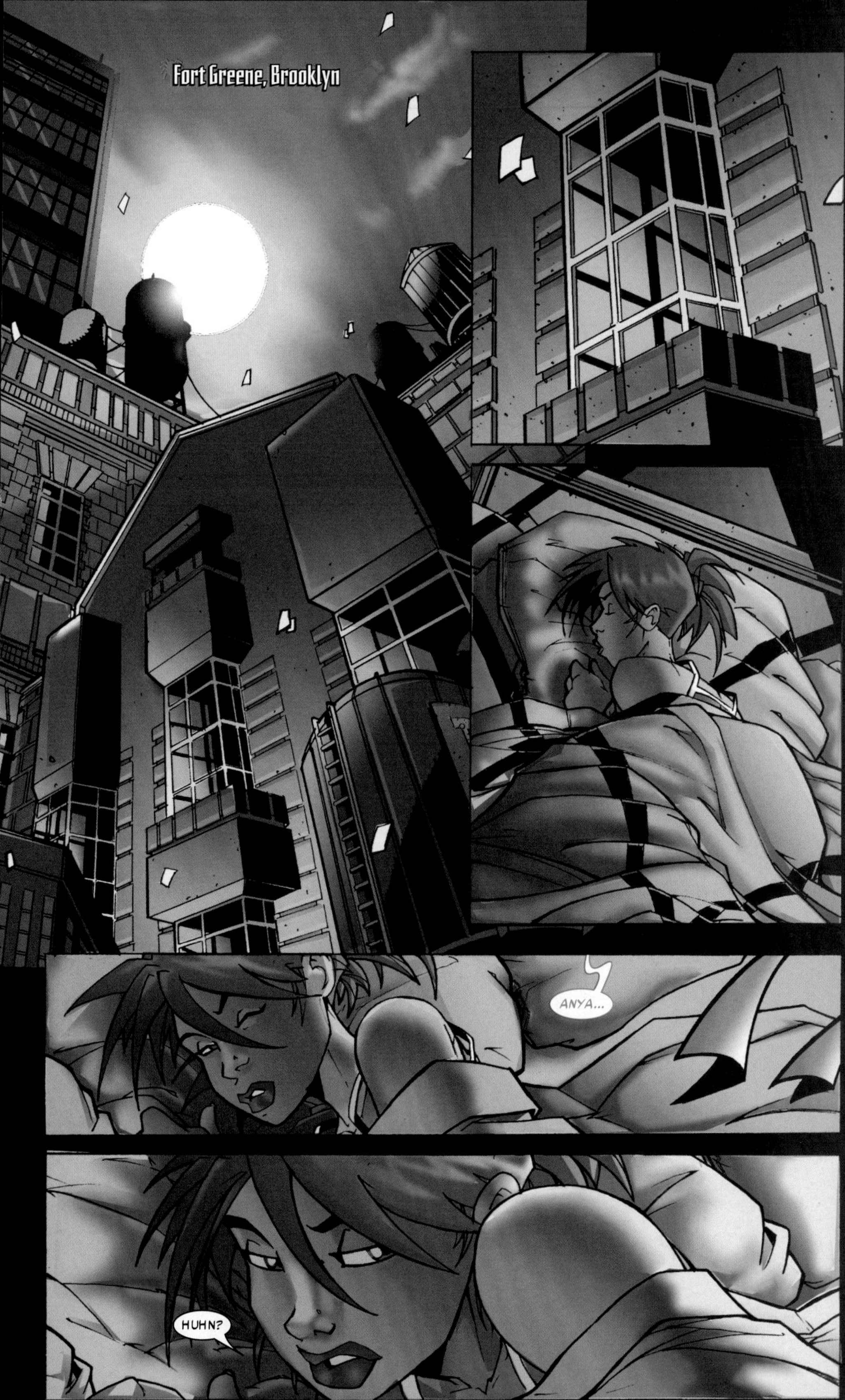
Fort Greene, Brooklyn
ANYA...
HUHN?

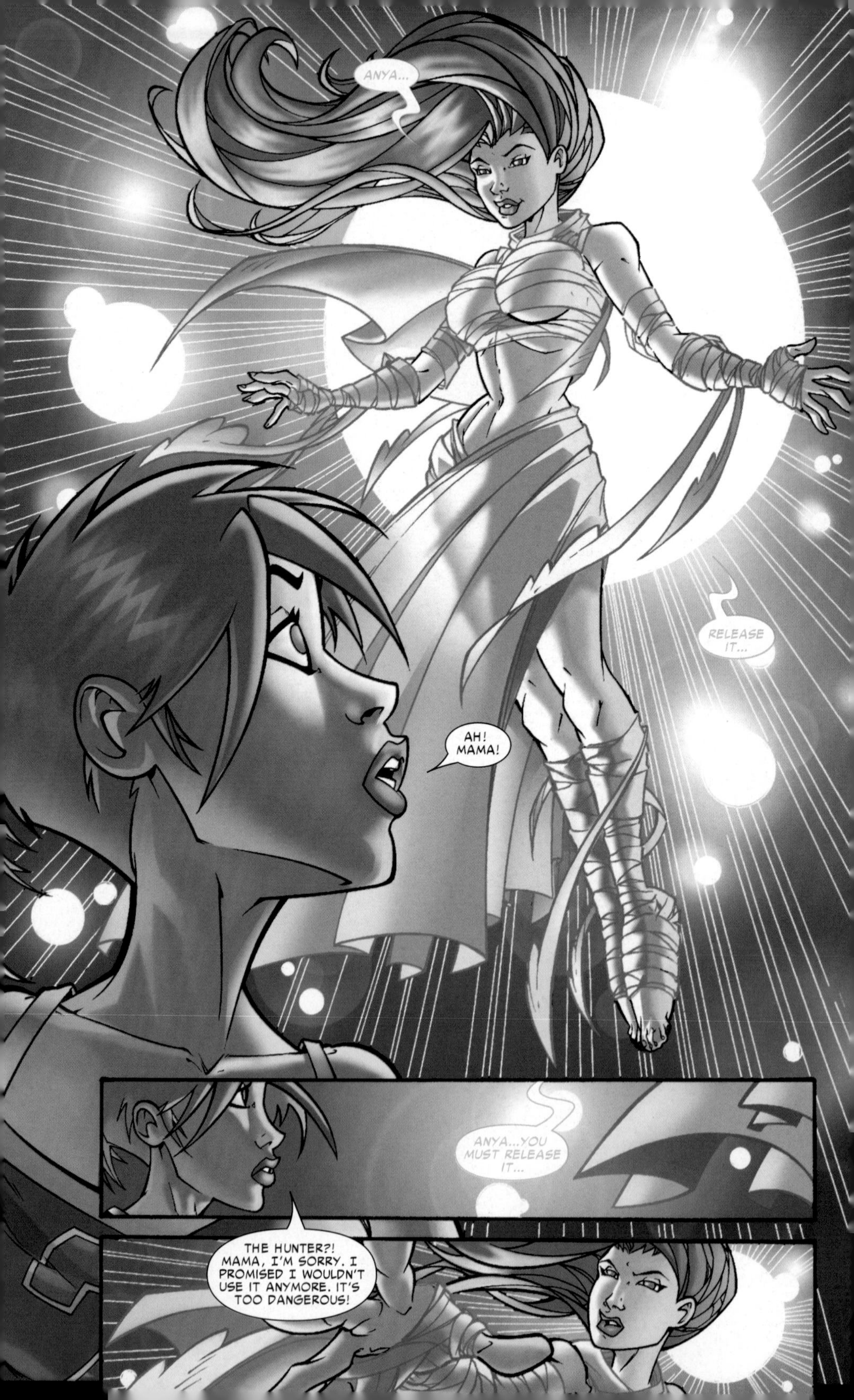
ANYA...
RELEASE IT...
AH! MAMA!
ANYA...YOU MUST RELEASE IT...
THE HUNTER?! MAMA, I'M SORRY. I PROMISED I WOULDN'T USE IT ANYMORE. IT'S TOO DANGEROUS!

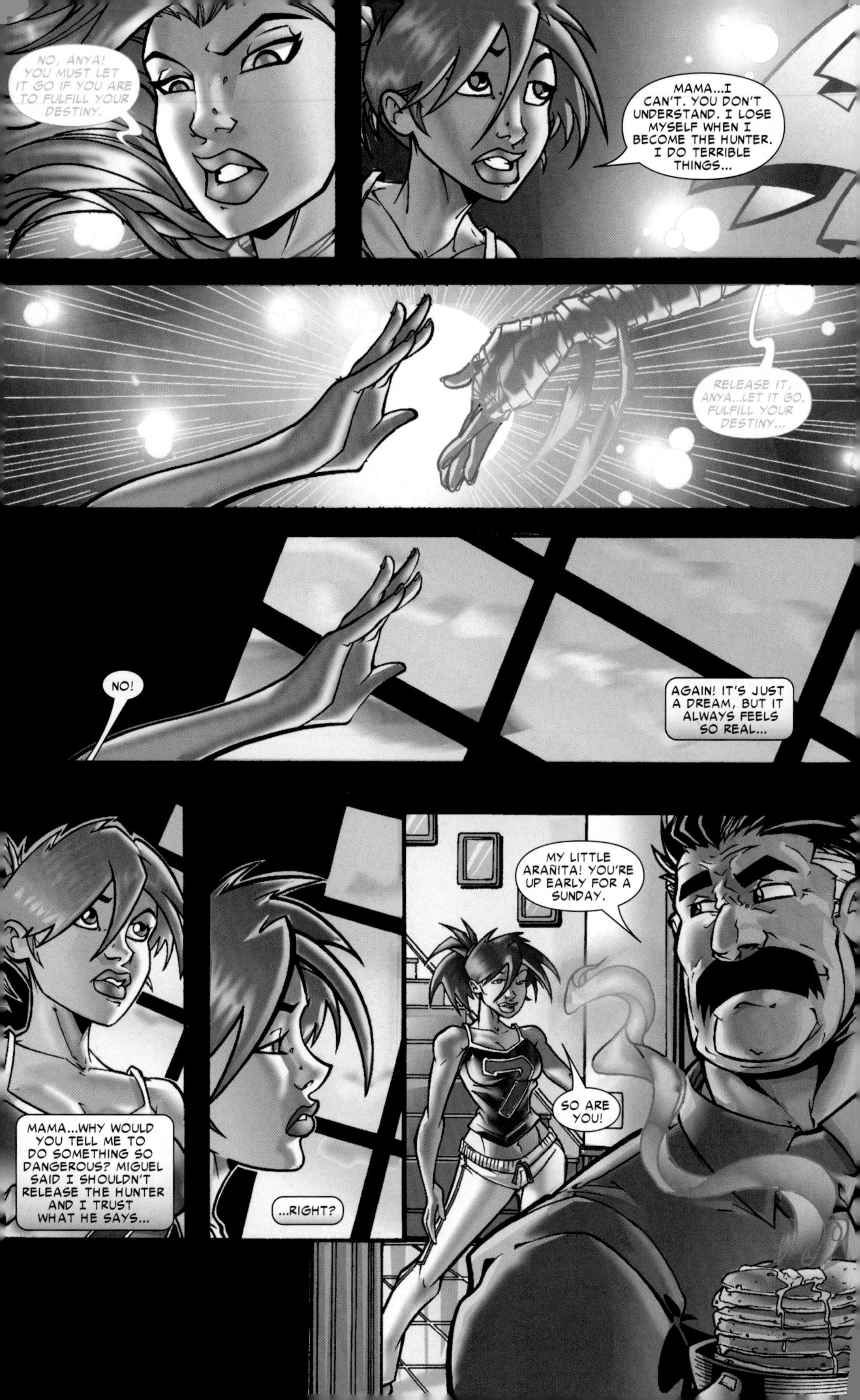
NO, ANYA! YOU MUST LET IT GO IF YOU ARE TO FULFILL YOUR DESTINY.
MAMA...I CAN'T. YOU DON'T UNDERSTAND. I LOSE MYSELF WHEN I BECOME THE HUNTER. I DO TERRIBLE THINGS...
RELEASE IT, ANYA...LET IT GO. FULFILL YOUR DESTINY...
NO!
AGAIN! IT'S JUST A DREAM, BUT IT ALWAYS FEELS SO REAL...
MAMA...WHY WOULD YOU TELL ME TO DO SOMETHING SO DANGEROUS? MIGUEL SAID I SHOULDN'T RELEASE THE HUNTER AND I TRUST WHAT HE SAYS...
...RIGHT?
MY LITTLE ARAÑITA! YOU'RE UP EARLY FOR A SUNDAY.
SO ARE YOU!

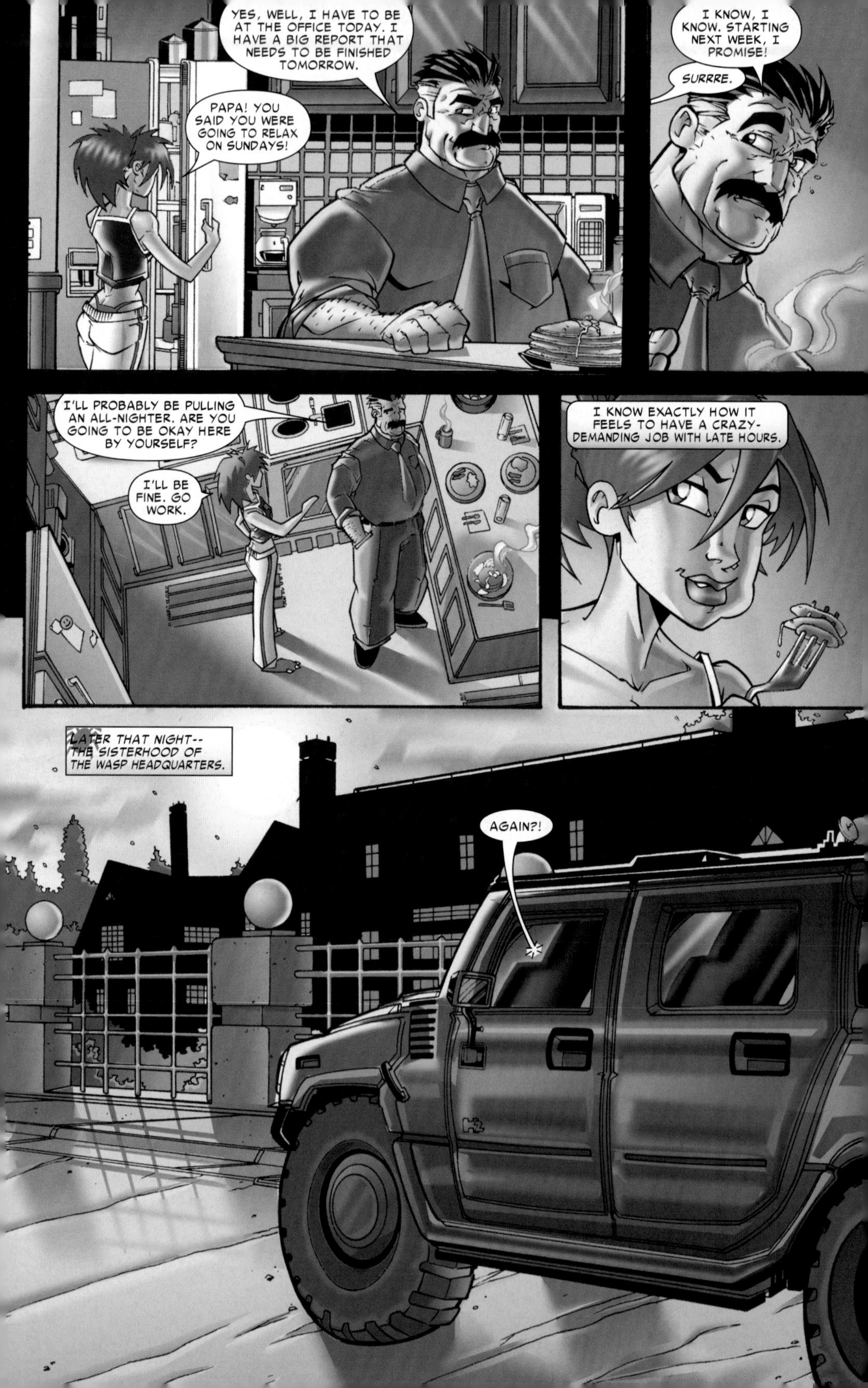

PAPA! YOU SAID YOU WERE GOING TO RELAX ON SUNDAYS!
YES, WELL, I HAVE TO BE AT THE OFFICE TODAY. I HAVE A BIG REPORT THAT NEEDS TO BE FINISHED TOMORROW.
SURRRE.
I KNOW, I KNOW. STARTING NEXT WEEK, I PROMISE!
I'LL PROBABLY BE PULLING AN ALL-NIGHTER. ARE YOU GOING TO BE OKAY HERE BY YOURSELF?
I'LL BE FINE. GO WORK.
I KNOW EXACTLY HOW IT FEELS TO HAVE A CRAZY-DEMANDING JOB WITH LATE HOURS.
LATER THAT NIGHT-- THE SISTERHOOD OF THE WASP HEADQUARTERS.
AGAIN?!

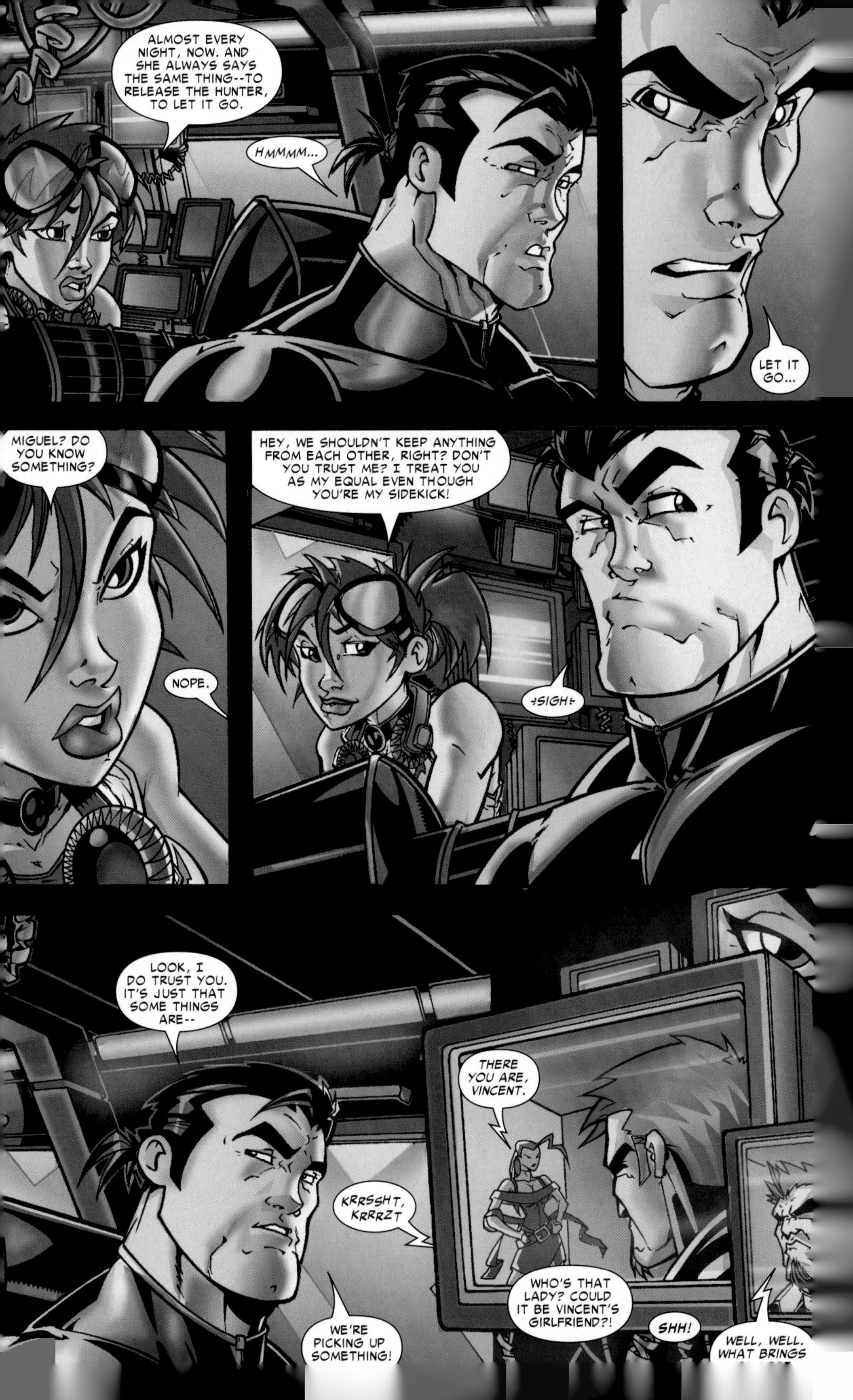
ALMOST EVERY NIGHT, NOW. AND SHE ALWAYS SAYS THE SAME THING--TO RELEASE THE HUNTER, TO LET IT GO.
HMMMM...
LET IT GO...
MIGUEL? DO YOU KNOW SOMETHING?
NOPE.
HEY, WE SHOULDN'T KEEP ANYTHING FROM EACH OTHER, RIGHT? DON'T YOU TRUST ME? I TREAT YOU AS MY EQUAL EVEN THOUGH YOU'RE MY SIDEKICK!
SIGH
LOOK, I DO TRUST YOU. IT'S JUST THAT SOME THINGS ARE--
KRRSSHT, KRRRZT
WE'RE PICKING UP SOMETHING!
THERE YOU ARE, VINCENT.
WHO'S THAT LADY? COULD IT BE VINCENT'S GIRLFRIEND?!
SHH!
WELL, WELL. WHAT BRINGS

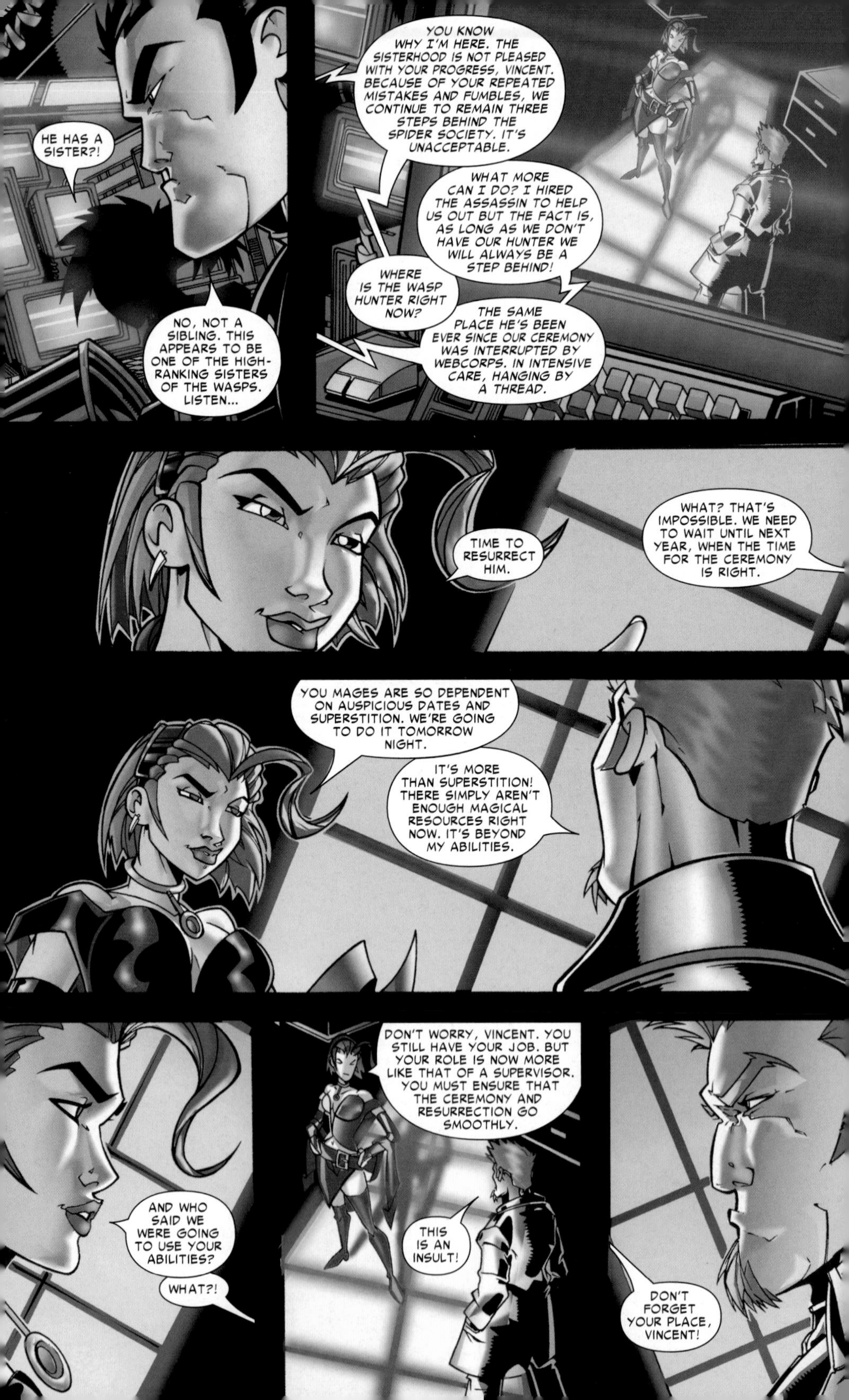
HE HAS A SISTER?!
NO, NOT A SIBLING. THIS APPEARS TO BE ONE OF THE HIGH-RANKING SISTERS OF THE WASPS. LISTEN...
YOU KNOW WHY I'M HERE. THE SISTERHOOD IS NOT PLEASED WITH YOUR PROGRESS, VINCENT. BECAUSE OF YOUR REPEATED MISTAKES AND FUMBLES, WE CONTINUE TO REMAIN THREE STEPS BEHIND THE SPIDER SOCIETY. IT'S UNACCEPTABLE.
WHAT MORE CAN I DO? I HIRED THE ASSASSIN TO HELP US OUT BUT THE FACT IS, AS LONG AS WE DON'T HAVE OUR HUNTER WE WILL ALWAYS BE A STEP BEHIND!
WHERE IS THE WASP HUNTER RIGHT NOW?
THE SAME PLACE HE'S BEEN EVER SINCE OUR CEREMONY WAS INTERRUPTED BY WEBCORPS. IN INTENSIVE CARE, HANGING BY A THREAD.
TIME TO RESURRECT HIM.
WHAT? THAT'S IMPOSSIBLE. WE NEED TO WAIT UNTIL NEXT YEAR, WHEN THE TIME FOR THE CEREMONY IS RIGHT.
YOU MAGES ARE SO DEPENDENT ON AUSPICIOUS DATES AND SUPERSTITION. WE'RE GOING TO DO IT TOMORROW NIGHT.
IT'S MORE THAN SUPERSTITION! THERE SIMPLY AREN'T ENOUGH MAGICAL RESOURCES RIGHT NOW. IT'S BEYOND MY ABILITIES.
AND WHO SAID WE WERE GOING TO USE YOUR ABILITIES?
WHAT?!
DON'T WORRY, VINCENT. YOU STILL HAVE YOUR JOB. BUT YOUR ROLE IS NOW MORE LIKE THAT OF A SUPERVISOR. YOU MUST ENSURE THAT THE CEREMONY AND RESURRECTION GO SMOOTHLY.
THIS IS AN INSULT!
DON'T FORGET YOUR PLACE, VINCENT!

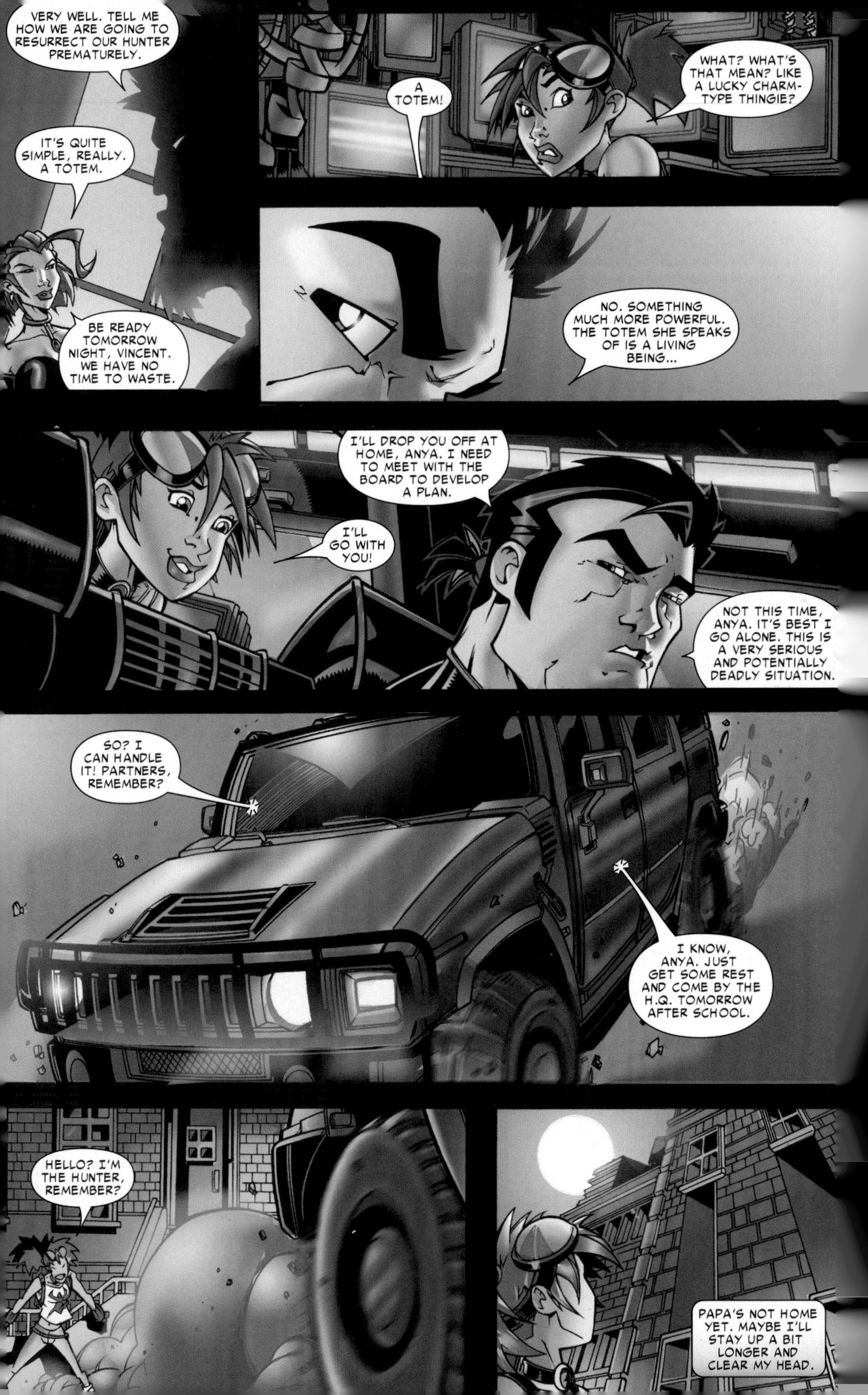
VERY WELL. TELL ME HOW WE ARE GOING TO RESURRECT OUR HUNTER PREMATURELY.
IT'S QUITE SIMPLE, REALLY. A TOTEM.
A TOTEM!
WHAT? WHAT'S THAT MEAN? LIKE A LUCKY CHARM-TYPE THINGIE?
BE READY TOMORROW NIGHT, VINCENT. WE HAVE NO TIME TO WASTE.
NO. SOMETHING MUCH MORE POWERFUL. THE TOTEM SHE SPEAKS OF IS A LIVING BEING...
I'LL DROP YOU OFF AT HOME, ANYA. I NEED TO MEET WITH THE BOARD TO DEVELOP A PLAN.
I'LL GO WITH YOU!
NOT THIS TIME, ANYA. IT'S BEST I GO ALONE. THIS IS A VERY SERIOUS AND POTENTIALLY DEADLY SITUATION.
SO? I CAN HANDLE IT! PARTNERS, REMEMBER?
I KNOW, ANYA. JUST GET SOME REST AND COME BY THE H.Q. TOMORROW AFTER SCHOOL.
HELLO? I'M THE HUNTER, REMEMBER?
PAPA'S NOT HOME YET. MAYBE I'LL STAY UP A BIT LONGER AND CLEAR MY HEAD.

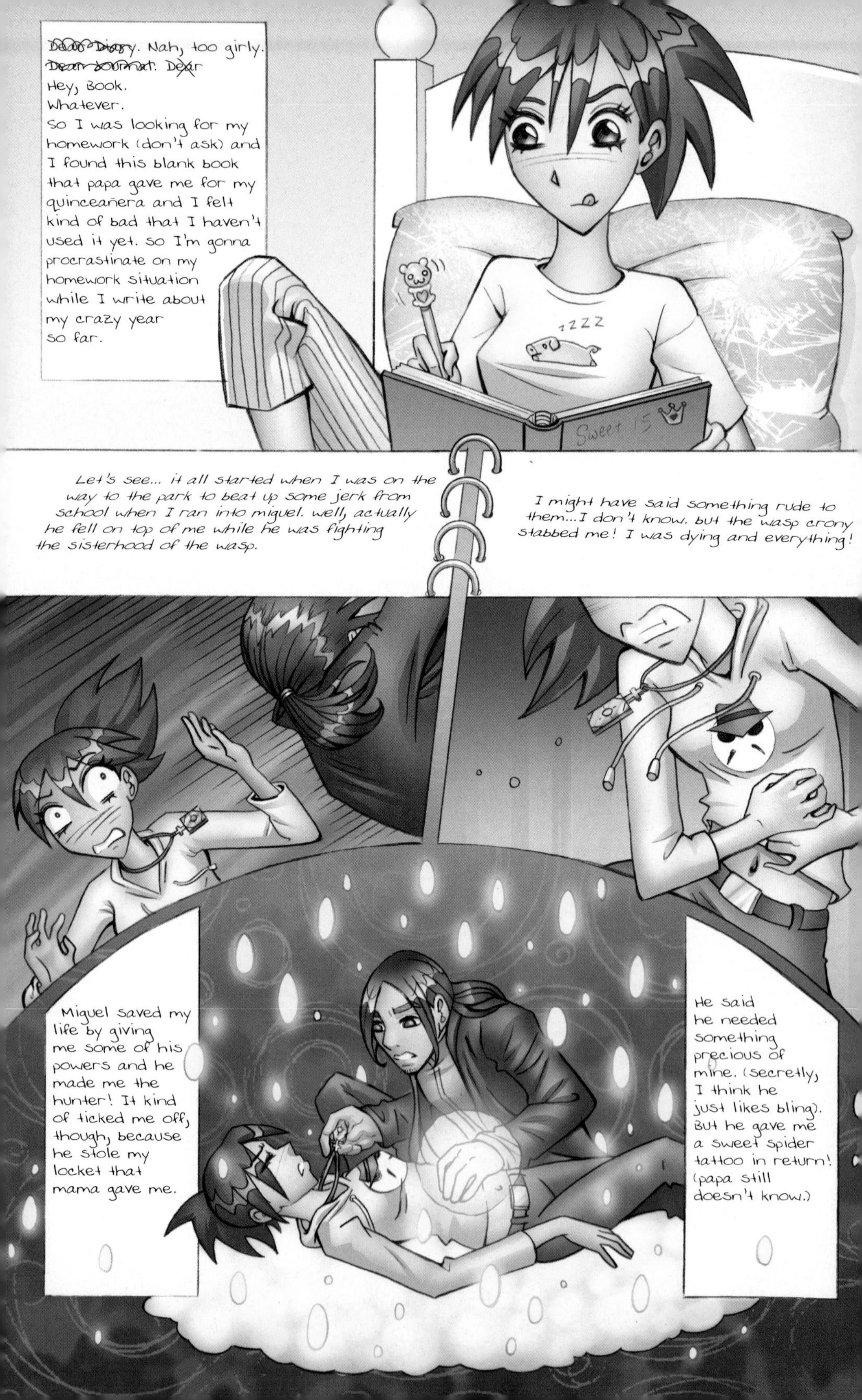
~~Dear Diary~~. Nah, too girly. ~~Dear Journal~~. ~~Dear~~
Hey, Book.
Whatever.
So I was looking for my homework (don't ask) and I found this blank book that papa gave me for my quinceañera and I felt kind of bad that I haven't used it yet. So I'm gonna procrastinate on my homework situation while I write about my crazy year so far.
Sweet 15
Let's see... it all started when I was on the way to the park to beat up some jerk from school when I ran into miguel. well, actually he fell on top of me while he was fighting the sisterhood of the wasp.
I might have said something rude to them...I don't know. but the wasp crony stabbed me! I was dying and everything!
Miguel saved my life by giving me some of his powers and he made me the hunter! It kind of ticked me off, though, because he stole my locket that mama gave me.
He said he needed something precious of mine. (secretly, I think he just likes bling). But he gave me a sweet spider tattoo in return! (papa still doesn't know.)

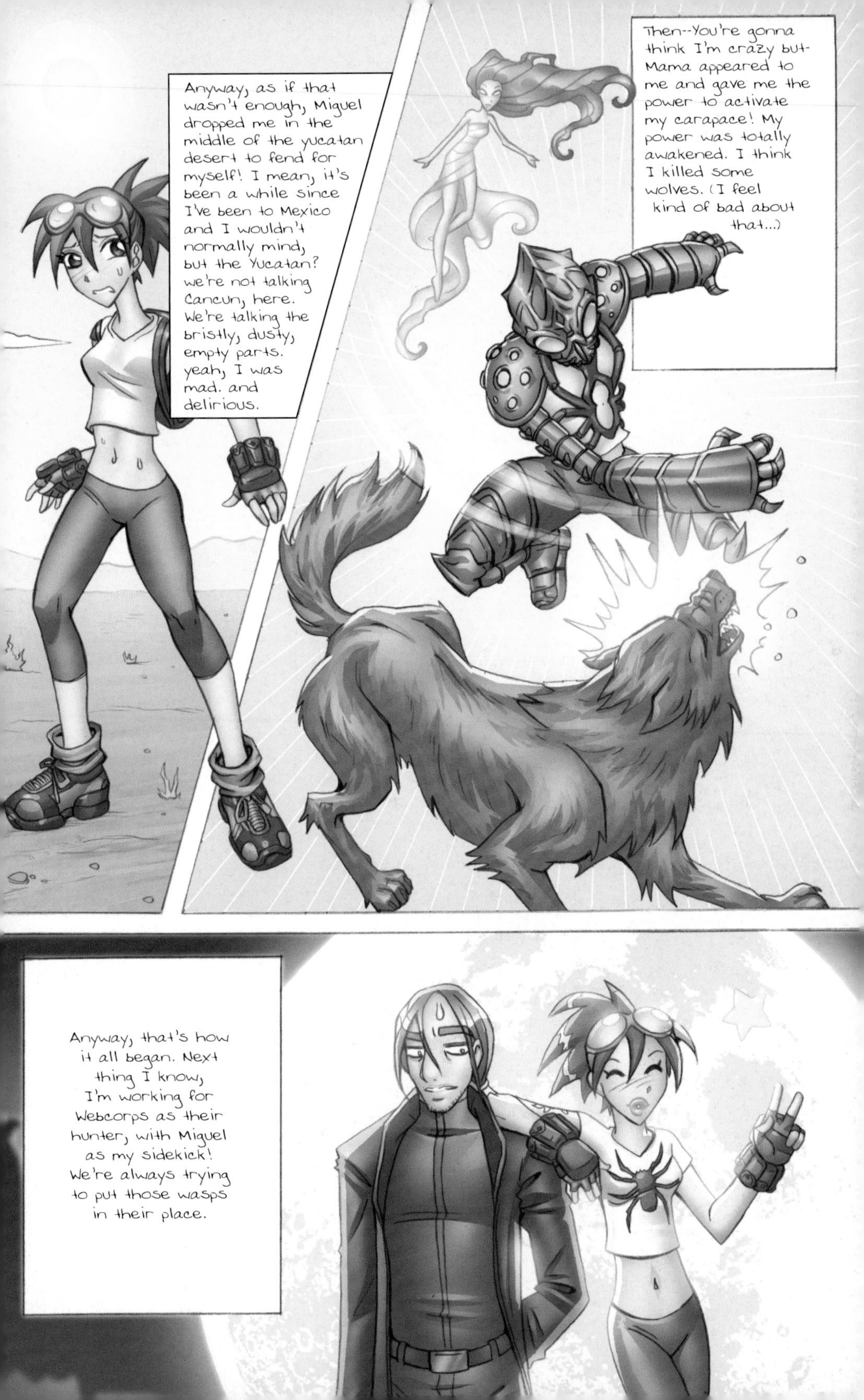
Anyway, as if that wasn't enough, Miguel dropped me in the middle of the yucatan desert to fend for myself! I mean, it's been a while since I've been to Mexico and I wouldn't normally mind, but the Yucatan? we're not talking Cancun, here. We're talking the bristly, dusty, empty parts. yeah, I was mad. and delirious.
Then--You're gonna think I'm crazy but-Mama appeared to me and gave me the power to activate my carapace! My power was totally awakened. I think I killed some wolves. (I feel kind of bad about that...)
Anyway, that's how it all began. Next thing I know, I'm working for Webcorps as their hunter, with Miguel as my sidekick! We're always trying to put those wasps in their place.

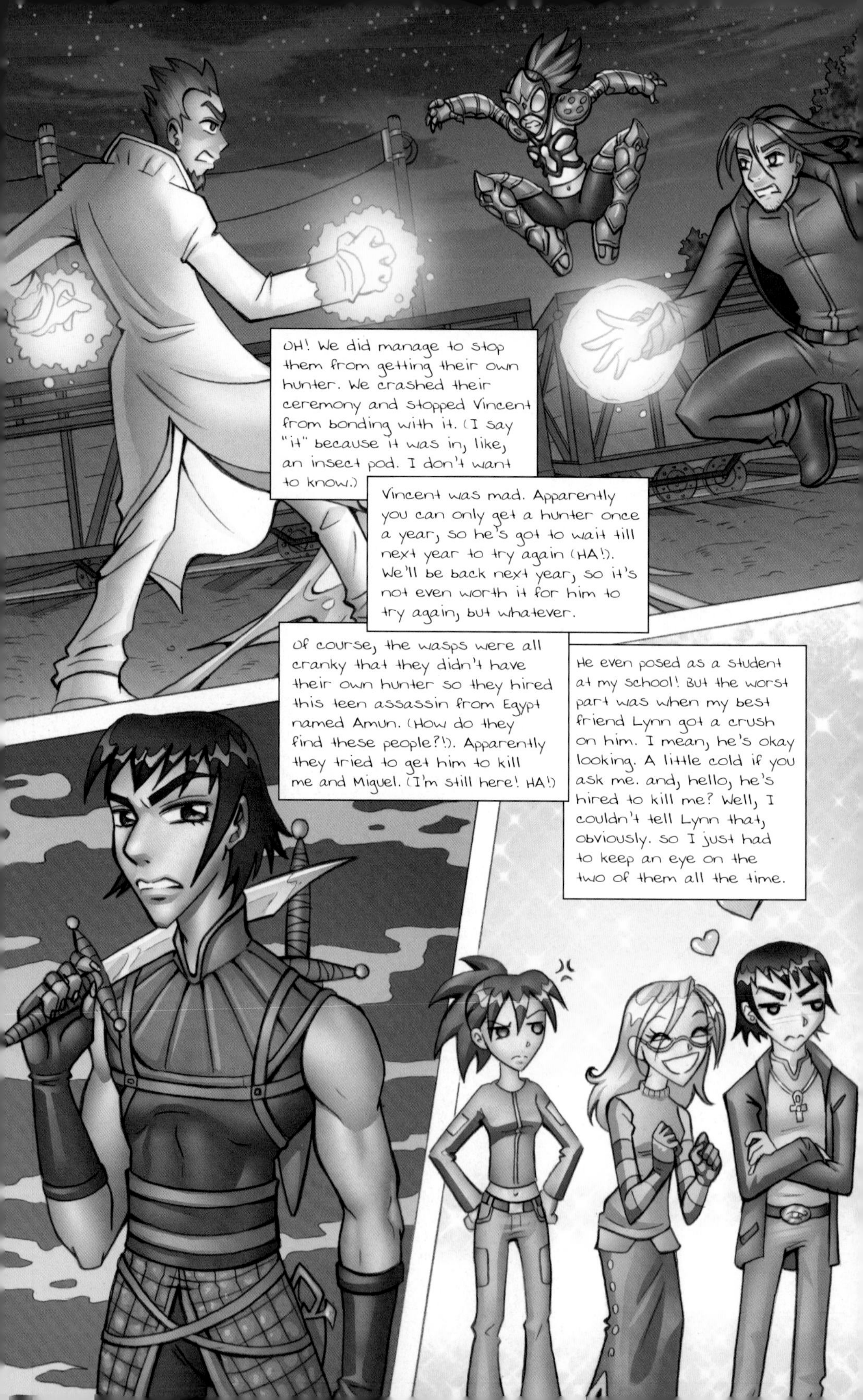
OH! We did manage to stop them from getting their own hunter. We crashed their ceremony and stopped Vincent from bonding with it. (I say "it" because it was in, like, an insect pod. I don't want to know.)
Vincent was mad. Apparently you can only get a hunter once a year, so he's got to wait till next year to try again (HA!). We'll be back next year, so it's not even worth it for him to try again, but whatever.
Of course, the wasps were all cranky that they didn't have their own hunter so they hired this teen assassin from Egypt named Amun. (How do they find these people?!). Apparently they tried to get him to kill me and Miguel. (I'm still here! HA!)
He even posed as a student at my school! But the worst part was when my best friend Lynn got a crush on him. I mean, he's okay looking. A little cold if you ask me. and, hello, he's hired to kill me? Well, I couldn't tell Lynn that, obviously. so I just had to keep an eye on the two of them all the time.

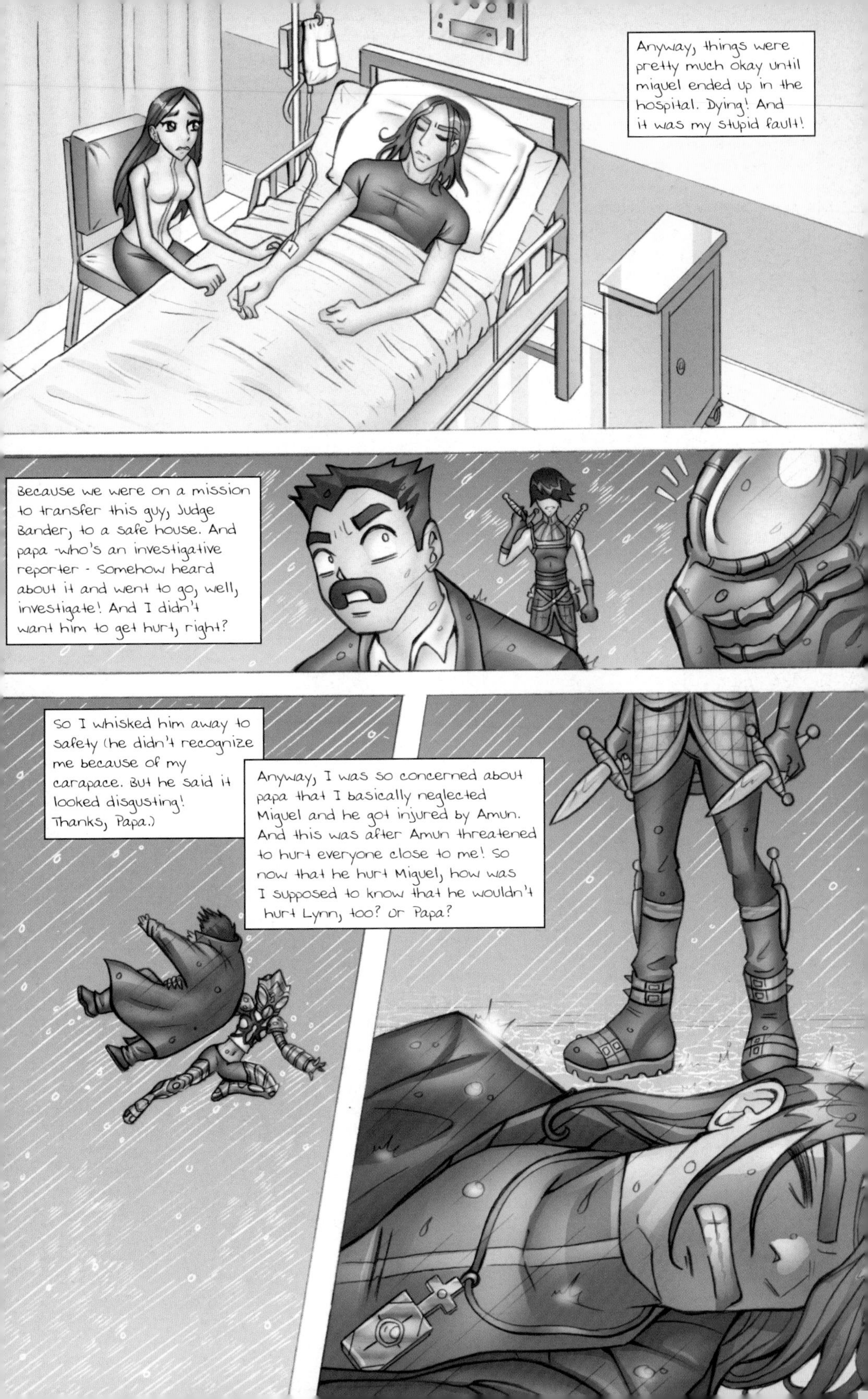
Anyway, things were pretty much okay until miguel ended up in the hospital. Dying! And it was my stupid fault!
Because we were on a mission to transfer this guy, Judge Bander, to a safe house. And papa -who's an investigative reporter - Somehow heard about it and went to go, well, investigate! And I didn't want him to get hurt, right?
So I whisked him away to safety (he didn't recognize me because of my carapace. But he said it looked disgusting! Thanks, Papa.)
Anyway, I was so concerned about papa that I basically neglected Miguel and he got injured by Amun. And this was after Amun threatened to hurt everyone close to me! So now that he hurt Miguel, how was I supposed to know that he wouldn't hurt Lynn, too? Or Papa?

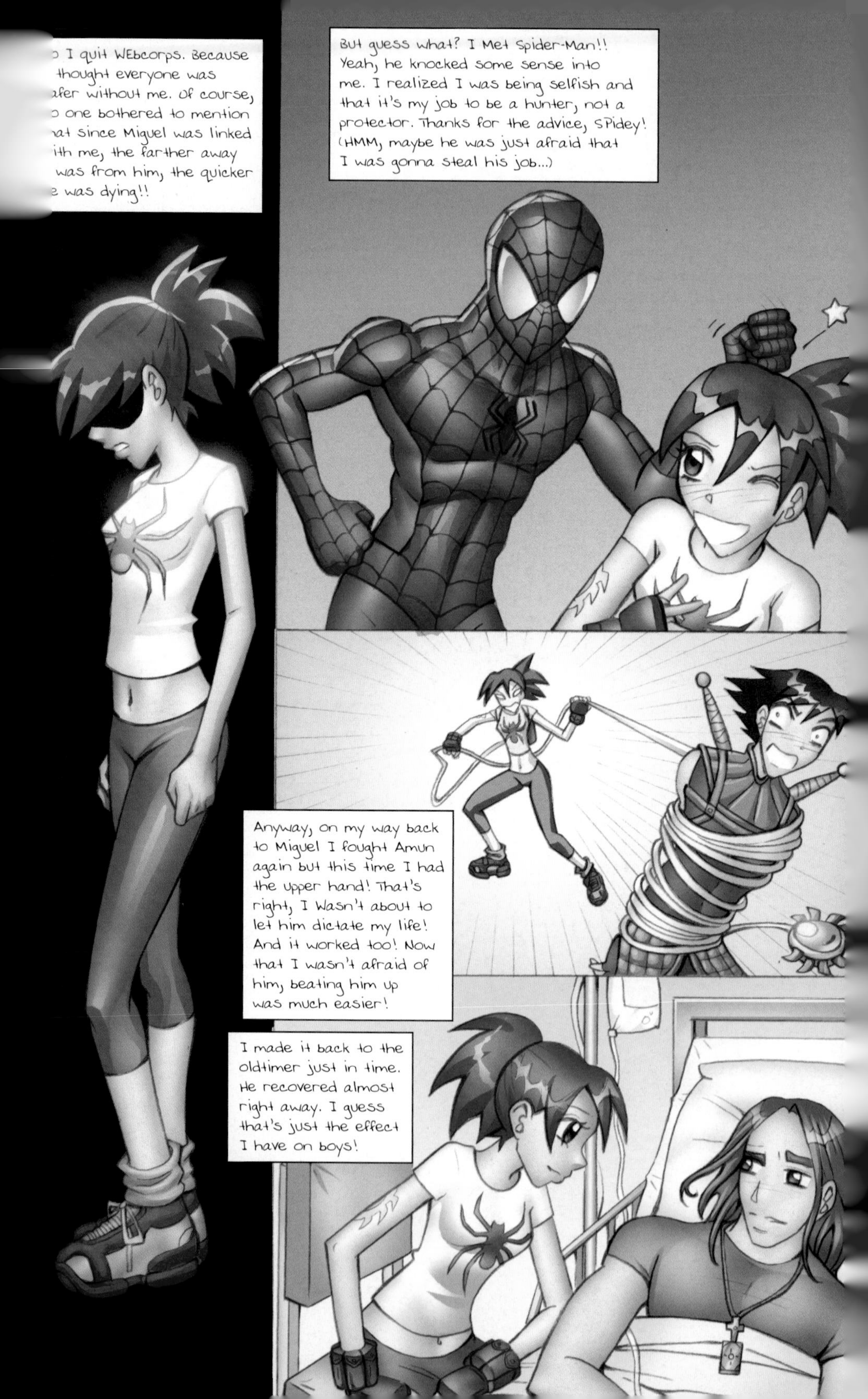
o I quit WEbcorps. Because thought everyone was safer without me. Of course, o one bothered to mention hat since Miguel was linked ith me, the farther away was from him, the quicker e was dying!!
But guess what? I Met Spider-Man!! Yeah, he knocked some sense into me. I realized I was being selfish and that it's my job to be a hunter, not a protector. Thanks for the advice, SPidey! (HMM, maybe he was just afraid that I was gonna steal his job...)
Anyway, on my way back to Miguel I fought Amun again but this time I had the upper hand! That's right, I Wasn't about to let him dictate my life! And it worked too! Now that I wasn't afraid of him, beating him up was much easier!
I made it back to the oldtimer just in time. He recovered almost right away. I guess that's just the effect I have on boys!

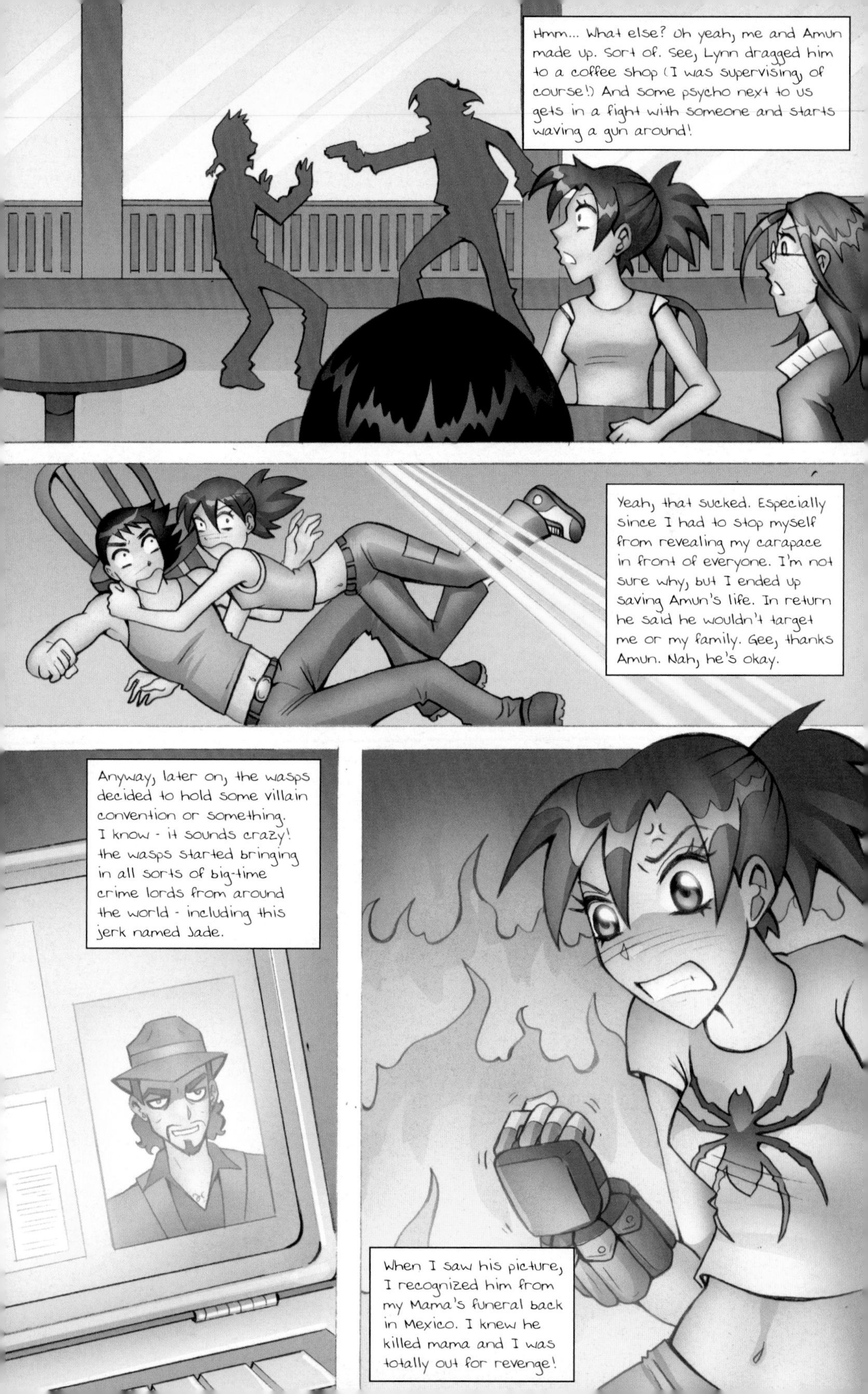
Hmm... What else? Oh yeah, me and Amun made up. Sort of. See, Lynn dragged him to a coffee shop (I was supervising, of course!) And some psycho next to us gets in a fight with someone and starts waving a gun around!
Yeah, that sucked. Especially since I had to stop myself from revealing my carapace in front of everyone. I'm not sure why, but I ended up saving Amun's life. In return he said he wouldn't target me or my family. Gee, thanks Amun. Nah, he's okay.
Anyway, later on, the wasps decided to hold some villain convention or something. I know - it sounds crazy! the wasps started bringing in all sorts of big-time crime lords from around the world - including this jerk named Jade.
When I saw his picture, I recognized him from my Mama's funeral back in Mexico. I knew he killed mama and I was totally out for revenge!

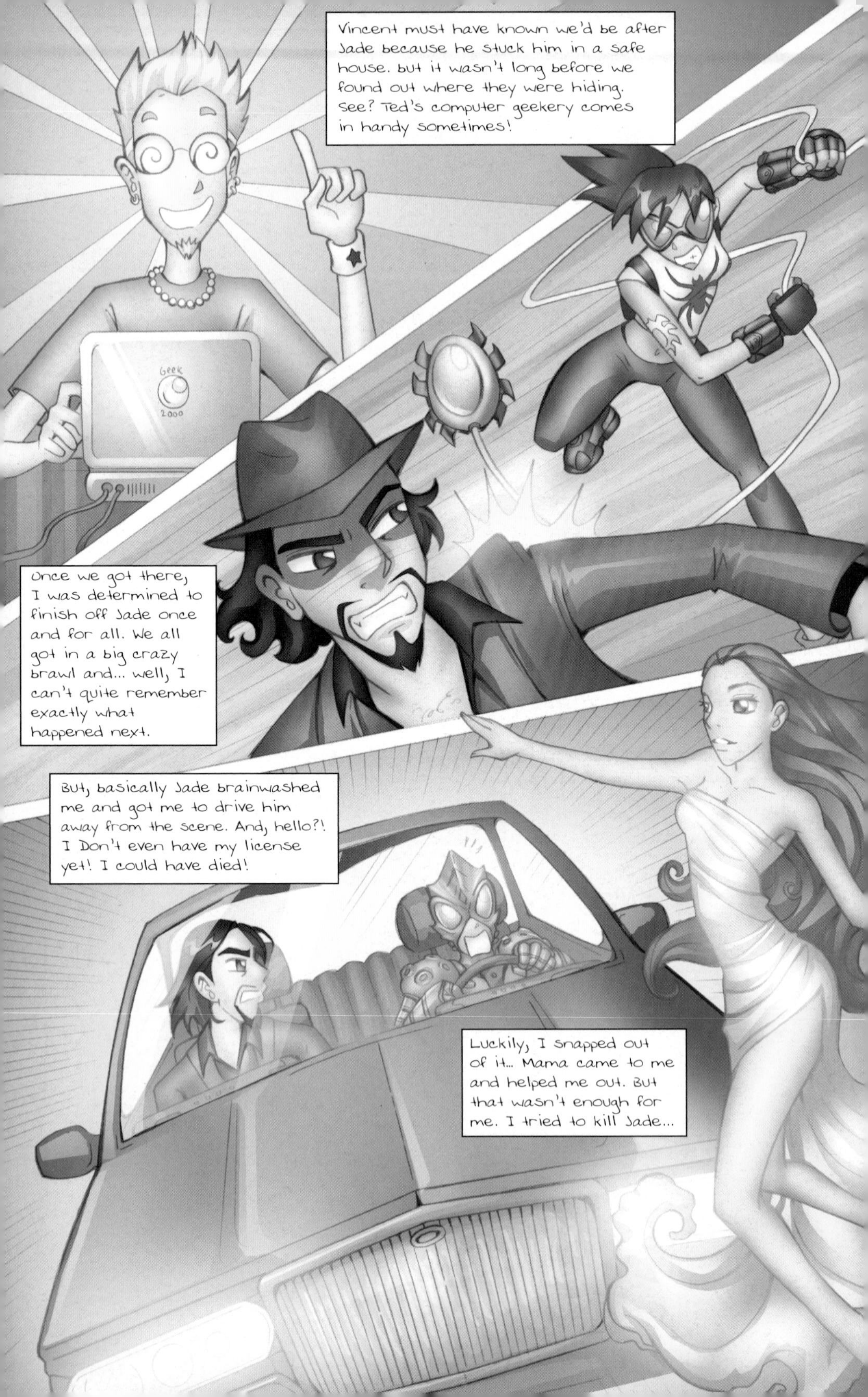
Vincent must have known we'd be after Jade because he stuck him in a safe house. but it wasn't long before we found out where they were hiding. see? Ted's computer geekery comes in handy sometimes!
Geek 2000
Once we got there, I was determined to finish off Jade once and for all. We all got in a big crazy brawl and... well, I can't quite remember exactly what happened next.
But, basically Jade brainwashed me and got me to drive him away from the scene. And, hello?! I Don't even have my license yet! I could have died!
Luckily, I snapped out of it... Mama came to me and helped me out. But that wasn't enough for me. I tried to kill Jade...

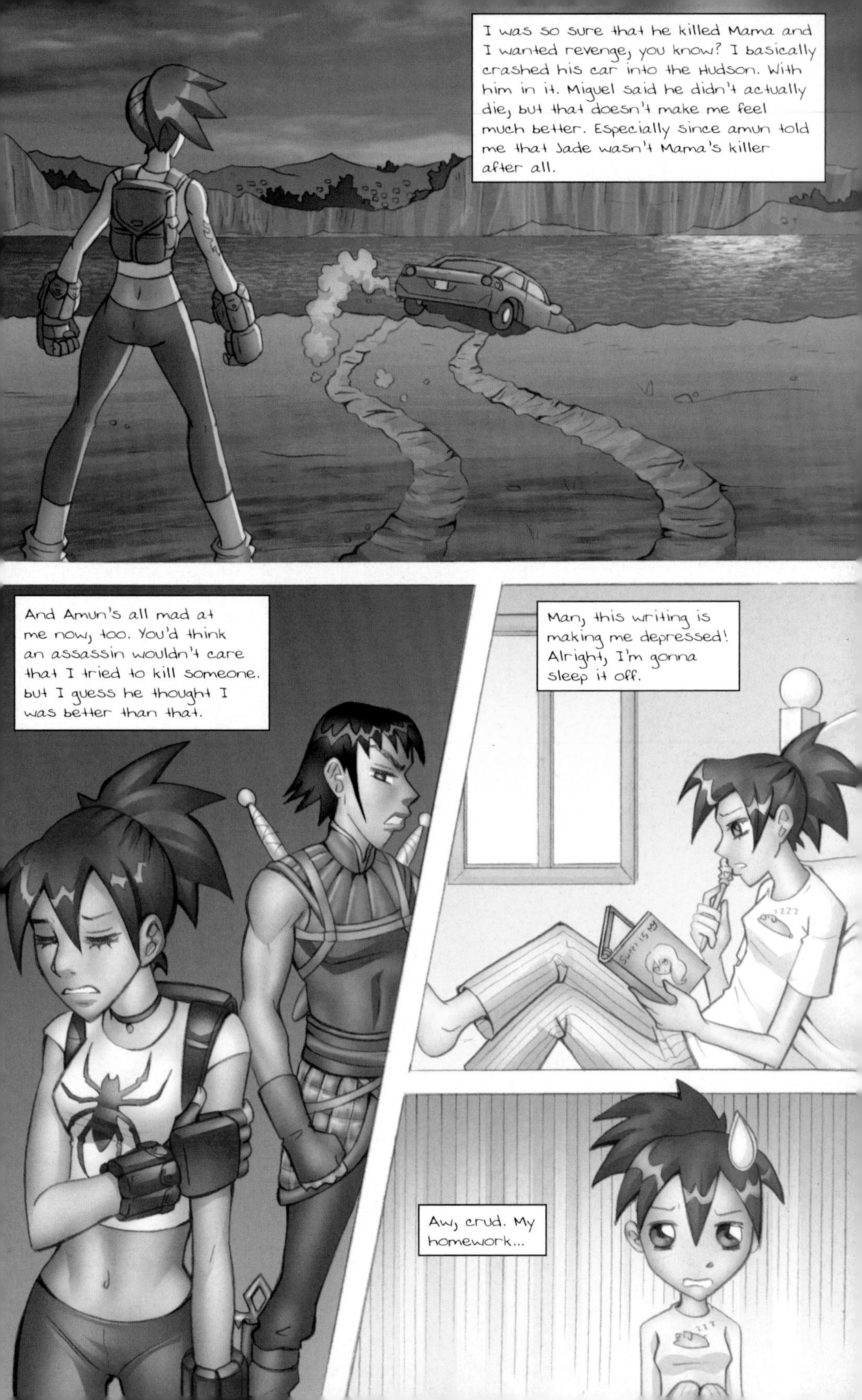
I was so sure that he killed Mama and I wanted revenge, you know? I basically crashed his car into the Hudson. With him in it. Miguel said he didn't actually die, but that doesn't make me feel much better. Especially since amun told me that Jade wasn't Mama's killer after all.
And Amun's all mad at me now, too. You'd think an assassin wouldn't care that I tried to kill someone. but I guess he thought I was better than that.
Man, this writing is making me depressed! Alright, I'm gonna sleep it off.
Aw, crud. My homework...

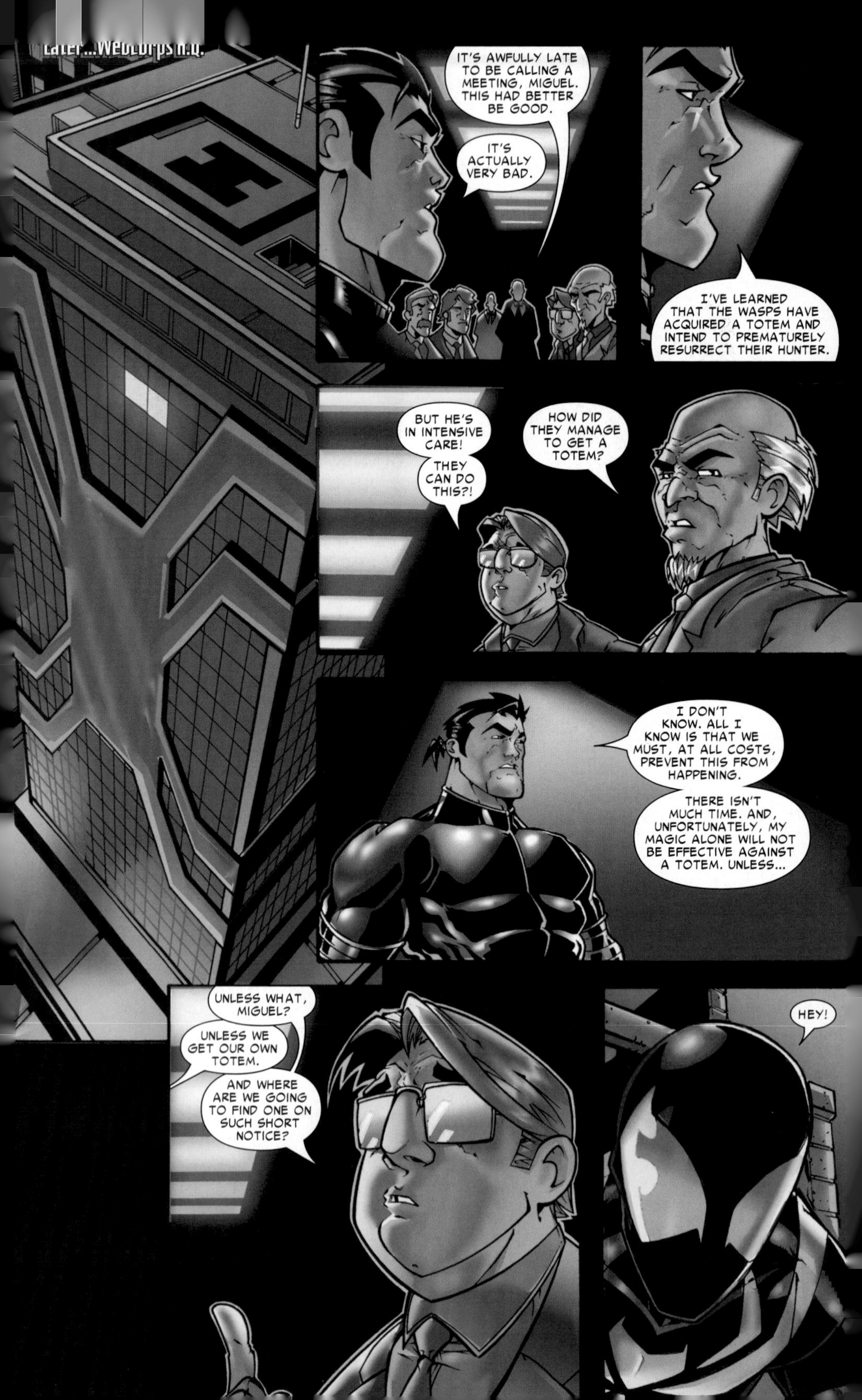
IT'S AWFULLY LATE TO BE CALLING A MEETING, MIGUEL. THIS HAD BETTER BE GOOD.
IT'S ACTUALLY VERY BAD.
I'VE LEARNED THAT THE WASPS HAVE ACQUIRED A TOTEM AND INTEND TO PREMATURELY RESURRECT THEIR HUNTER.
BUT HE'S IN INTENSIVE CARE!
THEY CAN DO THIS?!
HOW DID THEY MANAGE TO GET A TOTEM?
I DON'T KNOW. ALL I KNOW IS THAT WE MUST, AT ALL COSTS, PREVENT THIS FROM HAPPENING.
THERE ISN'T MUCH TIME. AND, UNFORTUNATELY, MY MAGIC ALONE WILL NOT BE EFFECTIVE AGAINST A TOTEM. UNLESS...
UNLESS WHAT, MIGUEL?
UNLESS WE GET OUR OWN TOTEM.
AND WHERE ARE WE GOING TO FIND ONE ON SUCH SHORT NOTICE?
HEY!

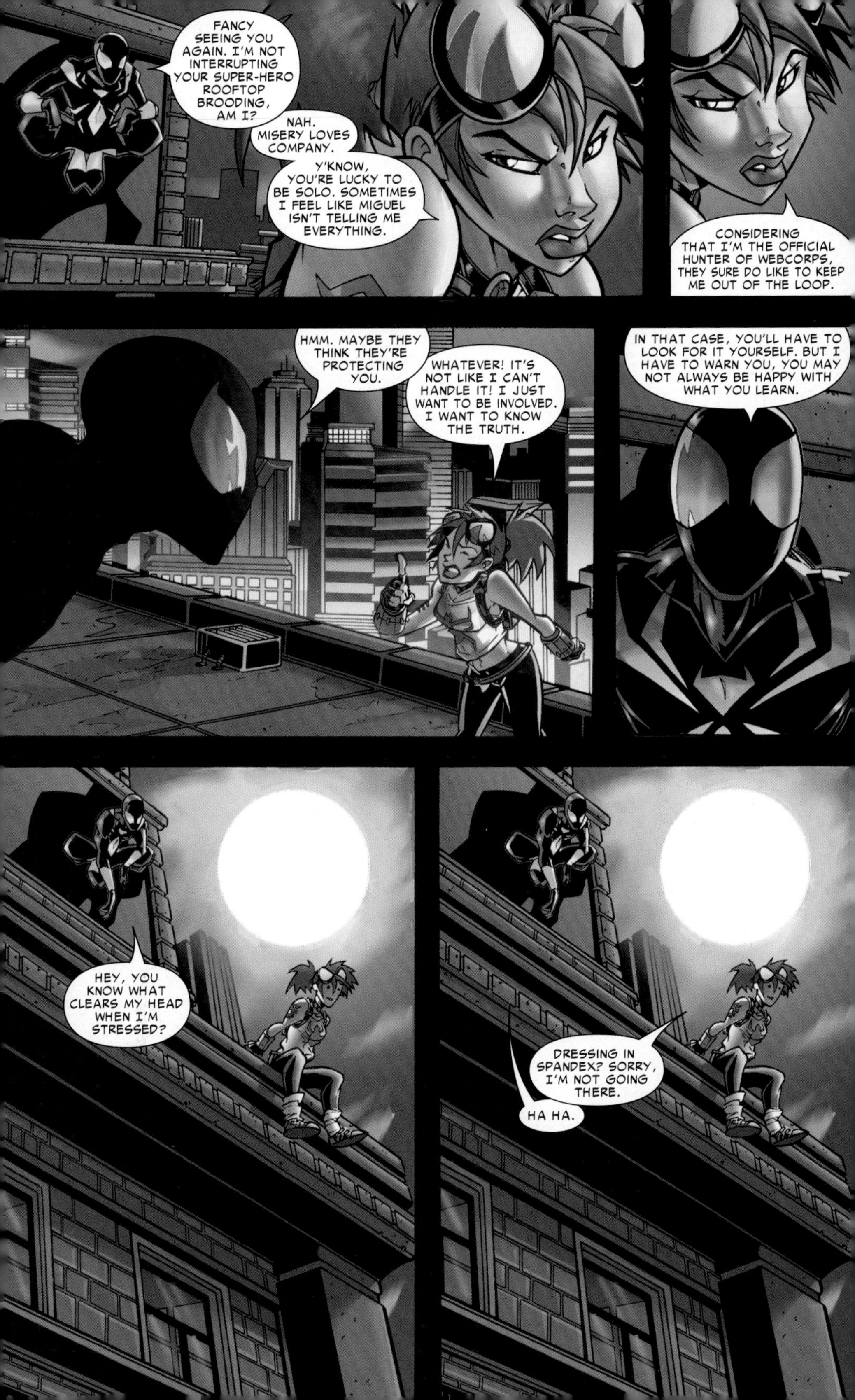
FANCY SEEING YOU AGAIN. I'M NOT INTERRUPTING YOUR SUPER-HERO ROOFTOP BROODING, AM I?
NAH. MISERY LOVES COMPANY.
Y'KNOW, YOU'RE LUCKY TO BE SOLO. SOMETIMES I FEEL LIKE MIGUEL ISN'T TELLING ME EVERYTHING.
CONSIDERING THAT I'M THE OFFICIAL HUNTER OF WEBCORPS, THEY SURE DO LIKE TO KEEP ME OUT OF THE LOOP.
HMM. MAYBE THEY THINK THEY'RE PROTECTING YOU.
WHATEVER! IT'S NOT LIKE I CAN'T HANDLE IT! I JUST WANT TO BE INVOLVED. I WANT TO KNOW THE TRUTH.
IN THAT CASE, YOU'LL HAVE TO LOOK FOR IT YOURSELF. BUT I HAVE TO WARN YOU, YOU MAY NOT ALWAYS BE HAPPY WITH WHAT YOU LEARN.
HEY, YOU KNOW WHAT CLEARS MY HEAD WHEN I'M STRESSED?
DRESSING IN SPANDEX? SORRY, I'M NOT GOING THERE.
HA HA.

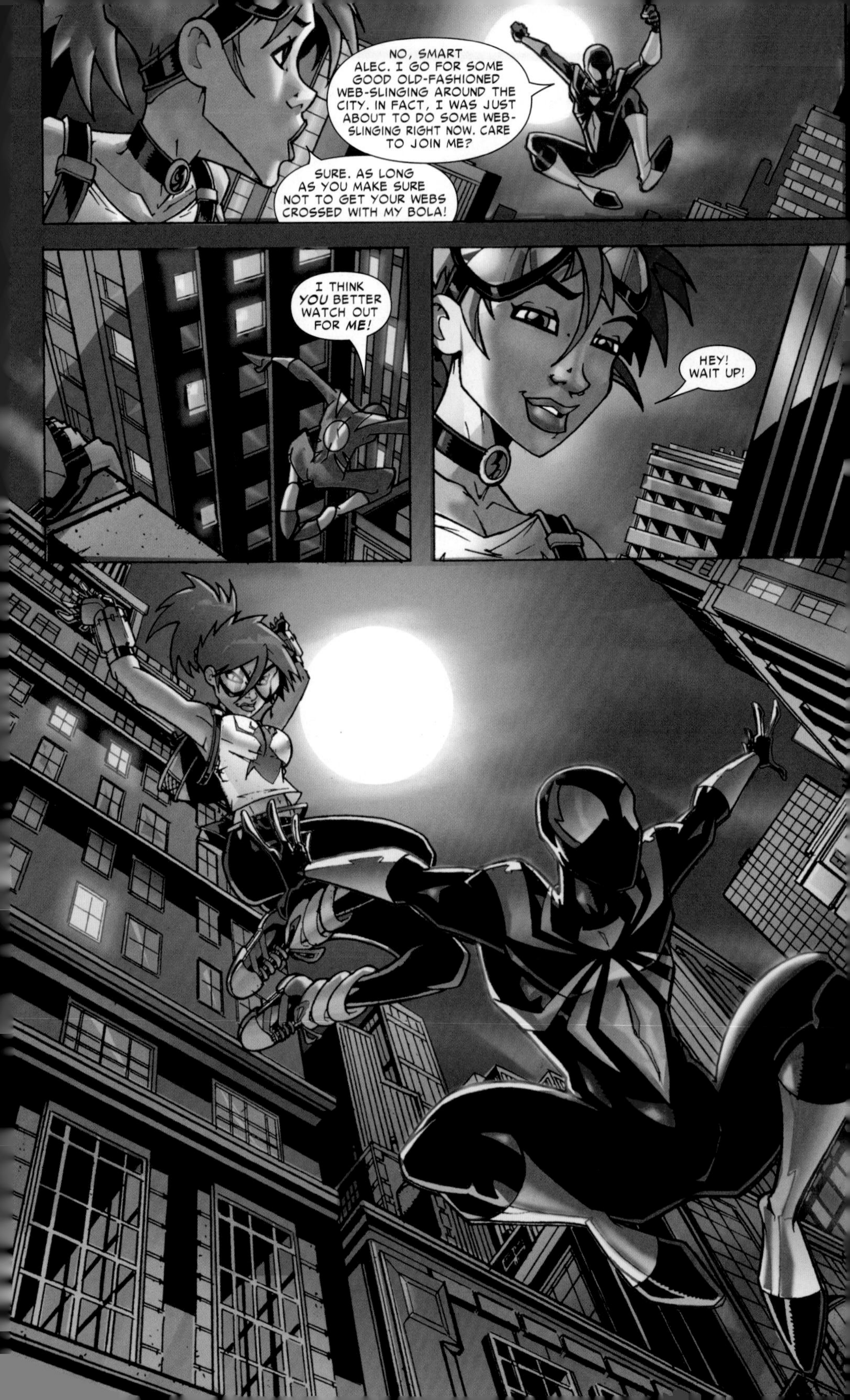
NO, SMART ALEC. I GO FOR SOME GOOD OLD-FASHIONED WEB-SLINGING AROUND THE CITY. IN FACT, I WAS JUST ABOUT TO DO SOME WEB-SLINGING RIGHT NOW. CARE TO JOIN ME?
SURE. AS LONG AS YOU MAKE SURE NOT TO GET YOUR WEBS CROSSED WITH MY BOLA!
I THINK *YOU* BETTER WATCH OUT FOR *ME!*
HEY! WAIT UP!

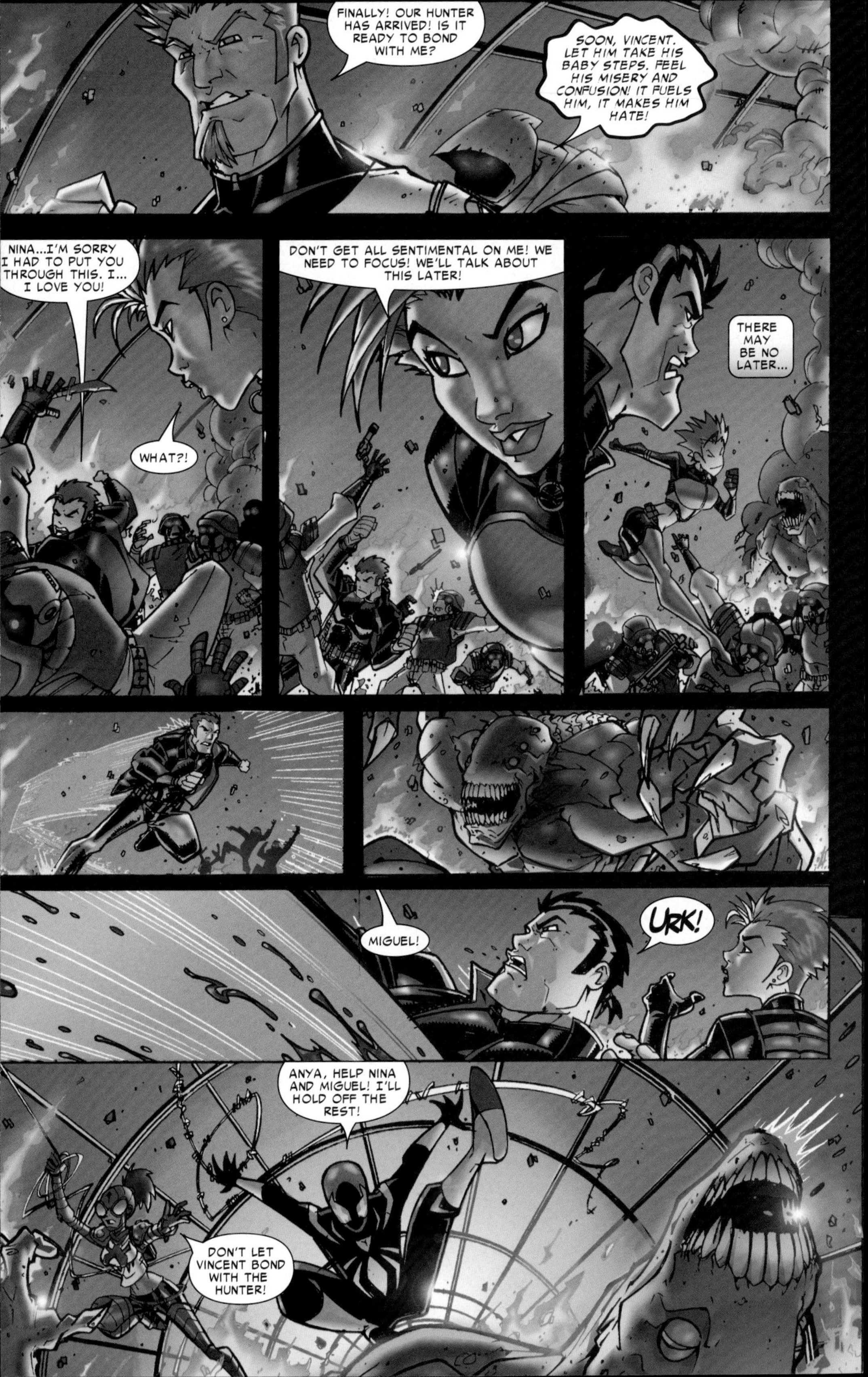
FINALLY! OUR HUNTER HAS ARRIVED! IS IT READY TO BOND WITH ME?
SOON, VINCENT. LET HIM TAKE HIS BABY STEPS. FEEL HIS MISERY AND CONFUSION! IT FUELS HIM, IT MAKES HIM HATE!
NINA...I'M SORRY I HAD TO PUT YOU THROUGH THIS. I... I LOVE YOU!
WHAT?!
DON'T GET ALL SENTIMENTAL ON ME! WE NEED TO FOCUS! WE'LL TALK ABOUT THIS LATER!
THERE MAY BE NO LATER...
MIGUEL!
URK!
ANYA, HELP NINA AND MIGUEL! I'LL HOLD OFF THE REST!
DON'T LET VINCENT BOND WITH THE HUNTER!

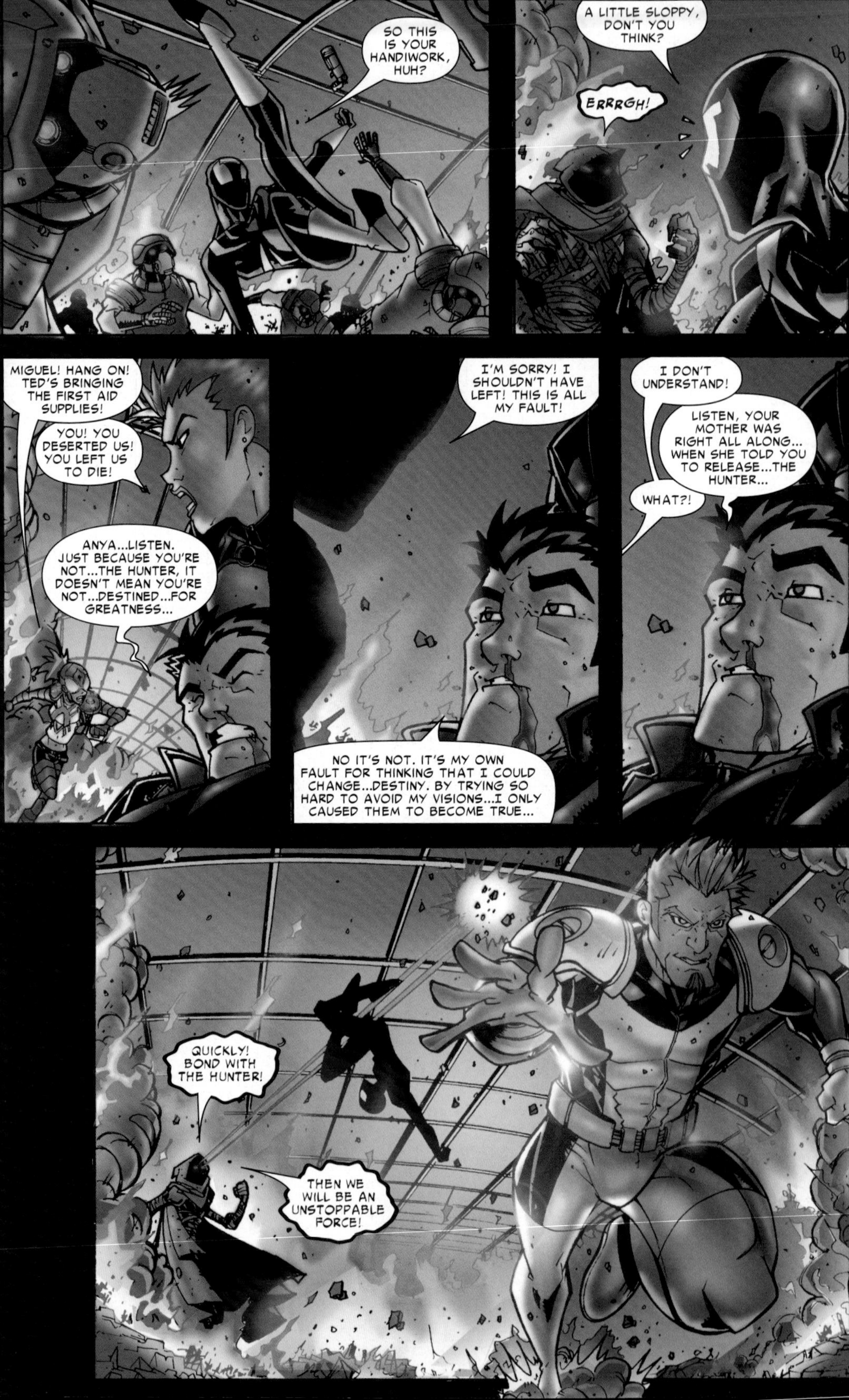
SO THIS IS YOUR HANDIWORK, HUH?
A LITTLE SLOPPY, DON'T YOU THINK?
ERRRGH!
MIGUEL! HANG ON! TED'S BRINGING THE FIRST AID SUPPLIES!
YOU! YOU DESERTED US! YOU LEFT US TO DIE!
ANYA...LISTEN. JUST BECAUSE YOU'RE NOT...THE HUNTER, IT DOESN'T MEAN YOU'RE NOT...DESTINED...FOR GREATNESS...
I'M SORRY! I SHOULDN'T HAVE LEFT! THIS IS ALL MY FAULT!
NO IT'S NOT. IT'S MY OWN FAULT FOR THINKING THAT I COULD CHANGE...DESTINY. BY TRYING SO HARD TO AVOID MY VISIONS...I ONLY CAUSED THEM TO BECOME TRUE...
I DON'T UNDERSTAND!
LISTEN, YOUR MOTHER WAS RIGHT ALL ALONG... WHEN SHE TOLD YOU TO RELEASE...THE HUNTER...
WHAT?!
QUICKLY! BOND WITH THE HUNTER!
THEN WE WILL BE AN UNSTOPPABLE FORCE!

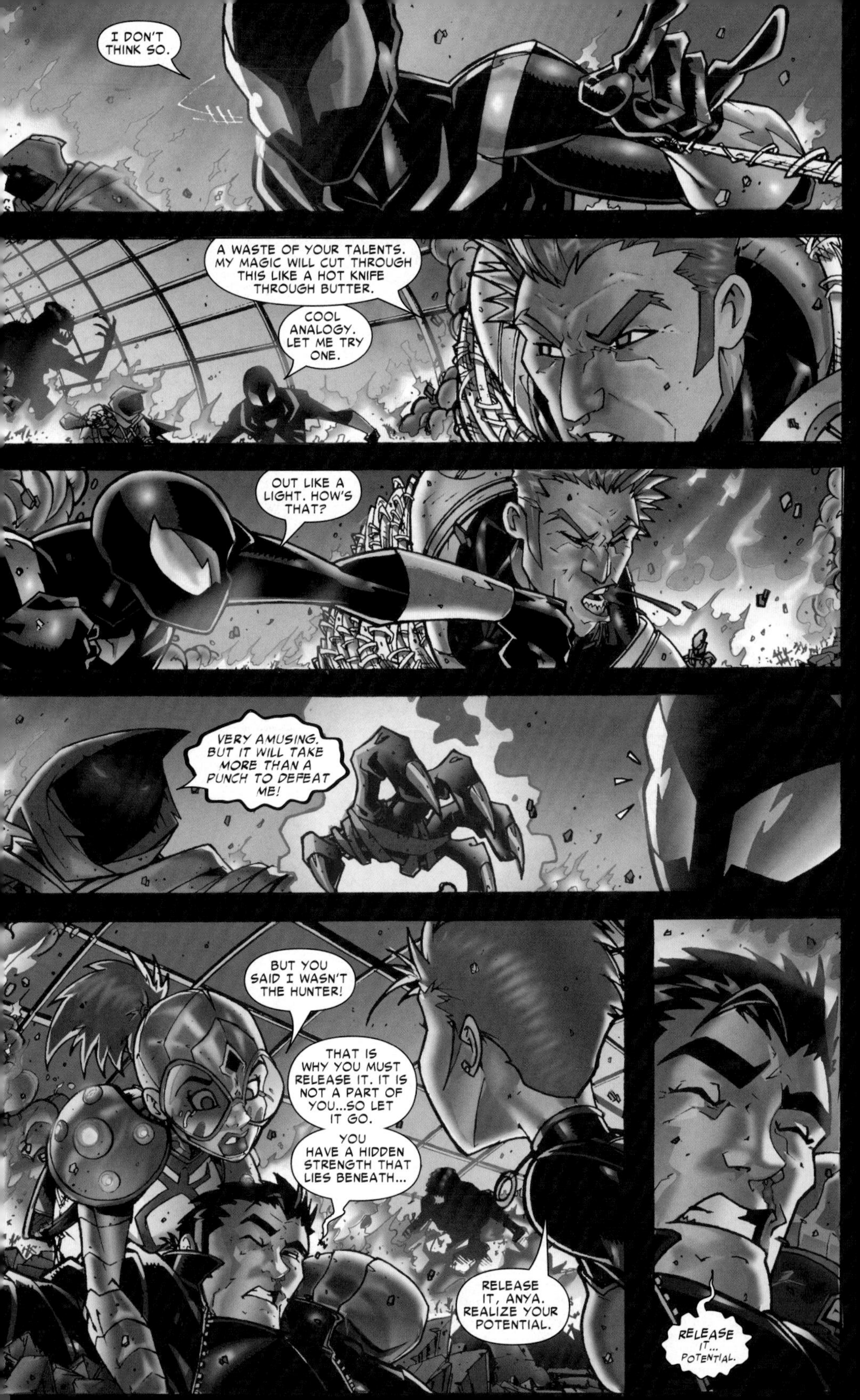
I DON'T THINK SO.
A WASTE OF YOUR TALENTS. MY MAGIC WILL CUT THROUGH THIS LIKE A HOT KNIFE THROUGH BUTTER.
COOL ANALOGY. LET ME TRY ONE.
OUT LIKE A LIGHT. HOW'S THAT?
VERY AMUSING. BUT IT WILL TAKE MORE THAN A PUNCH TO DEFEAT ME!
BUT YOU SAID I WASN'T THE HUNTER!
THAT IS WHY YOU MUST RELEASE IT. IT IS NOT A PART OF YOU...SO LET IT GO.
YOU HAVE A HIDDEN STRENGTH THAT LIES BENEATH...
RELEASE IT, ANYA. REALIZE YOUR POTENTIAL.
RELEASE IT... POTENTIAL.

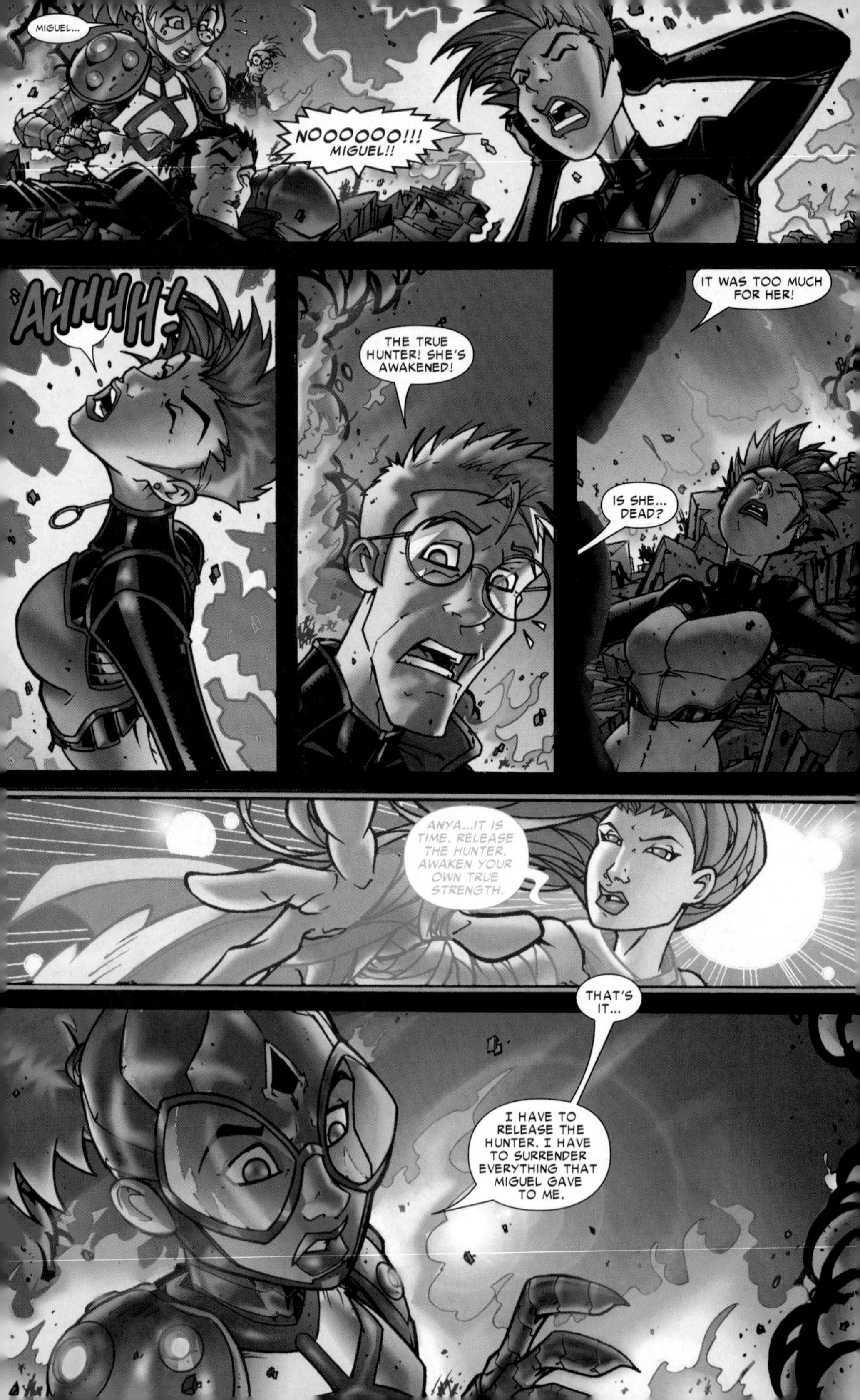
MIGUEL...
NOOOOOO!!! MIGUEL!!
AHHHHH!
THE TRUE HUNTER! SHE'S AWAKENED!
IT WAS TOO MUCH FOR HER!
IS SHE... DEAD?
ANYA...IT IS TIME. RELEASE THE HUNTER. AWAKEN YOUR OWN TRUE STRENGTH.
THAT'S IT...
I HAVE TO RELEASE THE HUNTER. I HAVE TO SURRENDER EVERYTHING THAT MIGUEL GAVE TO ME.

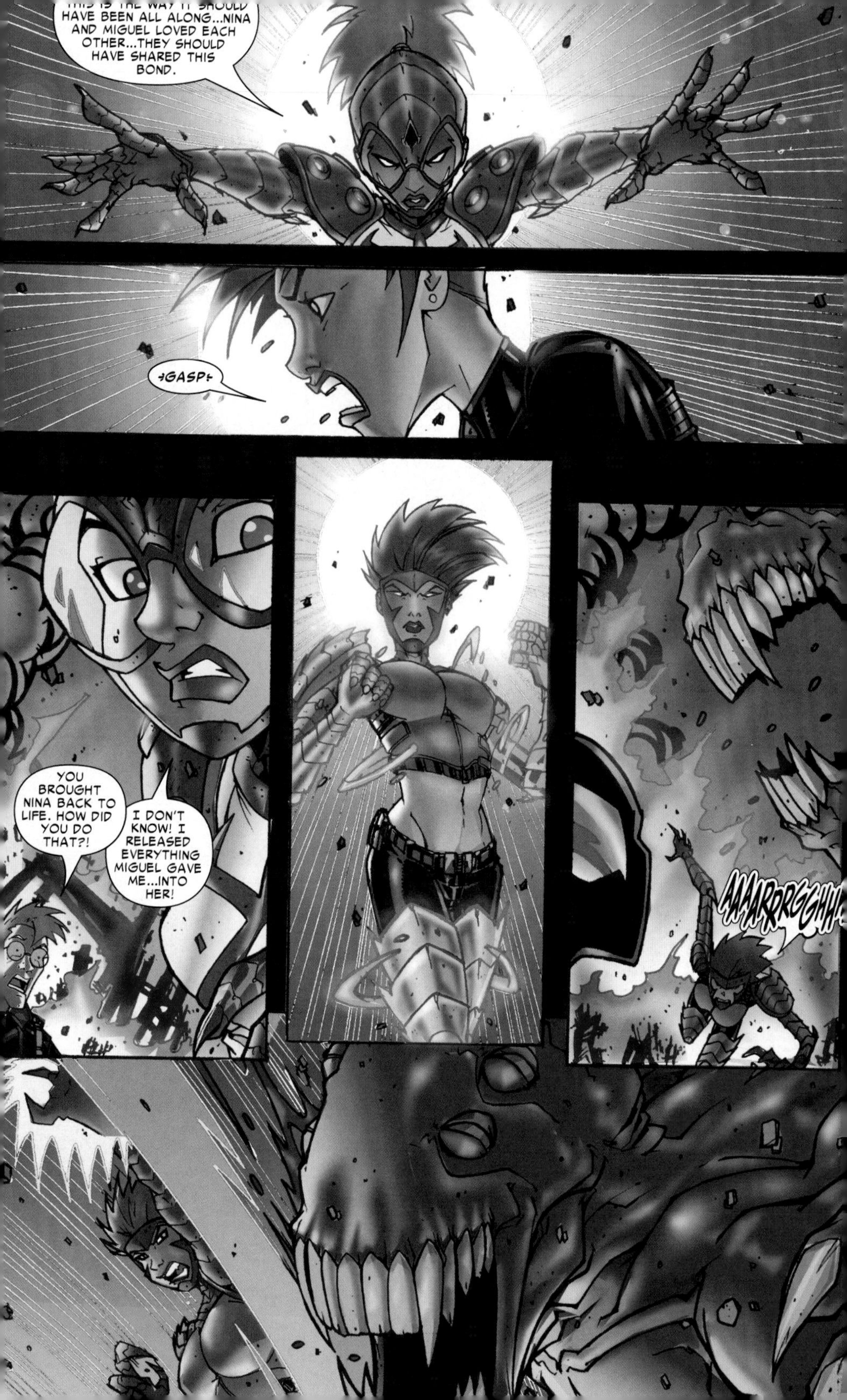
THIS IS THE WAY IT SHOULD HAVE BEEN ALL ALONG...NINA AND MIGUEL LOVED EACH OTHER...THEY SHOULD HAVE SHARED THIS BOND.
GASP
YOU BROUGHT NINA BACK TO LIFE. HOW DID YOU DO THAT?!
I DON'T KNOW! I RELEASED EVERYTHING MIGUEL GAVE ME...INTO HER!
AAAARRRGGHH

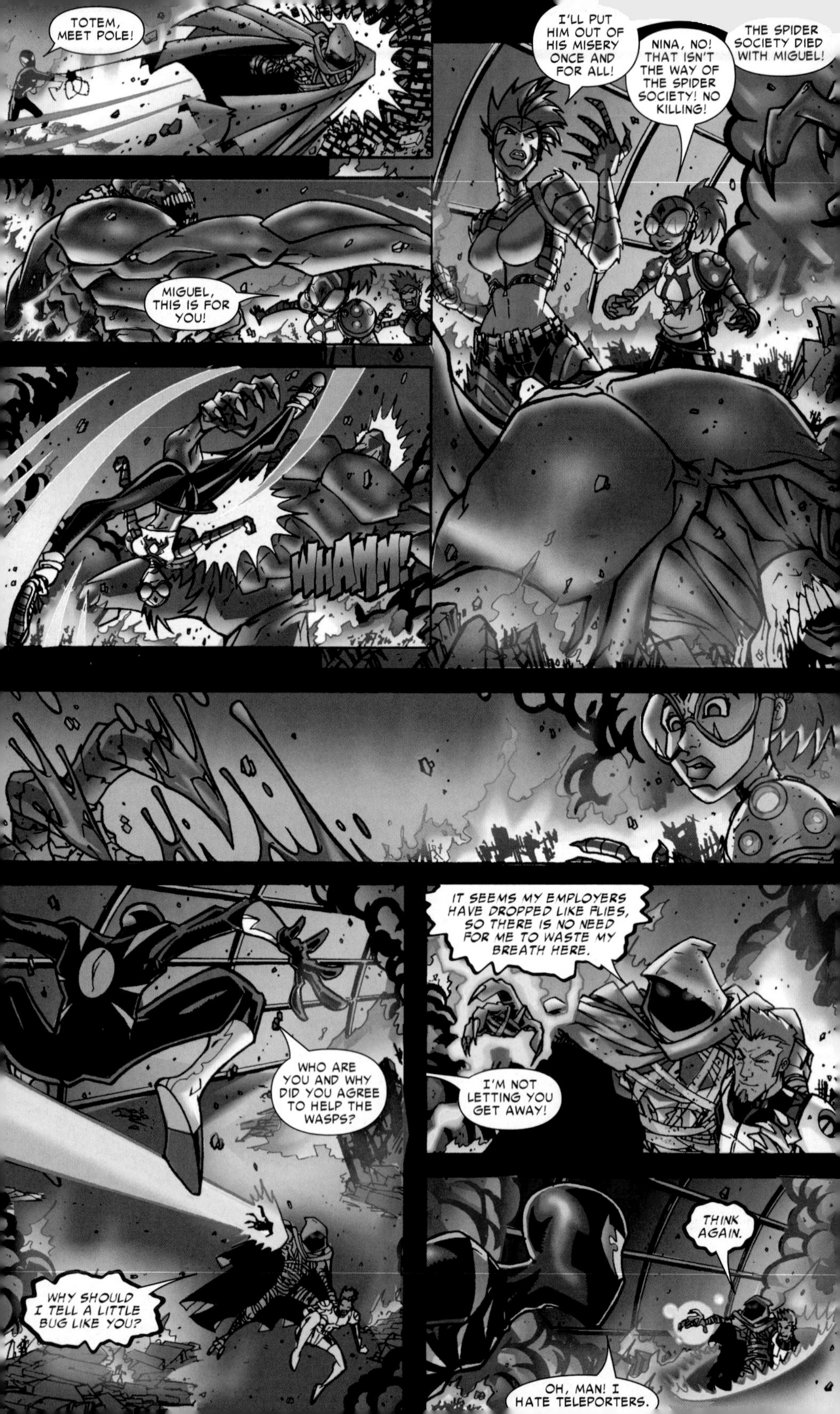
TOTEM, MEET POLE!
I'LL PUT HIM OUT OF HIS MISERY ONCE AND FOR ALL!
NINA, NO! THAT ISN'T THE WAY OF THE SPIDER SOCIETY! NO KILLING!
THE SPIDER SOCIETY DIED WITH MIGUEL!
MIGUEL, THIS IS FOR YOU!
WHAMM!
WHO ARE YOU AND WHY DID YOU AGREE TO HELP THE WASPS?
WHY SHOULD I TELL A LITTLE BUG LIKE YOU?
IT SEEMS MY EMPLOYERS HAVE DROPPED LIKE FLIES, SO THERE IS NO NEED FOR ME TO WASTE MY BREATH HERE.
I'M NOT LETTING YOU GET AWAY!
THINK AGAIN.
OH, MAN! I HATE TELEPORTERS.

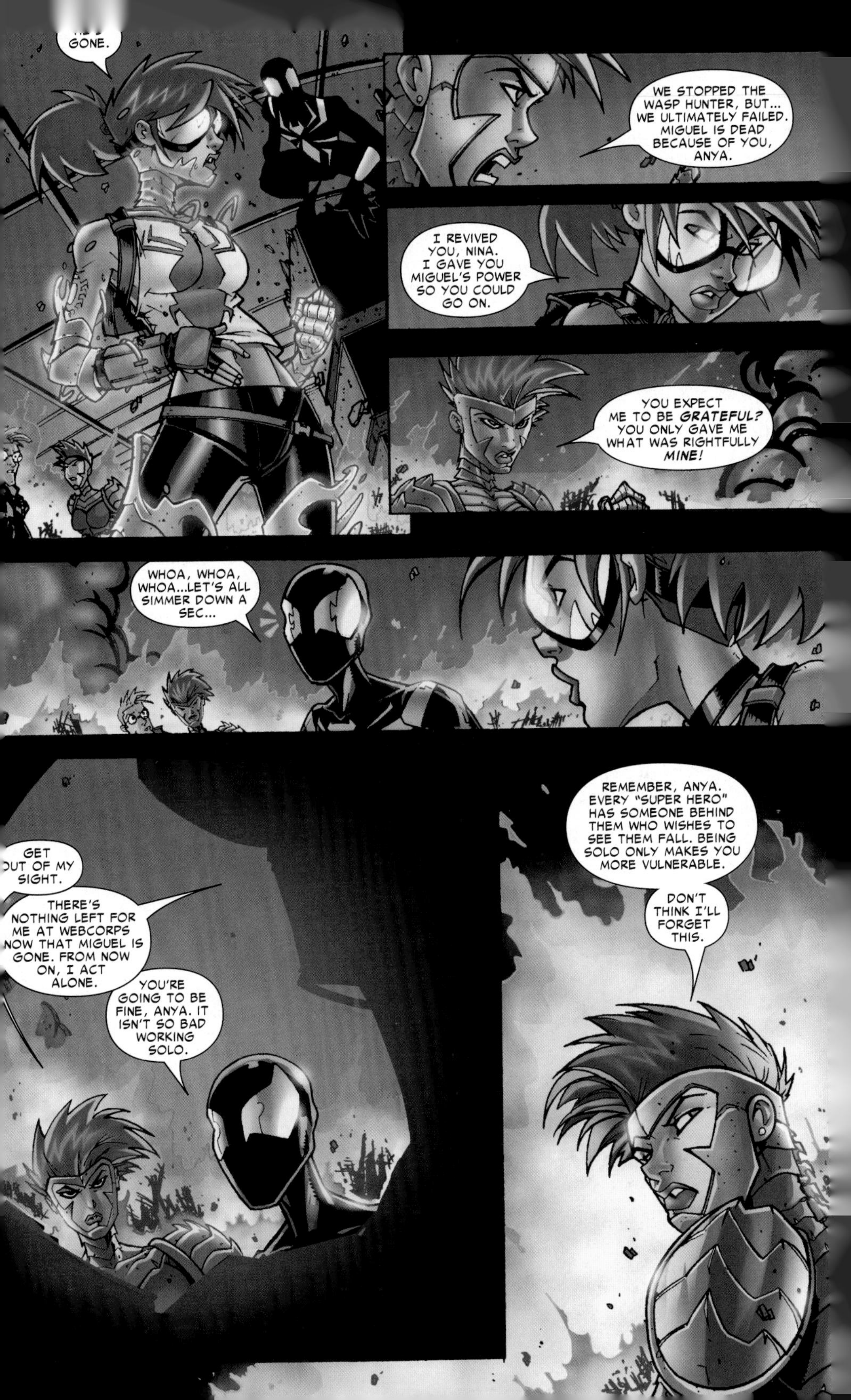
GONE.
WE STOPPED THE WASP HUNTER, BUT... WE ULTIMATELY FAILED. MIGUEL IS DEAD BECAUSE OF YOU, ANYA.
I REVIVED YOU, NINA. I GAVE YOU MIGUEL'S POWER SO YOU COULD GO ON.
YOU EXPECT ME TO BE GRATEFUL? YOU ONLY GAVE ME WHAT WAS RIGHTFULLY MINE!
WHOA, WHOA, WHOA...LET'S ALL SIMMER DOWN A SEC...
GET OUT OF MY SIGHT.
THERE'S NOTHING LEFT FOR ME AT WEBCORPS NOW THAT MIGUEL IS GONE. FROM NOW ON, I ACT ALONE.
YOU'RE GOING TO BE FINE, ANYA. IT ISN'T SO BAD WORKING SOLO.
REMEMBER, ANYA. EVERY "SUPER HERO" HAS SOMEONE BEHIND THEM WHO WISHES TO SEE THEM FALL. BEING SOLO ONLY MAKES YOU MORE VULNERABLE.
DON'T THINK I'LL FORGET THIS.

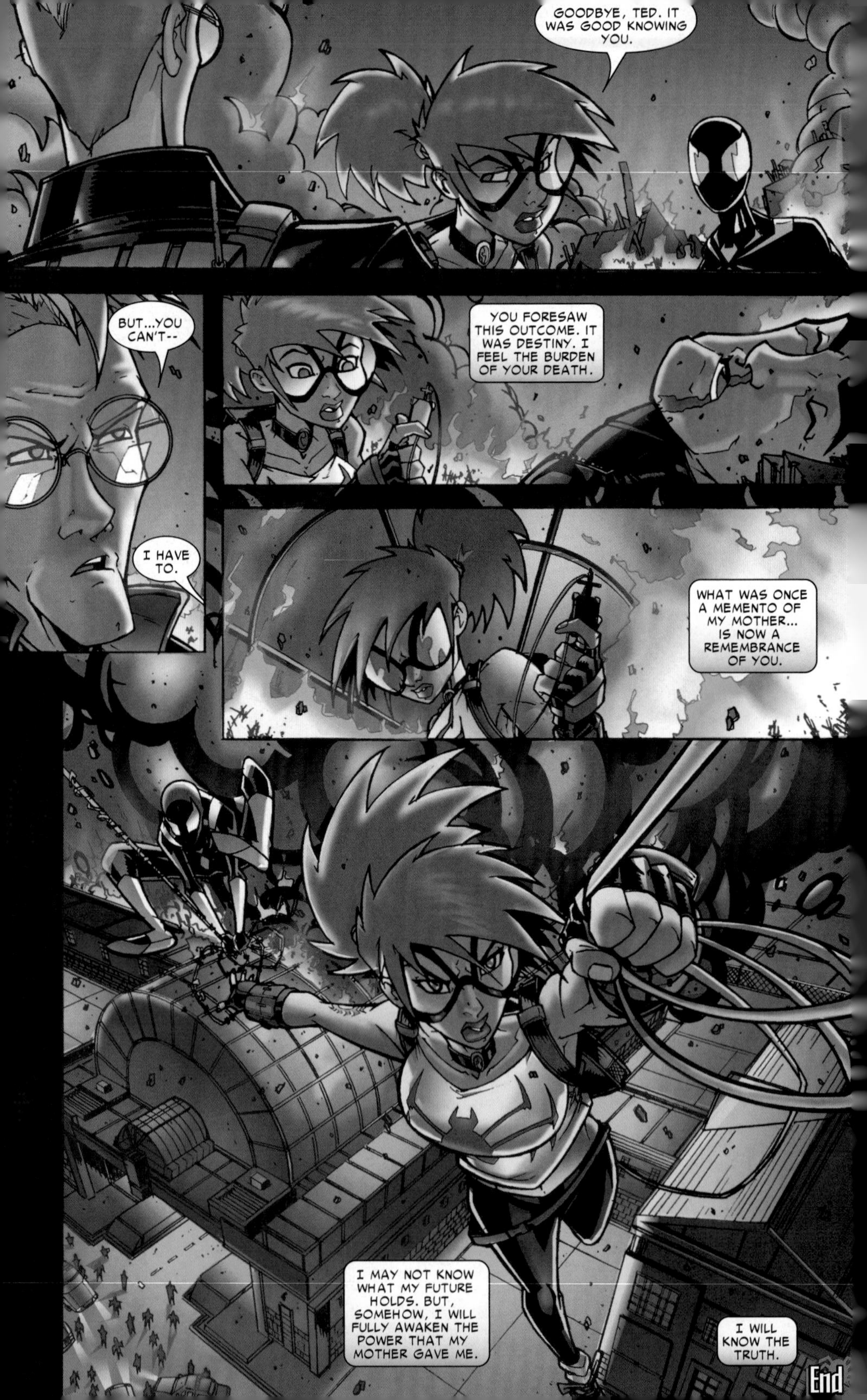
GOODBYE, TED. IT WAS GOOD KNOWING YOU.
BUT...YOU CAN'T--
I HAVE TO.
YOU FORESAW THIS OUTCOME. IT WAS DESTINY. I FEEL THE BURDEN OF YOUR DEATH.
WHAT WAS ONCE A MEMENTO OF MY MOTHER... IS NOW A REMEMBRANCE OF YOU.
I MAY NOT KNOW WHAT MY FUTURE HOLDS. BUT, SOMEHOW, I WILL FULLY AWAKEN THE POWER THAT MY MOTHER GAVE ME.
I WILL KNOW THE TRUTH.
End

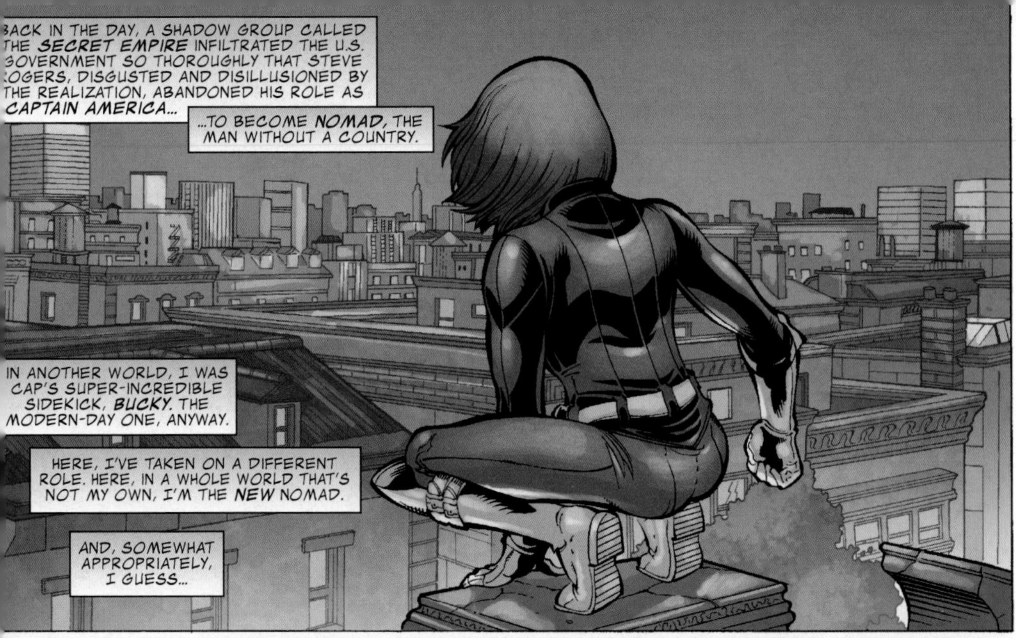
BACK IN THE DAY, A SHADOW GROUP CALLED THE SECRET EMPIRE INFILTRATED THE U.S. GOVERNMENT SO THOROUGHLY THAT STEVE ROGERS, DISGUSTED AND DISILLUSIONED BY THE REALIZATION, ABANDONED HIS ROLE AS CAPTAIN AMERICA...
...TO BECOME NOMAD, THE MAN WITHOUT A COUNTRY.
IN ANOTHER WORLD, I WAS CAP'S SUPER-INCREDIBLE SIDEKICK, BUCKY. THE MODERN-DAY ONE, ANYWAY.
HERE, I'VE TAKEN ON A DIFFERENT ROLE. HERE, IN A WHOLE WORLD THAT'S NOT MY OWN, I'M THE NEW NOMAD.
AND, SOMEWHAT APPROPRIATELY, I GUESS...

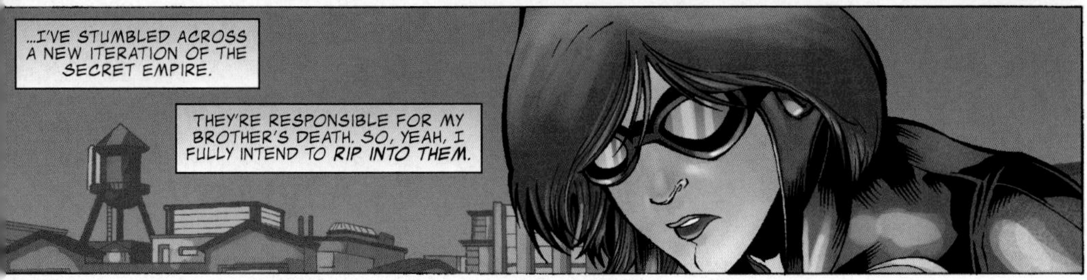
...I'VE STUMBLED ACROSS A NEW ITERATION OF THE SECRET EMPIRE.
THEY'RE RESPONSIBLE FOR MY BROTHER'S DEATH. SO, YEAH, I FULLY INTEND TO RIP INTO THEM.

NOMAD
IN CONJUNCTION PART 1

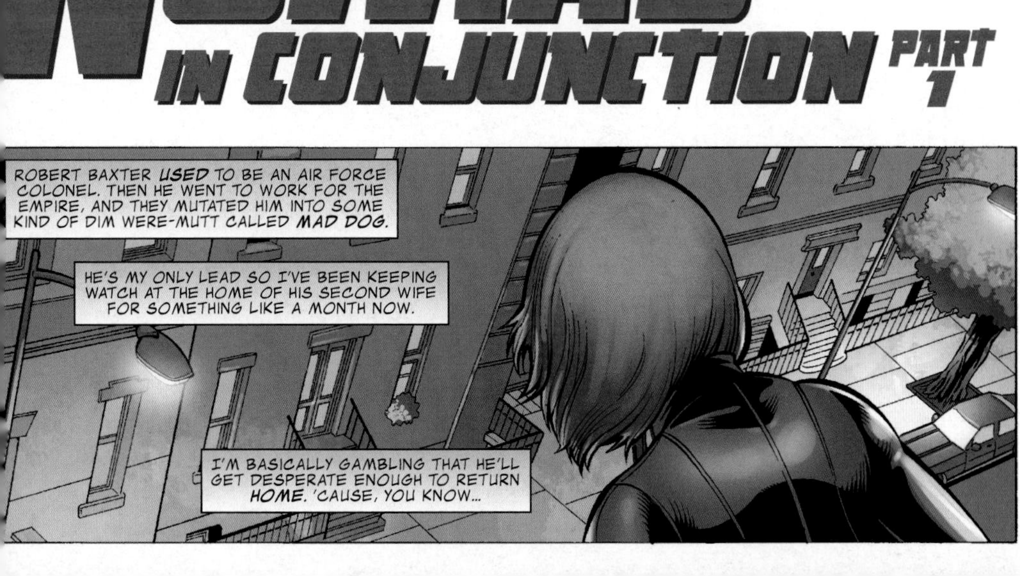
ROBERT BAXTER USED TO BE AN AIR FORCE COLONEL. THEN HE WENT TO WORK FOR THE EMPIRE, AND THEY MUTATED HIM INTO SOME KIND OF DIM WERE-MUTT CALLED MAD DOG.
HE'S MY ONLY LEAD SO I'VE BEEN KEEPING WATCH AT THE HOME OF HIS SECOND WIFE FOR SOMETHING LIKE A MONTH NOW.
I'M BASICALLY GAMBLING THAT HE'LL GET DESPERATE ENOUGH TO RETURN HOME. 'CAUSE, YOU KNOW...

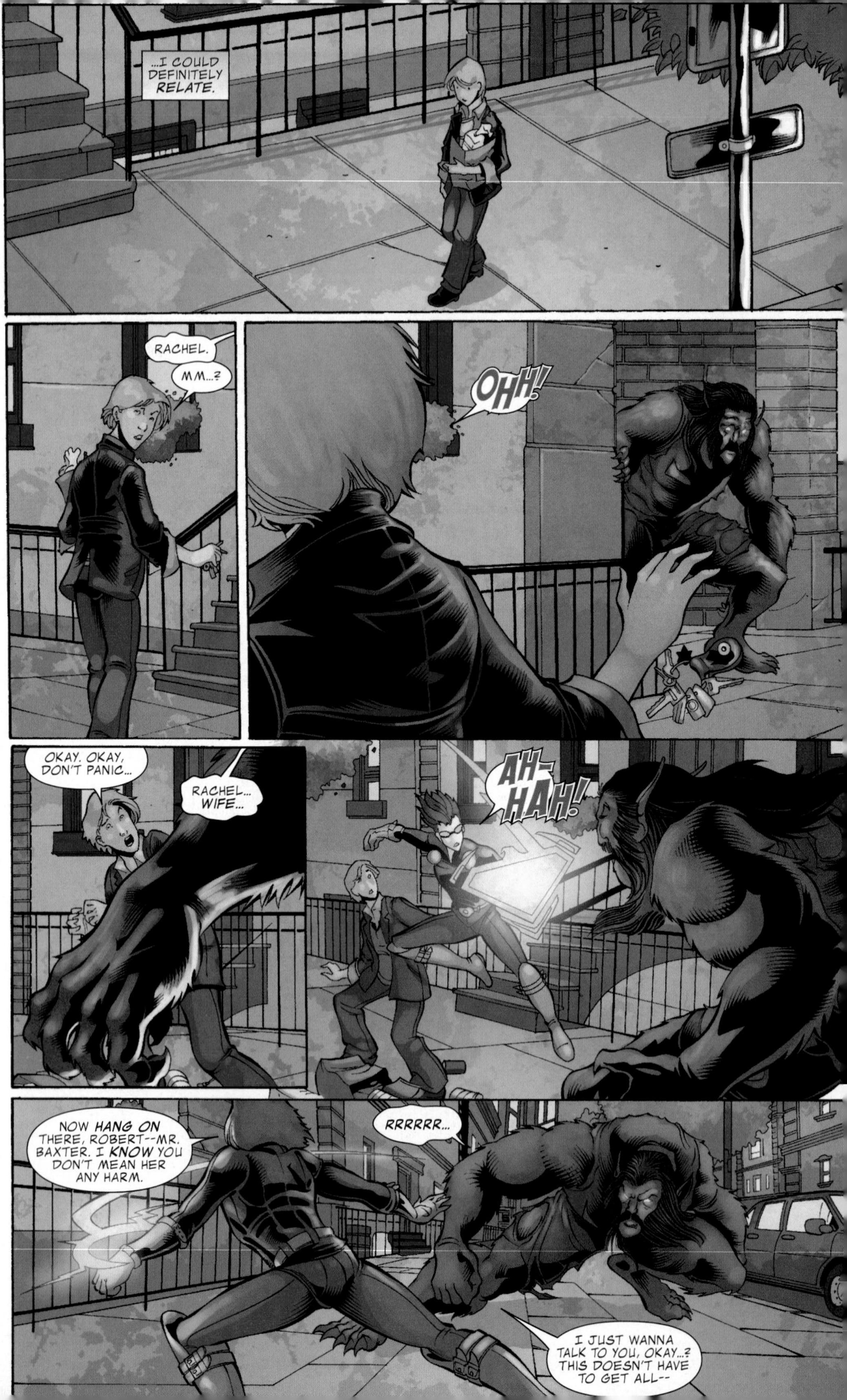
...I COULD DEFINITELY RELATE.
RACHEL.
MM...?
OHH!
OKAY. OKAY, DON'T PANIC...
RACHEL... WIFE...
AH-HAH!
NOW HANG ON THERE, ROBERT--MR. BAXTER. I KNOW YOU DON'T MEAN HER ANY HARM.
RRRRRR...
I JUST WANNA TALK TO YOU, OKAY...? THIS DOESN'T HAVE TO GET ALL--

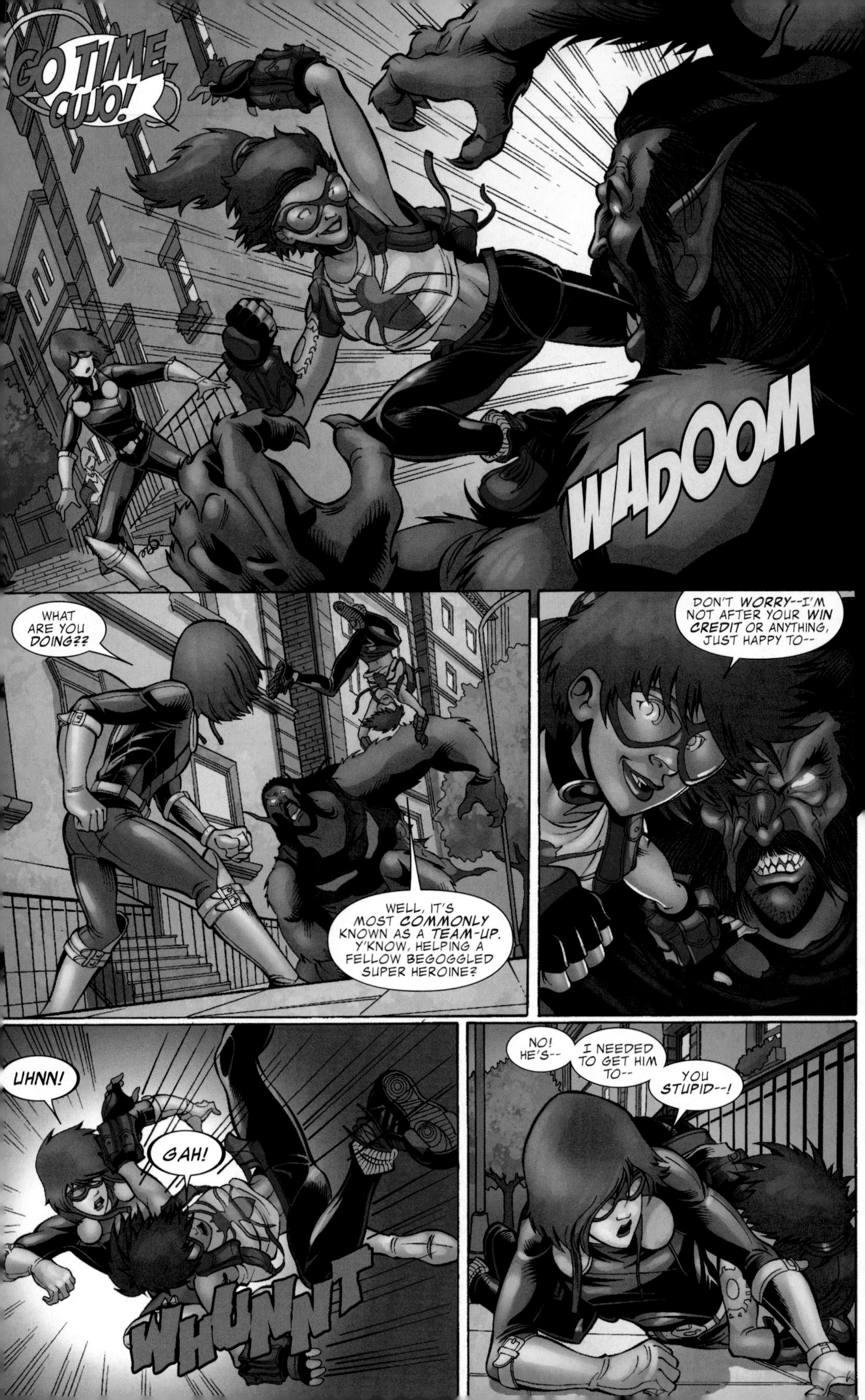
GO TIME, CUJO!
WADOOM
WHAT ARE YOU DOING??
WELL, IT'S MOST COMMONLY KNOWN AS A TEAM-UP. Y'KNOW, HELPING A FELLOW BEGOGGLED SUPER HEROINE?
DON'T WORRY--I'M NOT AFTER YOUR WIN CREDIT OR ANYTHING, JUST HAPPY TO--
UHNN!
GAH!
WHUNNT
NO! HE'S--
I NEEDED TO GET HIM TO--
YOU STUPID--!

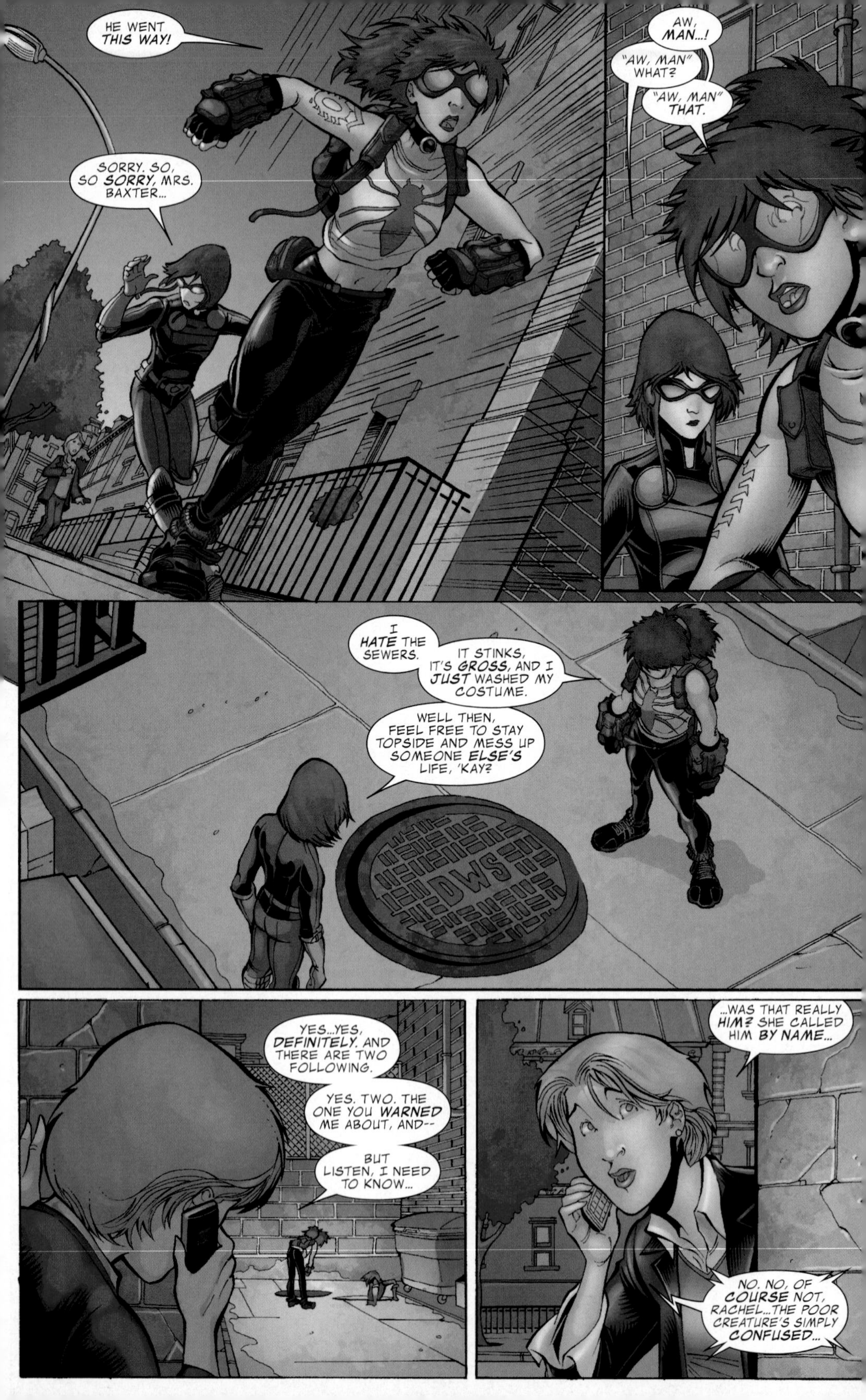
HE WENT THIS WAY!
SORRY. SO, SO SORRY, MRS. BAXTER...
AW, MAN...!
"AW, MAN" WHAT?
"AW, MAN" THAT.
I HATE THE SEWERS.
IT STINKS, IT'S GROSS, AND I JUST WASHED MY COSTUME.
WELL THEN, FEEL FREE TO STAY TOPSIDE AND MESS UP SOMEONE ELSE'S LIFE, 'KAY?
DWS
YES...YES, DEFINITELY. AND THERE ARE TWO FOLLOWING.
YES. TWO. THE ONE YOU WARNED ME ABOUT, AND--
BUT LISTEN, I NEED TO KNOW...
...WAS THAT REALLY HIM? SHE CALLED HIM BY NAME...
NO. NO, OF COURSE NOT, RACHEL...THE POOR CREATURE'S SIMPLY CONFUSED...

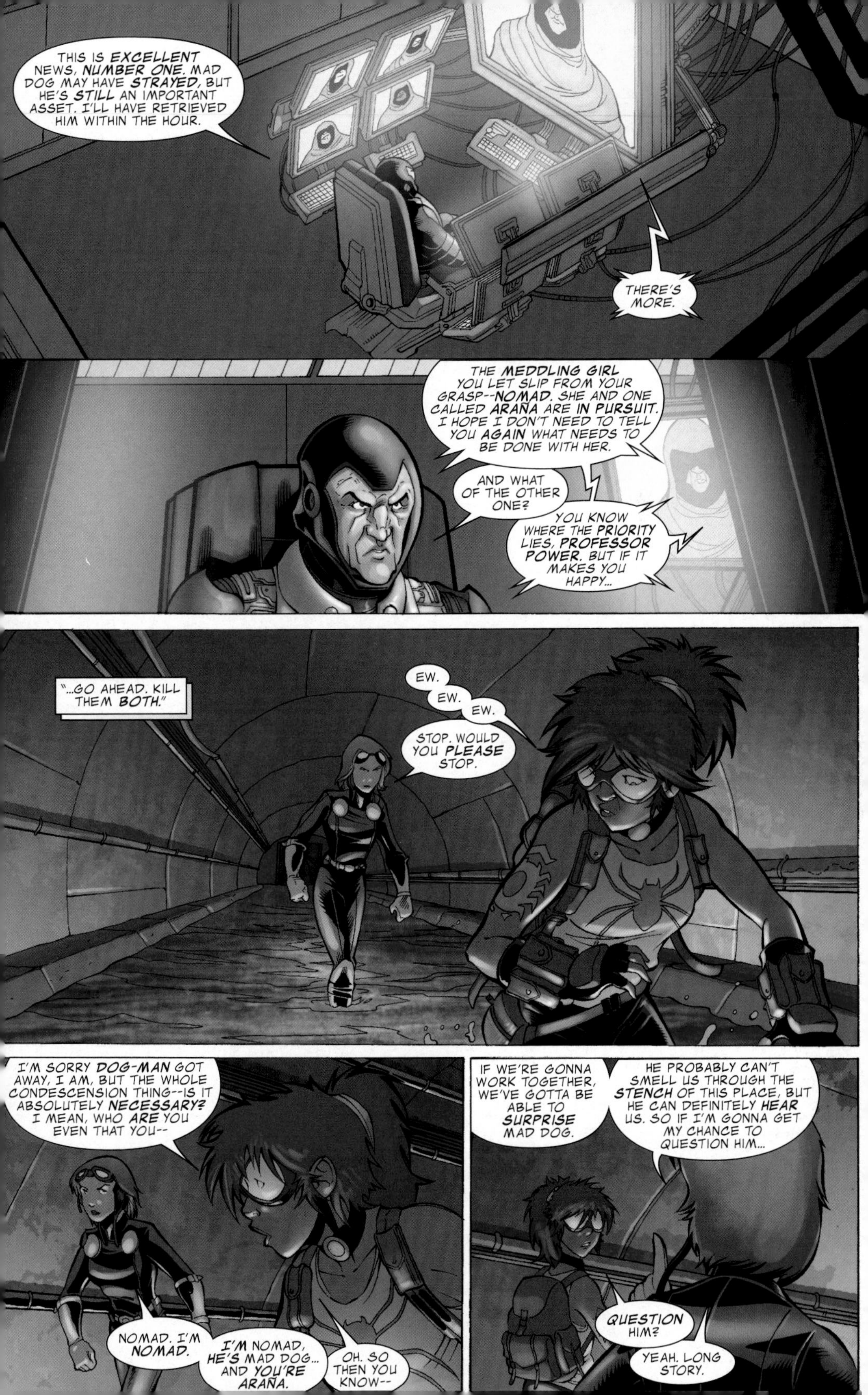
THIS IS EXCELLENT NEWS, NUMBER ONE. MAD DOG MAY HAVE STRAYED, BUT HE'S STILL AN IMPORTANT ASSET. I'LL HAVE RETRIEVED HIM WITHIN THE HOUR.
THERE'S MORE.
THE MEDDLING GIRL YOU LET SLIP FROM YOUR GRASP--NOMAD. SHE AND ONE CALLED ARAÑA ARE IN PURSUIT. I HOPE I DON'T NEED TO TELL YOU AGAIN WHAT NEEDS TO BE DONE WITH HER.
AND WHAT OF THE OTHER ONE?
YOU KNOW WHERE THE PRIORITY LIES, PROFESSOR POWER. BUT IF IT MAKES YOU HAPPY...
"...GO AHEAD. KILL THEM BOTH."
EW.
EW.
EW.
STOP. WOULD YOU PLEASE STOP.
I'M SORRY DOG-MAN GOT AWAY, I AM, BUT THE WHOLE CONDESCENSION THING--IS IT ABSOLUTELY NECESSARY? I MEAN, WHO ARE YOU EVEN THAT YOU--
NOMAD. I'M NOMAD.
I'M NOMAD, HE'S MAD DOG... AND YOU'RE ARAÑA.
OH. SO THEN YOU KNOW--
IF WE'RE GONNA WORK TOGETHER, WE'VE GOTTA BE ABLE TO SURPRISE MAD DOG.
HE PROBABLY CAN'T SMELL US THROUGH THE STENCH OF THIS PLACE, BUT HE CAN DEFINITELY HEAR US. SO IF I'M GONNA GET MY CHANCE TO QUESTION HIM...
QUESTION HIM?
YEAH. LONG STORY.

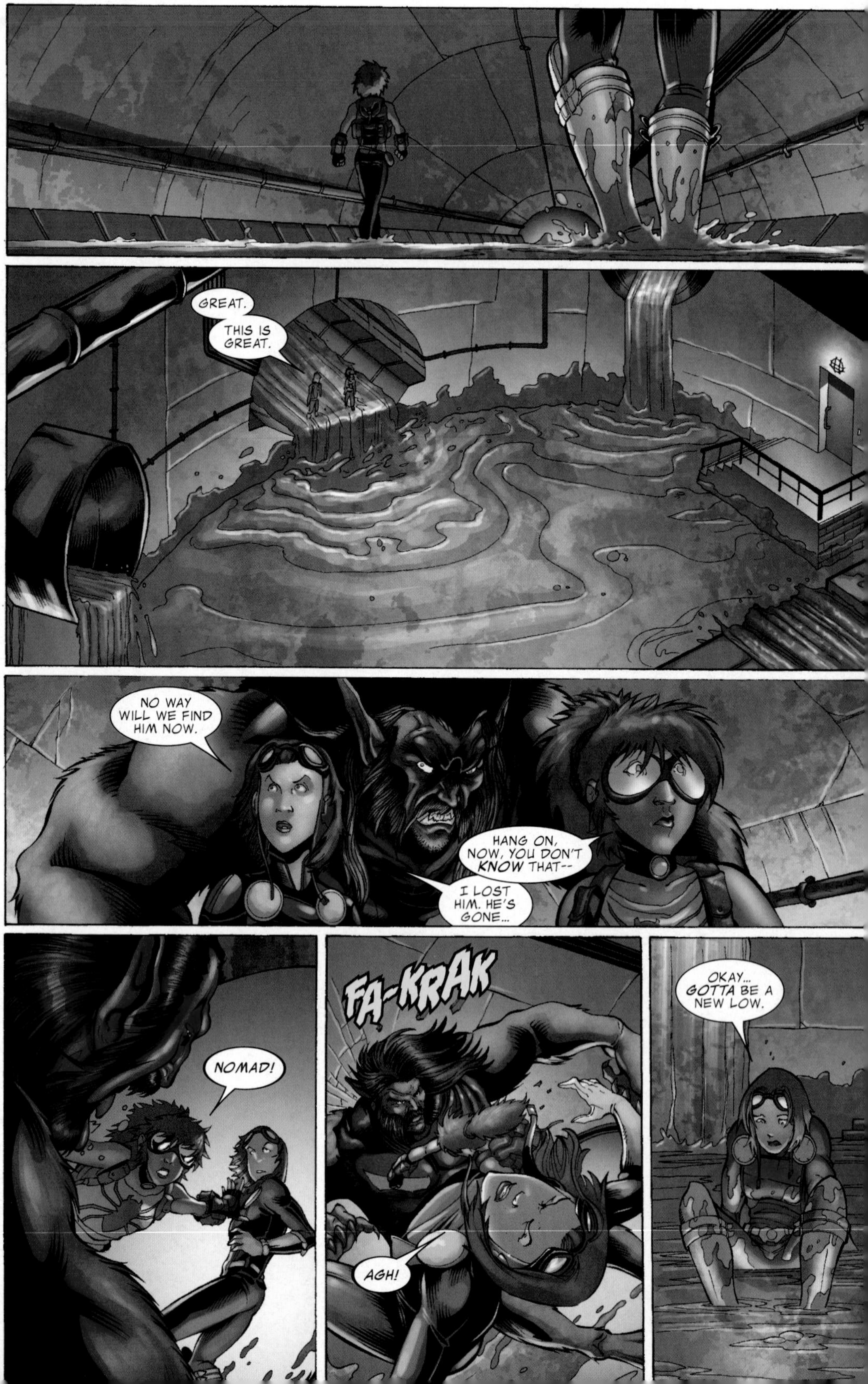
GREAT.
THIS IS GREAT.
NO WAY WILL WE FIND HIM NOW.
HANG ON, NOW, YOU DON'T KNOW THAT--
I LOST HIM. HE'S GONE...
NOMAD!
FA-KRAK
AGH!
OKAY... GOTTA BE A NEW LOW.

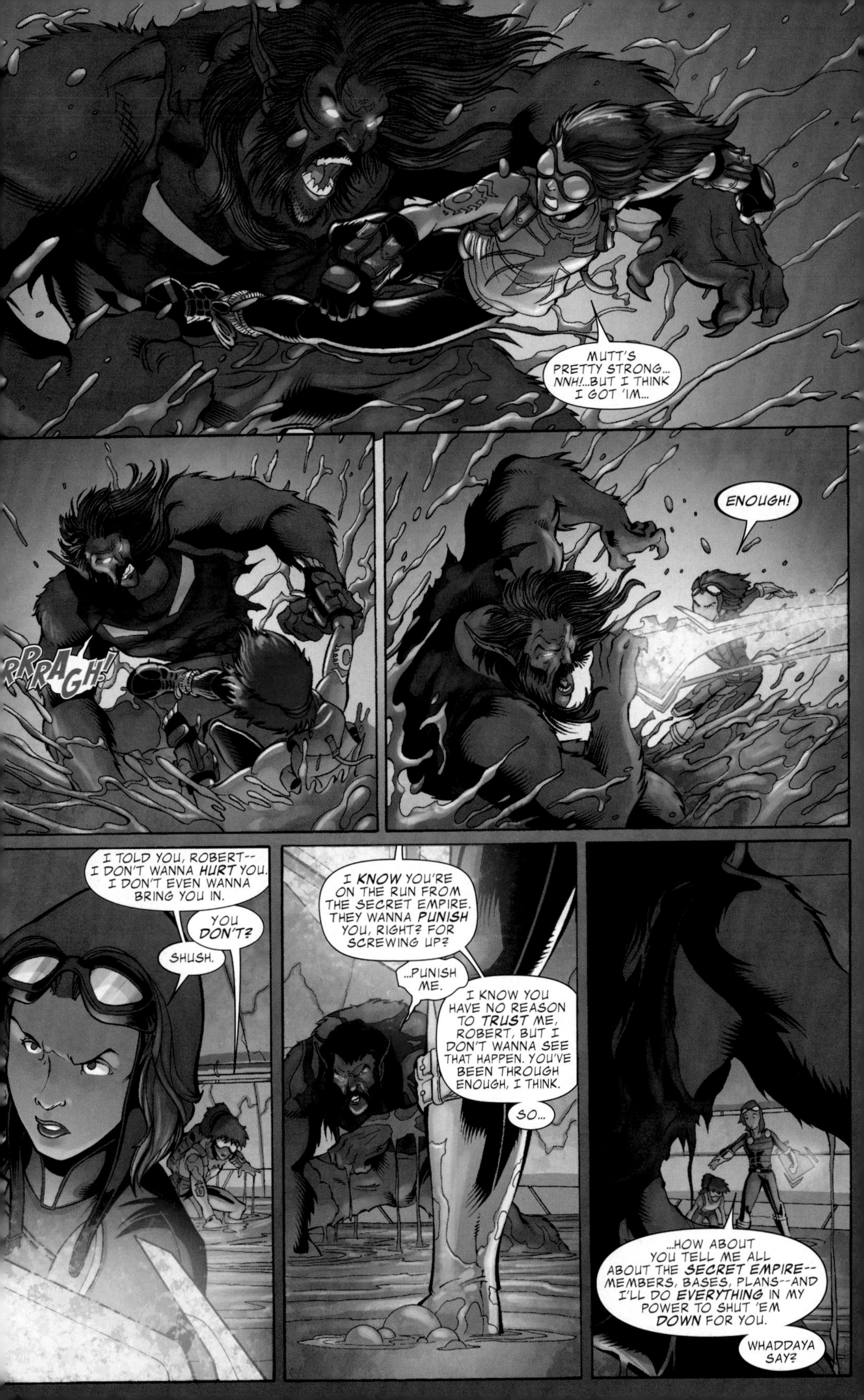

MUTT'S PRETTY STRONG... NNH!...BUT I THINK I GOT 'IM...
RRRAGH!
ENOUGH!
I TOLD YOU, ROBERT-- I DON'T WANNA HURT YOU. I DON'T EVEN WANNA BRING YOU IN.
YOU DON'T?
SHUSH.
I KNOW YOU'RE ON THE RUN FROM THE SECRET EMPIRE. THEY WANNA PUNISH YOU, RIGHT? FOR SCREWING UP?
...PUNISH ME.
I KNOW YOU HAVE NO REASON TO TRUST ME, ROBERT, BUT I DON'T WANNA SEE THAT HAPPEN. YOU'VE BEEN THROUGH ENOUGH, I THINK.
SO...
...HOW ABOUT YOU TELL ME ALL ABOUT THE SECRET EMPIRE-- MEMBERS, BASES, PLANS--AND I'LL DO EVERYTHING IN MY POWER TO SHUT 'EM DOWN FOR YOU.
WHADDAYA SAY?

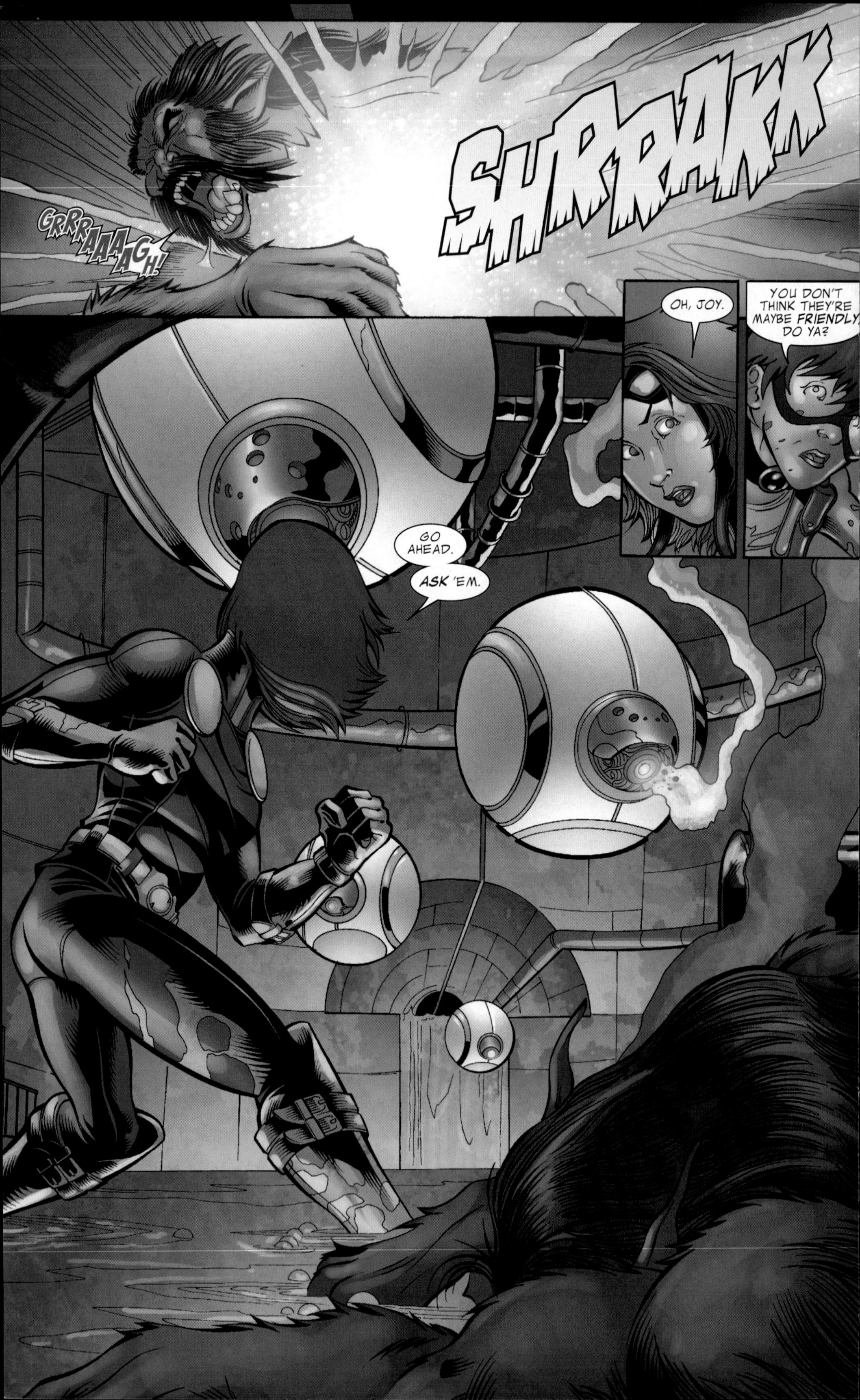
GRRRAAAAGH!
SHRRAKK
OH, JOY.
YOU DON'T THINK THEY'RE MAYBE FRIENDLY, DO YA?
GO AHEAD.
ASK 'EM.

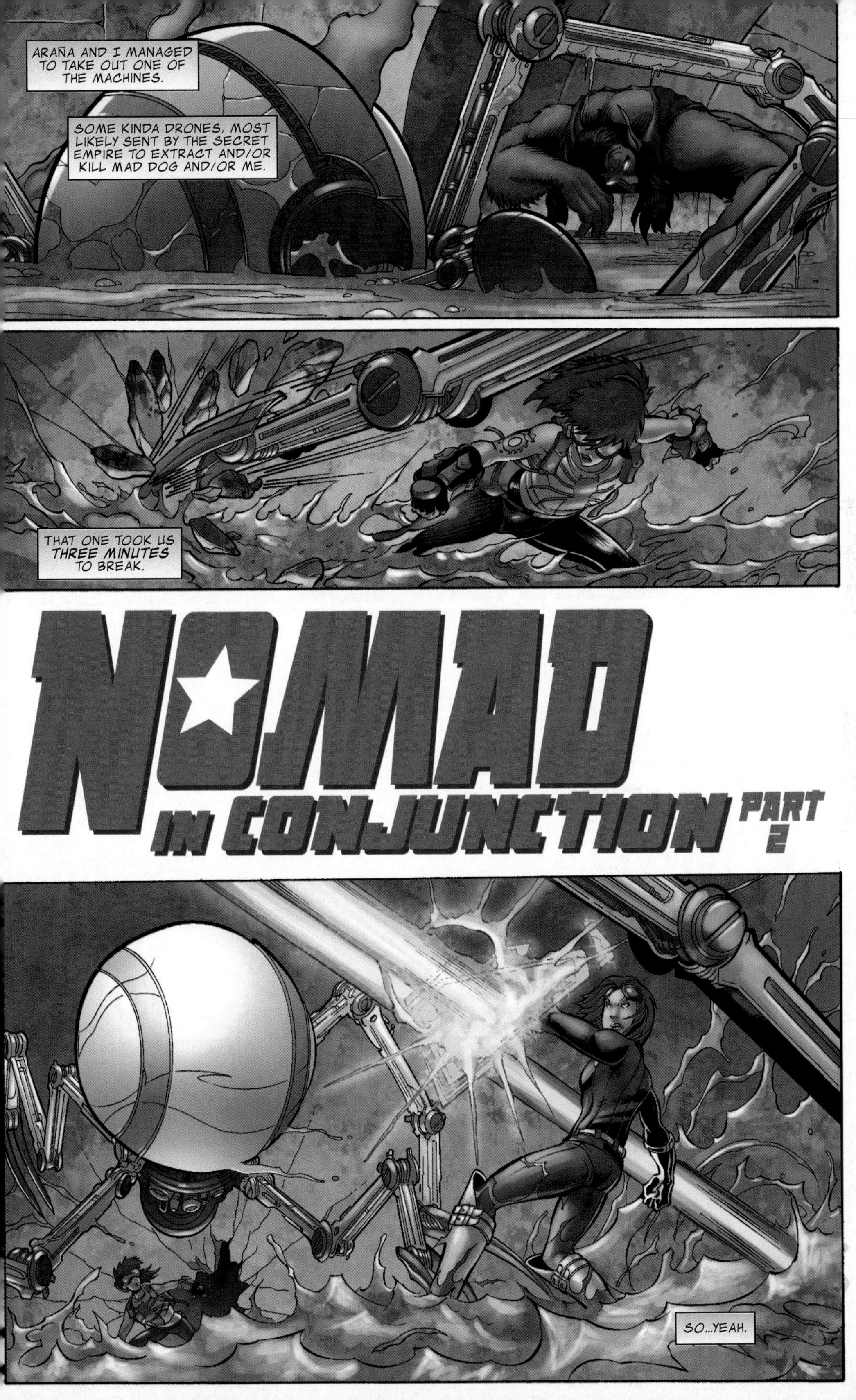
ARAÑA AND I MANAGED TO TAKE OUT ONE OF THE MACHINES.
SOME KINDA DRONES, MOST LIKELY SENT BY THE SECRET EMPIRE TO EXTRACT AND/OR KILL MAD DOG AND/OR ME.
THAT ONE TOOK US *THREE MINUTES* TO BREAK.
NOMAD
IN CONJUNCTION PART 2
SO...YEAH.

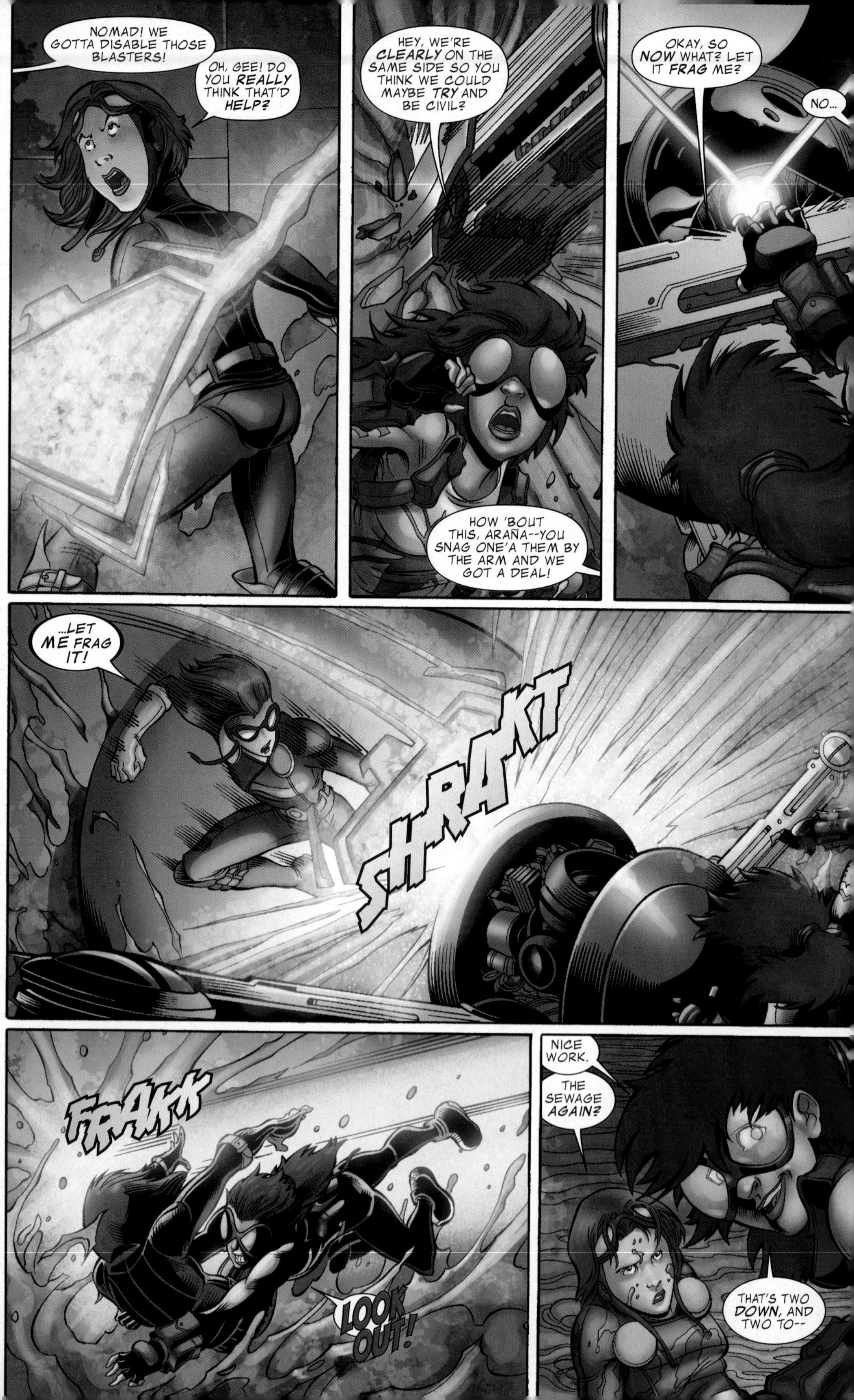

NOMAD! WE GOTTA DISABLE THOSE BLASTERS!
OH, GEE! DO YOU REALLY THINK THAT'D HELP?
HEY, WE'RE CLEARLY ON THE SAME SIDE SO YOU THINK WE COULD MAYBE TRY AND BE CIVIL?
HOW 'BOUT THIS, ARAÑA--YOU SNAG ONE'A THEM BY THE ARM AND WE GOT A DEAL!
OKAY, SO NOW WHAT? LET IT FRAG ME?
NO...
...LET ME FRAG IT!
SHRAKT
FRAKK
LOOK OUT!
NICE WORK.
THE SEWAGE AGAIN?
THAT'S TWO DOWN, AND TWO TO--

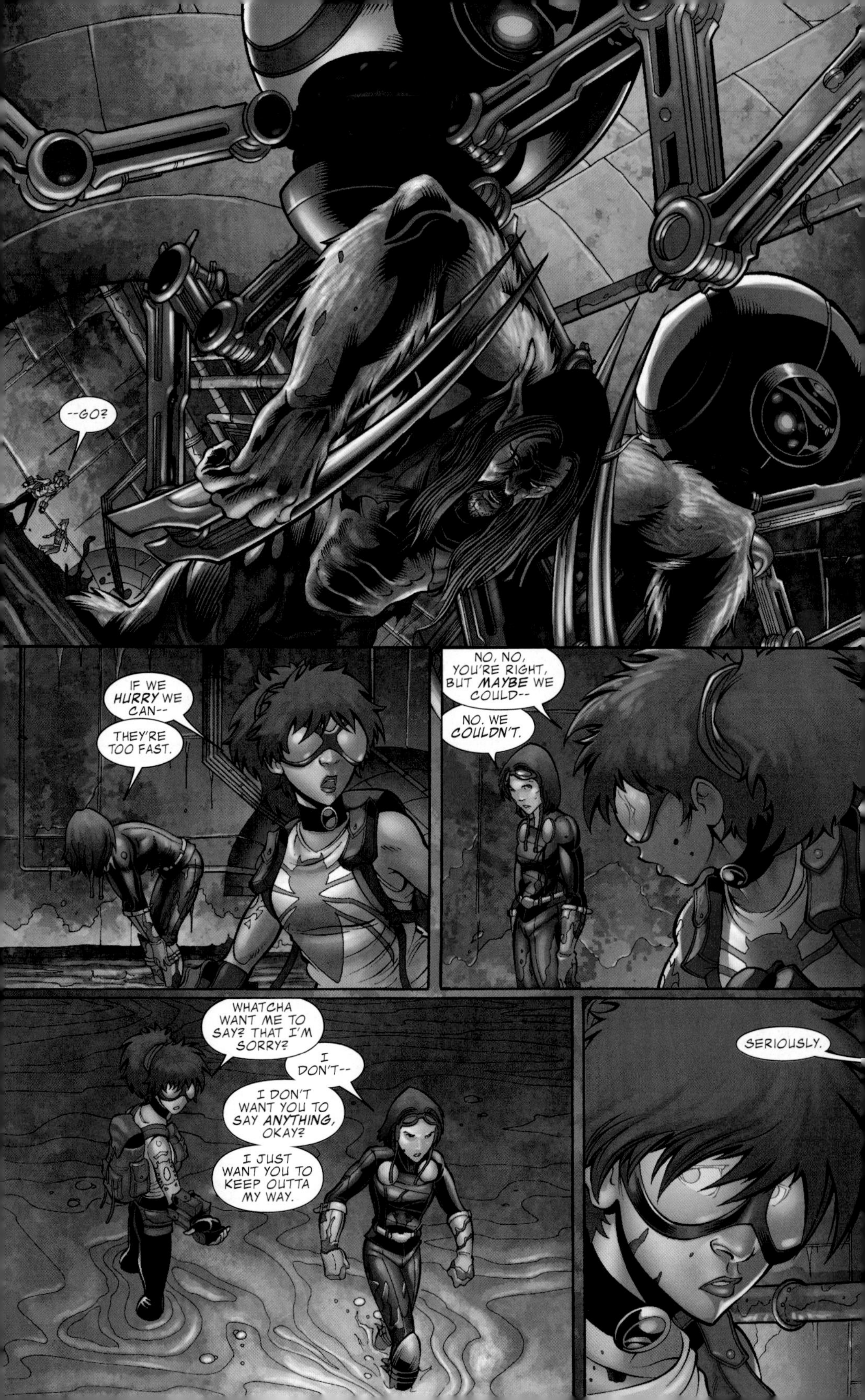
--GO?
IF WE HURRY WE CAN--
THEY'RE TOO FAST.
NO, NO, YOU'RE RIGHT, BUT MAYBE WE COULD--
NO. WE COULDN'T.
WHATCHA WANT ME TO SAY? THAT I'M SORRY?
I DON'T--
I DON'T WANT YOU TO SAY ANYTHING, OKAY?
I JUST WANT YOU TO KEEP OUTTA MY WAY.
SERIOUSLY.

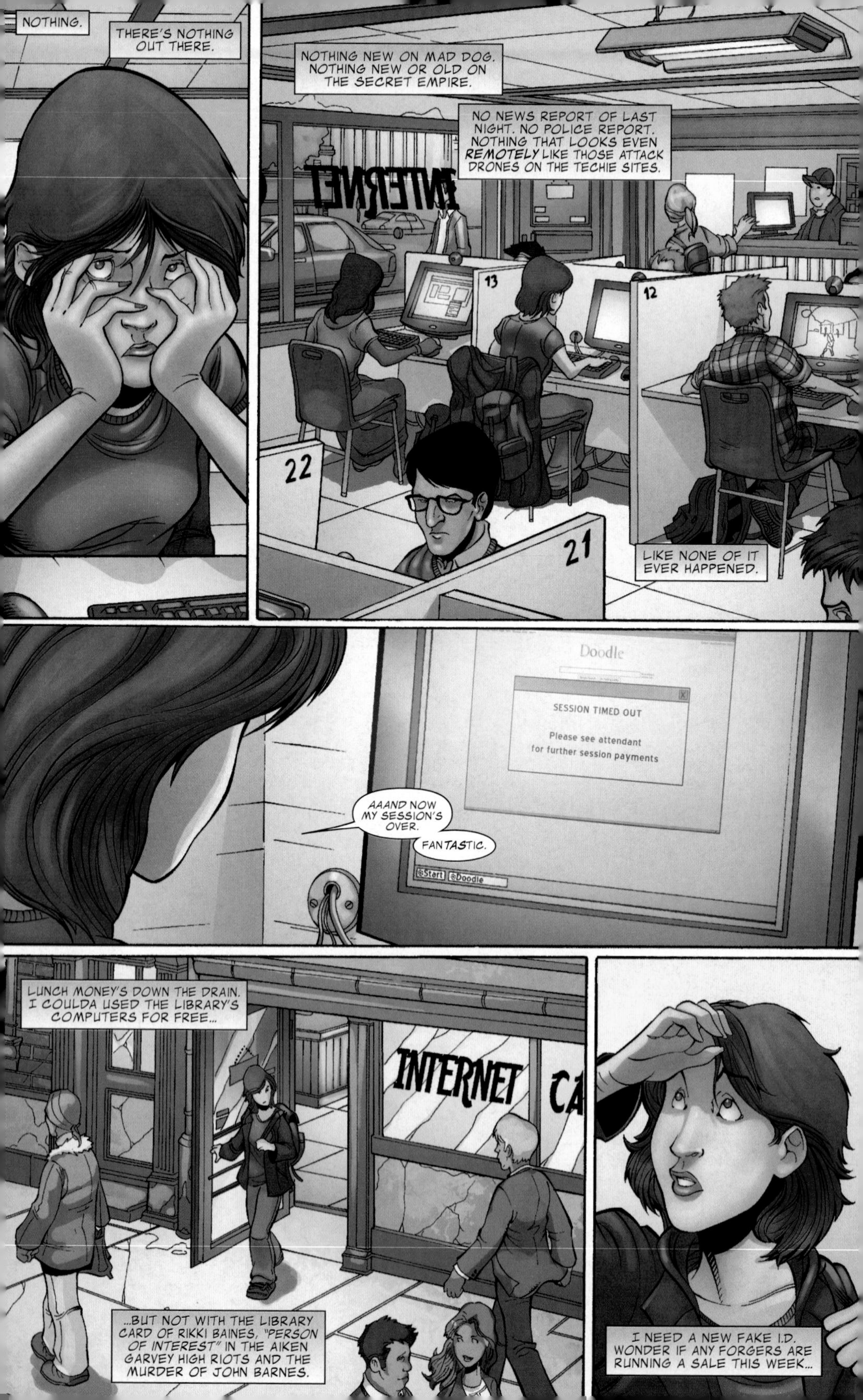
NOTHING.
THERE'S NOTHING OUT THERE.
NOTHING NEW ON MAD DOG. NOTHING NEW OR OLD ON THE SECRET EMPIRE.
NO NEWS REPORT OF LAST NIGHT. NO POLICE REPORT. NOTHING THAT LOOKS EVEN REMOTELY LIKE THOSE ATTACK DRONES ON THE TECHIE SITES.
13
12
22
21
LIKE NONE OF IT EVER HAPPENED.
Doodle
SESSION TIMED OUT
Please see attendant for further session payments
AAAND NOW MY SESSION'S OVER.
FANTASTIC.
Start
Doodle
LUNCH MONEY'S DOWN THE DRAIN. I COULDA USED THE LIBRARY'S COMPUTERS FOR FREE...
INTERNET
...BUT NOT WITH THE LIBRARY CARD OF RIKKI BAINES, "PERSON OF INTEREST" IN THE AIKEN GARVEY HIGH RIOTS AND THE MURDER OF JOHN BARNES.
I NEED A NEW FAKE I.D. WONDER IF ANY FORGERS ARE RUNNING A SALE THIS WEEK...

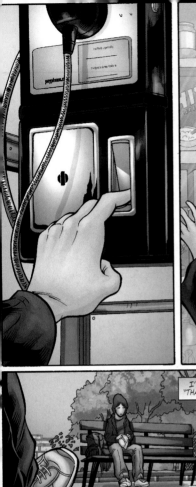

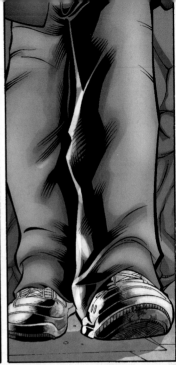

I'M THINKING TO MYSELF, "THANKS A WHOLE LOT, ARAÑA."

BUT THE THING IS, I KNOW I CAN'T PLACE THE BLAME ON HER.

GIVEN THE SAME SET OF CIRCUMSTANCES, I WOULDA DONE THE SAME, ESSENTIALLY.

HHH...

EVERY TIME THINGS START TO FEEL NORMAL, IT COMES BACK TO THIS.

THIS SEPARATION. THIS NON-EXISTENCE.

I START TO WONDER IF I REALLY *DID* SACRIFICE MY LIFE ON THE WORLD I'M FROM--LIKE I THOUGHT I *WAS* DOING--AND THIS IS JUST MY OWN LITTLE SLICE OF PURGATORY.

OR I'M ACTUALLY IN A COMA, AND THIS IS JUST A REALLY, REALLY, *REALLY* VIVID DREAM.

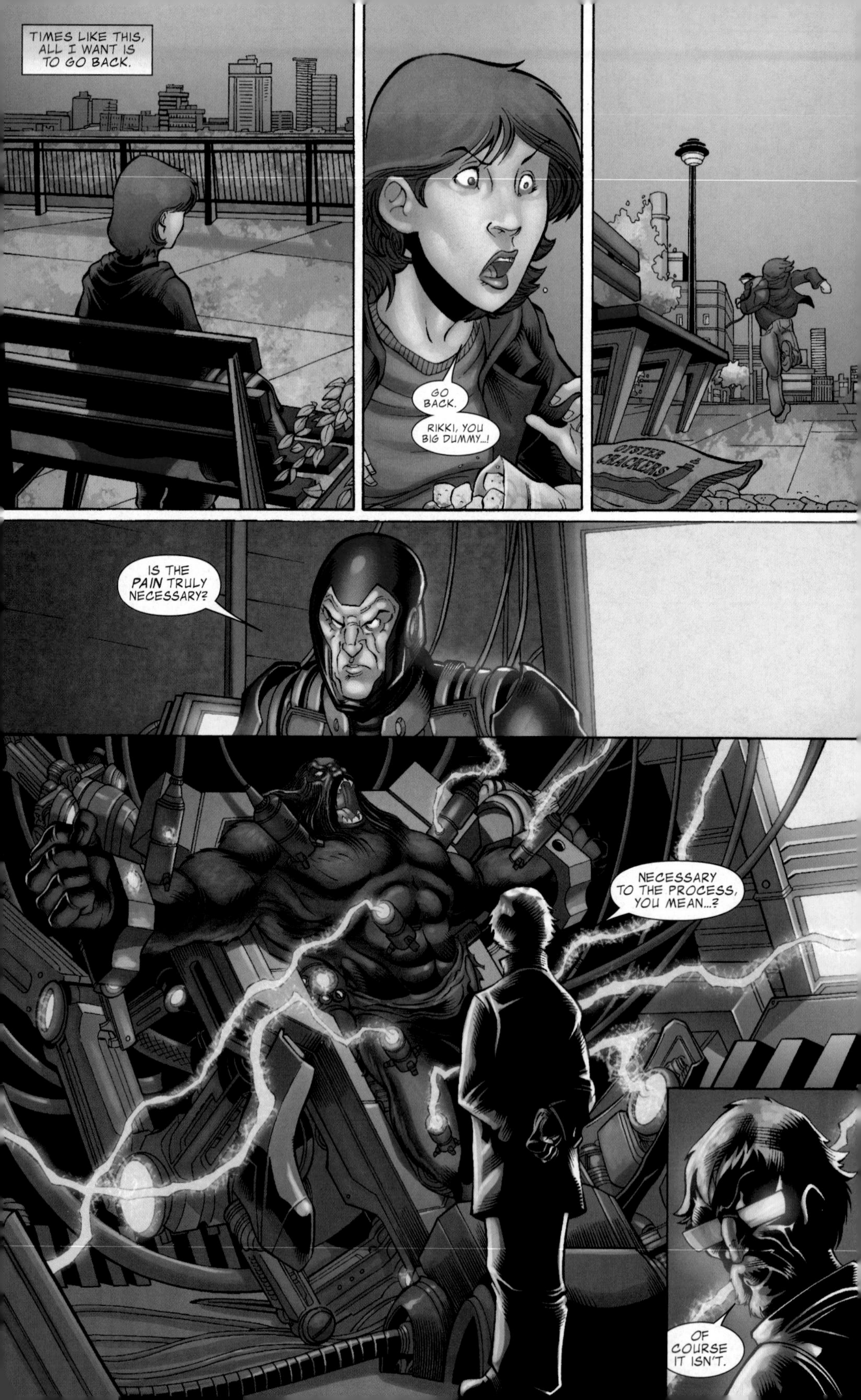

TIMES LIKE THIS, ALL I WANT IS TO GO BACK.
GO BACK.
RIKKI, YOU BIG DUMMY...!
OYSTER CRACKERS
IS THE PAIN TRULY NECESSARY?
NECESSARY TO THE PROCESS, YOU MEAN...?
OF COURSE IT ISN'T.

"THIS IS WHAT **NUMBER ONE** WANTS.

"THIS IS THE **PRICE** OF **DISOBEDIENCE**..."

...FOR **MAD DOG**, AT ANY RATE.

SOME OF US ARE APPARENTLY SPARED SUCH A FATE NO MATTER **HOW** MANY TIMES WE ERR.

SOME OF US ARE SIMPLY **INCARCERATED** UNTIL WE CAN REGAIN NUMBER ONE'S **TRUST**.

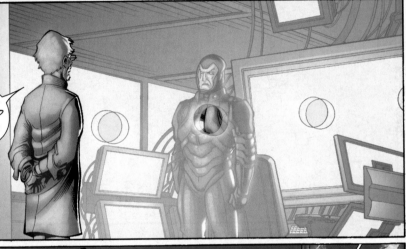

AREN'T YOU **FINISHED** WITH HIM YET?

HIS BODY NEEDS TO FULLY ACCEPT THE NEW **CATALYST** I'VE DESIGNED.

I MUST SAY, PROFESSOR POWER...

...YOUR CONCERN **WOULD** BE ADMIRABLE IF YOU WEREN'T SIMPLY CHANGING THE SUBJECT.

IT'S **TWICE** NOW YOU'VE LET THE GIRL LIVE IF I'M NOT MISTAKEN. DO YOU THINK NUMBER ONE WILL TOLERATE **FURTHER** INCOMPETENCE WITHOUT MAJOR REPERCUSSIONS FOR YOU?

GONE.

IT'S ALL GONE.

YEAH, I THOUGHT OF THAT, TOO...

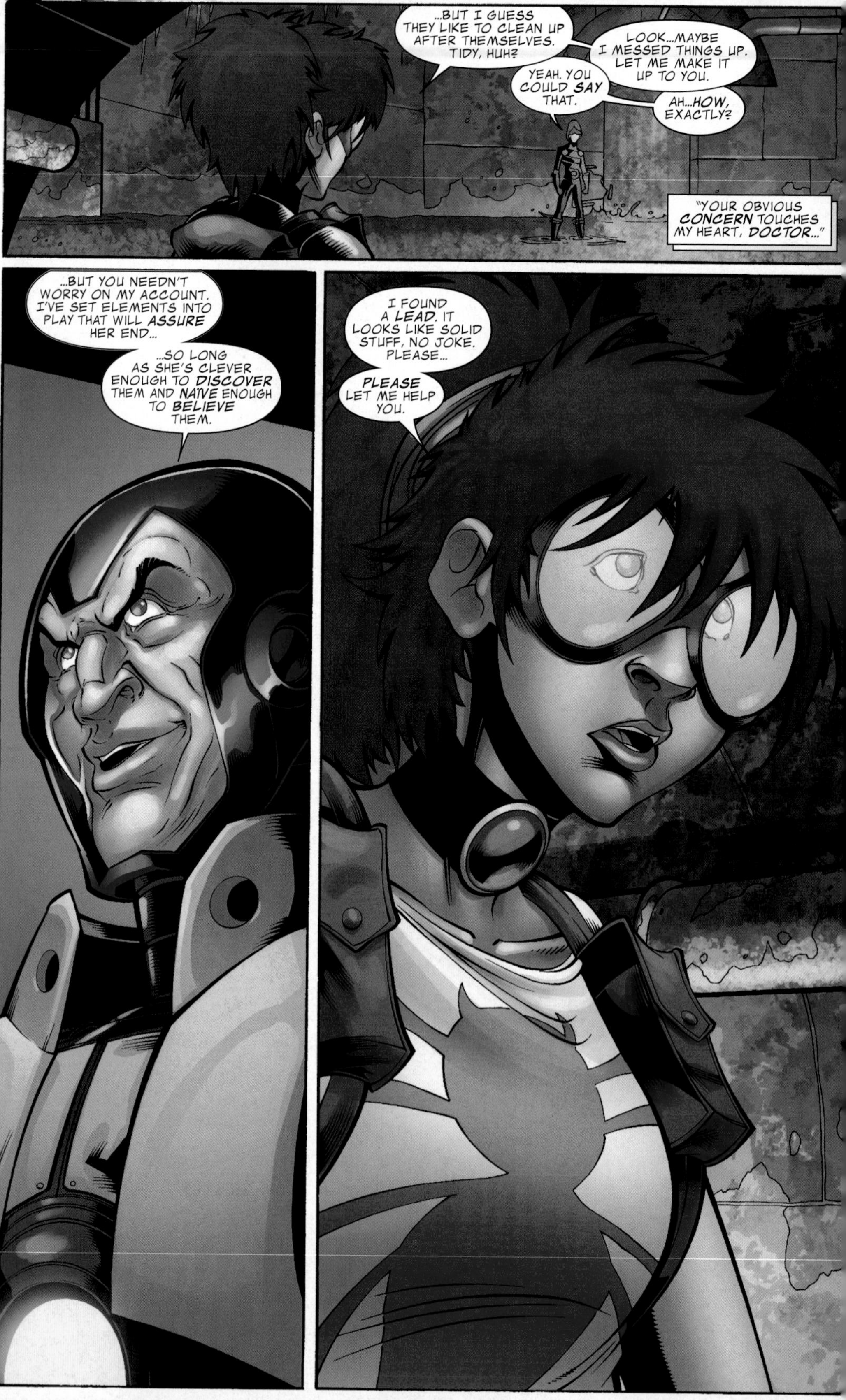
...BUT I GUESS THEY LIKE TO CLEAN UP AFTER THEMSELVES. TIDY, HUH?
LOOK...MAYBE I MESSED THINGS UP. LET ME MAKE IT UP TO YOU.
YEAH. YOU COULD SAY THAT.
AH...HOW, EXACTLY?
"YOUR OBVIOUS CONCERN TOUCHES MY HEART, DOCTOR..."
...BUT YOU NEEDN'T WORRY ON MY ACCOUNT. I'VE SET ELEMENTS INTO PLAY THAT WILL ASSURE HER END...
...SO LONG AS SHE'S CLEVER ENOUGH TO DISCOVER THEM AND NAÏVE ENOUGH TO BELIEVE THEM.
I FOUND A LEAD. IT LOOKS LIKE SOLID STUFF, NO JOKE. PLEASE...
PLEASE LET ME HELP YOU.

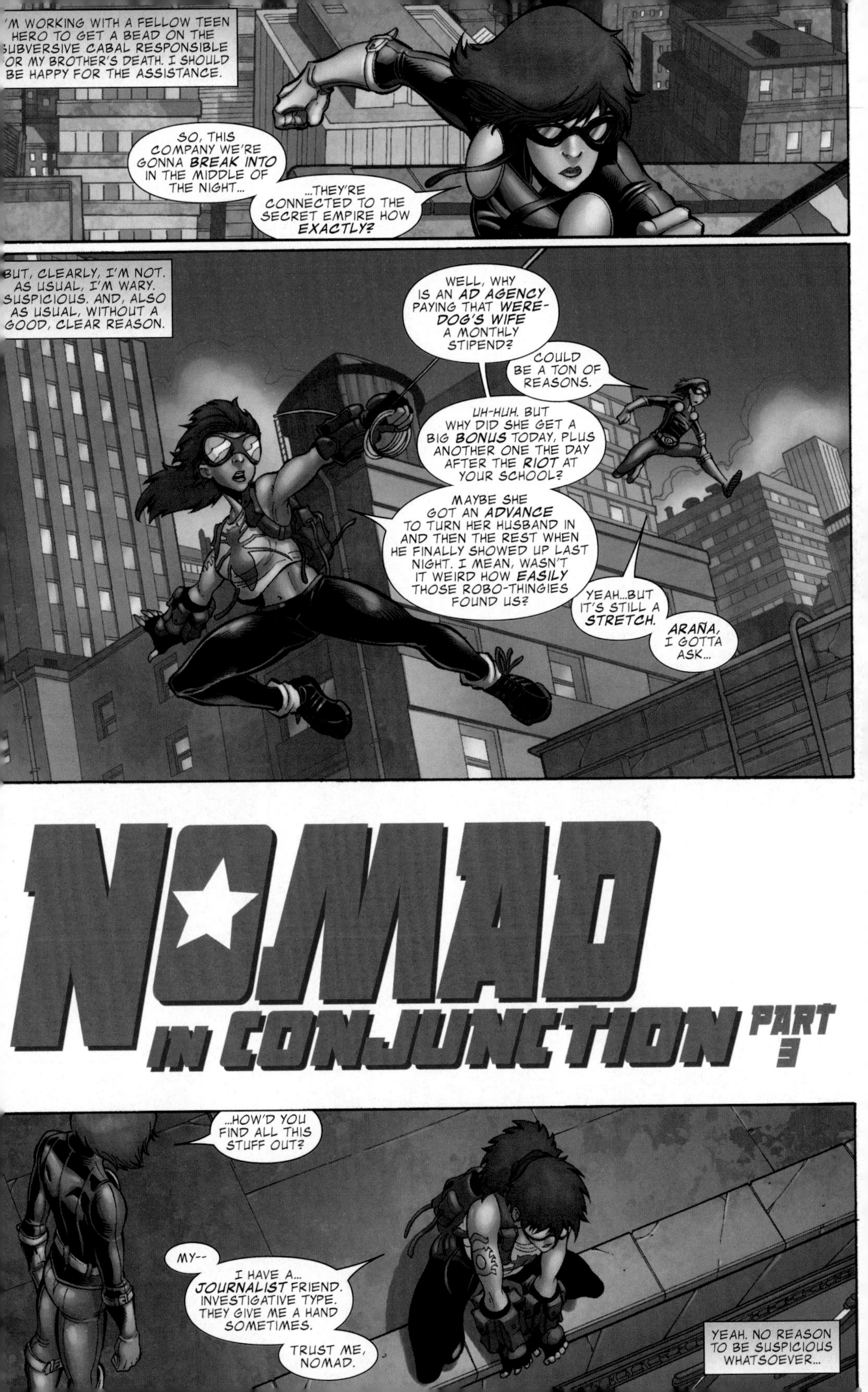
I'M WORKING WITH A FELLOW TEEN HERO TO GET A BEAD ON THE SUBVERSIVE CABAL RESPONSIBLE FOR MY BROTHER'S DEATH. I SHOULD BE HAPPY FOR THE ASSISTANCE.
SO, THIS COMPANY WE'RE GONNA BREAK INTO IN THE MIDDLE OF THE NIGHT...
...THEY'RE CONNECTED TO THE SECRET EMPIRE HOW EXACTLY?
BUT, CLEARLY, I'M NOT. AS USUAL, I'M WARY. SUSPICIOUS. AND, ALSO AS USUAL, WITHOUT A GOOD, CLEAR REASON.
WELL, WHY IS AN AD AGENCY PAYING THAT WERE-DOG'S WIFE A MONTHLY STIPEND?
COULD BE A TON OF REASONS.
UH-HUH. BUT WHY DID SHE GET A BIG BONUS TODAY, PLUS ANOTHER ONE THE DAY AFTER THE RIOT AT YOUR SCHOOL?
MAYBE SHE GOT AN ADVANCE TO TURN HER HUSBAND IN AND THEN THE REST WHEN HE FINALLY SHOWED UP LAST NIGHT. I MEAN, WASN'T IT WEIRD HOW EASILY THOSE ROBO-THINGIES FOUND US?
YEAH...BUT IT'S STILL A STRETCH.
ARAÑA, I GOTTA ASK...
NOMAD IN CONJUNCTION PART 3
...HOW'D YOU FIND ALL THIS STUFF OUT?
MY--
I HAVE A... JOURNALIST FRIEND. INVESTIGATIVE TYPE. THEY GIVE ME A HAND SOMETIMES.
TRUST ME, NOMAD.
YEAH. NO REASON TO BE SUSPICIOUS WHATSOEVER...

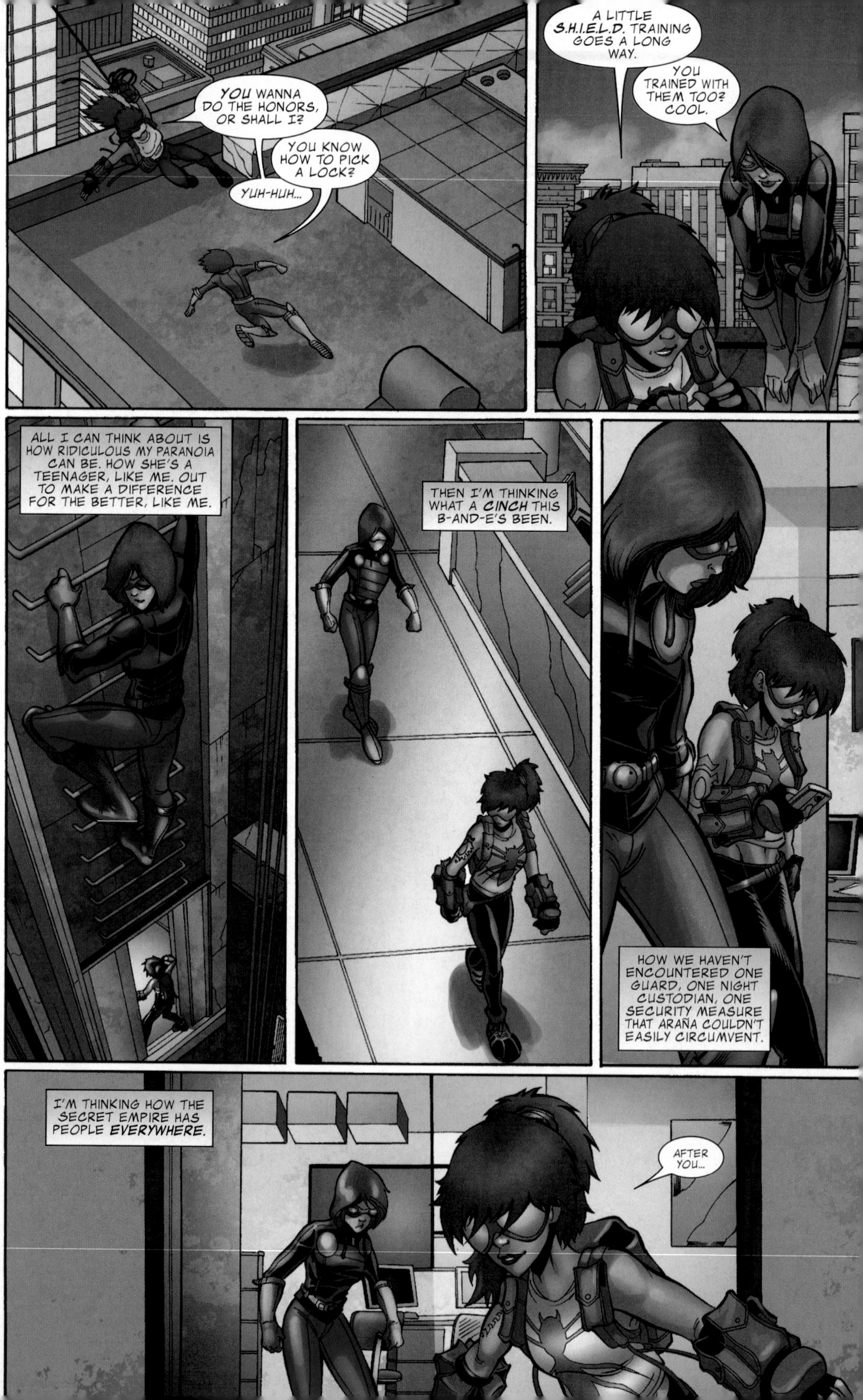
YOU WANNA DO THE HONORS, OR SHALL I?
YOU KNOW HOW TO PICK A LOCK?
YUH-HUH...
A LITTLE S.H.I.E.L.D. TRAINING GOES A LONG WAY.
YOU TRAINED WITH THEM TOO? COOL.
ALL I CAN THINK ABOUT IS HOW RIDICULOUS MY PARANOIA CAN BE. HOW SHE'S A TEENAGER, LIKE ME. OUT TO MAKE A DIFFERENCE FOR THE BETTER, LIKE ME.
THEN I'M THINKING WHAT A CINCH THIS B-AND-E'S BEEN.
HOW WE HAVEN'T ENCOUNTERED ONE GUARD, ONE NIGHT CUSTODIAN, ONE SECURITY MEASURE THAT ARAÑA COULDN'T EASILY CIRCUMVENT.
I'M THINKING HOW THE SECRET EMPIRE HAS PEOPLE EVERYWHERE.
AFTER YOU...

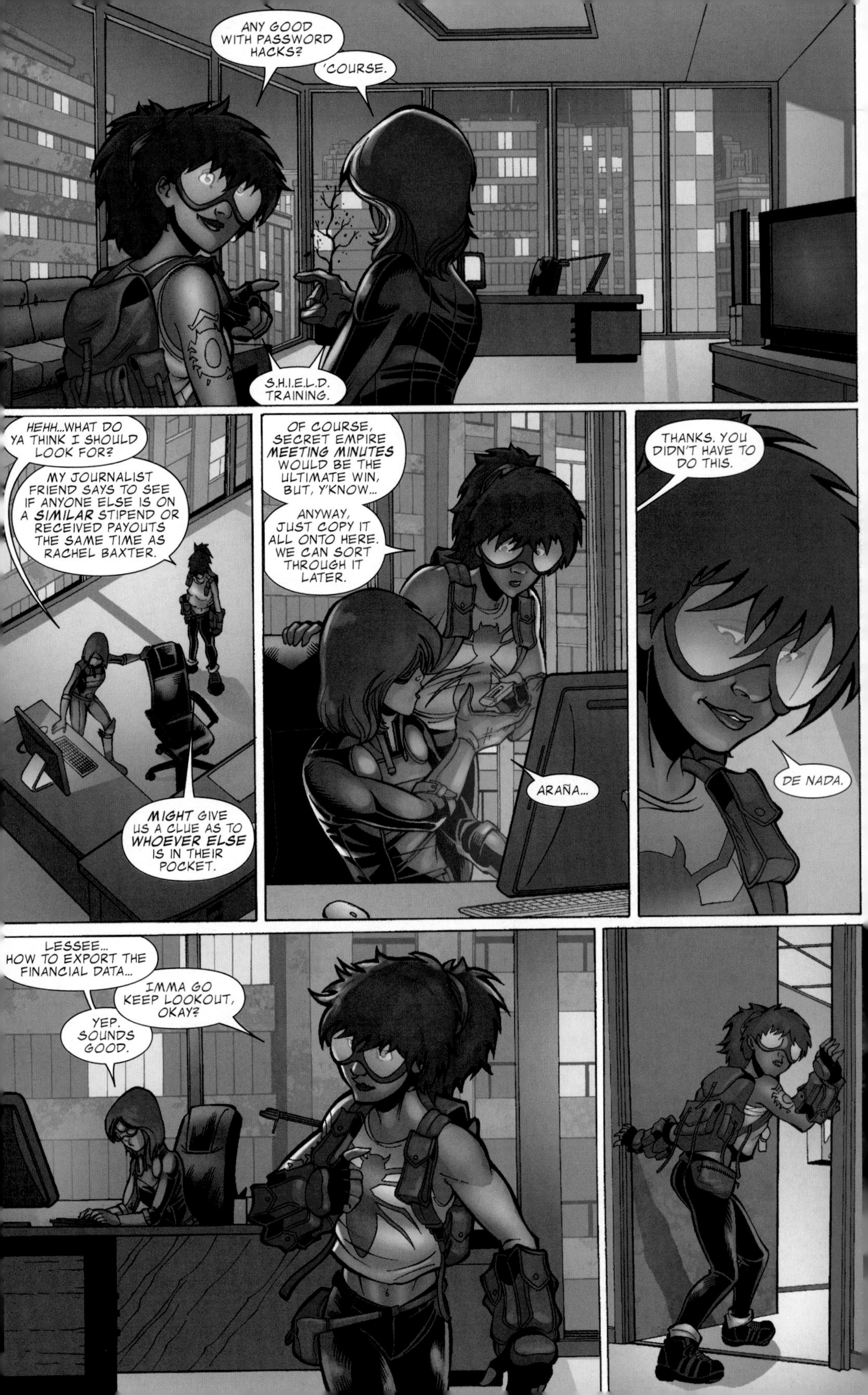
ANY GOOD WITH PASSWORD HACKS?
'COURSE.
S.H.I.E.L.D. TRAINING.
HEHH...WHAT DO YA THINK I SHOULD LOOK FOR?
MY JOURNALIST FRIEND SAYS TO SEE IF ANYONE ELSE IS ON A SIMILAR STIPEND OR RECEIVED PAYOUTS THE SAME TIME AS RACHEL BAXTER.
MIGHT GIVE US A CLUE AS TO WHOEVER ELSE IS IN THEIR POCKET.
OF COURSE, SECRET EMPIRE MEETING MINUTES WOULD BE THE ULTIMATE WIN, BUT, Y'KNOW...
ANYWAY, JUST COPY IT ALL ONTO HERE. WE CAN SORT THROUGH IT LATER.
ARAÑA...
THANKS. YOU DIDN'T HAVE TO DO THIS.
DE NADA.
LESSEE... HOW TO EXPORT THE FINANCIAL DATA...
IMMA GO KEEP LOOKOUT, OKAY?
YEP. SOUNDS GOOD.

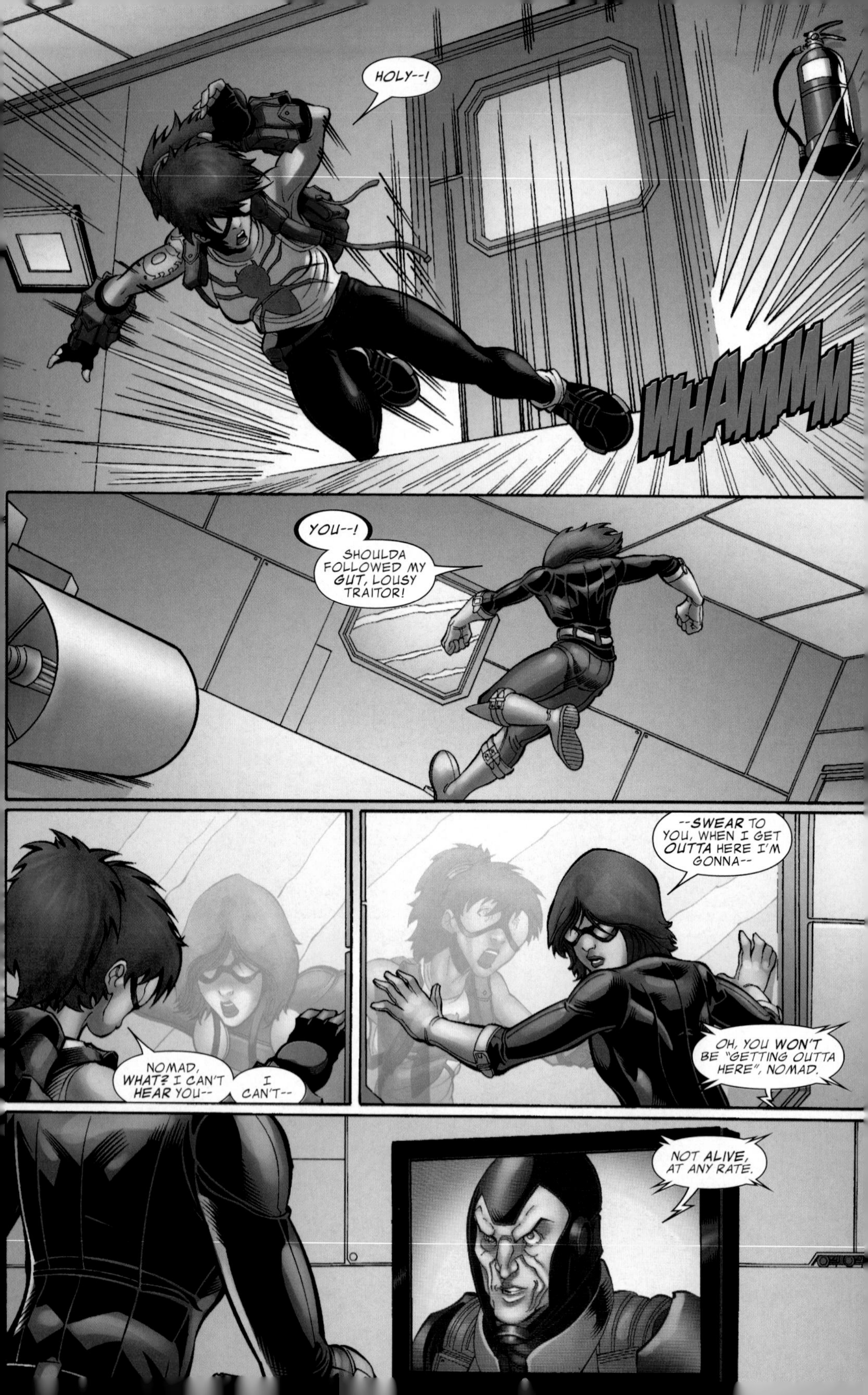
HOLY--!
WHAMMM
YOU--!
SHOULDA FOLLOWED MY GUT, LOUSY TRAITOR!
--SWEAR TO YOU, WHEN I GET OUTTA HERE I'M GONNA--
NOMAD, WHAT? I CAN'T HEAR YOU--
I CAN'T--
OH, YOU WON'T BE "GETTING OUTTA HERE", NOMAD.
NOT ALIVE, AT ANY RATE.

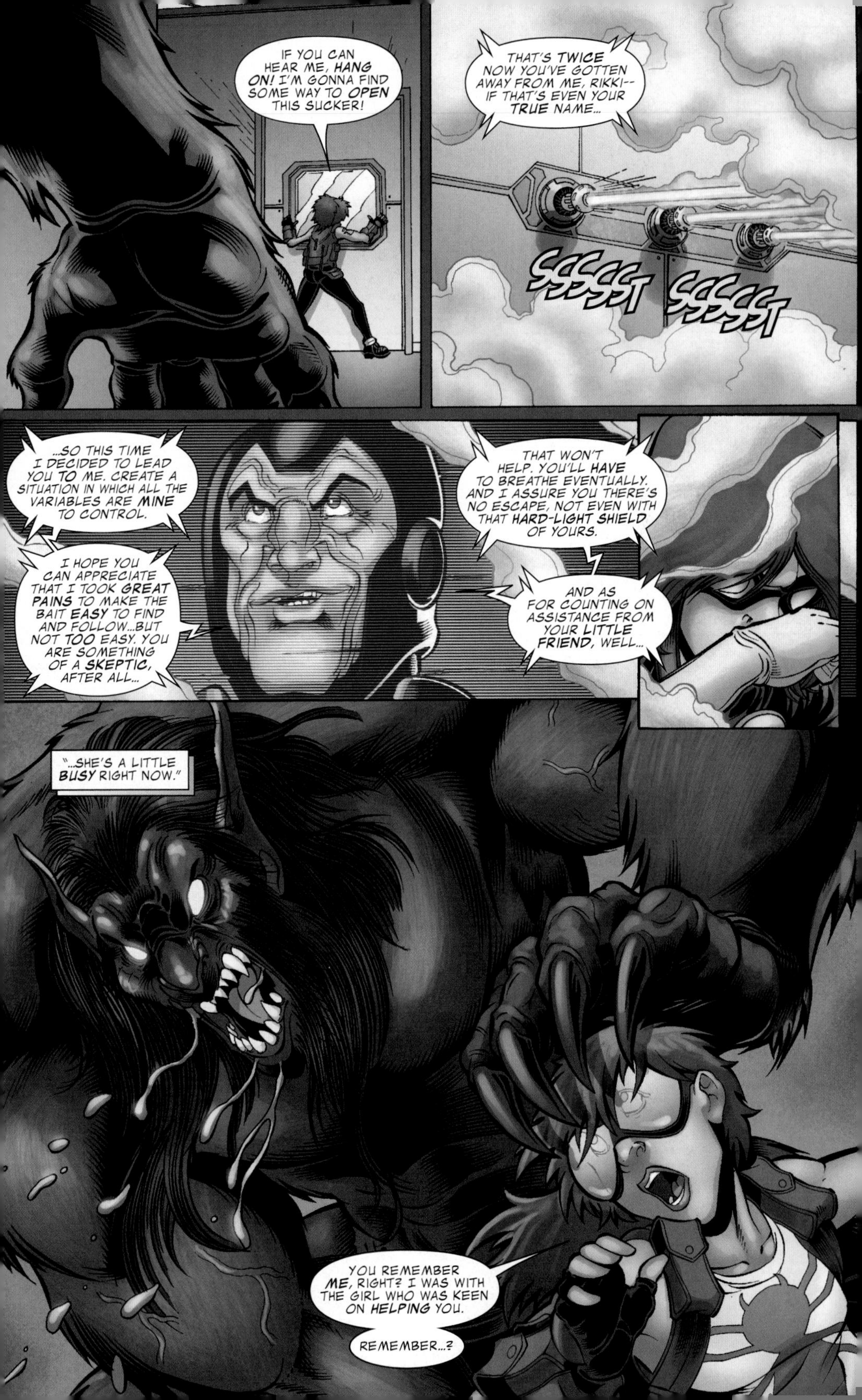
IF YOU CAN HEAR ME, HANG ON! I'M GONNA FIND SOME WAY TO OPEN THIS SUCKER!
THAT'S TWICE NOW YOU'VE GOTTEN AWAY FROM ME, RIKKI-- IF THAT'S EVEN YOUR TRUE NAME...
SSSSSST
SSSSSST
...SO THIS TIME I DECIDED TO LEAD YOU TO ME. CREATE A SITUATION IN WHICH ALL THE VARIABLES ARE MINE TO CONTROL.
I HOPE YOU CAN APPRECIATE THAT I TOOK GREAT PAINS TO MAKE THE BAIT EASY TO FIND AND FOLLOW...BUT NOT TOO EASY. YOU ARE SOMETHING OF A SKEPTIC, AFTER ALL...
THAT WON'T HELP. YOU'LL HAVE TO BREATHE EVENTUALLY. AND I ASSURE YOU THERE'S NO ESCAPE, NOT EVEN WITH THAT HARD-LIGHT SHIELD OF YOURS.
AND AS FOR COUNTING ON ASSISTANCE FROM YOUR LITTLE FRIEND, WELL...
"...SHE'S A LITTLE BUSY RIGHT NOW."
YOU REMEMBER ME, RIGHT? I WAS WITH THE GIRL WHO WAS KEEN ON HELPING YOU.
REMEMBER...?

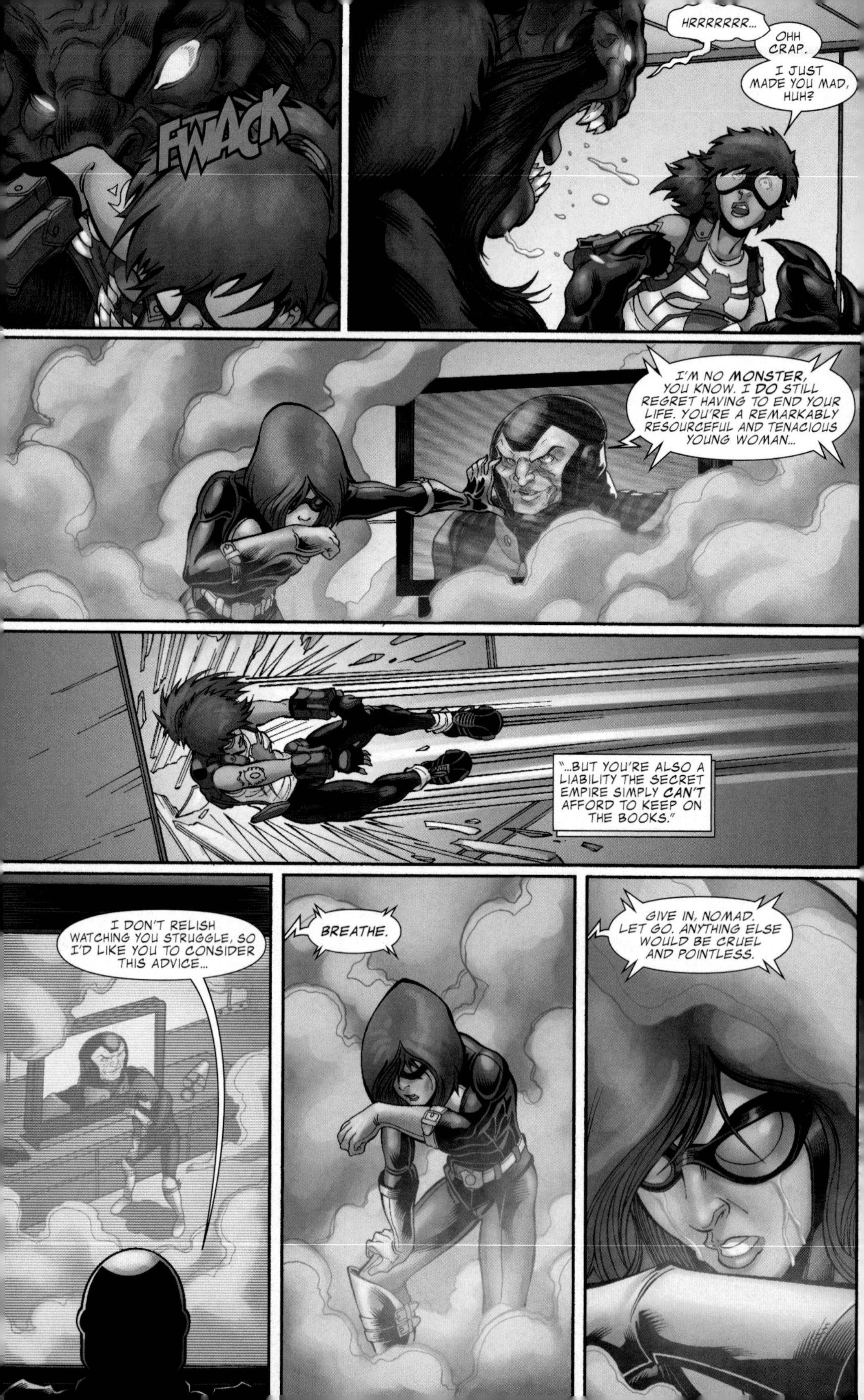
FWACK
HRRRRRRR...
OHH CRAP.
I JUST MADE YOU MAD, HUH?
I'M NO MONSTER, YOU KNOW. I DO STILL REGRET HAVING TO END YOUR LIFE. YOU'RE A REMARKABLY RESOURCEFUL AND TENACIOUS YOUNG WOMAN...
"...BUT YOU'RE ALSO A LIABILITY THE SECRET EMPIRE SIMPLY CAN'T AFFORD TO KEEP ON THE BOOKS."
I DON'T RELISH WATCHING YOU STRUGGLE, SO I'D LIKE YOU TO CONSIDER THIS ADVICE...
BREATHE.
GIVE IN, NOMAD. LET GO. ANYTHING ELSE WOULD BE CRUEL AND POINTLESS.

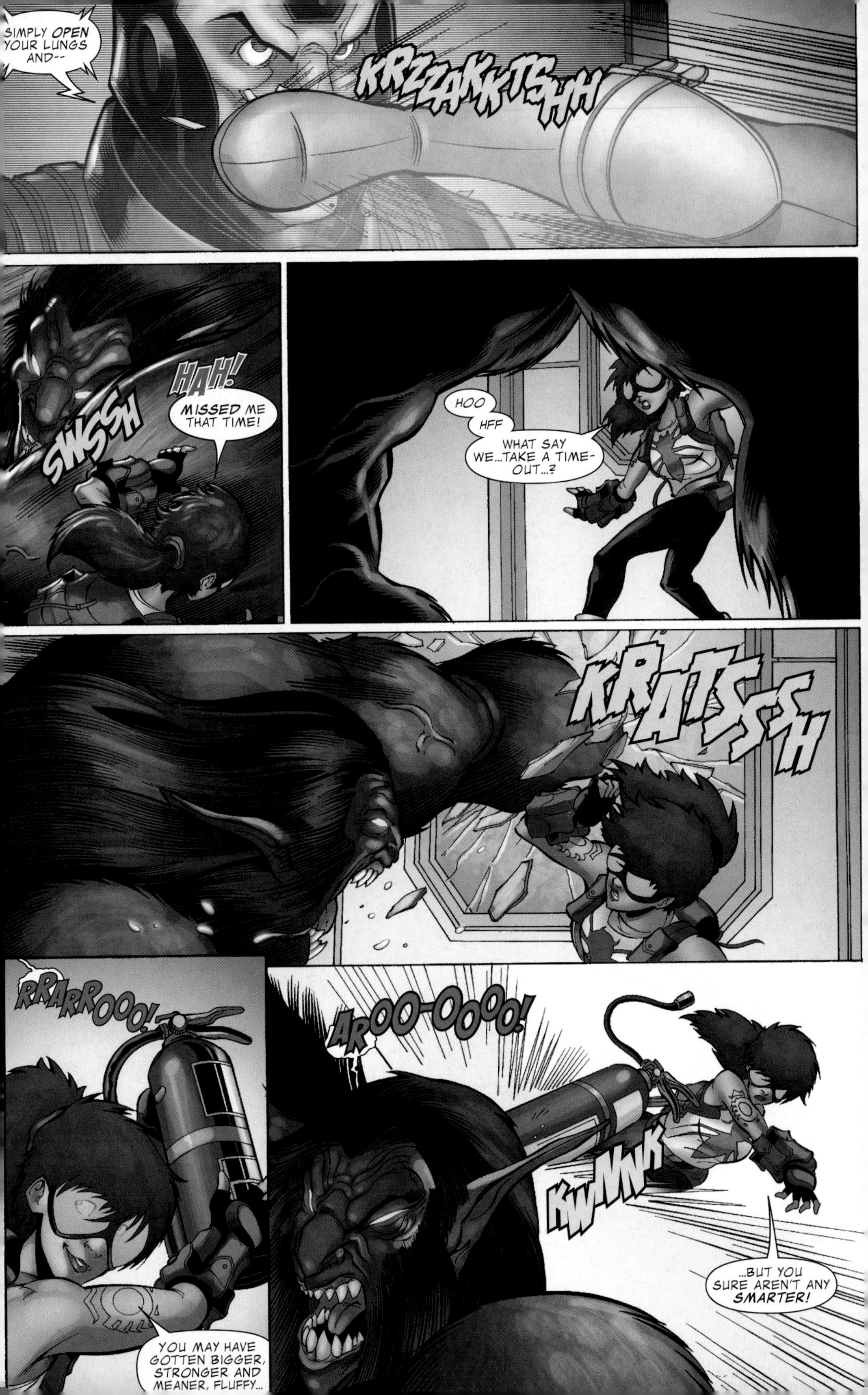

SIMPLY OPEN YOUR LUNGS AND--
KRZZAKKTSHH
HAH!
SWSSH
MISSED ME THAT TIME!
HOO
HFF
WHAT SAY WE...TAKE A TIME-OUT...?
KRATSSH
RRARROOO!
YOU MAY HAVE GOTTEN BIGGER, STRONGER AND MEANER, FLUFFY...
AROO-OOOO!
KWNNK
...BUT YOU SURE AREN'T ANY SMARTER!

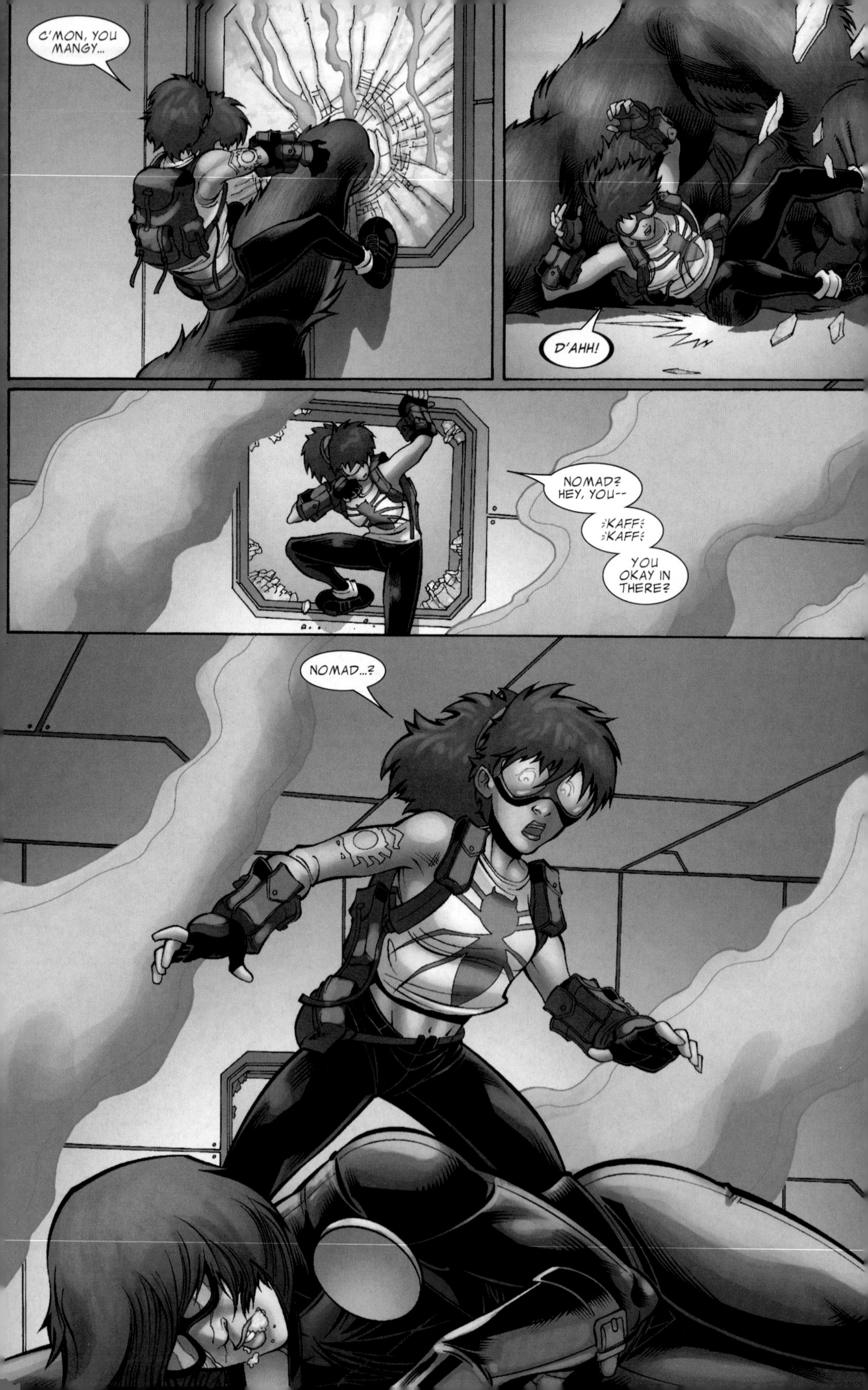
C'MON, YOU MANGY...
D'AHH!
NOMAD? HEY, YOU--
KAFF KAFF
YOU OKAY IN THERE?
NOMAD...?

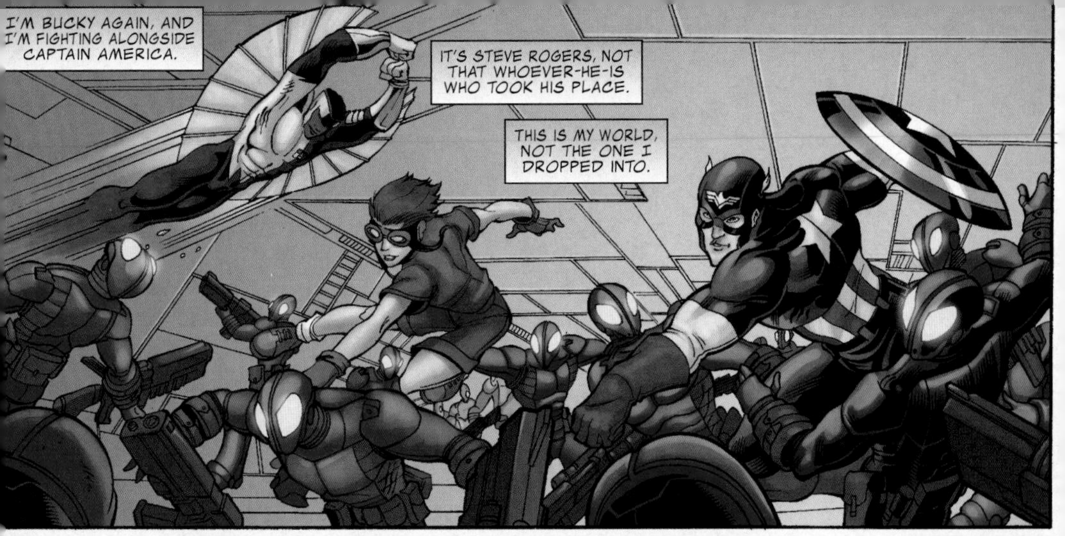
I'M BUCKY AGAIN, AND I'M FIGHTING ALONGSIDE CAPTAIN AMERICA.
IT'S STEVE ROGERS, NOT THAT WHOEVER-HE-IS WHO TOOK HIS PLACE.
THIS IS MY WORLD, NOT THE ONE I DROPPED INTO.

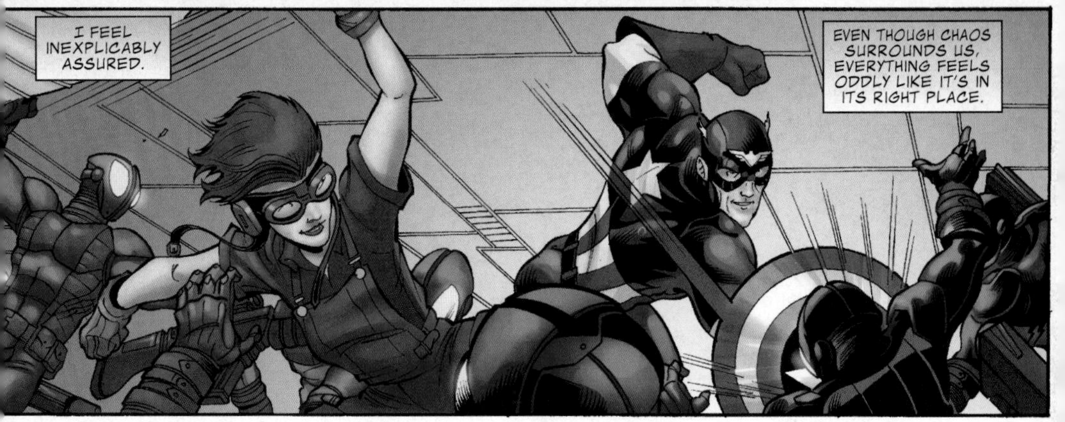
I FEEL INEXPLICABLY ASSURED.
EVEN THOUGH CHAOS SURROUNDS US, EVERYTHING FEELS ODDLY LIKE IT'S IN ITS RIGHT PLACE.

NOMAD IN CONJUNCTION FINALE

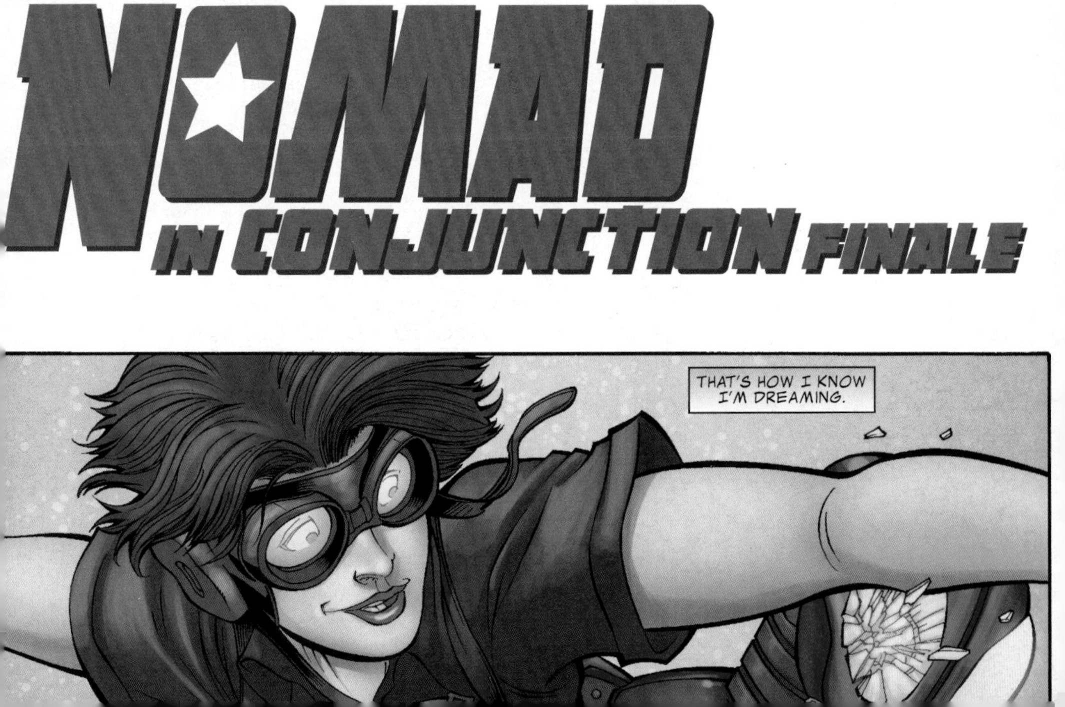
THAT'S HOW I KNOW I'M DREAMING.

AH. HELLO, *NOMAD.* IT'S NICE TO MEET YOU.

YEAH? IF YOU SAY SO...

THEY CALL ME *NIGHT NURSE.*

MY *CLINIC* HERE TENDS TO THE MEDICAL NEEDS OF YOUR *COMMUNITY.*

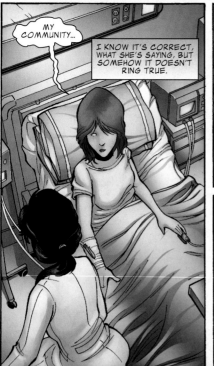

MY *COMMUNITY...*

I KNOW IT'S CORRECT, WHAT SHE'S SAYING, BUT SOMEHOW IT DOESN'T RING TRUE.

I HAD TO MANUFACTURE QUITE THE *COCKTAIL* TO COUNTER THE *CHEMICAL AGENT* YOU SUCCUMBED TO...

THE...?

OH. RIGHT. SO...HOW LONG HAVE I...?

FIVE DAYS. NO *SMALL* AMOUNT OF TIME, BUT BETTER THAN THE ALTERNATIVE, DON'T YOU AGREE?

YOU'RE *LUCKY* TO HAVE A FRIEND LIKE ARAÑA.

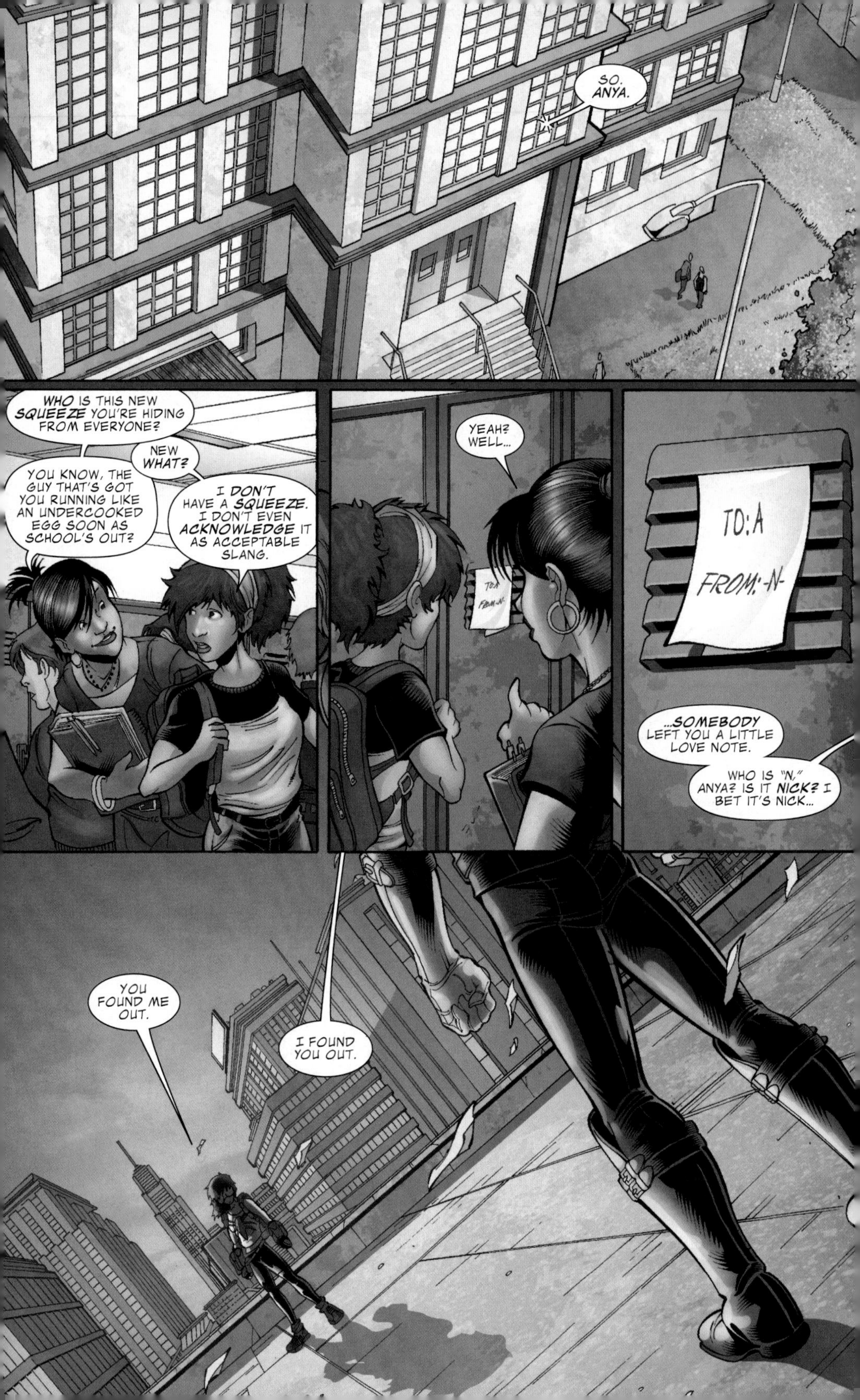
SO. ANYA.
WHO IS THIS NEW SQUEEZE YOU'RE HIDING FROM EVERYONE?
NEW WHAT?
YOU KNOW, THE GUY THAT'S GOT YOU RUNNING LIKE AN UNDERCOOKED EGG SOON AS SCHOOL'S OUT?
I DON'T HAVE A SQUEEZE. I DON'T EVEN ACKNOWLEDGE IT AS ACCEPTABLE SLANG.
YEAH? WELL...
TO:A
FROM:-N-
...SOMEBODY LEFT YOU A LITTLE LOVE NOTE.
WHO IS "N," ANYA? IS IT NICK? I BET IT'S NICK...
YOU FOUND ME OUT.
I FOUND YOU OUT.

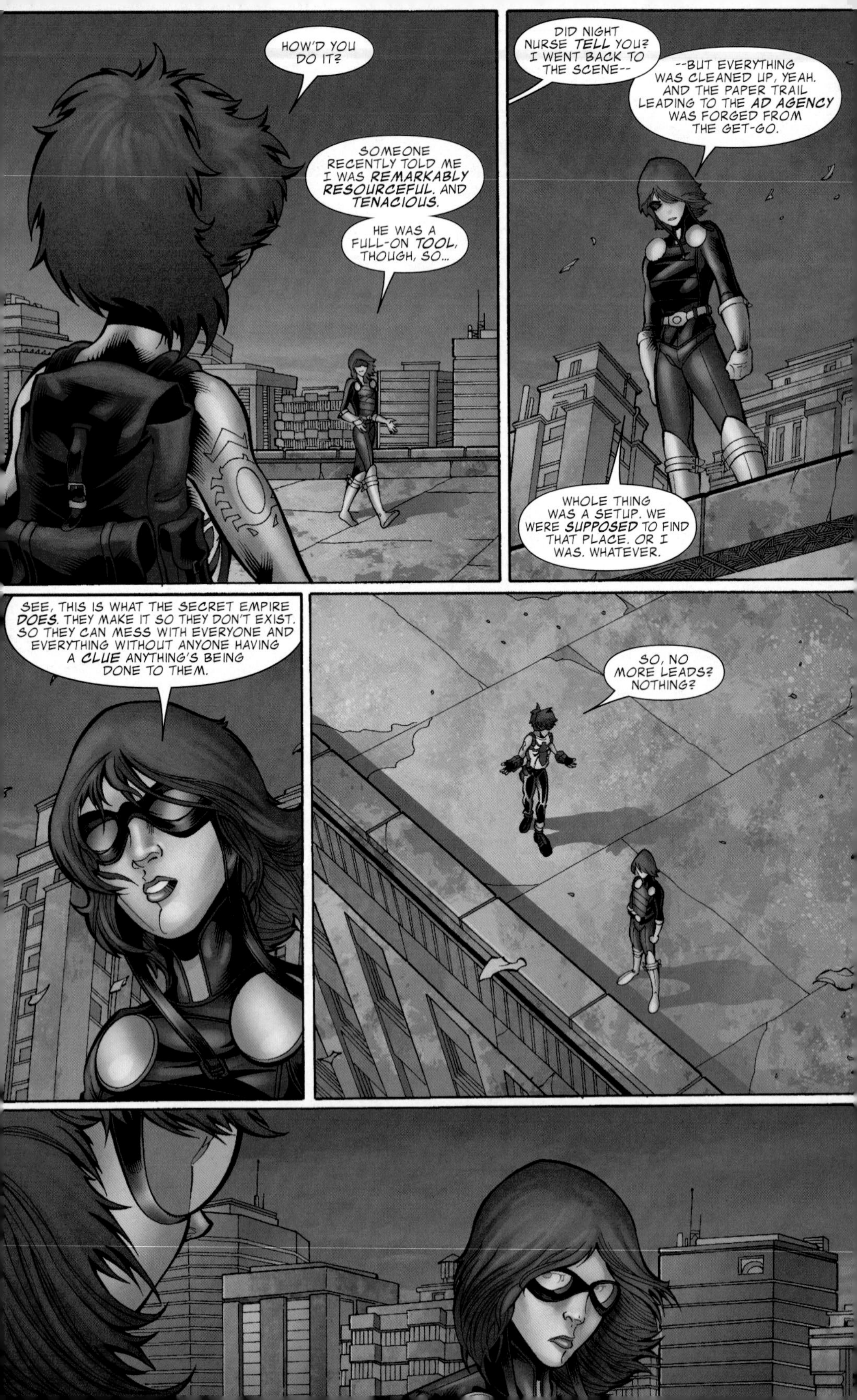
HOW'D YOU DO IT?
SOMEONE RECENTLY TOLD ME I WAS REMARKABLY RESOURCEFUL. AND TENACIOUS.
HE WAS A FULL-ON TOOL, THOUGH, SO...
DID NIGHT NURSE TELL YOU? I WENT BACK TO THE SCENE--
--BUT EVERYTHING WAS CLEANED UP, YEAH. AND THE PAPER TRAIL LEADING TO THE AD AGENCY WAS FORGED FROM THE GET-GO.
WHOLE THING WAS A SETUP. WE WERE SUPPOSED TO FIND THAT PLACE. OR I WAS. WHATEVER.
SEE, THIS IS WHAT THE SECRET EMPIRE DOES. THEY MAKE IT SO THEY DON'T EXIST. SO THEY CAN MESS WITH EVERYONE AND EVERYTHING WITHOUT ANYONE HAVING A CLUE ANYTHING'S BEING DONE TO THEM.
SO, NO MORE LEADS? NOTHING?

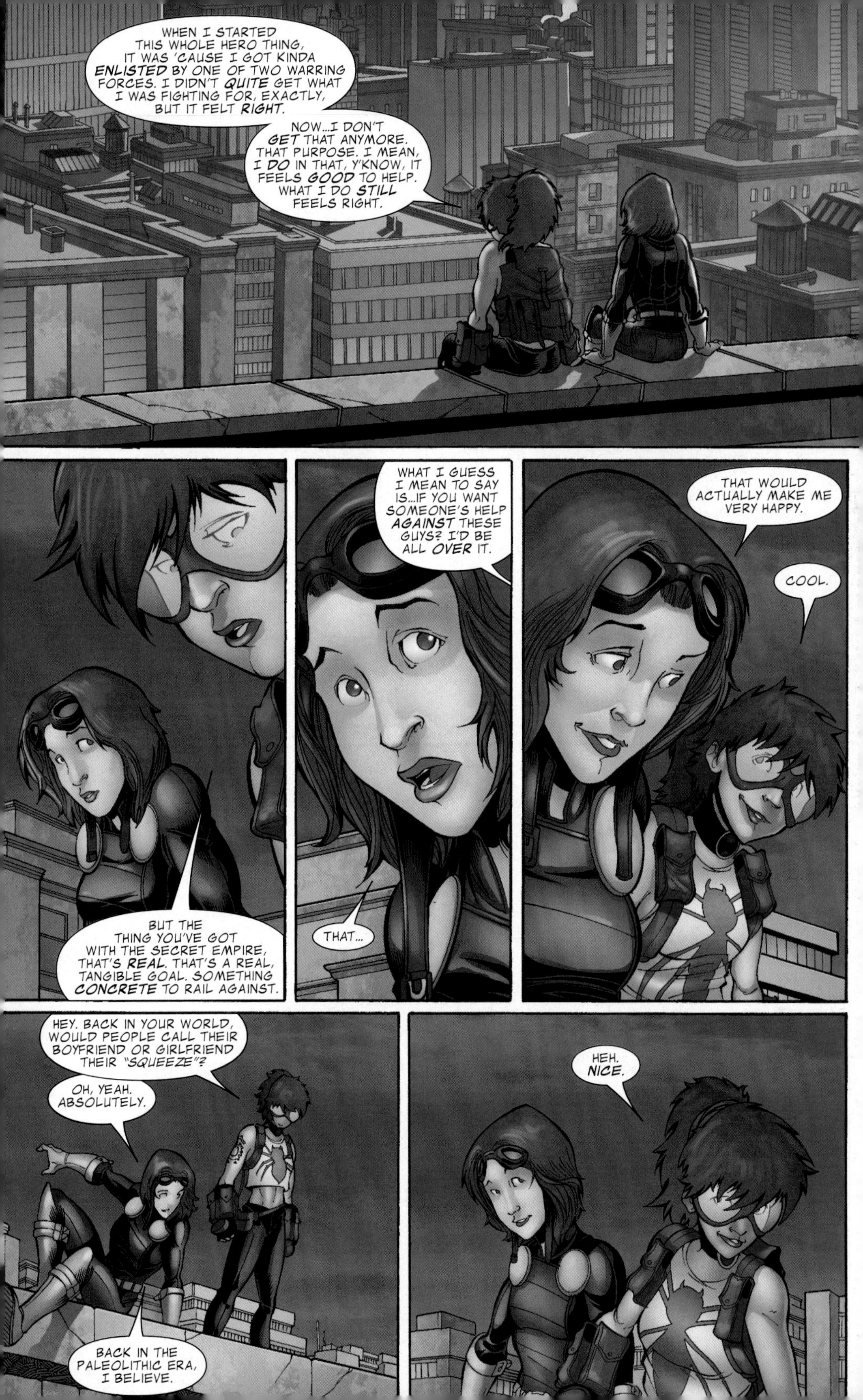

WHEN I STARTED THIS WHOLE HERO THING, IT WAS 'CAUSE I GOT KINDA ENLISTED BY ONE OF TWO WARRING FORCES. I DIDN'T QUITE GET WHAT I WAS FIGHTING FOR, EXACTLY, BUT IT FELT RIGHT.
NOW...I DON'T GET THAT ANYMORE. THAT PURPOSE. I MEAN, I DO IN THAT, Y'KNOW, IT FEELS GOOD TO HELP. WHAT I DO STILL FEELS RIGHT.
BUT THE THING YOU'VE GOT WITH THE SECRET EMPIRE, THAT'S REAL. THAT'S A REAL, TANGIBLE GOAL. SOMETHING CONCRETE TO RAIL AGAINST.
THAT...
WHAT I GUESS I MEAN TO SAY IS...IF YOU WANT SOMEONE'S HELP AGAINST THESE GUYS? I'D BE ALL OVER IT.
THAT WOULD ACTUALLY MAKE ME VERY HAPPY.
COOL.
HEY. BACK IN YOUR WORLD, WOULD PEOPLE CALL THEIR BOYFRIEND OR GIRLFRIEND THEIR "SQUEEZE"?
OH, YEAH. ABSOLUTELY.
BACK IN THE PALEOLITHIC ERA, I BELIEVE.
HEH. NICE.

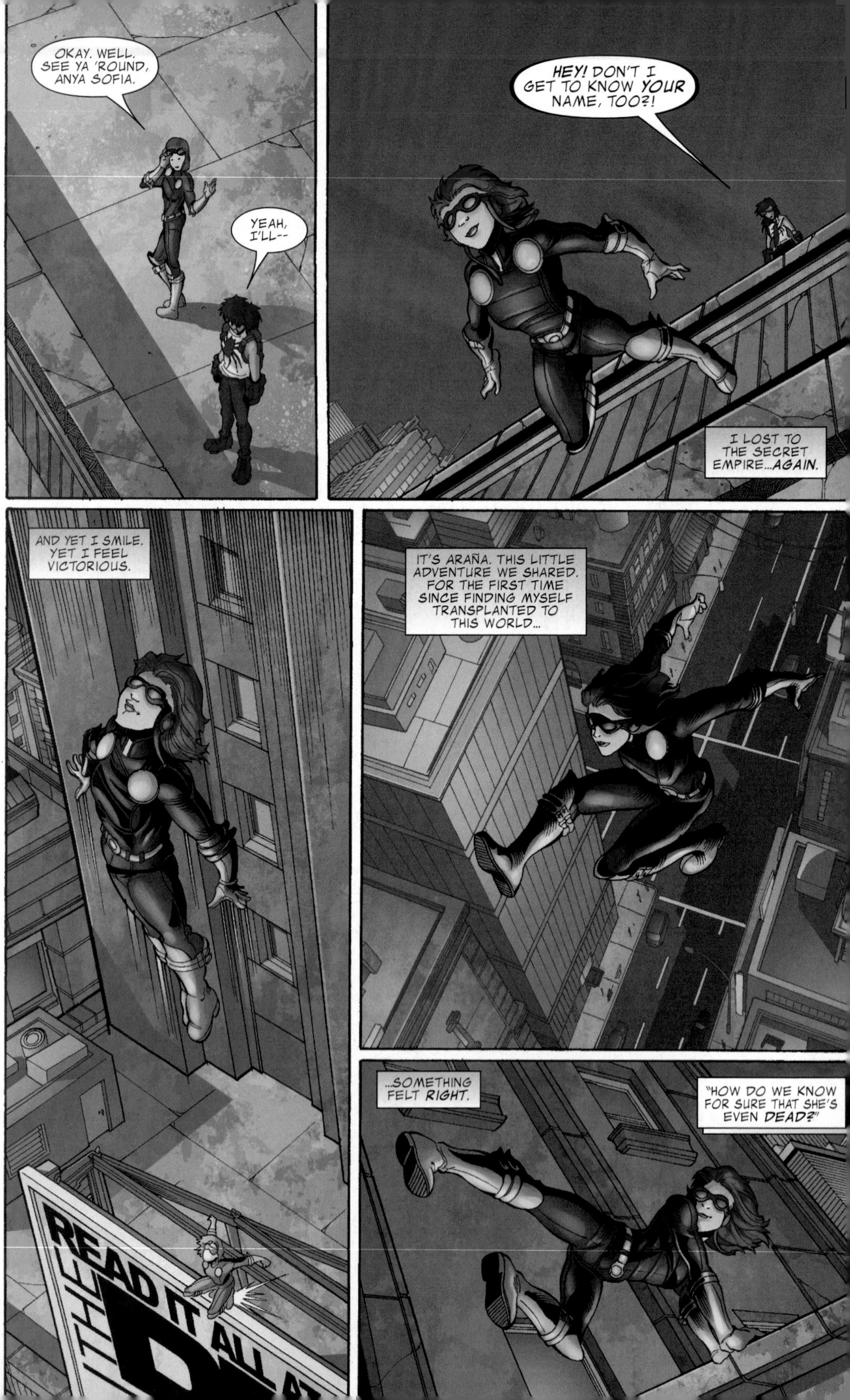
OKAY. WELL. SEE YA 'ROUND, ANYA SOFIA.
YEAH, I'LL--
HEY! DON'T I GET TO KNOW YOUR NAME, TOO?!
I LOST TO THE SECRET EMPIRE...AGAIN.
AND YET I SMILE. YET I FEEL VICTORIOUS.
IT'S ARAÑA. THIS LITTLE ADVENTURE WE SHARED. FOR THE FIRST TIME SINCE FINDING MYSELF TRANSPLANTED TO THIS WORLD...
...SOMETHING FELT RIGHT.
"HOW DO WE KNOW FOR SURE THAT SHE'S EVEN DEAD?"
READ IT ALL AT

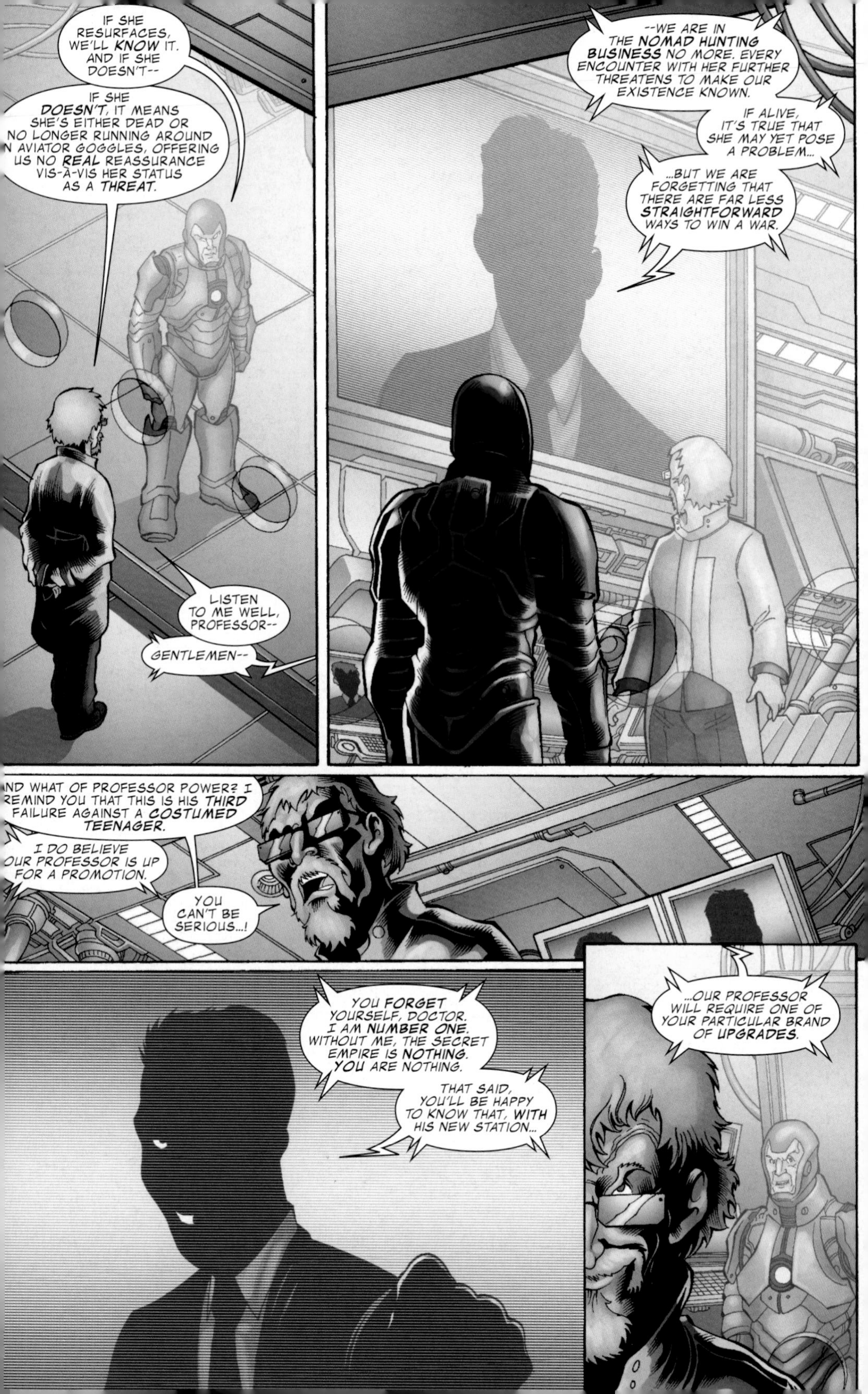
IF SHE RESURFACES, WE'LL KNOW IT. AND IF SHE DOESN'T--
IF SHE DOESN'T, IT MEANS SHE'S EITHER DEAD OR NO LONGER RUNNING AROUND N AVIATOR GOGGLES, OFFERING US NO REAL REASSURANCE VIS-À-VIS HER STATUS AS A THREAT.
LISTEN TO ME WELL, PROFESSOR--
GENTLEMEN--
--WE ARE IN THE NOMAD HUNTING BUSINESS NO MORE. EVERY ENCOUNTER WITH HER FURTHER THREATENS TO MAKE OUR EXISTENCE KNOWN.
IF ALIVE, IT'S TRUE THAT SHE MAY YET POSE A PROBLEM...
...BUT WE ARE FORGETTING THAT THERE ARE FAR LESS STRAIGHTFORWARD WAYS TO WIN A WAR.
ND WHAT OF PROFESSOR POWER? I REMIND YOU THAT THIS IS HIS THIRD FAILURE AGAINST A COSTUMED TEENAGER.
I DO BELIEVE OUR PROFESSOR IS UP FOR A PROMOTION.
YOU CAN'T BE SERIOUS...!
YOU FORGET YOURSELF, DOCTOR. I AM NUMBER ONE. WITHOUT ME, THE SECRET EMPIRE IS NOTHING. YOU ARE NOTHING.
THAT SAID, YOU'LL BE HAPPY TO KNOW THAT, WITH HIS NEW STATION...
...OUR PROFESSOR WILL REQUIRE ONE OF YOUR PARTICULAR BRAND OF UPGRADES.

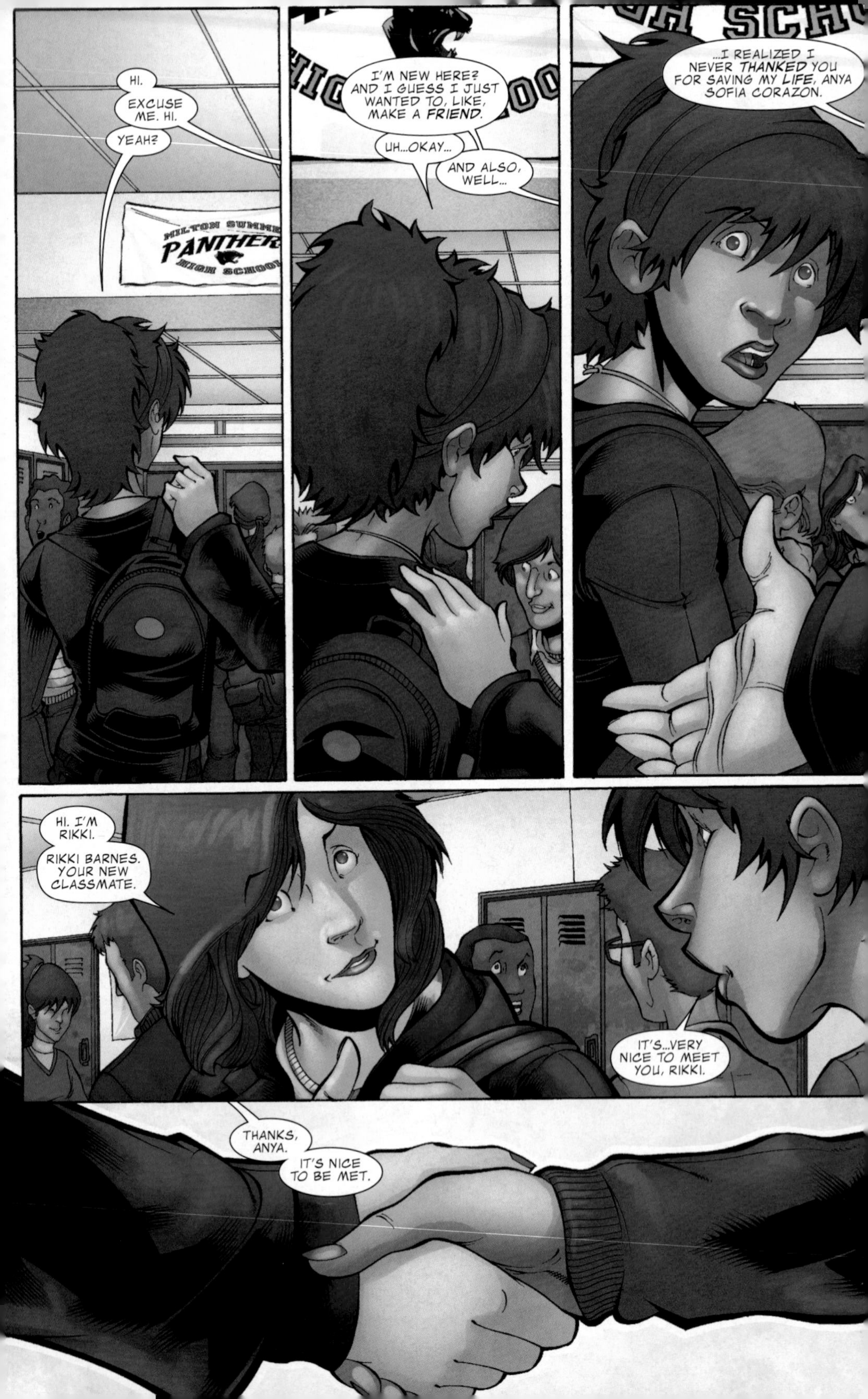
HI.
EXCUSE ME. HI.
YEAH?
MILTON SUMME
PANTHER
HIGH SCHOOL
I'M NEW HERE? AND I GUESS I JUST WANTED TO, LIKE, MAKE A FRIEND.
UH...OKAY...
AND ALSO, WELL...
...I REALIZED I NEVER THANKED YOU FOR SAVING MY LIFE, ANYA SOFIA CORAZON.
HI. I'M RIKKI.
RIKKI BARNES. YOUR NEW CLASSMATE.
IT'S...VERY NICE TO MEET YOU, RIKKI.
THANKS, ANYA.
IT'S NICE TO BE MET.

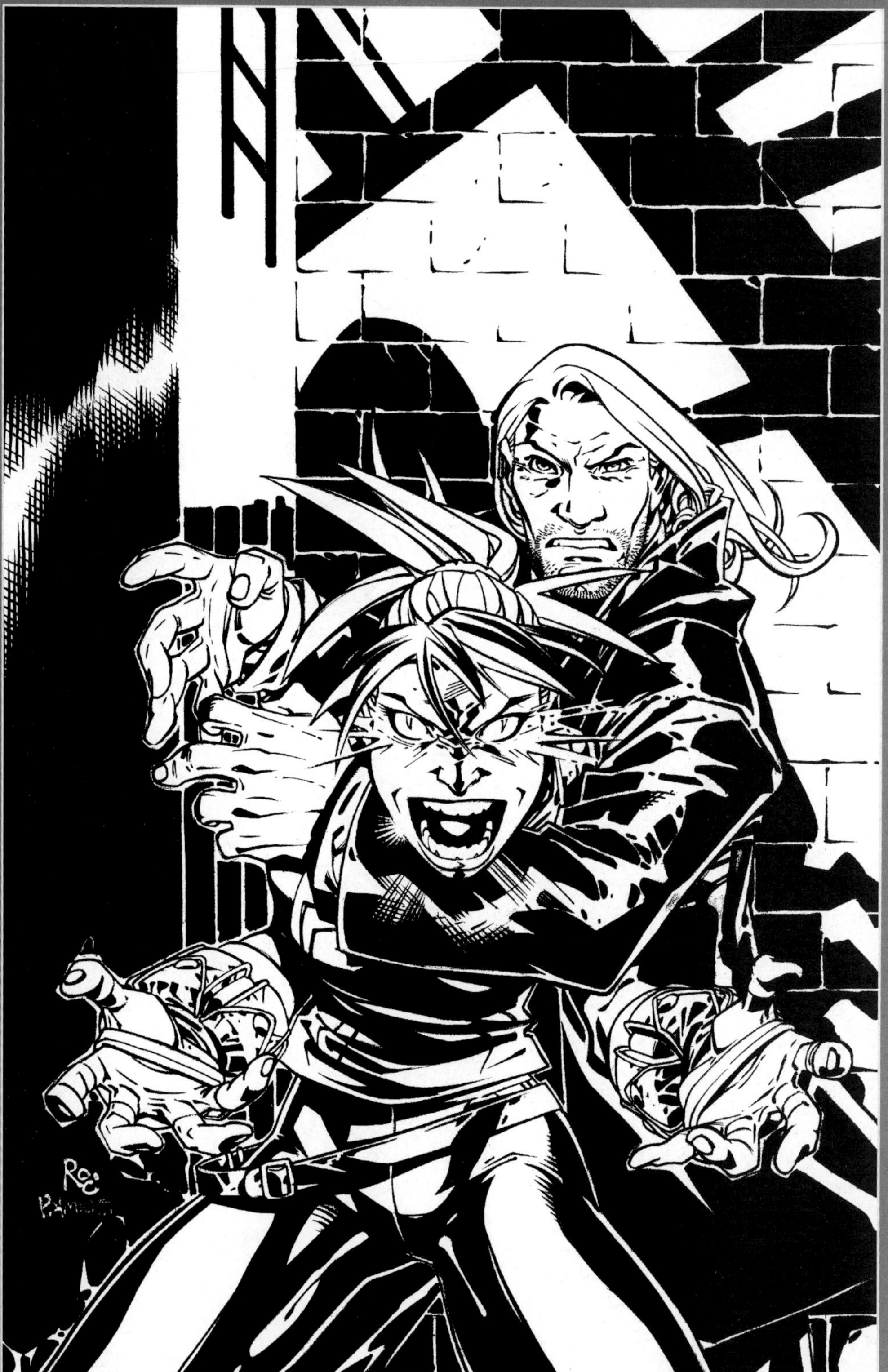

ARAÑA #11 COVER ART BY ROGER CRUZ

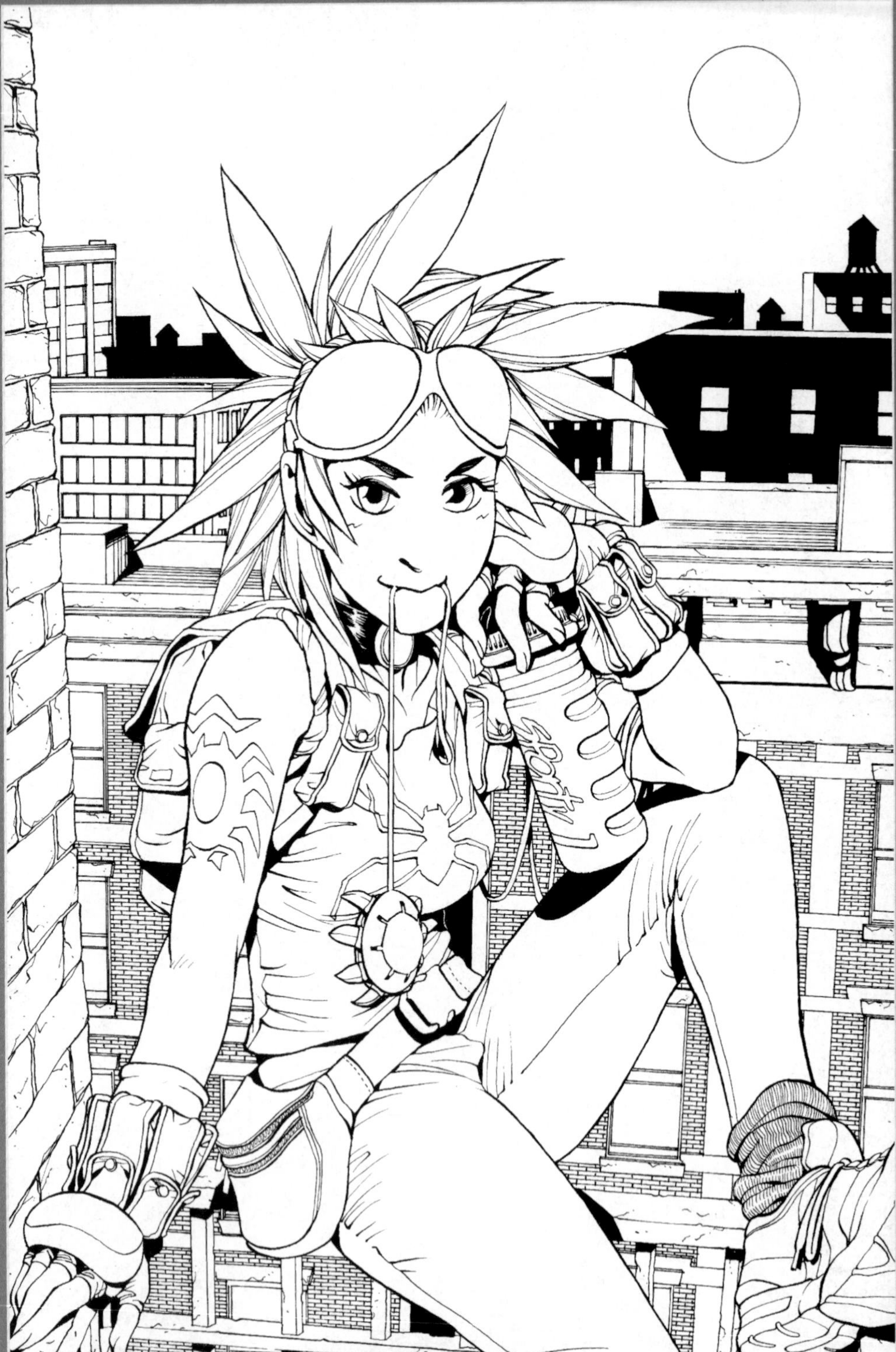

ARAÑA #12 COVER ART BY TAKESHI MIYAZAWA